WHITHER THOU GOEST

On a muggy August day in 2002, Alexandra Lind was unexpectedly thrown backwards in time, landing in the year of Our Lord 1658. Catapulted into an unfamiliar and frightening new existence, Alex could do nothing but adapt. After all, while time travelling itself is a most rare occurrence, time travelling with a return ticket is even rarer.

This is the seventh book about Alex, her husband Matthew and their continued adventures in the second half of the seventeenth century.

ANNA BELFRAGE

Whither Thou Goest

SilverWood

Published in 2014 by the author
using SilverWood Books Empowered Publishing®

SilverWood Books
30 Queen Charlotte Street, Bristol, BS1 4HJ
www.silverwoodbooks.co.uk

ISBN 978-1-78132-241-3 (paperback)
ISBN 978-1-78132-242-0 (ebook)

British Library Cataloguing in Publication Data
A CIP catalogue record for this book is available from the British Library

Set in Bembo by SilverWood Books
Printed on responsibly sourced paper

This book is dedicated to my sister, Sofia.
I am very fortunate to have her in my life, and
hope that one day she and I will once again play at
being dolphins in the warm waters of the Caribbean.
Te quiero, hermanita – montones!

Chapter 1

Uncharacteristically for Maryland, this winter had seen more snow than Alex Graham had ever experienced before. Huge, heavy snowfalls melted into a muddy sludge over a couple of days, and then there was a new blanket of snow, yet more mud.

Today was one of the muddy days. Alex had to tread carefully as she made her way across the yard to the laundry shed with a small bundle of linens under her arm. There could be no major wash until the weather improved, but a couple of shirts, some shifts and her single flannel petticoat she could hang to dry inside the shed, and, while she was at it, she was planning on submerging herself in a tub of hot water as well.

It was the first week of February 1686. The shrubs were beginning to show buds; here and there startling greens adorned the wintry ground. Alex lifted her face to the sky and drew in a deep breath. She could feel it shifting. Winter was waning, and soon it would be brisk winds, leaves on the trees, and weeks of toiling in the fields or the vegetable garden.

"About time," she muttered, slipped in the mud, took a hasty step forward, and had her clog sink with a squelch into a particularly soft spot. She stood like a one-legged stork, bending down to yank it loose.

"Bloody hell!" she said when she overbalanced and fell forward.

"Aren't you a wee bit too old to play in the mud?" Matthew grinned at her from some feet away.

Alex scooped up some mud and sent it to land like a starburst on his worn everyday coat. "Oops." She smiled, feeling a childlike urge to engage in a full-scale mud fight.

"Clean that off," Matthew mock-threatened, taking a few steps towards her.

"Make me." She managed to get her clog free, and sprinted like a hare on ice skates towards the laundry shed. Matthew came after, which made her run faster and laugh harder, so that by the time she'd broken the world record on the fifty-yard mud dash, she was gasping for air, her hair had come undone, and her cheeks were very warm.

"Got you." Matthew pinned her against the wall.

"…" Alex replied, struggling to get some air back down into her lungs. And the stays weren't exactly helping.

Matthew released his hold. "Hoyden," he said, rubbing at a streak of mud on her face. "All of fifty-three, and still incapable of keeping yourself neat and clean."

"You, mister, you're pushing fifty-six, and look at you! Mud all over the place!" She wiped her hands on his breeches.

Ian walked past leading Aaron, Matthew's big bay stallion, and shook his head at them. "You're old," he said, his lip twitching. "Very old, aye? Grandparents should act with more dignity."

"Huh, as a matter of fact, I was sedately crossing the yard to do some washing when your father here attacked me."

"Nay, he didn't. You fell flat on your face all on your own, Mama. Go and wash," Ian added before going on his way, clucking to Aaron to come along.

"Go wash, he said. What does he think we are? In our dotage and in need of a father figure?" Alex stuck her tongue out in the general direction of her stepson and pushed the door to the shed open, smiling when she entered this her almost favourite place.

Over the years, what had been a hastily constructed lean-to, meant mainly to house the huge kettle, the rinsing trough and all other paraphernalia associated with the tedious and heavy work of ensuring the laundry got done, had developed into a solidly built little house with soaped floors, broad wall benches and, standing in pride of place, the wooden tub – big enough to seat two. The small space was at present agreeably warm thanks to the fire Alex had lit earlier, the air suffused with the scents of lavender and crisp mints.

Along the back wall, drying herbs hung in bunches. On a small shelf stood stone jars of oils and salves, pots of soap, and an assortment of lanterns. The only things that were missing, in Alex's opinion, was a tap from which to turn on running water and huge terrycloth towels. Neither of those had been invented yet, as she was prone to reminding herself, just as cars and washing machines and phones were still centuries away from materialising.

"Are you just going to slouch against the wall and look decorative or are you going to help?" she asked Matthew, who had followed her inside.

"Oh, I don't mind looking decorative," he said, but came over to help her with the heavy cauldron. She set the few garments to soak with lye in a bucket, forcefully scrubbed the mud stains off his woollen breeches and coat, and then he helped her do the same with her skirts, stretching the fabric for her.

"I'll never get this off," she grumbled, inspecting the broad kneecaps of mud. "And look at my bodice!" The sleeves were encrusted with mud to halfway up the elbow, and once she had taken that garment off, the chemise beneath was just as dirty. Alex peeled it all off, hung her stays to sway on a hook, dunked the shift and petticoat in with all the other stuff, and found a bristle brush with which to attack the bodice. Matthew sat down on one of the benches and regarded her as she moved around, covered in her shawl and nothing else.

"It's impolite to gawk," Alex said sternly.

"Aye, but you're my wife and I can gawk at you as much as I want."

"Glad you like it." Alex arched her back and winked, making him laugh.

They talked about this and that while she did her washing, Matthew coming over to help her fill buckets with water when she needed it.

"It does him good, these long winters," Alex said.

"Who?"

"Ian. No limping, no shuffling." She smiled, thinking that Ian at present moved with the fluidity and ease one could expect of a man just over thirty. Not that it would last, she sighed, because with the advent of spring and summer, his damaged back, in combination with all the work, would at times leave him white-faced with pain, reduced to hobbling round the yard.

"Ah." Matthew sounded tense – but then he always did when they discussed Ian's injured back, the consequence of a failed ambush by those accursed Burley brothers. Understandably, her man sounded tense whenever the Burleys were mentioned. He bore scars of his own on account of them, as did their youngest daughter, while one of their sons was dead – all because of Philip and Walter Burley.

Alex concentrated on her scrubbing. They're gone, she reminded herself, they're dead by now – or if not dead, almost dead.

Matthew poured a couple of buckets of cold water over her scrubbed clothes, helped her wring them and hang them to dry.

"Look at my hands," she complained, holding them out to him: bright red, itching all over from the lye.

"Mmm," Matthew said, eyes glued to one of her breasts, quite visible now that the shawl had slipped. She let the shawl drop entirely, standing very still when his fingers grazed her flesh.

It shouldn't be this way, not when she was over fifty and had lived with him for almost thirty years, but it was, it still was. A current that surged between them, a heavy warmth spreading through her, breath that became shallow and rapid, knees that somehow lost stability, and all because of him, the man who stood fully dressed before her and ate her with his eyes. She fluffed at her hair, met his hazel eyes, and smiled.

"Da?" Ian's voice had an edge to it. "Da, are you there?"

"Aye," Matthew said, the attention he had been focusing on her wavering.

"You'd best come out."

Matthew threw a rueful look in the direction of Alex. "Stay here," he suggested, buttoned up his coat, and stepped outside.

"Stay here," Alex muttered, shivering in the chilly wind that he had let in. From outside came male voices, and from the agitated tone, they weren't exactly here for a natter and a biscuit. She threw the half-filled tub a longing look and, with a grimace, slid into stays, skirt and the dirty bodice, wrapping the shawl tight before going to join her husband.

Their visitors were still in the yard. Adam, her youngest son, had appeared from the stables to help with the horses, but remained hovering around the men, listening avidly. Alex smiled a greeting at Thomas Leslie, their closest neighbour, before nodding at the Chisholm brothers, also neighbours – a rather strange word to use for people that lived more than an hour's ride away.

"Scalped, I'm telling you! Not more than some hundred yards from my home!" Martin Chisholm was visibly upset, his normally placid exterior contorted into a hatchet face, small blue eyes staring like flints at his audience. "The poor bastards must have shrieked their heads off, and we didn't even hear them."

"Oh," Matthew said, sharing a worried look with Alex.

"Not Mohawk," Thomas Leslie hastened to assure them, and Alex's shoulders dropped an inch or two. Not her son, not his adopted Indian family. Grief rushed through her at the thought of her Samuel. He should be here, with her, not out in the forest with Qaachow and his tribe.

"Bloody nuisance is what they are," Martin went on, with Robert, his brother, nodding in agreement. "It would be best to enslave them all, put them to work on a plantation where they could be controlled."

"Maybe they don't want to." Alex picked some straw out of Adam's hair, cuddling him for an instant against her chest. All legs and arms, her not quite ten-year-old scrubbed his head affectionately against her shawl.

"Want to? What do we care what they want? Heathen is what they are, and to kill...oh, my God! My poor nephew!"

"Your nephew? They scalped a child?" In Alex's ear, Adam's tame raven, Hugin, cawed, seemingly as upset as she was.

"No, but he found them." Martin shifted from foot to foot, looking longingly in the direction of the Graham house, and with an internal sigh, Alex asked them all to come inside. On their way across the yard, Thomas leaned towards Matthew and whispered something, and her gut did a slow flip at the expression of shock that flew across Matthew's face.

"What?" She grabbed Thomas' arm.

"What? Oh, that. A matter between men. Nothing to concern you, my dear."

Alex pursed her mouth, unconvinced by Thomas' strained smile. "Never mind, I'll ask Matthew, and he'll tell me the truth if he knows what's best for him," she said, before wobbling off on her mud-caked clogs to ensure the guests were adequately fed.

"Yon men eat like horses," Mrs Parson said when Alex entered the kitchen. Alex gave the old woman an affectionate look. Mrs Parson was her best friend, an excellent midwife, but first and foremost the closest thing Alex had to a mother, a constant source of comfort and strength when Alex needed it.

"Lucky we have plenty of soup, then," Naomi said from where she was stirring the pot. Bean soup, from what Alex could make out. Not her favourite, but her daughter-in-law was partial to it, and it did have the benefit of being quite filling.

"I hate bean soup," Mark muttered from behind her.

Alex turned to flash her eldest son a grin. "Best tell your wife that, not me. She's the one who keeps on making it."

"I heard that." Naomi brandished the wooden spoon in their direction. "And I'll have you know my father loves it."

"Great, Thomas can have my share as well," Alex said,

laughing at Naomi's pretend scowl.

The Chisholms were solid men that took up a lot of room, but after some minutes the household and their guests were settled round the large table, albeit with less elbow room than usual. As always, Matthew sat at the head of the table while Alex had her chair at the other end, within easy reach of the hearth and the workbenches. Whitewashed walls and constant scrubbing of the floor and surfaces, ensured that the kitchen was clean and relatively light, the February sun streaming in through the two windows, both of them with horribly expensive glass panes.

"I had no idea that something so simple could be this good." Robert Chisholm stretched to spear yet another salt-baked beet on his knife, lathered the beet generously with butter, and bit into it.

"And it's good for you, full of vitamins and other stuff," Alex said, busy slicing bread.

"Vitamins?" Martin looked at her.

"That's what my father used to say," she temporised, which wasn't a lie, even if he'd said it in the late 1900s. "Maybe it's a Swedish expression."

Mrs Parson coughed loudly and placed the large pot of soup on the table before sitting down in the armchair reserved for her out of deference for her advanced age. She fiddled with her starched linen cap and turned her black eyes on the Spanish priest who had ridden in with the Chisholms. "Are you planning on staying to officiate at the funerals as well?" she asked, and Robert choked on his ale.

Carlos Muñoz blinked, an elegant hand coming up to smooth at his collar. "What funerals?"

"Well, you've wed most of the younger Chisholms almost two years back, you've baptised all the new weans, and so you can't have much cause to linger much longer, can you? Unless you're counting on them needing you for last rites and such nonsense before they pass on."

"Mrs Parson!" Alex glared at Ian and Mark who seemed to be on the verge of exploding with laughter.

"It is no nonsense, and I'll not have you disparage the

Holy Church," Carlos replied stiffly. "As to why I am still here, at present I find myself trapped due to inclement weather." He slid a look up the table to where Sarah usually sat, but now, in her last month of a most unwelcome pregnancy, their youngest daughter shunned the table when there were visitors. Alex stifled a sigh. The young priest had developed quite the crush on Sarah.

"You shouldn't tease him like that," Alex remonstrated with Mrs Parson once the men had gone outside to conduct their business, leaving them alone in the kitchen. "We both know why he's still here." She inclined her head in the general direction of Sarah's room. "If it hadn't been for him..." Alex left the rest unsaid. They both knew it was Carlos who had helped Sarah cope with her situation, chosen by Sarah as her sole confidant. Most unorthodox, given that Carlos was a Catholic priest.

Mrs Parson looked somewhat shamefaced. "He's a good lad, for all that he's a papist. But it's time he leaves, aye? For his sake, Alex. Yon lassie of yours won't want much to do with him once this is over."

"You think?" Alex was surprised by this assessment. In her opinion, Sarah was too fond of the priest, and at one point, Alex could have sworn Sarah was in love with him. She threw a distracted look out of the window, eyes lingering on Carlos, who was already mounted on his mule.

"She'll want to forget, all of this last year she'll want to bury, and wee Carlos is very much a part of it, no?"

"She can't forget. There will be a child." Alex watched the Chisholms and Carlos out of sight up the lane before turning to face Mrs Parson.

"She doesn't want it. She has said so for the last few months."

"She might change her mind once she sees it." Alex was in two minds about this: one part of her hoped Sarah would change her mind, the other couldn't quite see how a child with Burley blood would fit into the Graham household.

"I think not," Mrs Parson said. "You must start thinking about finding it a home elsewhere."

Alex was so busy mulling over her discussion with Mrs Parson, it took her some time to notice her entrance into the little parlour had effectively muted whatever conversation Thomas and Matthew had been having.

She set her tray down, handed them a mug of tea, took her own, and went to sit by the fire. First, she studied Thomas. Under her inspection, he fidgeted but by busying himself with his pipe, managed to avoid her eyes. Then she turned her attention to Matthew, and he calmly looked back, but she knew him too well, saw how his little finger twitched, how still he held his head, and the hair along her back began to rise.

"Something's wrong." It wasn't a question. It was a statement, directed at them both.

"We don't know," Matthew said.

Thomas gave him a sidelong glance, and sucked on the carved stem of his pipe, holding his tongue.

"What is it you don't know?" Alex asked, but there was a hollow feeling in her chest at the look that flared in her husband's eyes.

The men exchanged a look. Matthew sighed, beckoning that she should come over. She knew it was bad when he sat her on his lap, despite being in company, one strong arm encircling her waist.

"Philip Burley," he said.

"Oh, Jesus." The mug she was holding in her hands slid through numbed fingers to hit the floor.

Chapter 2

Alex paced their bedroom like a caged tiger, her hands twisting together.

"How?" she said, wheeling to face Matthew where he sat on the bed.

"I have no idea." He had thought them finally rid of the Burleys, that those days last May when they'd abducted their daughter, murdered his son, and almost killed him was the last time they'd ever hear of them. God, that he hadn't ensured they were dead! But he had been more dead than alive when the Indians saved him, and so the two surviving Burley brothers had been turned over to Qaachow and his Indian tribe for punishment.

"And where? Is he here?" She threw a wild look out of the window at the pitch-black night outside.

"Nay, not as far as we know." He concentrated on tracing the intricate woodwork with which he had decorated their bedstead, noting with detachment that his fingers trembled. "He was coming to tell us, Thomas, when he rode into the Chisholms. Thomas had it off one of his daughters' husbands, how a man in Virginia was attacked some weeks ago, his horse stolen from him. His attacker stabbed him and left him to die in the snow, but fortunately a trapper found him and managed to stem the blood flow. He insists he was attacked by a man with black hair and the light eyes of a wolf, a man whose face was grossly disfigured. And he couldn't talk properly...there was no tongue."

Alex moved her mouth soundlessly. Fingers tore at the fringes of her shawl, and even from here he could see the pulse at the hollow of her throat.

"But he's alone," she said, "and one Burley we can handle, right?"

"One Burley, aye." But Philip Burley – or it could be Walter, not that it made much of a difference – would never attempt full-fledged revenge on his own, and the woods were full of misfits, desperate men who would sell their souls for gold.

His brain grappled with this new, horrifying threat to his family. Thomas had suggested he turn to Qaachow for help, and mayhap that was not a bad idea, but how was he to find the Indian chief, his son's adopted father? He looked at his wife and attempted a smile. "He isn't at our door this minute, Alex."

But he would be. If Burley was alive, it was but a matter of time before he came here, and then what?

"No," she breathed, coming over to sit beside Matthew on the bed. He held out his hand and she rested hers in his, squeezing back with surprising strength when he closed his fingers over hers. In silence, they sat and held hands, both of them staring at absolutely nothing.

Finally, Alex turned towards him. "We can't tell Sarah."

"Nay, that we can't." If the notion of Burley made his guts twist and freeze, what would it do to his daughter? He pulled off his stockings and sat looking down at the gap in his left foot where the fourth toe should have been.

"He won't hurt you again," Alex said, following his thoughts.

Matthew smiled wryly. He hoped not. His back was criss-crossed by scars, on his buttock flamed a permanent brand, and his foot...

"He won't," Alex repeated, sounding very determined.

Come morning, Matthew had decided that his only option was to try and locate Qaachow.

"I think that's an excellent idea." Alex set down a bowl of porridge before him. He stretched himself for the butter and watched the knob melt into a puddle streaked with honey before beginning to eat. "After all," Alex continued, "Qaachow won't be thrilled to hear he's back either, will he?" Nay, probably not. The Burley band had been a scourge on the Indian communities as well.

"But as yet we don't know that he is — back, I mean," Matthew said.

"No," she nodded, eyes lightening with hope.

"But if he's alive, he'll come here," Mrs Parson put in, throwing a look at the door.

"Yes," Alex moaned, "he will." She averted her face for an instant. "So when do we set out?"

"We?" Matthew regarded her with some surprise. "You won't be coming with me."

"Oh yes, I will."

"You stay here," he insisted, but she shook her head.

"And if you get lost? If you never come back, or get eaten by a bear or fall into a precipice, how am I to live not knowing what has befallen you?"

"And is it better that we both get eaten by a bear?" he said with a slight smile.

"Yes," she replied and swallowed. "Yes, it is. I can't live without you anyway." And in her eyes stood a naked fear, a constant shadow ever since those days last May when she had watched him being dragged away by the Burleys to what she — and he as well — had assumed would be a long, protracted death.

"Ah, lass..." He collected her to him and kissed her unruly hair. "Bears hibernate."

"I was citing examples," she said, "and wolves don't, do they?"

"You can't leave Sarah," he tried, throwing in one last desperate card. "She can't, can she?" he asked, directing himself to Mrs Parson.

"She isn't due quite yet, and I don't think she'll be birthing before her time. The babe is far too restless, not at all settled." Mrs Parson narrowed her eyes at them. "But what will you tell her? That you just fancied a jaunt out into the unknown?"

"We'll tell her I have a need to assure myself Samuel is safe," Alex answered, "what with the dead Indians and all that."

"White Bear," Mrs Parson corrected, "that's his name now."

"Samuel," Matthew and Alex bit back instantly.

"Aye, Samuel," Mrs Parson said, looking sad. "Try to make it back within a week."

They left early next morning, leaving an upset and confused Sarah behind.

"Why now?" she'd demanded of Mama. "Why can't you wait another week or so, 'til after..."

"It may be three weeks more before the baby comes," Mama had said, "and I just have to make sure your brother's alright."

Sarah had stalked out, slammed the door to her room, and refused to speak to either of them throughout the evening. But in the morning she had come and hugged them both, clinging like a limpet to Mama.

"You won't leave me to do this on my own, will you?" she asked.

"I'll be back in time," Mama promised, kissing her brow before shoving her gently in the direction of Ian.

Sarah watched them ride away, biting her lip. Something was not right – she could see it in the way Ian and Mark followed their parents out of sight. She returned to the kitchen and sat down, regarding Mrs Parson sharply. She knew as well, Sarah could tell, even if the old woman tried to avoid her eyes by concentrating on the ubiquitous knitting that grew at a surprising speed from her hands. Sarah's whole belly moved, a series of bulges that came and went, and Sarah sat very still.

"A healthy babe," Mrs Parson commented.

"A Burley," Sarah hissed. For some months of her pregnancy, she had thought she might be able to forgive the child for its fathers, but these last few weeks had made it all so much worse, the child an invasive presence that she could never avoid, a constant reminder of what had been done to her under a canopy of green, sunlit trees. She ran her hands up and down her arms in a comforting gesture and turned towards Mrs Parson.

"Should I be loading the flintlock?"

"Whatever for?"

Sarah's body relaxed. "I'm going for a walk."

"You do that," Mrs Parson nodded, just as unperturbed. Sarah looked at her for some moments and then fetched her cloak. If it had been really bad, they would have stopped her going out.

It was a day of constant dripping, the heavy snow melting away under the rays of a brilliant spring sun. Matthew picked his way through the trees, trusting the mare he was riding to be sure-footed enough not to step into a crack or slip on a patch of ice. Alex was on one of their mules, a biddable beast that trotted along obediently.

Everywhere was the sound of water, from the drops that fell from melting snow overhead to the whispering little rivulets where water collected to run off dwindling drifts into creeks and hollows. Birds rustled in the undergrowth, here the flashing red of cardinals, there the more homely brown of a sparrow, and on a branch a cocky blackbird called that it was spring, and he was here and where were all the bonny lasses?

If it hadn't been for the purpose of their excursion, Matthew would have enjoyed every step of the way, but as it was he was concerned for Sarah, worried that they might be set upon by Indians once they ventured beyond the established borders, or, worst of all, suddenly turn the corner to find themselves face to face with Burley himself.

"Magnus would have enjoyed this." Alex broke their silence, gesturing at the surrounding forest, at the stands of as yet bare chestnuts that rose majestically sixty, eighty feet up in the air, interspersed with maples and sycamores and here and there groups of pine.

"Aye, he was mightily fond of trees," Matthew said, smiling at the memory of his father-in-law.

"Well, he would be. He was a trained botanist." She shook her head. "Actually quite a bad career choice in the future. No one really cares all that much about flowers and trees in the twentieth century."

"Mmm," Matthew grunted. He was never comfortable when they discussed her future life, the skin along his spine tingling every time he was reminded of the fact that his dear, very present wife was as yet not born. She wouldn't be, not for another three hundred years or so, and still here she was, riding by his side with her skirts tucked tight around her legs, her nose reddening with cold.

Alex must have seen something of this on his face, laughing as she rode up close enough to pat his leg. "I don't bite, and I'm very, very real."

He smiled back at her and craned his head back to look up at the distant, pale blue sky. "No thunderstorms brewing, no perfect right-angle crossroads. You're safe with me." He regretted his flippant remark the moment it was out of his mouth, seeing her face pinch together in real fear.

"Not funny," she said, and urged her mule past his mare.

He sighed. She'd been thrown from her time to this time in a gigantic thunderstorm, making her an impossibility, a person yanked out of one time to land in another, and he well knew that her constant fear was that one day time would yawn open and attempt to reclaim her.

Matthew put a hand on her reins and drew her mount to a stop. "I've told you. You belong with me. God meant for you to come tumbling down to me. He won't take you away from me."

"Huh," she said, "it would seem He has tried now and then."

"Or not. He's ensured I've been on hand every time." That was the right thing to say, he could see, almost smiling at how she relaxed.

"Yes, He has, hasn't He?"

They turned to other subjects, conversing about Daniel, their minister son in Boston, and their eldest married daughter, Ruth, in Providence.

"It's somehow so sad, isn't it?" Alex said. "One of our

girls lives through a pregnancy in constant terror, the other blooms with expectation."

"Life isn't fair," he reminded her. "God ordains."

"Sometimes He does a very crap job out of it, if you ask me."

"He does as well as He can, I reckon."

"You think?" She seemed about to say something more, but Matthew waved her silent. He held in his horse and looked about.

"This was as far as I came with them, back in January," he said, looking to where the river rushed to their right. "They forded the water here and rode off due north-west."

"Ford that?" Alex eyed the water dubiously.

"It isn't deep, it just runs swiftly."

"You can say that again," Alex said. "White-water rafting comes to mind."

He nudged his horse down towards the shore. It did look rather higher than he remembered it. He frowned, looking across the flowing, white capped water to the distant shore. "Flush with melting snow."

"I can see that," Alex said, "and I suppose that means it will be bloody cold."

It was – cold and fast, but also quite shallow – and a few hours later they were far into the western woods, with Matthew notching trees on a regular basis.

"What?" she teased. "You don't trust your inner compass?"

"Well enough, but why not take precautions if you can?" He glanced over at her and smiled. "If wee Hansel had done this instead of dropping breadcrumbs, they wouldn't have ended up with the witch."

"And God, what a boring tale that would have made," Alex said, making him laugh.

Chapter 3

There were serious drawbacks to travelling through the woods in late February, the main one being that it was cold and damp, with not an inn in sight. It was almost dusk by the time Matthew decided to stop for the day, and after some scouting, he found a huge hemlock under which they made uncomfortable camp.

Alex slept badly and woke with a start to find Matthew already awake.

"We have company," he said. Sure enough, the moment they stepped out from under the tree, they were surrounded by a group of Indians who regarded them with cautious reserve. Alex pressed closer to Matthew, but attempted a smile.

"Greetings," Matthew said in hesitant Indian speech, "I am White Bear's father."

The name obviously meant something to them because the whole group relaxed. One of the men said something to Matthew who held up his hands in an apologetic gesture.

"I don't know enough of your language," he said in English, "but I must see Qaachow." That name commanded respect, Alex saw, and after some moments of low-voiced debate amongst themselves, the apparent leader used his head to indicate they should follow them.

Several hours later, Alex was red with exertion, wet well above her ankles from walking in slush. The mule and horse were being led, and by her side walked Matthew, musket in one hand, her hand in the other.

"Bloody skirts," Alex said, hoisting them up to wade over yet another spontaneous little burbling stream. "My toes are freezing."

Matthew just grunted, his eyes flying from one side of the path to the other.

"What?" she asked.

"I can't very well go notching trees now, can I?"

"Oh." Alex scanned the endless forests that surrounded them looking for any kind of landmarks. A huge dead oak, there a boulder, trees, trees, trees...

She slipped in the mud up a steep incline, was steadied by Matthew, and together they crested the little hill that was the southern entry point to Qaachow's village.

There was smoke coming out of the two longhouses, children were playing among the trees, and a band of dogs came to bark at them. Alex nodded a greeting at an Indian woman with thick long braids who nodded back, she smiled at three little girls that had come rushing at the sound of the dogs, and then she saw her son, tall and loud among the other boys.

Samuel was a foot or two in the air when he noticed them. The ball dropped to the ground, her son landed in a crouch, and instead of hurrying over to greet them as she'd expected him to, he disappeared into the protective shadow of the longhouse. It cut straight through her, a final rejection that she wasn't sure quite how to handle. He's mine, goddamn you, she thought angrily when she saw Qaachow making his way towards them, mine and you've stolen him.

She greeted her son's adopted father politely enough and stood back a step to allow Matthew to talk to him alone. Not because Matthew expected her to, but because she had to collect her feelings. She peeked in the direction of the longhouse and there was Samuel, his hazel eyes seeking and finding hers. This time he smiled, a slow smile so like his father's, and someone pushed at him from behind, saying something that made him blush before beginning to move in her direction.

White Bear was shocked to see his birth parents here, in his village. It was one thing to go and see them and for some days or weeks step into being Samuel again, a totally different thing to have them encroaching here, where he was only White Bear and nothing else. It somehow made him ashamed, not wanting his new family and friends to see these awkward white people, so obviously not at home in the wilderness.

Da, with his hair tied back, his patched winter coat and dark breeches, looked surprisingly ineffectual here, while at Graham's Garden he was the undisputable master of it all. And Mama...well, she was pretty enough, even if she was much older than Thistledown, but her skirts were muddied to the knee, her thick winter cloak making her look fat and clumsy in comparison with his Indian mother.

She must have seen what he was thinking because he saw her look away, her hands smoothing back the hood and linen cap to uncover her thick dark hair, tied back in a soft bun. White Bear knew exactly how her hair would smell: of herbs and calendula, and if he were to rest his cheek against hers, her skin would release the scents of lemon and lavender. Soft, white skin, and hands that would rise to tousle his hair, the back of her fingers caressing his face.

"Mama." He stood before her, but instead of giving him the expected hug, she clasped her hands together. He gave her a wary look. What was the matter with her?

"Son," she replied with a careful smile. But she made no move to touch him, and he was strangely disappointed and secretly relieved, because he wasn't sure he wanted Little Bear and all the others see her make a fuss over him. Indian mothers were conscious of their sons' budding male pride in a way Mama had never been, hugging all her sons, no matter age, and kissing them as well. Still, it tore at him, this distanced greeting. Mayhap she no longer cared for him, he thought, and that made him reel with loss.

"Why are you here?" White Bear asked, and it came out like an accusation. He flinched at the hurt look in her eyes. He hadn't meant it that way, he tried to show her, stepping even closer. She backed away, and Samuel groaned into life inside of him, because he didn't want Mama to shrink from him, he wanted her to hug him.

"Your father has business to conduct with Qaachow," she replied formally. White Bear threw Da a look, noting how

25

serious he was as he stood talking intently with Qaachow.

"Bad business?" he asked.

Alex sighed and nodded. "You could say that again." She gave him a flashing blue look. "Otherwise we wouldn't have come," she said with a biting edge.

White Bear had no idea what to do. He mumbled something about being needed elsewhere, and loped back towards the longhouse.

Alex watched him go, already regretting that she hadn't pulled him into her arms, hugged and kissed him as much as she wanted to. Her son ducked out of sight behind one of the buildings, and Alex wanted to scream his name, call him back to her, but she didn't.

Instead, she fell into step with her husband, following Qaachow towards the closest longhouse. After the chilly air outside, it was comfortably warm if rather smoky inside, and Alex stared curiously at the long row of raised sleeping platforms that lined the wall, divided into several compartments by woven mats. A discreet count made it six compartments on either side, several hearths down the middle, and right at the bottom what seemed to be a communal area. It was all very neat, bedrolls stacked to one side, pelts for comfort and insulation on the platforms, and the space below them used for storage. Her stomach grumbled loudly at the smells of corn bread and squash soup, and Matthew smiled down at her.

"Hungry?"

"A bit," Alex said in a voice too low for Qaachow to catch. After all, she didn't want to force him to invite them to eat.

In the event, they were asked to sit down, close to the hearth, and bowls of fragrant, deep orange soup were brought to them. Alex stretched her feet as close to the fire as she could without actually setting her soles on fire, and her toes uncurled slowly from their frozen state. She saw Samuel again, standing with his Indian brother to the side, and in his arms he held a baby that she assumed to be Qaachow's latest child.

Bitterly, she regretted having let Qaachow take her son to begin with. Even more bitterly she regretted not having forced Samuel to stay with them when he came back after his one year with Qaachow, and now it was too late. It was them, Matthew and herself, that were the interlopers in his life now, and it showed plainly in how Samuel held himself, close to his Indian family rather than by their side. But what were they to do? Qaachow had demanded Samuel's fosterage in lieu of ensuring their home was kept safe from marauding Indians and the accursed Burleys. Alex sighed. It went back even further than that. She allowed her eyes to rest for an instant on Little Bear, the Indian boy she'd saved from imminent starvation by nursing him side by side with her own Samuel. To the Indians, this made them foster brothers, and watching them together she found it difficult to say which one of them was Indian and which one of them was white. She snuck her hand into Matthew's, and he squeezed before letting go to accept the pipe that Qaachow handed him.

"I don't smoke," he said some minutes later, still bright red from his coughing attack.

"I can see that," Qaachow replied with a smile in his voice, "but at least you tried.

"So," Qaachow settled back against the wall. "Philip Burley is still alive, you say."

"Either him or Walter," Matthew said. "And if he is, well then, it is but a matter of time before he returns here."

"Here?" Qaachow sucked at the pipe. "No, here I don't think he will return. Not unless he plans on bringing a great number of men."

"I meant here like my home," Matthew said, "and he will bring men with him."

Qaachow studied them both. "It was your daughter's wish that they not be killed."

"Aye," Matthew said, "and so she has nightmares every night where they return for her."

"And you?" Qaachow asked. "Do you have nightmares?"

"It happens," Matthew said in a casual voice. It did? Alex

27

gave her husband a long look, casting her mind back over the recent months. On occasion, she'd woken to find his half of the bed empty, but when she'd asked he had muttered something about having been thirsty, no more.

Qaachow smiled up at Thistledown when she came to serve him more to eat, a smile reciprocated in her dark eyes. Alex looked enviously at her clothes. A skirt ending mid-calf, leggings, moccasins and an elongated tunic in a darker shade than the skirt – all of it in deerskin, none of it muddy and torn after a day's hiking through the woods. She looked over to where her son stood, in a deerskin shirt, leggings and breechcloth. Samuel shifted under her eyes, said something in a low voice to his Indian brother, and sidled over to stand by Thistledown. Alex swallowed and swallowed to clear her throat of the sudden lump.

With difficulty, she returned her attention to the conversation where Matthew and Qaachow were now discussing different tactics to handle the Burley threat.

"…we will of course help you," Qaachow was saying. "Burley is an enemy of my people as well." He spat into the fire. "Far too many of our women has he stolen from us, selling them to white men far away from here."

"Aye," Matthew said. "He and his brothers enriched themselves on other people's misery – born warped, the four of them."

Qaachow nodded. "Only one left."

"Which is one too many," Alex muttered. One Burley intent on revenge. Oh God. Not here, he isn't here, she thought, and for all you know, Alex Graham, he might be dead in a drift of snow, or have stuck his foot in a bear trap, or maybe walked off a cliff in the dark.

She took a long, shuddering breath, took two, and to distract herself, she concentrated on the Indians around them, taking in the excellent needlework of their clothes, the beading that decorated sashes and moccasins, and the tattoos sported by the younger men. One of the braves grew irritated by her inspection and said something to Qaachow who raised a brow and turned to Alex.

"Is it not impolite among your people to stare?" he asked.

"I'm sorry," she mumbled. "It's just that I'm so impressed by your clothes."

"And the tattoos." Qaachow smiled.

"Well..." Alex said, "I'm not sure I'm impressed by them, but they are quite eye-catching. It seems to be a relatively new fashion, though."

"Fashion?" Qaachow's brows rose.

"You don't have them, nor do the other men of your age," Alex said.

"Susquehannock men were not tattooed as part of their coming of age, but Mohawk men are. And we are Mohawk now." Qaachow sounded curt.

Alex's eyes flew to where Samuel was listening.

"All Mohawk men are tattooed," Qaachow said, following her look.

This time it was Matthew's hand that snuck into hers.

White Bear nodded obediently at what his father said and went over to his birth parents.

"Are you tired?" he asked, kneeling down before them.

"A bit." Mama yawned.

"My fath—" he broke off, aware not only of their eyes but of Qaachow's eyes on him. He started anew. "My father says I am to show you where to sleep and stay with you that we may talk."

Da's brows pulled together. "I am your father, lad. It's from my seed that you spring. Don't forget that."

White Bear shifted on his knees, threw a helpless look in the direction of his Indian father who gave him a little smile.

"You're my Da," White Bear said at last, "and aye, you're my birth father. But I have two fathers now."

He rose to his feet, waited as they got up, and led them over to one of the sleeping compartments. On one side was a larger platform, covered in hides, on the other nothing but a woven mattress and a decorated quilt. White Bear sank down to sit cross-legged on the thin mattress and, now that it was only them and him, he could allow himself to be simply Samuel, bombarding them with questions about his brothers and sisters.

He crept successively closer, and finally snuggled up to them, his face rubbing affectionately at Da's chest. And when Mama at last hugged him and kissed him, he made a contented sound, relishing her fingers through his long hair, allowing himself to drift off into sleep in her arms, like a wee bairn.

"Maybe we did wrong," Alex said to Matthew as she kneeled to tuck the thick quilt closer round her sleeping son's body. "Maybe we should have refused to let him go."

Matthew stroked back a lock of her hair. "I don't know, lass. But when he's home, he's restless and edgy, wishing himself here, and, watching him tonight, I don't think he wishes himself with us when he's here. Not anymore."

"No, not anymore. But once he did." And maybe one day he will again, she hoped.

"Why haven't you told me?" Alex asked once they were snugly encased in a combination of pelts and quilts.

"Told you what?" Matthew yawned.

"About your dreams, the nightmares." She raised herself on her elbow to look down at him.

"I don't want to talk about them," he said, closing his eyes.

"But if you're having nightmares…" Alex rested her hand against his cheek, "…maybe I can help."

"Not with these," he told her in a definite tone.

Alex looked down at him a little while longer. She had a pretty good idea what it was he was dreaming about, having been an unwilling witness to the final degradation the Burleys submitted him to when they raped him. "At least I can warm you some milk."

His mouth twisted into a sad smile. "Aye, that you could do." He rolled her over on her side, spooned himself around her and kissed her nape. "Sleep, aye?"

"Sleep," she agreed.

Chapter 4

"So, by the time he's thirteen, he'll be considered a man?" Alex stared at Qaachow.

"Yes," Qaachow said, "man enough to go on raids, man enough to bed a woman."

"At thirteen?" Alex squeaked.

Qaachow looked at her and smiled. "Boys come to that at different ages. Myself, I was well over fourteen, but my brother was a year younger."

"You make sure it's well over fourteen for Samuel," Alex said.

"White Bear," Qaachow corrected. He threw the boy a look laden with possessive pride, and Alex alternated between wanting to kick him in the balls or elbow him in the gut, anything to wipe that look off his face.

"Samuel, he's my Samuel Isaac." Whom you stole, you bastard. Something shifted in the tall Indian's face — a fleeting expression of shame? Compassion?

"I am sorry," he said.

"No, you're not," she said, angry at hearing the wobble in her voice. "After all, you achieved what you wanted: you seduced him to your way of life."

"You could have stopped him. When I brought him back, you could have told him he had to stay with you, and he would have obeyed."

Alex studied her husband and her son, talking together on the other side of the clearing. "No, we couldn't, because that would have killed something inside of him." She settled the cloak tighter around her shoulders. "It's like Solomon and the baby," she said, and walked over to bid her son goodbye.

★

31

"Who was Solomon?" Qaachow asked White Bear once Da and Mama had dropped out of sight.

"He's a king in the Bible," White Bear said. "A king renowned for his wisdom." His eyes were still stuck to the spot where he had last seen Mama, a very unwelcome feeling of homesickness stirring inside of him. She hadn't hugged him when she left either; just an attempted cheerful smile that stood in horrible contrast to the dark in her eyes and her crossed arms.

"Ah. And what is this about Solomon and a baby?"

"Why?"

"It was something your birth mother said."

White Bear gnawed at his lower lip. "Two women quarrelled over the same child," he said, struggling to remember the story, "and Solomon said that, as they couldn't agree, well then he'd split the child in two. So he took the baby, a swordsman was brought, and the woman who was the true mother fell to her knees and begged for the child, saying she would rather have him go to the other woman than see him torn apart..." He came to an abrupt stop and wheeled, running wildly for the trees before anyone should see the tears coursing down his face.

Matthew and Alex didn't say much on the long trudge back to the ford, but after having thanked their Indian escort, Matthew decided they had gone far enough for the day and set about making camp while Alex focused on the food.

She was heavy with loss. Seeing her son so at ease and so obviously not hers anymore had been like having six-inch nails driven into her heart. Her head thudded with his name, with a gallery of images of him, from babyhood to the stringy ten-year-old he had been that first time Qaachow came to claim him.

Morosely, she set the small kettle to boil over the fire, so sunk in her reminiscences that she didn't hear Matthew's warning call, not until it was almost too late, a large, dark hand closing over her arm. Without stopping to think, Alex threw the kettle at her assailant, and with knife in one hand, a rock in the other, whirled to where her husband was fending off three black men while a fourth was kneeling by the man – no, boy – she'd scalded.

Matthew was an accomplished fighter, and on top of that he was tall and fit, while the three men facing him were undernourished and much the worse for wear. But still, three against one was uncomfortable odds.

"Go!" Matthew panted. "Run, Alex!" He swung his musket in a wild arc, ducked a large fist, and retreated a pace or two.

"In your dreams, Superman," she replied, rushing over to join the free-for-all.

"Superman?" One of the black men straightened up, surprised, and Matthew's musket crashed into his head, bringing him to his knees. "Fucking hell," the large man moaned. "Jesus, man! You've split my skull."

"Stop!" Alex yelled when it seemed Matthew was going to clobber the kneeling man again. "Don't!" She dropped to her haunches beside the man. "Are you okay?"

"Okay? Of course I'm not okay!" The large man met her eyes. "And he sure as hell isn't Superman, is he? No blue leotards, no cape…"

"No phone booths," Alex said, smiling at him. Leon White, aka Noah, branded slave and now apparently a fugitive Maroon, smiled back.

"No." He nodded. "I haven't seen any in years. Unfortunately." It came out very bitter. Alex was still trying to grasp the fact that the man she had last seen hogtied and covered in welts after an unsuccessful attempt to run away was sitting at her feet, bleeding profusely from his head.

"Get away," Matthew warned when one of Leon's companions made as if to come over to join them.

"You know these whiteys?" the man demanded of Leon, keeping a wary eye on Matthew and his musket.

"They're good people," Leon said.

"Good? How good? Benji is hurtin', he is, all bubbly his skin is, and you, well look at you. Bleedin' like a pig, you is, and it's him's fault." The man spat in Matthew's direction,

33

said something in a guttural language to the other men who moved towards Matthew, sharpened sticks and knives at the ready.

"No," Leon barked, and with a grumble the men lowered their weapons, but Matthew kept his loaded musket in his hands, eyes never leaving them.

An hour or so later, the tension had dissipated somewhat, helped along by the fact that Alex had fed the starving men, bandaged Leon's head, and even coaxed Benji into letting her look at his burn which she pronounced must hurt like hell. She took the lad by the hand and led him closer to the fire, insisting she treat his blistered skin.

Matthew looked Leon over. "So you absconded again." Having witnessed the exceptionally cruel punishment Leon had lived through nearly six years ago after his previous attempt to run away, he couldn't but admire the man.

"Well, he didn't exactly let me go voluntarily, the son of a bitch," Leon said, "and the right word is escape, not abscond, as I was never his slave to begin with, was I?"

"Nay." Matthew had never really spoken to a black man before, and it was disconcerting to listen to the well modulated, educated voice that emanated from the man before him. A musician, Alex had told him all those years ago, an unfortunate soul who'd had the misfortune to fall back in time to land in a day and age where any coloured person by definition was unfree unless capable of proving otherwise. And now the man sitting before him had all the hallmarks of a fugitive slave: dressed mostly in rags, barefoot, and with scars around ankles and wrists after heavy fetters, he regarded Matthew with apprehension.

"Is he looking for me?"

"I don't know. I haven't seen Mr Farrell lately. But I suspect that aye, he is. It's a special thing between the two of you."

"Special thing?" Leon spat, holding out his hands to show how all his fingers were badly twisted. "You can say that again… The first time I met the bastard he called me a slave, and so I punched him in the face. The second time I met him, Farrell claimed me as his slave, stripping me and branding me on the spot, and now, six years on, I've been whipped so many times I can't remember them all." He closed his hands into loose fists, a tremor rippling through him. "And if he catches me this time—"

"He'll kill you," Matthew said. "Over many days, he'll whip the skin off you."

"Yeah. But he won't. Catch me, I mean."

"No, best not let that happen." Matthew studied Leon and his knife, let his eyes rove over the other equally badly armed men, and moved over to his saddlebags. He rooted around and pulled out one of his snaphance pistols, handing it to Leon who accepted it gingerly.

"I have some powder and shots to go with it," Matthew said, "and it isn't much use against a musket, but at times it might be better than a knife." There was a whisper of admiration among Leon's companions, and they thronged around to study the weapon.

"Why?" Leon asked Matthew, turning the beautifully engraved gun round in his hands.

"Why?" Matthew shrugged and looked away. "Because there was nothing I could do for you the day you were made a slave, and yet I knew you weren't. I heard it in how you spoke, and saw it in how you moved. And so did he, Mr Farrell."

"He did?" Leon gave him a surprised look.

"Mr Farrell has been trading in slaves as long as we've lived here," Matthew told him. "He knows a slave when he sees one. But you humiliated him, and on top of that you were tall and healthy – and black."

Alex had by now finished salving Benji's burn, and after further making the boy's day by giving him her last biscuits, she came over to talk to Leon.

"So now what?" Alex asked.

"I want to go back," Leon said, his voice breaking with longing. "Back to my wife and my life, to hours spent in the recording studio with the Philharmonic Orchestra."

"That may be difficult," Alex said. "Time only tears itself apart by chance."

"Yeah, I know, you already told me, remember? How we're stuck here." He sighed and looked about his surroundings with a displeased frown. "At any rate, I have no plans on staying in this area. The Indians don't like us, and I'm not made for sleeping out in the open." He coughed as if to underline his statement. "Shit," he groaned, "don't you miss it? The highways, the cars, the way you flipped a light switch and, wham, there was light? Or just imagine opening the door to your bathroom..." He allowed his lids to drop down over his dark eyes, a small smile forming on his mouth. "...you turn the tap, and there's hot water pouring over you, and then you just wrap yourself in a thick towel and wander over to the scale to see if you can eat those chicken wings you've got sizzling in the oven." He laughed shortly. "Weight isn't exactly an issue here, is it?"

"No," Alex said, "there's a dismal lack of comfort foods."

"But you don't miss it," he stated.

"No, I don't." Her eyes went to her husband.

"Lucky you," Leon said bitterly, following her gaze.

"Very." She gnawed her lip. "Maybe you should go further west, deeper into the wilds."

"You think?" Leon shook his head. "I want a house, a bed. I want..." His voice tailed off.

"Staying here is risking capture," Alex said. "Sooner or later, someone might find you and take you."

"They can try." Leon sounded belligerent. He sighed, dropping his eyes to his hands. "I'll die before I go back to him. Anyway," he added, straightening up, "first they have to find us, and it isn't as if these parts are full of settlers, is it?"

"Not really." Six families within a three-hour ride didn't exactly qualify as being densely populated. She placed a hand on his arm, making him start. "Take care, okay? And stay well away from Providence and Mr Farrell."

She gave them what food she had left, wrapped Benji in her shawl, and stood to the side as the men prepared to leave.

"Do you think they'll make it?" Alex asked, waving for one last time to Leon before the big man was swallowed by the night.

"Make it?"

"Will they be alright, I mean."

Matthew looked at her as if she had completely taken leave of her senses. "They're fugitives, Alex. They live half-naked in the woods, with no hunting skills to talk of, no home, no nothing."

"He said they did. He said how they had built themselves a shelter."

"They can't risk staying too long in one place. Those five men are valuable." Matthew looked in the general direction they had left and sighed. "So alone, so utterly alone for all that they are five."

In the morning, they found the mule gone, with SORRY written in coal across the mare's saddle. Matthew cursed for a very long time, words like ingrates, bastards, scum and swine dropping from his mouth, before giving a resigned sigh and helping Alex up on the horse.

"At least they left the mare," Alex said.

Matthew snorted, not at all mollified. Mules were versatile animals, he muttered, far more useful in the sheer drudgery of farm work than his precious horses and easier to handle than the pair of oxen that only he could truly manage.

"They'll eat it, I reckon." He sat up and set the horse to walk.

"He wasn't glad to see us," Alex suddenly said.

"Samuel, you mean?"

"No, Leon," Alex replied sarcastically. She rested her open hand on his thigh, and he covered it with his own.

"We don't belong in that world. It confused him, to see us there."

"Nor does he. He belongs with me, with us," Alex said.

Matthew didn't reply. He just gave her hand a comforting squeeze.

★

Mark had obviously been keeping lookout, appearing rather abruptly from a screen of trees when they closed in on Graham's Garden.

"Alright then?" he asked, eyes drifting over the double-mounted mare.

"Aye," Matthew replied.

"The mule?" Mark smiled a swift greeting at Alex, and a sudden shaft of sunlight lightened his eyes into a greenish brown, making him look remarkably like his father. A throwback on Matthew when she first met him, Alex reflected, leaning over to pat her son's cheek.

"Alex!" Matthew warned, making a grab for her, but it was too late, and in an undignified welter of skirts, flailing legs and arms, she slid off the horse to land on the mossy ground. A gust of laughter, hastily swallowed, and Alex glared up at her son and husband, both of them with identical and straight faces, and slowly got to her feet, shrugging off Mark's helping hand.

"I'll walk the rest of the way," she informed Matthew. "I felt like some exercise."

"Of course," he replied with a grin and with a slight wave urged the horse on.

"They stole it," Alex said to Mark.

"Stole what?" Mark asked, confused.

"The mule. Some runaway slaves stole it."

Mark's features hardened. "Runaway slaves?"

"Yes, and God help them, half-naked and alone in all that," Alex said, waving a hand at the surrounding forest.

"I don't like it," Mark said. "Desperate men so close to our home."

They came out of the woods, and before them the ground sloped upwards, all the way from the river to where the main house stood safe against the hillside, framed by stables and barns, meadows and fields. To the right stood the three separate cabins that housed Ian and Mark and their respective families, with the smallest of them being home to their servants, Agnes and John. As if on cue, Agnes stepped

38

out of her doorway holding her daughter, Judith, by the hand. Alex waved at her, and Agnes shone up at the sight of her mistress and waved back.

"They might steal our beasts or scare our bairns," Mark said, eyes flying over to where his three eldest children were playing by the rope swing.

"Well, they have a bloody big mule to eat first. And I don't think they're dangerous – frightened and hungry, but definitely not dangerous." She laughed when Hannah, Mark's eldest, succeeded in tipping her brother Tom off the swing only to have little Lettie steal the coveted seat.

"'Tis the frightened dog that is the most dangerous, Mama. Corner it and you don't know what it will do to fight itself free."

"With the fundamental flaw being that we're talking about men, not dogs," Alex said, frowning at him.

"Still." He shrugged, giving her a kiss before striding off to where John was calling for his help.

It was a nice day, and once Alex had verified Sarah was okay – if in an even fouler mood than when they left – she decided to take a quick walk up to the graveyard.

Ian joined her halfway across the yard, wondering how things had gone with the Indians.

"…so Qaachow will be on the lookout as well," Alex finished.

"Well, that's good," Ian said.

"The more the merrier." She studied him out of the corner of her eye. Something was troubling him, and at first she'd thought it was his back, but he walked easily up the steep slope, and Betty had been taking good and thorough care of his lumbar region, at least to judge from the strong peppermint scent that hung around him.

Alex smiled at the thought of Ian's wife: small and slight, stubborn like a mule, and with quite nondescript looks if it hadn't been for her hair and her eyes. Betty hated her wild, vigorous hair, a constant fuzzy cloud around her head no matter how hard she braided it. A deep, reddish brown, it matched her eyes, wide and thickly fringed with dark lashes.

Like maple syrup her eyes were, shining with luminous pride whenever they rested on her husband or her children.

Alex began by giving Magnus' headstone a swift little pat. Her father shouldn't have died and been buried here, centuries before his birth, but that's what you got when you suddenly decided to do some time diving. It made all of her itch: one parent a time travelling witch of some sort, littering the world with small, painted time portals, and the other had been sufficiently desperate to brave the void of time on purpose to come looking for her, skydiving through a magic picture the size of a normal pocketbook. Bloody, fucking unbelievable, as she was prone to say to herself. She gave a bark of nervous laughter, closed a mental door on all this, and moved over to the other grave.

Alex said hello to Jacob, running her fingers over his headstone while she talked to him. Most mornings, she came to tell him of her life, a few moments when she allowed herself to hope that he was still around, somehow, her son. But he wasn't. In the ground beneath her feet, his remains were slowly decaying, and what had been a tall and strong young man was now at best a skeleton.

"Bloody berserk," she said to the stone, tracing the scrolled *J* in his first name. Shot through the heart when he rushed to his sister's rescue, his eyes blazing with hatred as he charged the Burleys. "Do you think—?" Alex broke off with a rueful smile.

"Do I think what?" Ian prompted, settling himself on their favourite perch: the bench that afforded a view all the way to the river.

Alex came to sit beside him. "Is he in heaven, do you think? Or is he forever gone?"

"As long as he lives here," Ian placed a hand over her heart, "and here," he placed a hand on his own chest, "then how can he be gone?"

A trickle of warmth flew through her at his words, and for an instant, she thought she could hear Jacob's laughter in the air, a happy, vibrant sound that made her smile in response.

"Betty's with child," Ian told her as they strolled the long way back through woods beginning to burst with spring.

Alex came to an abrupt stop. Not good, not good at all.

"I've tried, but she has begged and wept for yet another babe, and I want one too, and—" He looked away, his cheeks mottling into red as he described just how much he'd fought this, how she'd begged and pleaded, telling him that she'd be alright, of course she'd be alright, and she so wanted another child.

"And now... Oh God, Mama, what have I done? I couldn't help myself, I swear..." There was an edge of desperation to his voice, his eyes surprisingly dark as he looked entreatingly at her.

"Shh," Alex interrupted. "How long gone?"

"A month?" His mobile mouth quivered somewhere between pride and a gesture of despair.

"So not until October," Alex calculated, sounding very much calmer than she felt. "It'll be fine," she said, even if she had no idea, "but this time she does exactly as Mrs Parson tells her, okay?"

"Okay," Ian said.

Chapter 5

Sarah went into labour in the last week of February. For six hours straight, all she did was scream and curse, shrieking that she didn't want it, that she hated it, that it hurt. Two hours later, and her ordeal was over. The room had been aired and cleaned, Sarah had been washed and fed, and the baby had been inspected and pronounced healthy by Mrs Parson.

Alex was very ambivalent towards this latest grandchild. It wasn't the baby's fault, she reminded herself as she studied the sleeping boy, wishing that it at least could have been a girl. Nor did the shock of black hair help, or the way his ears stood straight out from his head – just like Philip Burley's.

"What do you want to name him?" she asked Sarah.

"Nothing," came the dull reply. "I don't want him." Sarah refused to touch the child, defensively crossing her arms whenever the baby was close. Alex looked for help in the direction of her husband, but Matthew avoided her eyes, just as he had so far avoided holding the baby.

"So what should we do then?" Alex said. "Roll him into a blanket and place him in a basket like Moses?"

"Why not?" Sarah shrugged.

"He's innocent, look at him – a helpless child." The little body squirmed, the face darkening into a ferocious scowl, and a damp spot appeared in the swaddling.

"I know that," Sarah said, "but it doesn't help."

"He's your son as well," Alex insisted.

Sarah rolled onto her side, turning a stiff back to her. "Nay, he isn't. I never wanted him, and I don't want him now. Give him away."

"Give him away?" She placed the restless boy in Matthew's reluctant arms and went over to sit on the bed beside her daughter. "Honey, that's a very big step to take."

Sarah just hitched her shoulders. "Mayhap someone else can love him – I never will."

"It isn't your decision," Sarah said to Carlos next morning. She was groggy with lack of sleep, and in substantial discomfort on account of her sore and heavy breasts, bandaged tightly.

"No, of course not, *hija*. But I'm asking you to consider the implications."

"The implications?" Sarah gave a short laugh. "I have considered the implications. I don't want a constant reminder of what his fathers did to me, I don't want to see him open eyes the same light grey as theirs, I don't want to see all my life stolen from me by them. By them! By the accursed Burley brothers."

Giving birth had been hell. Having Mama's hands on her inner thighs had thrown her into a panic, making her recall those other hands, forcing and hurting her. Dead, she reminded herself when her throat began to close, they're dead, by now they're dead. They won't come back, ever.

"But he isn't them," Carlos insisted, smoothing down the front of his new cassock, "and raised in love, he will grow into an entirely different man."

"Aye," Sarah agreed, "which is why I won't keep him. I can't love him." She dropped her eyes to her rosary beads, a gift from Carlos, and caressed them with her fingers. "I tried. I prayed and I prayed that I wouldn't hate him, but it hasn't helped." She kept her eyes on her beads until she heard him sigh and leave the room.

"She remains obdurate," Carlos said, accepting a mug of herbal tea and a biscuit from Mrs Parson. He sat down with a little sigh, extending his peg leg before him.

Matthew just nodded. His Sarah had made up her mind several months ago, and he thought it most unlikely that she would have a change of heart.

"She has it from both sides," Mrs Parson said. "Stubborn as mules, the both of them."

"I'm not stubborn," Alex protested, making Matthew bite back on a grin, "not like he is." She jerked her head in Matthew's direction and went back to the time-consuming work of feeding the baby with a cloth dipped in milk.

"Naomi can nurse him, can't she? She's nursing a baby of her own, isn't she?" Carlos said.

"She doesn't have enough," Mrs Parson explained, "so this one gets one meal a day from her, no more."

"This one?" Carlos extended his hand to stroke the wee head from which hair sprouted in a spectacular mop.

"As yet unnamed." Matthew felt sorry for the wean, to be born into a family that didn't want it, and even more that no one should have chosen a name for him, now that he was well over a day old.

"So what will you do?" Carlos asked.

"I don't know for sure." Matthew sighed. "I'll wait a while and give the lass a chance to change her mind, and if not, well then I must find him a home. Far away from here." He looked away from Alex's eyes. She wished him somewhere close, had even suggested the babe could stay with them, but Matthew considered that to be unfair not only to the wean but also to his daughter.

"At least he must have a name." Carlos dug into a side slit in his cassock and extracted a small wooden cross attached to a braided piece of twine. "I made this for him, something to protect him against the vagaries of the cold world he now has entered." There was an element of accusation in his voice, and Matthew narrowed his eyes at him.

"Are you suggesting we are doing less than we should by him?"

"Yes," Carlos replied, "it is difficult enough to be a bastard without being shunted out at once. I'm in a position to know, having had the dubious experience of growing up an unwanted child in my uncle's home."

"If we have to, we'll find him a good home," Matthew said defensively.

Carlos lifted the infant out of Alex's arms. "Your name is Jerome." Carlos used his finger to draw a cross on the wean's head. "May your namesake keep you safe, *hijo*." In an undertone, he blessed the child in Latin and handed him back to Alex.

"Jerome?" Alex said.

"After the patron saint of orphans," Carlos informed her. "It seems like a good choice, given the circumstances."

"You had no right," Matthew said.

"Yes, I did. As a priest, I have an obligation to safeguard this innocent soul." Carlos finished tying the cross in place around the baby's neck and straightened up. "I'll be back in some days to see how they fare."

They fared badly, the both of them. Sarah threw tantrums when the wean cried, screeching at her parents that she wanted it gone, and that made the babe scream even more, as if it understood his mother's rejection of him, and that in turn made Sarah rush off to hide in her bed, the pillow pressed hard over her head.

She looked at the child and she saw Philip Burley leering at her; she saw it fast asleep on its back and there was Walter, eyes regarding her hungrily.

"Take him away!" she screamed. "Make him stop his infernal crying, aye?"

Every time the wean cried, her breasts strained against the linen bands. Every time that thin voice rose in a plaintive wail, her womb contracted in painful cramps and she hated it that even now, when the wean was birthed and safely out of her, it should still have such an effect on her.

"Please, Da," she sobbed one evening, "I can't bear it, aye? Just—" Kill it, she was going to say, but she bit back on that, and, anyway, she didn't necessarily want the babe dead, just gone. She slid covert glances at Mama, and something black and toothy crawled through her guts at the look in Mama's eyes when she held the detested bairn. How could she smile and coo at him, bastard son of the Burleys that he was?

At night, she heard her parents argue as she'd never heard them argue before, and with each day, Mama grew more and more pinched around the mouth, blue eyes sunk to lie like dull pools in dark, bruised hollows. Da looked but little better: sun would strike a tired face, etched with grooves that made Sarah realise that he was, in fact, quite old.

And then finally, after well over a fortnight, Mama gave up.

"Fine," she said one morning, "take him away. But promise me you'll find him a good home." She looked utterly dejected, her spine curved into a heavy C. "Poor kid, all alone in the world." From where she stood, just outside the room, Sarah threw the wean eyebolts. He shouldn't even exist, should he?

"I'll do my best," Da promised. "Mayhap Julian will know of a family willing to take him." He went over to where Mama was sitting and crouched down to rest his head against her. "Won't you please come with me? Help me?" Mama's hand came up to smooth at his hair, rest on his unshaven cheek.

"Of course I will."

It was a cavalcade that set off in the direction of Providence the next day: not only her parents and the wean, but also Thomas Leslie, one of his men and a nanny goat. The babe was crying, a reedy sound that floated back with the breeze and then abruptly stopped.

Sarah crossed her trembling arms over her chest. It was gone. The uninvited guest that had lived for months inside of her was borne out of her life, and Sarah slumped into Mrs Parson's capable arms and cried with relief. Afterwards, she straightened up and gave Mrs Parson a wobbly little smile. "Am I terrible for being so glad to see him go?"

Mrs Parson stroked her cheek and shook her head. "Nay, you're not, lassie."

To celebrate, Sarah went out into the woods. For the first time in nearly a year, she could move unencumbered, free at last. With Viggo the dog at her side, and her brother's musket in her hand, she walked for hours among the chestnuts and the maples, running hands down the uneven bark of oaks and the papery stems of birches. She clambered up onto a boulder, filled her lungs with crisp, cold air, and yelled out loud.

"Sarah!" she cried to the trees, to the sky. "I'm Sarah!" And then she lapsed into a wordless howl that reverberated in the air around her.

"Where are you going?" Ian's voice was sharp with irritation.

"Out," Sarah replied, grabbing for the musket. She was still cross with him for yesterday – he'd been very upset when she returned after her long walk, yelling at her that she was an irresponsible fool to wander off like that without ensuring someone went with her.

"I told you," Ian said, towering over her, "you go nowhere without me or Mark."

"Why?" she demanded, stamping her foot. "I can take good care of myself."

"Because I say so," Ian barked back, "and you'll do as I say." He pointed in the direction of the stables. "Now that the cows have calved, there's milking to do."

Sarah glared at him, at Mrs Parson, and even at the unfortunate cat before flouncing off.

She leaned her flushed, angry cheek against the prickly warmth of one cow after the other. Agnes sat some stalls away, and the early evening was filled with the sounds of ruminating cows, the soft whooshing of milk hitting the sides of the buckets, and the occasional scrape of a milking stool against the underlying floor. None of them spoke, except for the odd word as they moved from cow to cow.

From the yard came a faint wail, and all of Sarah stiffened until she recalled that this was Naomi's babe, not hers. Hers? Most certainly not hers. She adjusted the damp bands around her chest and forced all thoughts of weans out of her head. Instead, she busied herself analysing Ian's uncharacteristic irascibility. Something was troubling him, and not only him but Mark as well. With a frown, she went back to her milking, staring without seeing at the milk bucket between her feet.

Chapter 6

Philip Burley remained for a long time in the fringe of trees bordering his brother-in-law's busy little place on York River. He brushed at the breeches he'd stolen a few days ago, let his hand slide over the worn wood of the musket he'd had off the trapper he'd knifed back in January, and went back to scanning the yard.

Too many people, and so he settled down to wait, leaning back against a tree trunk. He had to do so gingerly – just as he had to do most things carefully these days, his body a patchwork of scars and chronic pain after the ordeal the damned savages had put him through. His knuckles stood stark against the skin of his hands, an instinctive reaction to the recollection of all that torture. No man should be capable of surviving what had been done to him – Walter hadn't, dying in his arms some months back – and then to brave that long, endless march towards the east, interminable days and weeks through wintry forests.

At times, he had even forgotten who he was and why he was walking so determinedly towards the rising sun, sinking down to stare blankly at nothing for hours, days on end. Those had been the dangerous times, stretches of inertia when his weakened body had begged him to give up, lie down and die under the closest pine. But he hadn't...oh no, he hadn't, stumbling to his feet with the name Graham ringing in his head. His mouth stretched into a mirthless smile. No doubt Graham thought him well and truly dead, for how was someone to survive disfigurement and pain such as the one he had been subjected to?

It was late evening before Philip was convinced only his kin remained on the premises, and with the reins of the nag he'd appropriated a few weeks ago in one hand, he took a step into the open. The setting March sun lingered on a haphazard collection of houses and sheds, and to the furthest right stood the cabin set aside for his use, a well-built little house that not only housed his bed and other pieces of furniture, but also the secret place in which he kept his gold, his coins and other valuables. Assuming, of course, that none of his long-fingered nephews had helped themselves in his absence, but Philip was relatively certain they hadn't, none of them wishing to risk his ire.

Halfway across the yard, he was hailed, a warning note in the voice of the speaker. Philip turned towards the stables, took in the familiar outline of his favourite nephew, complete with that bristling head of black hair, so like his own. He doffed his hat, his dark hair tumbled as it always did to fall like a curtain over his right eye, and the young man lowered his musket.

"Uncle Philip?"

Philip nodded, attempting to enunciate a greeting. It came out as a guttural sound.

"What..." Joseph Connor stood before him, eyes narrowing to light blue slits as he took in his uncle's face. "Jesus and all his saints, what happened to you?"

Philip shrugged. It would keep. Instead, he indicated the tired horse, his dirty self and ragged clothes.

Joseph nodded that he understood. "Go on, I'll bring up water and clothes."

"Emma?" It actually came out correctly, and Philip looked towards the main house, hoping to see his eldest sister appear in the doorway.

"Dead," Joseph said. "Mother died just before Christmas."

Michael Connor was, in both his defunct mother's and his own opinion, by far the brightest of the Connor lads. So when his uncle, looking like a man risen from the grave, began to speak – well, mostly to write, given his lack of a tongue – of vengeance, he listened but said little, watching with amusement how his older brother fawned on Uncle Philip.

To Michael, Uncle Philip's sorry tale was full of holes the size of mine pits, painting this unknown man Matthew Graham as the devil himself, a man who without just cause had persecuted Uncle Philip and his brothers over very many years, all of it ending when Graham had handed Philip and Walter over into the keeping of the Indians.

Michael didn't much like the detailed descriptions of what the Indians had done to his uncles, and it had to be admitted that Philip had accomplished something of a feat in returning alive from his hellish experiences. He listened with half an ear as Philip laboriously recounted yet again what had been done to him, and how he planned to exact his revenge.

"We don't know," Michael said to his brother next morning.

"Know? What else do we need to know? Our kinsman, our uncle, has been disfigured, and all at the behest of this Matthew Graham."

"But why, Joseph?" Michael gave his piebald stallion one last pat over the rump and backed out of its stall. "What man would do something like that without a reason? If the girl went willingly, then why?" This was the major flaw in his uncle's story. No matter how often he mulled this over, Michael found it incredible that a young girl – and a pretty, marriageable one at that – should gladly go with his outlawed uncles and, after what Philip termed mild convincing, freely give up her body to them.

"Who cares about the why? He'll pay us, Michael, and handsomely at that."

"I don't know," Michael muttered, throwing a look through the open stable door to where his father was talking to his uncle.

"A lot of gold, Michael, a sizeable chunk towards that printing press you so dream about." Joseph gave his brother a brief, one-armed hug. "Mother would have wanted that for you, that you could break away from this, set up on your own."

"Umm," Michael replied, not at all convinced that

50

Mother would have wanted him to achieve his dreams by murdering this unknown Graham.

"Family," Joseph said, "our uncle needs us, little brother. And who was it that paid for your years in London?"

Michael squirmed, threw yet another look at his uncle. Propitiously, Philip chose this exact moment to take off his hat, thereby baring his destroyed countenance to the sun.

"And it's only this one man, Matthew Graham, right?" he asked.

"Of course," Joseph said. Michael wasn't quite sure he believed him – but it was a lot of gold.

"If you ride with him, don't bother coming back," Paul Connor told his two youngest sons. "And don't expect me to intercede for you should you be arrested." He shook his head at them. "Your uncle is a violent man, as were his brothers, and I myself find it doubtful he didn't bring all this upon himself, a just retribution for wrongs done."

"That's not what he says," Joseph said, "and all he wants is revenge."

"Hmph!" Paul Connor said. "You're too old not to know what kind of man he is. A rogue, an unscrupulous man that trades in whatever will further line his pouch, no matter the cost to his victims."

"He'll pay us," Michael said, "and God knows we both need the money."

"Blood money," Paul said, shaking his head.

Michael looked away from the disappointed look in his father's eye.

"Gold is always gold," Joseph said, "and it isn't as if you have any to spare, is it?"

"That's how it has to be," Paul Connor said defensively. "What we earn has to be reinvested in the business."

Joseph raised his brows, looked over the ramshackle sheds and the stacked, finished barrels. "That's how it is because you're a dismal businessman, and if it hadn't been for Mother and her brothers, we'd all have starved to death."

"Hold your tongue, lad. Be grateful for what we've given you."

"For what? For this? A little cooperage in the middle of nowhere?" Joseph sneered.

"Go then! Go and never come back."

Michael flushed at his father's tone. "Now that Mother isn't here, there's no reason to return here anyway."

"Ingrate! We sent you overseas, we did, we've had you educated, and this is how—"

"You didn't. Mother did, with money Uncle Philip gave her."

"Ill-gotten gains," Paul spluttered, "gold soiled with the blood of innocents, with—"

"You don't know that!" Joseph retorted.

"Of course, I do, and so do you." With that, Paul swivelled on his toes and stalked off.

"He's right, you know," Michael told his brother.

"Maybe." Joseph shrugged. "But I don't care. This time, he has a legitimate reason, and that's all that matters."

"Hmm," Michael said. But he knew he'd ride with them anyway, if nothing else for the promised gold.

Two days later, Philip Burley sat up on his horse and scanned his new companions. Wolves, the lot of them – his wolves, and at their head rode his nephews. Philip Burley made a sound that nowadays passed for a chuckle, and with his hand motioned for them to fall in line behind him. He settled his broad-brimmed hat on his head, and his ravaged face was hidden in its shadow. The horses raised a cloud of dust behind them as he set a steady pace due north. It was a long ride from the warmth of the Virginia coastlands to the north of Maryland, and he itched with suppressed expectations. This time, he would kill them all, every single Graham male, and Matthew he would save for last.

Chapter 7

Alex looked doubtfully at her brother-in-law. "You?" she said, unable to keep the incredulity out of her voice.

"Why not?" Simon Melville challenged, smiling at the baby he was clutching to his chest. Matthew and Alex shared a look. This they had never considered an option, and when Julian had suggested that maybe Simon would make a good father to the boy, both of them had just stared at him. Simon let his eyes flit from one to the other and tightened his hold on poor Jerome who let out a displeased squawk.

"Sorry," Simon cooed, and hefted the boy against his shoulder instead.

"But…" Alex cleared her throat. "You're too old!"

"Too old? I'm not too old!" Simon stood to show off his physique. "Not yet sixty, and as healthy as a frolicking bull calf in spring."

"Hmm," Alex replied, not at all impressed. Simon had always been round, but since Joan's death some years ago, his girth had expanded worryingly, giving him an unflattering similarity to a spinning top. Simon followed her glance and made a futile effort to pull in his stomach.

"Most of it is brawn," he tried, and Alex burst out laughing. Simon gave her a hurt look, and turned his attention instead to Matthew. "I would make him a good father, you know I would. The lad would be well raised and schooled."

Undoubtedly, Alex smiled, seeing as Simon himself was an educated man, a lawyer no less.

"But why?" Matthew asked. "A wean is a lot of effort."

Simon looked away, a shadow crossing his face. "I have nothing. My dearest Joan, my daughter, both gone from me, and my wee grandchildren…well, it isn't the same, is it?"

He sighed and kissed the dark head of the child he was still holding. "I'll love him for who he is, not blame him for who his father was."

"You know nothing of taking care of children," Alex protested, more out of rote than anything.

Simon beamed at her. "Esther has promised to help."

Esther Hancock confirmed that this was the case, and even her husband, William, assured them that the baby would be welcome in their home.

"What's his name?" Esther asked, folding back the shawl to get a proper look at the baby. Wide open eyes met hers.

"Err..." Alex shifted from foot to foot.

"Carlos named him Jerome," Matthew broke in, "but I can't say I much like the name."

"Carlos?" Simon gave him a curious look. "The wee priest?"

Esther was frowning down at the wooden cross around the baby's neck. "Is he baptised a papist?" she asked, her voice heavy with censure.

"He gave him a name and a cross to keep him safe," Alex said. "I'm not sure that counts as being baptised into anything."

"It sounds like a baptism to me." William eyed the baby as if he expected him to sprout horns at any moment.

Alex stifled a sigh. She liked Betty's parents, and for the most part, William was a reasonable man, open to rational argument – except when it came to his faith. His wife was just the same: devout well beyond what Alex considered normal, with hours spent each day on her knees with her nose in the Bible.

At times, Alex suspected William considered her flighty, eyes wandering over her, all the way from her head to her toes, before flitting over to his own wife, always most modestly dressed. At other times, like now, she suspected the man had the hots for her, his gaze locking down on her breasts. It made her smile, rather pleased that she could still entice a man into gawking, so she straightened her back ever so slightly and leaned towards him – by chance, like.

"We'll have him baptised into the kirk, and I'll name him Duncan, after my Da." Simon clapped himself on the knees and straightened up. "Are we in agreement then?"

"I'm not sure how Sarah will react." Alex adjusted the baby's coif.

"She won't need to see him," Simon said. "It isn't as if we run into each other often, is it?" And so the matter was concluded, and Simon Melville became a father again, proudly carrying the basket up to the room he rented from the Hancocks. In celebration, a toast to Duncan was drunk in good Scots whisky.

"You flaunt yourself," Matthew said with some asperity when Alex and he made their way back through the gathering March dusk to Julian's house and the little attic room there.

"I do what?" Alex dragged back against his hand.

"He drools, William, and you sit back and raise your breasts even higher in his direction."

"I do no such thing!" Alex was very affronted. Was it her fault that William gawked at her? Besides, the man was about as exciting as a doornail.

"Aye, you do, and I don't like it. Not one bit do I like it." He yanked her close and surprised her by kissing her, hard. "He devours you with his eyes," Matthew went on when he let her go, "and you preen."

"Preen?" Alex tried to pull her hand free from his hold. "For him? Don't be ridiculous!"

His eyes were very close, only inches from her own. "So for whom is it that you smooth down your skirts to lie close to your thighs, for what eyes is it you fiddle with your hair, adjust your bodice over your chest?"

Alex felt caught out. Okay, so at times she enjoyed teasing poor William, flattered by his obvious infatuation. "For you, I suppose. I never see any other man but you. Not like that."

"Don't you?" he said softly and his nose brushed once, twice, against hers.

"No," she breathed against his cheek, "never." Which, after all, was true. It made him smile, his mouth coming down to cover hers in the softest of kisses, while his hand, as if by chance, brushed over her breasts.

"My woman," he murmured into her ear before kissing her just below it, which made her inhale, her insides contracting pleasantly. "My woman," he added, biting her ear lobe a tad too hard. "Best you don't forget it, wife." Once again, his lips, his tongue, caressed the sensitive spot below her ear, and Alex shivered, leaning into him. He laughed. "Behave," he said, straightening up. "Later," he promised as he took her hand again.

Supper took too long – far too long. Alex tried to act normal, conversing with her thirteen-year-old son David about his schoolwork and his newfound friends, but her thoughts were elsewhere, like two feet away from David, where Matthew was sitting with Malcolm, Ian's son. She hummed and hawed at adequate intervals, shared a fleeting, hungry look with Matthew, and forced her attention back to the boys.

David was doing well in school, but Malcolm was finding it all rather difficult, Julian had confided before supper, saying that Ian's son spent a lot of time looking out of the window and longing for home.

"A farmer's lad," Julian had said with a slight smile. "That Malcolm is happier among beasts and fields than he is here."

Throughout the meal, Matthew made distanced love to her. He handed her the cabbage dish, and his fingers caressed her hand. He dropped his napkin and, when he bent to retrieve it, his hand rested on her thigh. She leaned forward for the salt and, as if by chance, his hand stroked the underside of her arm. She blushed and he grinned, eyes dropping casually to her bosom before flashing back up to lock into hers. Alex was dry-mouthed with desire, and when Ruth snatched the last of the pie away from under David's and Malcolm's speculative eyes, Alex was about to stand and hurry up to their room.

"Whisky?" Julian asked Matthew, sweeping with his arm to suggest they should repair to the parlour.

"I wouldn't mind," Matthew replied, smiling teasingly in Alex's direction. He took her hand for an instant in the narrow hallway, his thumb moving in slow circles over her wrist a couple of times before he resumed his conversation with Julian. Not entirely unperturbed, Alex noted, seeing how gingerly he crossed his long legs before adjusting the skirts of his coat over his lap. She arched her back and smiled widely at him. By chance, he extended his leg so that the toe of his shoe nudged at hers. She could feel the current leap between them and sat back before she did something thoroughly inappropriate, such as sitting on his lap and... Her imaginations were brought to an abrupt end by the entrance of Ruth, balancing a huge tray before her.

"Are you alright?" Alex asked Ruth after having accepted a cup of tea. Ruth blew at her tea and nodded. Pregnancy became her, and Ruth, in her sixth month, was the epitome of blooming womanhood, round and generous of body, with permanent roses on her cheeks and an air of contentment about her that spread like rings over water to lap at the feet of anyone close to her.

"Julian says I was born to motherhood," Ruth said. Now a married woman, she wore her dark red hair braided and coiled high on her head, covered by a starched cap, and in keeping with her husband's profession, she was sedately dressed in a becoming shade of muted green that served to highlight her eyes, a lighter, greener version of her father's hazel.

Quite the exemplary minister's wife, Ruth was, and on the small table beside the armchair where she usually sat were stacked a set of small volumes, mostly biographies of devout women who had made it their mission in life to support their husband and birth his children. Alex flipped through one of them, reading with some compassion about the by now defunct unknown Mrs Sydney, who had given birth regularly as clockwork and still had not one live child to show for it at the end.

"Oh my God...one a year, almost," she muttered, snapping the book closed to look at her daughter. "That's too close, and even while you're breastfeeding, you have to take precautions."

Ruth looked away, muttering that this was a subject best discussed between husband and wife.

"It saps your strength, Ruth," Alex said, "and you have very many fertile years before you." At which her eighteen-year-old daughter smiled, a hand settling on her swelling belly.

Alex was distracted from her conversation with Ruth by Matthew's sudden stillness.

"What?" She looked from Julian to her husband.

"I...err, well, I thought it best to tell you," Julian said.

"Tell us what?" Alex asked, even if she already knew. The pleasant buzzing in her veins stilled, she set a hand on Matthew's thigh, not to arouse him but to reassure him.

"Burley." Matthew's eyes lightened into an opaque green. "It's confirmed, aye? He's alive."

"But not here," she said, sinking her fingers into his flesh.

"Oh no," Julian hastened to say. "Of course not here. Down in Virginia, as we hear it, and still with a price on his head."

"Far away," Ruth put in.

"Very," Alex tried, smiling. But in her chest her heart was banging so hard against her ribs that she feared it would break out of her body and plop wetly to the floor.

They retired to bed early, Matthew with that vacant look on his face that indicated he didn't want to talk – he was wallowing in memories he preferred to handle on his own. He undressed in silence, cleaned his teeth in silence, and slid into bed in silence. Alex tried to talk to him while she did her evening things, but he replied in monosyllabic grunts, no more, and when she was ready for bed, he had already rolled over on his side, eyes firmly closed. Alex sighed and nestled up as close as she could to his back.

"I'm here, you know," she said, kissing his nape. "I'm always here."

In response, he nodded.

She was already wide awake in the predawn when he turned to her, his hands moving questioningly over her legs. She shifted closer and opened her arms, and he came into her, urgent and hard. He pounded into her, head thrown back, eyes squished close, and this had nothing to do with making love: it was more about assuaging fears and laying demons to rest. She held him without saying anything, her hands caressing his shoulders, the small of his back, the outline of his arms through his shirt.

He shuddered in release and fell forward to rest his full weight on her, his head pillowed only inches from hers. His face relaxed, lines smoothing out, the long mouth reverting to its natural softness, and with a contented noise, he buried his nose in her neck and exhaled, warm breath tickling her skin. She lay with her sleeping man in her arms and watched over him, fingers repeatedly touching his hair, the back of his neck, the bristle on his unshaven cheeks. Only as the sun rose, patterning the bed and floor with reassuring blocks of light, did she fall asleep.

"Don't be silly," Alex said later that same morning, smoothing back Ruth's hair from a worried face. "We'll be alright."

"But Burley—" Ruth began.

"We'll fix it." Alex smiled with confidence she didn't at all feel. She patted Ruth on her stomach and stood back. "You take care of yourself and the baby, sweetheart."

Ruth gave her a blinding smile. "Julian does that."

"I imagine he does." Alex smothered a smile, her eyes on the love bite on Ruth's neck. She hugged her daughter close.

"Had a good time?" Alex asked Thomas once Providence had dropped behind them. Thomas gave her a guarded look and confirmed that yes, he had. She looked over at their old friend and smiled. Some years short of seventy, Thomas Leslie sat his horse with ease and still carried a sword by his side, as he had done since, as a young man, he fought in the English Civil War.

"Pistols and such are not for me," he had confided to Alex

at one point. "I'm a bad marksman, but a good swordsman, Alex, even now."

Thomas had pushed his hat down firmly on his head to shield him from the sun, and on his large gelding he still cut quite the figure, albeit that he was all in grey, effectively matching his horse.

"The beer as good as always down at Mrs Malone's?" Alex asked, tongue-in-cheek. She knew for a fact Thomas frequented Mrs Malone for other itches than those for good beer.

"Mmm," he replied vaguely and spurred his horse to join Matthew, riding some paces ahead on a restive Aaron.

Around noon, Alex began to feel ill, and by evening, she was damp with fever, her stomach turning itself inside out whenever she attempted to eat something. They made camp in a grove of white oaks, and repeatedly, she stumbled away into the woods, refusing Matthew to go along as her guts voided themselves both ways, leaving her shivering and stinking and ridiculously weak.

It was sheer luck that she was lucid enough in the middle of the night to understand what she was seeing when a band of men rode down the western slope towards the narrow dirt track that passed for the road from Providence to Leslie's Crossing and beyond. She remained where she crouched for a long time, trying to calm her racing heart back from its present thundering rate. A weak moonbeam had hit one man squarely in the face, and even at this distance she had known him at once: Philip Burley, eyes glinting like droplets of brittle ice

"Don't be a fool!" Thomas Leslie snapped, and all of a sudden he was back to being a renowned and trusted senior officer in the New Model Army, face set in stern, grim lines. "Alex says there were many men, very many men, and how do you plan on taking them on by yourself?"

"But she also says they were riding hard! I must stop them before they…" Matthew broke off, dragging his hands desperately through his hair. Alex sat huddled into herself, trying to force her brain into coming up with one – at least one – good idea as to what to do.

"Matthew!" Thomas' voice was sharp with authority, and Matthew turned to face him. "You take Aaron and ride for the Chisholms but for God's sake, keep well off the road. I will follow with Alex once she is somewhat more recovered." Matthew nodded in reluctant agreement with this plan.

"No!" Weakly, Alex pushed herself up on her knees and then to stand. "No, Thomas. I'm going with Matthew." Never again would she let him out of her sight – look what had happened to him last time!

"Lass," Matthew groaned, grabbing at her as she swayed, "I have to ride fast, and Aaron can't go full speed with a double load."

"No…" Her hands knotted themselves into his coat.

"I have to go," Matthew whispered to her. "I must get help before they ride into Graham's Garden."

"No," she repeated uselessly, and he had to unclench her hands before hurrying off to his horse. Halfway there, he wheeled and rushed back, swept her into his arms and kissed her hair.

"I love you," he said, and a minute or so later, he was swallowed into the dark.

Chapter 8

Ten days in the company of his uncle and the men riding with them had further increased Michael's doubts about this whole venture. Besides, he was no fool, and to ride more than a dozen men strong seemed excessive if the intention was to rid the world of only Matthew Graham.

Whenever he tried to raise the subject with Joseph, his brother shrugged, saying that Uncle Philip was taking no chances this time, and, as he heard it, this Graham fellow was wily as a fox. Still, Michael was hungry for his promised gold, and on top of that he had the definite impression that his uncle would take it badly should he choose to leave. Very badly. Michael swallowed.

They were two days or so from their intended target when they found the slaves, five of them sitting huddled round a fire that announced their presence to the wolves of this world – men such as them. It was an uneven fight, and by the time it was over, Michael had a huge grin on his face. Philip glared at him, attempted to speak, but all that came out was a long stream of inarticulate sounds. The tenor of it all was clear: Philip Burley was an angry man, and his hands twitched with the need to hurt someone.

"They're worth money, a lot of money, even." Michael dismounted from his piebald horse and followed his brother over to inspect the five captured men.

Four of them stood meekly while their mouths were forced open, their arms and legs probed. The fifth struggled wildly, screeching through the rag someone had stuffed into his mouth to shut him up. Michael smiled when he found the elegant pistol on him, made as if to tuck it in his belt but thought better of it, offering it to his uncle instead.

"Are they branded?" he asked, and one by one the men

were stripped. All of them were, an F standing visible against their skin.

"Hmm." Michael frowned. Escaped slaves were always claimed by their owners, and in this case the brands clearly showed where they belonged – this confirmed by the youngest of the slaves.

"Do you know this Farrell?" Joseph asked Philip, who gave him a sullen nod. Well enough, Philip managed to convey, a small self-important man with a thriving slave business and a couple of large tobacco plantations south of Providence.

Michael inspected them again. Strong men, all of them, but the worse for wear after living badly in the woods. They had a friend who sailed regularly down to Jamaica, he explained to Philip, and bucks such as these would bring in good money there. Philip nodded grudgingly. Gold never came amiss.

"We'll rebrand them," Joseph suggested, and indicated for one of the men to stoke some life back into the fire.

It all took too long, according to Uncle Philip, and by the time they set off again, Philip was glaring at Michael and Joseph in a way that made Michael shiver and Joseph laugh.

The black men were running in halters behind them. Stripped and bound, Michael could see the play of muscle beneath their skins. Yes, strong men all of them, and in his head he calculated the neat profit they would make on them once their friend had his share. Philip sneered when Michael mentioned a round number. That was nothing compared to what the Grahams would bring in, he indicated.

"The Grahams?" Michael gave him an uncomprehending look.

Beside him, Joseph laughed. "What did you think, little brother? That we'd ride all this way, fifteen strong, just to kill one homesteader? No, no, Uncle Philip has a far more complex plan in mind." He grinned at his uncle who grinned back, a grimace that forced Michael to suppress a shudder.

"Slaves," Joseph went on. "We'll sell them all as slaves

– bar the adult males – and you have no idea what a white woman – or a white child – can bring in on the slave markets, do you?"

A distinct feeling of unease rippled up Michael's spine. It was one thing to capture and sell blacks – they were, after all, slaves – quite another to contemplate doing the same to white people. There and then, it dawned on him that his uncle was planning for the total eradication of this unknown Graham family. Michael chewed his cheek. To kill this Matthew Graham to avenge the deaths of his other three uncles seemed fair, but a whole family...no, that had to be wrong.

Joseph just laughed when Michael voiced his concerns, saying he didn't care one way or the other as long as he returned substantially richer than when he set out, and then he clapped his spurs into his horse to bring it abreast with Philip's mount, an eager second-in-command on this punitive expedition.

Michael threw a long look at his brother. Cut from the same cloth, his mother used to say when she regarded Joseph and his maternal uncles, and Michael knew for a fact his mother had not meant that as an accolade. His musings were brought short by an angry sound emanating from Philip, a sound clearly indicating they had to hurry, and Michael had better keep up.

Philip pushed them to ride most of the day, well into the evening and, after but a few hours' respite, again through the night. When one of the slaves gasped that they had to rest, Philip brought the handle of his whip down on his face before ordering them all gagged, and now, just as dawn was breaking, Michael walked his exhausted horse down a wooded slope, coming to a halt at his uncle's raised hand.

"It's not right," Michael whispered to his brother, "to destroy an entire family like this." He shook his head, throwing a worried look at his uncle. In the returning light, he looked a veritable monster, and Michael was no longer sure he wanted to take part in the coming atrocities.

Joseph gave him a patronising smile. "It will make us

rich. And who will ever know, little brother? There will be no one left to tell." He snickered at Michael's shocked face and moved away with a shrug, eyes glued to the farm spread out before them.

"I'll know," Michael whispered to his back, and stepped a few feet further away. He should leave, distance himself from this place before it was too late.

Philip Burley stood looking down at the Graham farm where all was still sunk in sleep, and his mouth drew back in a stiff and painful smile. In the dawn light, the solid, grey buildings gave the impression of having sprung seamlessly from the ground, permanent and indestructible. Philip sneered. By tonight, it would all be gone, the Graham family slaughtered or carried off to slavery, and he intended to keep the Graham girl for himself.

He was overwhelmed by an urge to ride his men down there now, torch the buildings and set about with musket and knife, but forced himself away from these tempting images. First to know where they all were, then to plan the way each and every one of them would end. Matthew Graham he would tie to the large oak that stood in solitary splendour in the yard, and force him to watch as his family was eradicated, his women and children branded slaves before his eyes. Philip swallowed back on a surge of black joy. Today, Matthew Graham would pay, kept alive until his entire home lay in smouldering embers around him.

Philip couldn't believe his luck when the kitchen door to the big house opened and Sarah Graham stepped out on the stoop, her hair still in its thick night braid. She stood in the morning sun, raised her arms to her head and undid her hair, shaking it out to lie heavy and unbound. Philip's hand knotted itself around air, a bodily recollection of how it had felt to sink his fingers into that thick glistening hair, how he had used it to rein her back, force her into obedient stillness while he...

The girl stretched, stepped off the stoop, and strode off straight towards him. Philip shrank back into the bushes, but realised she was making for the kitchen garden, and watched her avidly as she walked up the gentle slope. He wondered if she remembered him as he remembered her and snickered. Of course she did, and if he were to appear before her she wouldn't even try to run. He had taught her just how much it hurt to attempt to flee.

Philip returned his attention to the waking farm: women making for the stables and the lowing cows, men appearing at the doors of the cabin, dressed for a day of heavy work in the fields. Three men, Philip counted, and his teeth ground together as he waited and waited but no Matthew Graham appeared. He scowled, twisted his head a fraction of an inch, and there was Sarah, now halfway up the hill, and he decided he wouldn't wait – he'd destroy what was here and come back later to finish Graham off.

"We can share her," Joseph suggested, eyeing the young woman lasciviously.

Philip's fist struck him full on the mouth. Mine, Philip thought, mine and if you touch her you're dead, nephew or not. He adjusted his breeches and stalked off towards the girl.

Michael had been on the point of mounting his horse when the girl had stepped outside, and once he'd seen her, it was inconceivable that he should ride away and leave her to her fate – not that he had any idea how to wrest this creature from his uncle. He moved stealthily through the fringe of the woods, his eyes never leaving the girl. She was light on her feet, the general shape of her legs discernible through the cloth of her skirts, and when she turned to the side, he saw a well-shaped ear, the line of neck and shoulder, and a nicely rounded bosom.

The tip of his tongue slid out to wet his lip, and like an eel Michael wiggled into the protective depths of a blackberry bramble. She stopped at the entrance to the kitchen garden, and when she raised her hand to her hair it trembled wildly, a soft sound escaping through her nose. One hand disappeared into the side slit of her skirts, reappearing holding a dagger. A dagger? The other hand clutched at her skirts, and she frowned as she threw repeated looks down the hill. Well, she didn't see him, hidden as he was in a cloud of spiny greens and browns, but he pressed himself even closer to the damp ground and tried to find what she was looking for.

Michael swallowed when he finally did, and his grip on the smooth ivory butt of his pistol slipped. He had to get out of here, find his brother and warn him that this was a trap, but before him the girl – Sarah, he recalled her name was – took a step out into the full sunlight, and he just couldn't move, transfixed by the sun in her hair, the vivid blue of her eyes.

"Da!" Ian yanked at Matthew's sleeve, nodding his head to where Philip was climbing the slope. "Sarah, he's going after Sarah!"

"As planned," Matthew replied, deeply ashamed for putting his daughter so at risk, no matter that he'd given her his best dirk. But with only an hour or so in which to plan his defences, this had seemed the best strategy: to lure Philip away from his men by presenting him with the enticing picture of Sarah, barefoot and with her hair undone.

"Now then?" Ian said, musket already resting against his shoulder.

"Now," Matthew said, and with a ringing yell he leapt out into the open, pistol in one hand, sword in the other.

For all that they were taken by surprise, the ruffians regrouped at impressive speed. Matthew staggered back when someone butted him full in the gut, went down on one knee, and was suddenly fighting for his life against three men. Philip – where was Philip? With a roar, Matthew regained his feet, threw the discharged pistol to the side and pulled his dirk instead. A man toppled down the slope, hatless, with thick, dark chestnut hair. His son? Merciful Lord, was he dead?

"Mark!" He parried a blow to his head, tried to locate his son.

"Here, Da." Mark was bleeding and limping but he was alive, and hale enough to snatch a sword from a wounded man and charge up the slope again.

Matthew followed him. Philip – he couldn't see the bastard. Was he mayhap hiding? Or had he run, spineless coward that he was at heart? But no – well to the top of the slope, Philip was standing, and even at this distance, Matthew could see every movement he made. Burley pulled a knife, mimed a slashed throat, and turned towards the kitchen garden.

"No!" Matthew gasped. "No, goddamn it, not her, not Sarah!" He redoubled his efforts to fight his way up the slope, but there were too many men between him and his daughter, too many raised swords, swinging muskets and expertly wielded knives.

"Ah!" A short blade slashed at his arm. Matthew forced his attention back to his opponent, but in his head all he could hear and see was Sarah, oh God, his wee lass! The man before him bore more than a passing resemblance to Philip Burley – the same messy dark hair, the same general good looks, the same build – and with a surge of black rage, Matthew lunged, sword at the ready.

"Get out of my way," he hissed, but the man just shook his head.

"It's you," he panted. "It's you that's Matthew Graham, and I'll have the pleasure of killing you myself, in revenge for my uncles."

"I think not." Matthew blocked a well-directed thrust, wheeled, rose on his toes and with a tearing sound his blade sank deep into the younger man's right shoulder, neatly slicing off his arm.

He ran. Like a stag in flight, he bounded up the hill, and his amputated toe shrieked in agony, his exhausted body pleaded with him to slow down, but Matthew pushed on, driven by the image of his daughter bleeding out on the ground.

"Sarah!" He gasped, had to struggle to fill his lungs. "Sarah! Run, lass, run!" Too late, his warning came too late. He could see Philip entering the garden, the sun glinting on his knife, on the silver buckle of his hat. "Oh God, oh God," Matthew moaned. What was he to tell Alex, how was he to live with himself, and Sweetest Lord, please hold Your hand over Sarah now, please protect her today, because damn You, God, You didn't help her last time, did You?

The last fifty yards were the worst. He could see her now, his daughter screeching in terror as she backed away from Philip. Matthew tried to call her name, assure her he was coming, but his mouth had gone dry, his vocal chords had frozen in an 'aaaah', like the bleating of a desperate ram.

Sarah went for Philip with the dirk. At first, Philip staggered back, but where Sarah should have taken the opportunity to flee, she screeched and flew at him again. This time, Philip blocked her thrust, wrenched the weapon from her hand and threw it to the side. She kicked at him. Philip got hold of her and twisted his hand into her hair, forcing her down to the ground. Sarah collapsed, kneeling like a supplicant at Philip's feet.

Oh God, what had he done? How could he have been foolish enough to believe Sarah would be capable of defending herself against Burley? How could he have thought she'd be fuelled by righteous rage when in fact she was incapacitated by fear?

Sarah grovelled on the ground. Philip Burley walked around her. He set his hands on Sarah's hips, he kneeled behind her, and his daughter was trembling uncontrollably, but she didn't move away.

"No!" It came out as a croak. Matthew watched mesmerised as Philip Burley pressed his groin against his daughter's posterior, grabbed hold of Sarah's hair, and held her still. The knife. It flashed in the light. Philip Burley laughed – no, he cackled. The knife came down. Slowly, Philip lowered it so that it rested almost at Sarah's throat. Matthew fell to his knees. There was nothing he could do. Any moment now, his daughter would be dead, and all because of him.

Sarah's hand closed on a stone. Matthew stumbled to his feet and ran, praying as he had never prayed before, begging the good Lord for a miracle, a bolt of divine intervention that would guide Sarah's hand. He could see Sarah tense, fingers whitening on the stone. There was a shot. Philip Burley grunted, the knife fell unhanded, and with a gurgling sound Philip collapsed on top of Sarah.

She screamed. "Da!" she shrieked. "Help me, Da!"

Matthew was already hurtling towards her, covering the remaining yards as fast as he could. The man on top of her jerked. For an instant, Matthew thought Burley might be still alive, and his hand closed on the hilt of his dirk in anticipation of slicing the man's throat from ear to ear. But no, Burley was dead as a rock, his large frame pinning a frantic, screaming Sarah to the ground. Matthew heaved Burley to the side and collected Sarah to his chest.

"You're alright, Sarah," he crooned, holding his distraught daughter as gently as if she were a cracking egg. "You did right well, lassie. You were very brave." Sarah scrabbled even closer to him. He overbalanced and sat down heavily in the cabbage patch, still holding her, and all the time he murmured her name, smoothed her hair, assuring her she was alright.

"Mama," Sarah whispered against him. "I want Mama."

Matthew tightened his hold. So did he, now that the anxiety that had been surging through him for the last thirty hours was quickly waning.

"She'll be here by tonight," he said, throwing a look in the direction of the lane. He got to his feet and helped her to stand. "You must dare to look at him, or else he will live forever in your nightmares."

"He already does," she answered bitterly.

"Aye, in mine as well," Matthew replied, and between them flew a look of total understanding. "But it will help, to see him truly dead. It will for me, at least."

She slipped her hand into his and took an unsteady gulp of air.

"A well-sprung trap," Robert Chisholm commented later, rubbing his hands together. Matthew grunted, surveying the men before them. Seven were dead, and of the remaining six, two were badly wounded. And then there was Philip, dead in the kitchen garden. Over his heart bloomed a circle of blood – a perfect shot that must have killed the man immediately. Too easy a death, the bastard should have been roasted slowly to death. "And quite the catch," Robert went on, his eyes glued to the captive blacks.

"Aye," Matthew said.

"I counted one more." Ian studied the men. "The one on that distinctive horse, the piebald."

Matthew narrowed his eyes at the horses. No piebald – not anymore. "Aye, I think you're right."

Robert walked over to one of the captive men and questioned him in a low threatening voice, returning with his brow heavily creased. "A man named Connor, Michael Connor, and he isn't here – nor is his horse."

"If he knows what's good for him, he will be halfway back to Virginia by now," Matthew said, but he didn't like it, not at all. He stood staring out towards the west for a couple of minutes, debating with himself whether to set off after the man or not. Irrelevant, he decided, a mercenary, no more.

"Doesn't it feel hypocritical?" Matthew asked, watching Carlos close the eyes of the man he had just administered confession and last rites to.

"Hypocritical?" Carlos cast him an edgy look.

"Well, aye, you have just absolved a self-confessed murderer and rapist of his sins, and tomorrow he'll stand before the gates of heaven. That is what you believe, right?"

"Not quite as simple," Robert put in. "He'll spend many lifetimes in purgatory first."

"And yet, one day, his victims may find themselves face to face with him in heaven." Matthew shook his head at the notion. "Won't they be upset?"

"They will have learnt to forgive," Carlos said, "and if God can forgive him, then how can we simple humans not?"

Matthew spat. "Right easy, and I won't forgive Burley or his brothers, ever, for what they did to me and mine."

"And so they may pass into the magnificence of heaven while you remain outside," Carlos said.

"According to you," Matthew said.

"According to the Holy Church," Carlos corrected.

Matthew hitched his shoulders. "On account of him being Virginian, I reckon he was an Anglican." He jerked his head towards the dead man in the kitchen garden.

"He died unshriven in any case," Carlos said, "and unrepentant, I suspect."

"So he goes to hell," Matthew stated with satisfaction.

"To hell." Robert and Carlos nodded in chorus.

Chapter 9

It was well into the afternoon by the time Matthew rode into Leslie's Crossing.

"Alex?" he said as he leapt off his horse. "How is she?"

"Asleep." Thomas had to trot to keep up with Matthew's long strides. "Still feverish, but somewhat better." He led Matthew through the kitchen and up the narrow stairs and took a step back to allow Matthew to enter the little room first.

"She's uncommonly fond of you," Thomas said, coming to stand beside Matthew, who was looking down at his sleeping wife. "I can't begin to count the times she's said your name."

"That's good." Matthew stooped to brush a long, curling tendril off Alex's face. "A wife should be devoted to her husband."

"Devoted?" Thomas said. "That's not what you have, and you know it. It's a rare thing to see, such as what grows between Alex and yourself."

Matthew was acutely embarrassed by this comment – as was Thomas – and after a further moment or so, Thomas left Matthew alone with his wife.

Her mouth curved into a smile. "A rare thing indeed," she murmured and opened an eye, "and he doesn't know the half of it." They shared a low laugh, and he sat down on the edge of her bed. "You smell of blood, but I suppose it isn't yours."

Matthew hadn't thought to wash properly, changing only his shirt, and now that she mentioned it, he could see dark stains on his breeches.

"Some of it is, but most of it isn't." He flexed his bandaged arm. A gash, no more, according to Mrs Parson.

"Oh," Alex replied and shifted closer to him. "Tell me everything."

So he did, describing how he had ridden like the wind for the Chisholms and how, anyway, he'd have been too late if it hadn't been for the Burley band running into the luckless Maroons.

"Maroons?" Alex opened both eyes. "Leon?"

"I come to that," he said, and waited until she settled back into the pillow before continuing with his story, telling her how he and their Chisholm neighbours had set a trap for the would-be pillagers.

He had known she wouldn't like it, but quailed all the same at the look in her eyes when he described how he'd used Sarah as a decoy. And because he had no choice, he had to tell her just how close a thing it had been, with their daughter immobilised by fear and that accursed Philip... He choked, wiping clammy hands up and down his breeches, and somehow his despair softened her face, and he found the courage to tell her the rest: how the knife had come down, and... He frowned.

"He just dropped dead, shot through the heart." Who had fired that shot? Certainly not him, nor any of his comrades. He knuckled himself in the eyes and blinked. God, he was tired. The men with Burley had been easily defeated, he told her, and now nine of them were dead – ten if you counted that damned Burley – while four remained healthy enough to be taken south to hang. The Chisholms had already set off towards Providence, taking the five Maroons along as well.

"You just let the Chisholms take them?" Alex said.

"Of course not. I slipped yon Leon a knife to cut himself and his friends loose come night, and I told him I forgave him for the mule." He yawned so widely his jaws cracked. He had actually done a wee bit more than that, insisting even slaves had a right to food and rest as well as clothes.

"Oh," Alex said, clearly not all that impressed.

"What was I to do? Fight Robert and Martin over

them?" He pinched himself over the bridge of his nose and yawned again.

"No, I suppose not," she sighed. "I hope they make it."

Matthew just nodded, too tired to talk anymore, and when she moved over and patted the bed beside her, he gratefully fell into it.

"I told you," Alex said through her teeth. "I'm fine. I've been fine since yesterday." Not that either Matthew or Mrs Parson had believed her, bundling her off to bed the moment she was off the horse.

"You'll stay in bed one more day," Mrs Parson said, "and then we'll see."

"See? I'm old enough to decide myself!" She tried to stare Mrs Parson down, but that was like trying to make an elephant levitate, and with a loud, protesting grumble, Alex sank back against the feather mattress. She sulkily accepted the mug of herbal tea Mrs Parson extended her way.

"I'm hungry," she whined, and her stomach loudly agreed.

"Tonight," Mrs Parson promised, "but not before." She waited until Alex had finished her tea and with a quick pat left the room.

"Cow," Alex said to the closing door.

"I heard that," Mrs Parson shot back, "and it takes one to know one, no?"

Alex decided to stay on the safe side and just stuck out her tongue.

She woke some hours later with a start to find Carlos sitting beside her. In her fuzzy, still half asleep state, she uttered a gasp of fear and threw herself away from him, a pillow clutched to her chest.

"Alex?" Carlos leaned towards her. "*¿Qué pasa? ¿Una pesadilla?*"

"A nightmare," Alex agreed and gave him a weak smile.

It was still very disconcerting that this mild, sweet priest should be an exact copy of the future Ángel Muñoz, first-class bastard and father of her son, Isaac, born in 1999. If she looked at Carlos through her lashes, she could see her future tormentor, some years older than the young priest, but essentially the same, slight and fine boned, borderline feminine if it hadn't been for the square jaw and the dark, well-defined brows. Alex shook her head to clear it of these hallucinations, aware of the priest's worried eyes on her. She gave him a reassuring smile and sat up in bed, hunting about for her bedjacket.

Carlos averted his eyes while Alex adjusted the soft, knitted garment over her thin shift, smiling instead at the squares of bright coloured light that patterned the floor. Nine panes in the window consisted of stained glass, six red and three green, and on a day like this, the reflections created a very pleasing effect on the scrubbed floorboards.

"Matthew bought them for me," Alex said, having followed his eyes. "He knows I am overly fond of red."

"A very nice colour," Carlos said with a smile.

"I guess you'll just have to work harder then," she teased, "so that one day you can flash around in cardinal robes."

His face darkened, and he ruefully shook his head. "Too late for that. I'm doomed to be an inconspicuous priest far away from the true seat of power."

"You're only twenty-six."

"And very far from Rome."

"Are you and your cousins much alike?" Alex asked, throwing him by this very abrupt change in subject.

"My cousins? Why do you ask?"

She shrugged, not about to tell him that she sincerely hoped it wasn't his direct descendant who would hurt her so badly three centuries from now.

"Just curious, I suppose. After all, you're very like your father." She smiled at the memory of Don Benito, long dead – and very disgraced – Catholic priest.

Carlos regarded her with the expression of mingled dislike and curiosity he always wore when she mentioned his father. "I hope it's only superficial. He was a weak man. So weak he broke his holy vows."

Alex just looked at him. "It burdened him until the day

he died. So, your cousins." She reclined against her pillows and nodded for him to start.

"My uncle and father were brothers," Carlos began, and smiled at her exasperated eye roll. "I mean they were *gemelos*, twins, and Raúl María was born when the bells for morning Mass rang, while my father, Ángel Benito, entered into the world just before Vespers. Their mother died of the ordeal, and the boys grew up with a grieving father and an aunt, Doña Isabel. Quite the termagant..." Carlos straightened up. "We come from an old Seville family. We have lived there since well before the *Reconquista* back in the fifteenth century, and one of our long dead relatives, the saintly Alonso de Hojeda, was instrumental in ridding our land of the nefarious Jews – and other heretics, of course."

"Not something I would brag about," Alex muttered.

"What?" Carlos asked.

"Never mind," Alex said. "Go on."

Carlos gave her an irritated look and bent down to scratch at his peg leg. "Alonso de Hojeda established the Inquisition in Seville and rooted out more false converts, *marranos*, than anyone else—"

"By torturing them, by threatening their children! A man confesses to anything if enough pain is applied to him."

"The Jews killed Jesus. Is it not just that they be punished for this?"

"If we're going to be quite correct, the Romans executed Jesus," Alex said, "and no, I don't think it's fair, and I suspect God is with me on this."

"God? Why would He be? It's His son they killed! They chose – Barabbas before Jesus."

"But they're his chosen people," Alex said.

"Were, Alex, were. They refused to welcome the Messiah."

Alex snorted, but decided to drop the subject before it all became too infected. Besides, she'd bet Carlos had *marrano* blood in him – most of the hoity-toity Seville families did, however reluctant to admit it. She waved for him to go on with his story.

"In our family, one son is always given to the Church, in honour of our saintly relative, and my father was sent from an early age to study with the monks, knowing always he was destined to be a priest."

"Did he want to be?" Alex asked.

Carlos shrugged. "How am I to know? I never met him, did I?"

"I think he did, and he must have been a good priest, a compassionate man."

"He was a bad priest," Carlos said with uncharacteristic vehemence. "Surely he burns in hell by now."

Alex gave him a long, pitying look. Now the bastard son to this disgraced priest was trapped in a web of carnal desires, drawn like a helpless moth to the flame, to Sarah. Most ironic – and very sad.

Carlos dropped his eyes to the rosary beads he was twisting round and round in his hands.

"*Sevilla* is a beautiful place," he murmured, his voice heavy with longing.

"I know," Alex said. "A city stretched out along the Guadalquivir *de saliente a poniente*, from east to west, and over it all stands la Giralda."

"You know my city?"

"I used to. I'm sure it has changed since I saw it last."

He nodded and went back to his rosary. It was probably much changed since he had last seen it too, he said, first all those months in sodden Ireland and now here. "Our family lived close to the royal palace, and my uncle and father ran wild through the courtyards, and as they were impossible to tell apart, it was difficult to punish them. Well, Doña Isabel punished both of them, just in case," he added with a certain dryness that made Alex laugh.

"I think they loved each other, those two small boys, but then my father was taken to the monastery, and Raúl was set to learn his father's trade, and when they met the common ground between them had shrunk to childhood memories of hot days in the shade, stolen oranges they shared behind the rosebush, and slowly they grew into two very different men."

Carlos cast a thoughtful look in her direction. "You say my father was a compassionate man. My uncle, unfortunately, isn't. He took me in to salvage the family's reputation, and ever did he look askance at me, this constant reminder of his brother's fall from grace. I suppose he tried at first, but then his wife gave him a son, a mere year after my arrival, and then two more in as many years. Raúl, Ángel, and Carlos – my namesake. His wife didn't like me, and especially as I and my cousins were so alike we were always taken for brothers." He smiled wryly. "So yes, Alex, to answer your original question, my cousins and I look just the same."

"And do you like them?"

"Like them? I was sent away before I was six, and after that I saw them but once a year at most. I don't know them, but what little I know of them..." He hitched his shoulders. "It seems they take after their father." They sat in comfortable silence for a while, and then Carlos stood.

"I suggest you sleep," he said with a small smile, "or else that dragon you have downstairs may eat us both alive."

"Huh," Alex said, "I'd like to see her try." But she closed her eyes all the same, thinking that a little nap was just what she needed.

She woke to the sensation of hands on her body. Big, warm hands that slid down her arms, up her legs, doing a most thorough inspection of her body. Alex opened an eye and smiled.

"Hi," she said, licking her lips.

"Hi, yourself." Matthew was lying very close, his eyes that amazing golden green that always made her think of sunlit water. "Feeling better?"

"Much." She raised her arms to help him pull her shift off, relishing the sensation of his naked skin against hers. His hand travelled down her back, rolling them both so that she ended up on top, her breasts squished against his hairy chest.

"Your arm?" she asked, bending to nip her way along his jawline.

"It was nowt but a scratch," he said, fiddling with her

braid. Her hair came undone, falling like a curly curtain round her head. She smiled, moved downwards, trailing her hair over his body. His nipples, his navel, the darker line of hair that travelled towards his groin… She kissed and bit, she licked and teased, and Matthew sighed, his hands lying open and relaxed on her head.

"Well, hello there," she murmured, dropping a kiss on his penis. It twitched and thickened under her gentle touch. She cupped his balls and took him in her mouth, liking how his thighs tensed beneath her when she did.

"Aaah," he sighed, his hands no longer quite as relaxed. His fingers sank into her hair, his buttocks rose towards her. "Alex," he whispered, "my Alex."

"That's me," she said, releasing him. "Kiss me," she demanded, and he raised his back off the bed, cradled her head with his hands and kissed her until she had to break away and gulp for air.

"More?" he asked, flipping her over so that she was on her back, pressed into the bed by his weight.

Alex licked her lips again and nodded. "Much more."

"More?" he asked a couple of minutes later, and she wasn't quite as coherent anymore, because she was out of breath and her blood was boiling through her veins, and his fingers were doing things to her that made it difficult to think straight. So she just nodded, hands clutching at the quilt when he slid down to use that oh, so expert mouth on her sex.

"Matthew," she groaned some time later, "no more, Matthew."

"No more?" He laughed, his exhalation a rush of hot air that tickled her.

"No more," she gasped. "I just want…"

"Me," he said, flexing his hips against her.

"Yes," she said, "I want you."

"Now?"

"God, you're a horrible tease at times!" She raised her hips towards him. "Please, Matthew…"

At last, he took pity on her, entering her in one swift

movement that pinned her to the mattress. The size of him inside of her, the words he murmured in her ear, the way his hands tightened their hold on her. He moved a couple of times. She gripped at his back, his buttocks. So close, so very, very close. Oh, yes, yes, yes...

Matthew held still. "Open your eyes," he said.

So she did, staring into his as she came.

Chapter 10

Qaachow came by a few days into April, and with him came his two sons.

"Are you staying?" Alex asked Samuel, and Matthew could hear the hope in her voice.

"Nay," the boy replied, "we're but stopping by. My father is taking us north for some weeks."

"Oh." Alex nodded, and retreated a step or two, pulling wee Adam to stand before her, as if she were using their youngest son as bulwark. Matthew could but sympathise, inundated by an acute sense of loss that washed through him at seeing his son – his, goddamn it! – standing so unreachable for all that he was only a foot or so away. Something shifted in Samuel's eyes, a dark shadow flashed through the light hazel, the mouth wobbled for an instant, and it tore at Matthew to see his son so confused. Alex has apparently seen it too because she extended her hand to touch the boyish shoulder.

"I thought you'd be here for the spring planting," she said.

"We've said twice a year," Qaachow interrupted, "and he was here for your winter feasts."

In reply, Alex walked away, with Samuel running after her. Matthew followed at a slower pace.

"Mama?" Samuel caught up with her by the smoking shed.

She waved a hand at him, averting her wet face. "Just go," she said, breaking into a half run.

"Mama," he groaned, made as if to go after her but was stopped by Matthew.

"Leave her be, lad. I'll talk to her, aye?"

"I don't want her to hurt," his son mumbled.

Matthew gave him a sad little smile. "But she does, Samuel. We both do. Do you find that surprising?"

Samuel hitched his shoulders, scuffed at the ground with his worn moccasin. "I thought…" he muttered but then shut his mouth.

"That it would be easy?" Matthew drew him close. Samuel nodded, sighing into Matthew's shirt, and, for a brief moment, Matthew allowed himself to pretend things were as they should be, with Samuel back where he belonged. The daydream was shattered by Qaachow's voice, and in his arms Samuel began to fidget. Matthew released him, even managed a little smile.

"Go then, lad, they're waiting for you." He gave his son a gentle shove, but couldn't find it in himself to accompany him back to where Qaachow was waiting. Instead, he went to find his wife.

"I can't stand it, I just—" Alex used her shawl to wipe at her face. "I want him back, he should be here, with me!"

"Shh." Matthew kneeled down beside her, gathered her close enough that he could kiss the top of her head. "So do I, lass. Every day I wake, and there is a hollow in my heart, a constant aching for him." And since that visit to the Indian village back in February, if possible his longing for his son had increased, made all the worse by seeing how easily Samuel had fitted into his new life and family. The lad was his Samuel, not White Bear, not a soon-to-be Indian brave whose face would be permanently marked by tattoos, who'd slip further and further away from them.

"Yes," Alex said, "it's awful. And to see him, like today, it tears my heart out."

"Mine too." He rested his head against hers.

"Maybe he'll come back," Alex said.

"Mayhap," Matthew agreed with zero conviction.

They sat in silence as the sun rose to its zenith, and around them spring stood green and bright, but Matthew didn't notice. He saw a lad in breechcloth and moccasins that should have been here, with them.

★

"Do you mind?" Alex threw Sarah a worried look, already regretting her decision to tell her. "He very much wanted him," Alex continued, now with her nose to the ground where she was seeding bed after bed with vegetables, submerging all the emotions woken by Samuel's visit the day before by throwing herself into an extended cycle of work.

"How can he?" Sarah said, thrusting garlic cloves into the soil.

"He sees the baby, not the father," Alex answered, "and maybe he also sees the mother."

Sarah leapt to her feet and threw her wooden trowel to land in the soft, dark earth. "I'm not a mother, you hear? It doesn't count when you are forced and…" She whirled, glaring at her mother, her sisters–in–law, her little nieces who were staring at her open-mouthed. "Oh bloody hell!" she said and ran off, clogs and all.

"She does mind," Mrs Parson said from where she was sitting on the bench.

"No," Alex said sarcastically, "I would never have guessed." With a sigh, she sat back on her heels. "Were we wrong? Simon so wanted him, and the boy…well, it isn't his fault, is it?"

"I think you did right," Naomi voiced staunchly. "And with time she will think so too."

Betty shook her head. "She wants to forget him – this whole last year she wishes to erase completely from her head, and how can she do that if the boy still lives on the fringes of her life?"

Alex gave her daughter–in–law an impressed look. "Very eloquent," she said, making Betty duck her head. "But if you're right, then we may have done right by the boy, but not by Sarah."

"It's done, no?" Mrs Parson pointed out. "So why waste time discussing it? I presume you don't plan on riding down to Providence and tearing the hapless lad away from Simon, do you?"

"No," Alex said, "that alternative hasn't occurred to me."

Sarah had by now reached the stables, and Alex watched her duck inside.

"She'll do," Mrs Parson told her. "Just give her time, aye?"

Sarah had expected the stables to be empty – at least of humans – and was somewhat thrown to find her eldest brother there. Hastily, she rubbed at her face, wiping her nose with her sleeve.

"Why are you here? Shirking, are you?" All the men were out in the fields, as were the oxen and the mules. A cloud passed over Ian's face, and belatedly Sarah realised what she'd said. "Sorry," she mumbled, studying him from under her lashes.

Ian made a guttural sound that Sarah translated to mean he heard but didn't accept her apology. "And you? Aren't you supposed to be working in the garden?"

Sarah grunted and came over to watch him curry Aaron into a shining bronze. "I can do that," she offered in an attempt to compensate for her previous blunder.

If anything, her comment made it worse, two angry eyes regarding her across the horse's broad back. "I'm not entirely useless."

"Useless? Of course you're not useless. I've seen you, you know. You've been out working full days for the last week, from just after dawn 'til dusk. Does Betty know how hard you work out there? Does Da?"

Ian muttered something under his breath along the lines that he didn't appreciate being spied on.

"I wasn't spying," Sarah retorted. "I just happened to be passing." She'd seen him collapse one day, his hands on his lower back, and she had hesitated between rushing to help him and waiting to see what would happen. In the event, it had not taken long before he was back on his feet, his shirt sticking to his sweating skin. Now, she watched how carefully he moved, each step a conscious effort to overcome pain, and moved towards him.

"You have to rest," she said.

"I haven't finished!"

"I don't care. You're coming with me this minute or I'll call Mama down to see you."

He glared at her but threw the currying comb to clatter on the stamped earth of the stable floor. "Fine," he said, crossing his arms, "and where are we going?"

"You are going to bed, and I'll fetch Betty."

"Better?" Betty asked, wiping her hands on her apron. Ian grunted, half asleep on the sun-warmed wooden floor.

Sarah remained by the door, not wanting to intrude as Betty ministered to her husband, but she smiled at how relaxed Ian looked, his dark hair tousled, his face near on buried in the small rug below him.

"Why didn't you tell me?" Betty asked, and Sarah could hear how hurt she was. Because he hates being so dependent on you – on all of us – Sarah thought, stepping inside the dark room.

"I…" Ian fell silent.

"Because he's a stubborn daftie of a man," Sarah cut in. She plunked down to sit cross-legged on the floor some feet away from her brother. "Do you hate them for it? The Burleys?"

Ian lifted his head to properly see her and nodded. "Aye, I do. Although, to be fair, this wasn't their intent, was it?"

"No, their intent was to kill Da, and you stopped that from happening but damaged your back instead." She held out her hand to offer him some of her purloined apricots, and Ian took one, popping it in his mouth to chew slowly. Betty shook her head in refusal at the dried fruits, smoothed down Ian's shirt, and got to her feet.

"I'll be back shortly," she said and left brother and sister alone.

Sarah swallowed the last of the apricots. "I thought it would be better, now that I know they are dead, but I still hate them, and I still dream."

"It takes time," Ian said.

"And I hate the wean too," Sarah went on. "I hated it while it was inside of me, I hate it for how much it hurt to

86

birth it, and I hate it because Mama and Da are sorry for it."

"Him," Ian corrected. "It's a wee lad, Sarah."

"I don't care! I don't want to know it exists, and now they've given it to Uncle Simon to raise, and I will never, ever get away from it!" She looked at him in despair. "How can I forget, if he's there? And I want to forget it, all of it, but now I never will." She clutched at herself and curled together, crying noiselessly.

"Sarah..." Ian's hand closed on hers. "Sarah, lassie." He held her hand and waited until she achieved some control. "You won't forget, but you'll live with it, and hopefully there will be other men and other bairns, and then one day you'll no longer hate the laddie." She gave him a very doubtful look, and he smiled. "I promise, little sister, you won't forget, but it won't hurt as much." He turned his head away, muttering that in his case it would always hurt, a constant reminder of what he lost the day he was shot and fell off his horse.

Sarah sat and held his hand until he fell asleep.

When the Chisholms and Carlos rode in just before noon, Alex was more than thrilled to interrupt her work in the garden. It was apparent at first glance that the three Chisholm brothers were very unhappy men. On the first leg of the trip down to Providence, the five Maroons had escaped, their ropes neatly cut, and on top of that, they'd made off with a musket and enough powder to blow a barn sky-high.

"...so there we were," Robert said, "and we couldn't set off after them, what with the prisoners. And it's no comfort to know they're still in the area."

"Oh dear." Alex tut-tutted and set plates of warm, fragrant bread on the table.

Carlos sniffed appreciatively at the scent of rosemary while the Chisholms regarded the herb-dotted bread with some misgivings. When dinner was served, they looked positively depressed, stirring the dark green soup with dislike.

"Nettles?" Martin Chisholm said.

"All spring," Adam piped up mournfully from his end of the table. "At least once a week we get it on account of Mama saying it's full of iron."

"Iron?" Robert Chisholm shook his head. "Are you expecting to find nails in the soup, Alex?" He laughed at his own jest. "My mother uses nettle water for her hair."

"Aye," Mrs Parson nodded, "nettles and comfrey together makes a very nice hair wash."

"Oh." Robert sounded uninterested. "They won't hang the men," he said, and the whole table looked at him in confusion. "Our prisoners."

"Ah." Matthew nodded. "Why not?"

"Farrell suggested selling them as indentures instead," Martin said, "and we had no reason to disagree. Let them be of some use before they die." He handed a small cloth pouch over to Matthew. "Your share."

Over pudding, the mood relaxed, and conversation turned to planting and crops, to the new bull the Chisholms had recently bought, and to the pleasing news that Providence now had its first physician in residence.

Alex listened with only half an ear, most of her attention on Carlos and Sarah who were conducting some kind of silent conversation across the expanse of the kitchen table – or rather Carlos seemed to be attempting communication with a very evasive Sarah.

Abruptly, Sarah stood and, with a mumbled excuse, escaped the room, leaving Carlos to look after her with eyes the size of saucers. He made an effort to return to the conversation, but after a few minutes he too left the room, and Alex watched him go, cassock swinging round his peg.

Carlos knocked on Sarah's door. He remained standing by the door once she'd opened it, unwilling to compromise either her or himself by entering further into her room. He swallowed, ran a tongue over his lips and cast about for something to say. Since the birth of her child, Sarah had avoided being alone with him, and where before their conversation flowed as easily as water through a millrace, lately it had become a thing of silences, heavy pauses and desperate attempts from his side to catch her eyes.

"I just..." He smiled hesitantly. "I wanted to make sure you are alright, *hija*."

"Alright? As well as I can be." She gave him a shy look, and in his chest his heart did cartwheels of hope. "I couldn't have done this without you."

"That's what I'm here for," he replied. For you, Sarah, only for you...

She nodded and just stood there, her hands clasped before her, her head demurely bent. She had taken off her cap, and from where he stood, he could catch the scent of her, clean and somehow sparkling, as if she had dipped herself in a river of icy water. The silence became oppressive, and after a further few minutes, Sarah went over to her bed.

She slid her hand in under her pillow and pulled out the dark rosary beads he had once given her, and held them out to him.

"I don't think I'll be using these much more," she said with a small smile.

Carlos felt as if someone had slammed him with a barrel in the stomach. She was telling him goodbye, shedding him from her life just as she had done with the newborn child. He tried to catch her eyes, but saw only slits of blue in her downturned face.

"Keep them. They were a gift, not a loan." He watched her hands caress the beads, long fingers running over them, and every breath was a painful effort. Without really thinking, he had her face between his hands, and then he kissed her.

"I will always love you, Sarah," he whispered, and then he fled, thinking that it shouldn't be possible to live or breathe, not when your heart had just been shattered into thousands upon thousands of painful shards.

The Chisholms left some time after dinner, rather disgruntled at having to ride off without Carlos, who seemed to have gone up in thin air. No matter that they called for him repeatedly, the little priest did not appear, and while normally Alex would have been worried, this time she wasn't, having caught a glimpse of Carlos when he stumbled out of the house. The man's face had been wet with tears, and she assumed he needed time alone.

Alex was proved right when Carlos reappeared some hours later. He muttered something about not feeling well and escaped to the little room he normally stayed in when visiting the Grahams. Alex shared a look with Matthew and shook her head, before returning to their conversation.

"What will we do with it?" Alex touched the small pile of guineas reverently.

"We'll set it to Sarah's dowry," Matthew told her, letting the coins disappear back into their pouch. "She'll need to come well dowered."

"What do you mean by that?"

Matthew shrugged, telling her there was no way to keep secrets in a colony like Maryland, and likely any young man of good enough background would have heard of the misfortunes of the Graham girl.

"Maybe she doesn't want to marry anyone of them either. She might prefer to remain single."

Matthew raised his brows. "She will want a family of her own."

"Who knows? Maybe she decides to become a nun instead."

Matthew looked as if he was about to burst. "A nun?"

Alex hitched one shoulder. "Well, she does that a lot. Tell the rosary in Latin and all that…" Her voice trailed off at his expression.

"Are you telling me our daughter has taken to papist ways?"

"Umm," Alex hedged. "I…well, I'm not sure, but she does have—"

"How long?" he interrupted. "How long have you known her to be doing this?"

Alex looked away from his penetrating eyes. "Since last summer."

"Dearest, sweetest Lord," Matthew muttered. "Help me, God, that I don't lose my temper with my witless wife."

"Witless?" Alex glared at him. "Who are you calling witless?"

"You," he said, and his hands were hard on her arms. "Don't you see, Alex? She's in risk of losing her immortal soul!"

"Bullshit," she snapped, "and let go of me, okay?"

He did, dropping his hands to his sides. "You should have told me."

"And what would you have done? Forced her to turn over the rosary beads?"

"Aye, and I would have forbidden the priest to come over."

"That would really have helped, given that he was the only person she truly spoke to."

Matthew exhaled loudly, his eyes tight with anger, and turned for the door.

"Where are you going?" Alex asked.

"To see my daughter," he said and banged the door shut behind him.

Sarah seemed to have been crying, even if she insisted that she hadn't, it was just the pillowcase not having been properly rinsed of lye.

"Hmm," Matthew said sceptically and sat down on the single stool, waving with a hand to show she could sit on the bed. "Your mama tells me you've been saying the rosary."

"Aye, I have. It helps, at times."

"We don't hold with such, you know that."

Sarah looked away from his eyes. "Do you think it truly matters? The form of the prayers as such? Is it not the sincerity that counts?"

"Aye, of course it is," Matthew answered, somewhat taken aback. "But you don't need popish prayers to talk to God."

Sarah hitched her shoulders. "*Hail Mary, full of grace, the Lord is with thee,*" she said, and gave him a very blue look that reminded him of a young Alex. "I had no words, Da.

And these words helped, just as it helped to hold the beads in my hands, feel the weight of God's presence in them." She hugged herself, her eyes locked on the embroidered sleeve of her chemise, an intricate pattern of daisies and dipping bluebells carefully executed by Alex. "I won't be doing it anymore. I've put them away."

"And the priest?"

"Carlos?" Sarah looked away. "He was my friend, and today I broke his heart." Her lower lip trembled for an instant before she caught it with her teeth. "I had to. He was in love with me."

"And you? Are you in love with him?" Matthew asked as gently as he could.

Sarah gave him a watery smile but shook her head. "Not as he is in love with me, not enough that he should break his vows for me."

"I don't think I'll be coming back," Carlos said with some formality next morning. He looked awful, Alex reflected, his cassock rumpled as if he'd slept in it, but from the state of his hair and the pouches under his eyes, she doubted he'd done any sleeping at all.

"No, I don't suppose you will." Matthew took Carlos' hand and pressed it. "I can't thank you for what you did for her."

Carlos extricated his hand and stretched his lips into a smile, his eyes black with misery and loss. "I'm glad I could be of help." He turned towards Alex, and bowed. "*Señora Alex.*"

"*Padre*," she replied and slipped her hand under his arm to lead him some feet away. "What will you do now?"

"Santo Domingo, and then we'll see." His eyes drifted over to where Sarah was standing halfway up the slope. "*No sé que hacer.* I have no idea what to do. I love her, and I'm not allowed to. God won't forgive me, I fear."

"Of course He will. If anyone knows about love, it's Him." She looked over to her daughter and then back at Carlos. "She loves you too, Carlos. But it's a fearful thing to tear a man away from his holy vows, a burden far too heavy for a young girl to carry." A low, pained sound escaped Carlos' mouth, and Alex squeezed his arm.

"*Vaya con Dios, Padre*," Alex said, "and talk to your confessor. Maybe he can help you find your way." She reached forward and thumbed a lock of his hair behind his ear. "And for what it's worth, I love you as well," she said, and kissed him softly on his cheek.

Chapter 11

Mrs Parson made a satisfied sound, and Alex sat back and studied Betty with a smile. "According to our resident expert, everything is okay."

Betty smoothed her clothes back into place and came to her feet. "Of course it is, and it's a girl this time," she said, making Mrs Parson laugh.

"A lass? Nay, Betty, I think not. A lad, as lively as his brothers."

Betty looked over to where her two small sons were helping their older cousins with the piglets, which involved a lot of running about in the muddy pigpen. Alex smothered a grin. Little Timothy kept on falling over, and as a consequence his smock was muddier than the pigs, streaks of mud adorning his bright red hair.

"A girl," Betty sighed. "A sweet child who stays clean."

In reply, Alex pointed at Lettie, Mark's soon four-year-old daughter who came crawling out between the slats of the pigpen covered entirely in mud.

"Lettie doesn't count," Betty said.

Alex was prone to agree: quick-witted, stubborn and scarily inventive, Lettie was a catastrophe waiting to happen no matter where one put her. Little Maggie appeared next, just as dirty, if not more, swinging her six-year-old legs easily over the stile.

Betty groaned at the sight of her stepdaughter. "A boy," she sighed in resignation, and went to collect her children and scrub them into some semblance of cleanliness.

"Will it be alright, you think?" Alex asked, following Mrs Parson into the kitchen.

"She's convinced, no?" Mrs Parson said. "In my experience, that helps. She doesn't seem at all frightened, does she?"

"No, but Ian is." Alex bent down to pick up the green leaf that lay on the kitchen floor, rearing back with a loud explosion of expletives when the leaf bounded away.

"I swear, Adam Graham, the next time I find one of your frogs in my kitchen, I'll kill it and fry it and make you eat it!" Her youngest son hastily collected his escaped pet and promised it wouldn't happen again.

"You said that last week as well. And, you," she said to Hugin, "how about making yourself useful and eating the pesky things!" From the interested gleam in the raven's eye, he was all for complying with her suggestion, leaning forward from his perch on Adam's shoulder to study the frog intently.

"Mama!" Adam exclaimed, stuffing the frog into the relative safety of his shirt.

"I told you I wouldn't stand for any amphibians inside my house." She shooed at him with a broom. "Take your menagerie with you, and make sure it stays away. God, that boy has a thing about animals," she complained with a smile once Adam had escaped outside.

From where she was busy dicing carrots and onions, Agnes laughed. "A veritable Noah, all those wee creatures he collects..." She shook her head in the direction of Adam who dropped to his haunches beside little Judith to show the girl the frog.

"Maybe he could build an ark to keep them in," Alex muttered, "instead of littering my house with all those half-dead animals he finds."

Alex went over to inspect Sarah's cinnamon buns, earning herself a sharp rap over the fingers when she tried to nick a piece of dough. Her daughter was slowly becoming herself again, the constant tension of the last year dripping away by degrees. She worked in the garden and the stables, she spent hours in the woods with Viggo and a musket, she played long, heated chess games with her father and her brothers, and she sulked as much as she always had when Alex set her to mending and sewing.

It was different when they had visitors: Sarah retreated

into a shy, mute person, constantly ducking her head to avoid any kind of eye contact.

"Why?" Alex had asked her last time the Leslies had come over.

"I don't like the look in their eyes," Sarah had explained. "Half pity, half condemnation."

"Huh," Alex said, "if I see anything like condemnation, they'll be looking at castration."

"The women too?" Sarah had inquired mildly, causing Matthew to give both of them a disapproving eye.

Alex heard Sarah mutter under her breath, and a quick look out of the window indicated they were about to have visitors – again. Yet another quick look and Alex muttered as viciously as Sarah had just done, wiping her hands on her apron before stepping outside to greet the men making slow progress down the lane, five of them on horseback, four on foot.

Shit, Alex thought, meeting Leon's panicked eyes. He and three of his companions were being towed along behind the horses, and from the look of them, it had been a violent fight, covering all of them in bruises and slashes.

The lead rider held in his horse, small eyes staring at her until she dropped him a minimal curtsey. Alex actively disliked Minister Macpherson, a sentiment returned in full by the minister who now dismounted with ponderous grace, his eyes sweeping the well-tended farm. He gave her the slightest of nods, pursed his mouth into a spout, and just stood there. Alex sent Hannah off to find Matthew, and from the displeased wrinkle that appeared on the minister's brow when Hannah set off at speed, braids flying and skirts held high, she gathered this was most unseemly behaviour in a little girl.

Matthew had no fondness for the minister, and even less when he saw the man snub his wife, but opted for being polite, inclining his head in greeting.

"Brother Matthew," Minister Macpherson said, his multiple chins wobbling with every word, "I trust I find you well?"

"As well as can be expected," Matthew replied. "And you?" An unnecessary question: the minister looked like a cat in a saucer of cream, a very obese cat to be sure, but still. The minister's eyes alighted briefly on Alex, swept over Ian and Mark, who had joined them, and came to rest on Adam and his raven.

"A corbie?" he asked, his brow puckering.

"Aye," Adam replied.

"Nasty birds," the minister said. "Carrion eaters, all of them."

"Not Hugin," Adam assured him. The minister sniffed but let the subject drop.

"I come recently from Ingram's place," he said, returning his attention to Matthew.

"Oh aye?" Matthew let his eyes travel over the captive men. "Any particular reason?"

The minister followed his eyes and chuckled. "Nay, Brother Matthew, I have not taken up slave-hunting as a pastime. I was there on spiritual matters, and these wild, dangerous creatures attempted a raid on the place."

"Men," Alex cut in. "They're men, not creatures. Men just like you or Matthew here."

Minister Macpherson regarded her coldly for some moments. "I can assure you, Mrs Graham, that I carry no likeness to such as those. Anyway," he continued, directing himself to Matthew, "it was fortunate I and my servants were there, otherwise who knows what bloodshed would have taken place. Instead, we killed one and subdued the others – as you can see." He smirked. "Mr Farrell will be most pleased to have his property returned to him, I think."

"No doubt," Matthew mumbled, wondering what on earth the minister was leading up to.

The minister pulled at his ear, bushy eyebrows coming down in a 'v' over the piercing eyes. "It's mightily strange, but according to Ingram, these same men were led off down south a month ago."

"Aye," Matthew said, "the Chisholms took them with them."

"And they escaped," the minister stated.

"It would seem so." Matthew nodded.

"Despite being trussed up like chickens," the minister pushed.

"Aye," Matthew said.

"Someone must have handed them a knife – someone from here." He produced a small, very sharp knife with a bold G carved into the handle.

"From here?" Matthew shrugged. "It may be that the G stands for Gregor."

"Gregor?" the minister spluttered. "Are you implying that I have helped these...these..."

"Men," Alex supplied.

"...slaves," the minister finished somewhat lamely.

Matthew raised his brows. "Is that not what you just insinuated I did?"

"Insinuate? I say you did! And one of the slaves bears me out!" He beckoned to the tallest of his men who dragged one of the bound men to his feet and shoved him in their direction. The laddie, the one Alex scalded with her kettle.

"Go on," Minister Macpherson barked, "tell me again. Was it Mr Graham who helped you?"

The lad moaned a yes, avoiding looking at Matthew.

"How?" Minister Macpherson demanded.

"He give us clothes," the slave mumbled through a broken mouth, "and food."

"And did he give you a knife?" the minister asked. "This knife?"

The slave twisted, mumbling something unintelligible.

"Answer your betters!" the minister roared, and the lad hunched together, raising his hands to deflect the blow the minister aimed at his head. "It wasn't him, was it?" the minister continued. "Of course it wasn't Mr Graham. It was her," he said, pointing at Alex. "She was the one who handed you the knife, wasn't she?"

The slave began to shake his head, but the minister's face in combination with his raised hand made him nod instead.

"She did, yes, she did," he whined.

Alex opened her mouth to protest. Nay, Matthew warned, giving his head a minimal shake. She didn't understand, not at first, but after a few seconds a smile flashed through her eyes. Aye, let the fat minister dig himself into a very deep hole.

The minister was near on skipping with glee, eyes darting triumphantly from Alex to Matthew and back again. "It grieves me, but I must request that your wife accompany us south. To help and abet fugitive slaves is a serious offence – I dare say it will be a long stretch in the pillory."

Alex's eyes flew to Matthew's. For a moment, she looked quite fearful, and the minister smirked.

"You heard him, Mistress Graham," the minister said, "and so did my men. He pointed you out as being the one who gave them the knife."

"And if I say I didn't?"

"Well, you would say that," the minister retorted. He shook his head in mock sadness. "It grieves me, truly, Brother Matthew."

"Nay, it doesn't," Matthew said, "nor is it true. But we will go south with you nonetheless."

"Oh, of course you will." The minister had an edge of steel to his voice. "It would be unwise not to."

"Da!" Ian caught up with him just inside the house. "Why don't you just tell him? Mama wasn't even here that day!" He said something foul about overweight men with hearts the size of sheep turds.

"But I was," Matthew reminded him, "and the fine would be very heavy." No pillory for him, not for a senior member of the congregation, but Farrell would most certainly demand compensation. At least the value of the dead slave, and that sort of money was not readily available – not without breaking into the funds he had set aside for future needs, and that was not something he wanted to do. "So, instead, I reckoned I'd let yon minister talk himself into a corner, discredit himself, like."

Ian swiftly worked this through, looking with some admiration at Matthew. "He won't like it," he said, but promised to ride over to Leslie's Crossing and talk to Thomas.

"And I don't like him coming here to drag my wife off like a common criminal," Matthew threw over his shoulder, hurrying up the stairs to gather some clothes together.

He found Alex sitting on the bed, looking very tired. "What is it, love?" he asked, smiling at how she started at his uncharacteristic endearment.

She rested her head against his shoulders and sighed. "Sometimes it's a bit too much, you know? And even if I know this particular charge won't stick, I'm not exactly looking forward to having yet another appearance before the ministers." Distractedly, she massaged her hands. "Why can't we just retire and go live in a bungalow somewhere, just you and I?"

He laughed softly. He found the concept of retirement ludicrous, and he had no idea what a bungalow was, but thought it sounded like something rather small and nasty.

"I can build us a wee cabin down by the river, up beyond the old Indian village."

She smiled at the idea. "Not exactly Florida, but it will do just fine: you and me, the river and nothing else."

After several hours riding in rain, they made camp in a little clearing. Once he'd seen to Aaron, Matthew came over to help Alex by the fire, noting out of the corner of his eye that the minister seemed most disgruntled, glaring at them from where he sat wet and cold under a chestnut.

"He can do his own bloody cooking," Alex protested when Matthew told her to prepare a plate for the man.

"He's your spiritual guide," he said with a teasing smile. "Surely you want him fed?"

"If you ask me, he's padded enough to survive a day or two without food."

"Aye, well, but feeding the lion before entering its den is a wise move."

"Huh," she said, handing him a heaped plate.

The minister shone up at Matthew's approach. "Thank you."

Matthew shrugged. This was done out of a sense of obligation, nothing else.

"Fortunate it isn't soup," Minister Macpherson commented.

"Soup?"

The minister nodded, mouth full of hot eggs. He swallowed noisily and gulped some water from his water skin. "Aye, or she might have gone after me with the soup ladle like she did with Richard Campbell."

Matthew gave him a guarded look. "That was a long time ago."

"And forever engraved in poor Richard's memory," Minister Macpherson said. "For a woman to do such – and to a minister at that." He shook his head. "Wayward, oh yes, Brother Matthew, wayward and opinionated, loud and disrespectful." He leaned forward as if to share a secret. "Richard has no fond memories of your wife."

"I dare say my wife has no fond memories of him," Matthew said icily, "and nor have I. We don't take to ignorant fools, no matter they come in minister garb."

Minister Macpherson choked on the last of his food. "Ignorant? Richard isn't ignorant!"

"Oh yes, he is," Alex said, having come over to offer the minister some beer. "He has no geography, very little history, no languages to talk of, and is about as well-read as my youngest son."

"Well-read? And you are?" Minister Macpherson sneered.

"A hell of a lot more than he is," Alex snapped, making Matthew wince at her choice of words.

Minister Macpherson snorted, seemed on the verge of saying something more, but Matthew was already halfway across the clearing, wife in a very firm grip.

"God, I hate his guts," Alex said to Matthew. "He reminds me far too much of that little turd of a man, Richard bloody Campbell."

"Richard Campbell was a wee man, all skin and bones," Matthew protested.

"But they have the same eyes," Alex said, "cold and

censorious – in particular when it comes to women – and the same constant displeased twist to their mouths, as if life is a lemon they must unfortunately suck dry before passing on to the spiritual joys of heaven."

Matthew recalled with some discomfort that long ago summer when he'd returned home from a visit to Providence with Richard Campbell in tow, proudly pronouncing that the minister had undertaken to teach their sons in the Bible. Alex had disliked the minister on sight, making it very clear just what a fool she thought Matthew for assuming this man could teach her precious boys anything.

He met her eyes, reliving weeks of estrangement following on the evening when Alex had threatened Richard with the ladle and Matthew had forced her to apologise for calling him a shit-spouting cretin, thereby siding with the minister against his wife.

"Many years ago," Matthew said, extending his leg to nudge at her. "And I was young and foolish."

Alex laughed. "You were over forty!"

"As I said, a wee daftie."

Alex woke next morning to angry shouts, and when she crawled out from under Matthew's cloak, she found the minister arguing with two of his men.

"Has something happened?" she asked Matthew, who was busy shaving. In reply, he waved his razor in the direction of the slaves.

"One of them is missing."

"Oh dear," she muttered.

"Oh dear, indeed," he agreed, and folded his razor shut. He pulled at some hemp fibres that had caught in the handle before returning it to its little leather case. "He isn't made for a life in the wild, but I suggested he go and find Qaachow and bring him greetings from me."

"Only Leon?" she asked.

"I didn't dare to do more than that, and I don't think the others want to run. They're too afraid."

The minister strode over towards them, pudgy hands

clenched into impressive fists. "Did you do this?" he barked at Alex. "Was it you?"

"What makes you think that?"

"He was securely tied last night. I myself inspected the lines, and now..." The minister waved his arms. "Gone! Just like that!"

"Well, it wasn't my wife," Matthew told him. "She has slept like a babe through the night."

"Och aye?" the minister said. "And you would notice, would you, if she slipped off?"

"Aye," Matthew assured him, "on account of us sharing the same cloak."

The minister's small eyes narrowed into pale blue slits, the pupils pinpricks of black, no more. "Someone cut him free, and I will make it my business to find out who!"

Matthew strolled over to where the slaves were being held, and studied the coils of rope left behind by Leon.

"This wasn't cut," he said, holding up a rope end. "It was untied. Mayhap you didn't check the knots as well as you should have."

The minister's face acquired an unflattering, red hue. Without a further word, he stalked off, calling for his men to follow him.

In less than five minutes, two of the men were astride, nodding repeatedly at whatever it was that the minister was saying. Three overexcited dogs milled round them, and at the minister's curt command, they set off, the dogs leading the way.

"Shit," Alex said.

"Aye." Matthew threw a long look after the departing men. "God help him if they ride him down."

"What, you think they might kill him?" Alex said.

"Nay. Unfortunately."

They had stopped for an extended midday break when the men returned, dragging what looked like a carcass behind them.

"Leon!" Alex was on her feet, was already rushing towards him.

103

"Stay away!" the minister said, blocking her way. "Brother Matthew, control your wife!"

Leon was heaved to stand. His shirt was in shreds, the skin on his chest and back had been scraped raw, one arm hung awry from the shoulder as if it had been dislocated and there were multiple bites on his legs. A deep cut on his forearm was welling blood, it looked as if he'd raised his arm to block a sword or something. He swayed, crashed into the closest man, and collapsed.

"Let me through," Alex said, glaring at the minister while trying to free herself from Matthew's hold on her arm. "The poor man is seriously hurt – thanks to your brutes."

"Brutes?" One of the minister's men frowned. "He's the brute, not us." As if to demonstrate this, he kicked Leon. Leon jerked, no more.

"And if he dies?" Alex said. At that, Leon opened his eyes, looking straight at her.

"Oh, he won't," Minister Macpherson assured her.

"You think?" Alex had by now reclaimed her arm, shoved the minister out of the way, and knelt beside Leon.

"Aaaa…" he said.

"Shhh, here." Alex held the water skin to his mouth.

"Back away, Mrs Graham," the minister said. "My men will ensure he gets adequate care."

"Adequate care?" Alex rose. "Is this adequate care? To drag a man behind a horse, to let the dogs get at him, is that adequate care?"

"Alex," Matthew said.

"Don't Alex me! Help me! We can't let him die, can we?" She crouched down again, wondering where on earth to start. Poor Leon was a patchwork of welts and scrapes, and as to his arm… Matthew knelt down beside her.

"And if he lives, Alex?" he whispered.

Leon opened his eyes wide. "No," he moaned.

"My men will take care of the slave." The minister shoved at Alex and gestured for his men to lift Leon to sit.

"Hey!" she said, overbalancing to land heavily on her backside.

"Touch my wife again, minister, and I'll—" Matthew said, helping Alex up.

"Touch her? If ever a woman lived that would benefit from a good belting—"

"Hold your tongue!" Matthew snarled. He squared his shoulders and advanced on the minister who retreated, and with every step the minister took went his men, except for the one standing guard over Leon.

"Brother Matthew, calm down," the minister said. "It was not my intention—"

"Aye, it was!"

Alex frowned. What was the matter with him? Matthew rarely let his temper get the better of him, and for him to behave as he was doing over a mere trifle was very out of character.

There was a scuffle behind her. She wheeled just as Leon sank his teeth into the leg of his guard. Jesus, but the man screamed! Leon wound his good arm round the man's leg, and for all that the man tried to beat him off, Leon just wouldn't let go. Alex rushed towards them, and from the other side of the clearing came the minister and his men.

With a wrench, Leon toppled the man to the ground. He grabbed for the man's dirk, pulled the blade just as the other men reached him. Leon disappeared in a welter of arms and legs.

"Grab hold of his arm, fools," the minister said, dancing on his toes around the men. "Take hold of his hand before—" There was a yelp. One of the men threw himself backward, blood running down his cheek.

"Leon!" Alex hollered. She kicked at the backside closest to her. The man squealed and half sat up. She did it again, and had a glimpse of Leon. One of the men was holding on to his arm, but as Alex watched, Leon pulled free and sank the knife straight into his own gut.

"No," Alex whispered, falling to her knees. "No, Leon, don't."

There was blood everywhere. One by one, the men scrambled to their feet while on the ground Leon writhed.

She crawled towards him, and when the minister made as if to stop her, she just looked at him, and something in her eyes must have made him decide not to intervene.

"It's okay," Leon managed to say. "I'm dead anyway," he reminded her in gasps. "That son of a bitch would whip me to death over the coming months." He struggled with his breathing, eyes closed tight in concentration, and his hold on her hand hardened. "I...wanted..." He opened one eye, looked at Alex. "I..." He convulsed, heels drumming against the ground, hand clenched so tight around her fingers she feared they would break.

"Clara!" he screamed. He slumped into stillness. A slow smile spread over his bloodied mouth. "Clara," he breathed, and died.

"You did it on purpose," she said some hours later. They were back on the horse, and several yards in front of them rode the minister, now and then swivelling to glare at them.

"Hmm?" Matthew said.

"The quarrel."

He sighed, very softly, and pressed her to sit even closer to him, her arse wedged between his thighs. "Aye, it was the only thing I could think of, to give him the opportunity to..." He broke off, and she heard him murmur a prayer. A sin. It was a grievous sin to take your own life. Somehow, Alex suspected Leon didn't care. He was free again, at last.

Chapter 12

Providence – Anne Arundel's Town, if one was to use its official name, but none of its Puritan inhabitants did – in late April was a nice enough place, still not panting under the dense summer heat that would plague it during the summer months. A sensation of spring freshness remained in the air, and from the Chesapeake Bay a steady south-easterly breeze blew, carrying with it salt and oxygen.

Alex breathed in with relish, and studied the neat little town with affection. In the eighteen years they'd lived in the colony, the nondescript little settlement they had arrived to had developed to have a meetinghouse, an Anglican church, four inns – five if one counted Mrs Malone's thriving whorehouse, but Alex wasn't sure one should – several small shops, a complement of craftsmen, three lawyers, and now one physician.

Unfortunately, Alex reflected an hour or so later, the town also had more than its fair share of ministers, and all three of them now sat ranged before her, with her son-in-law seated to the far left and looking as if he wished he could be anywhere else but here. That makes two of us, Alex thought, going back to her idle study of the floor before her, listening with only half an ear while Minister Macpherson expounded on her sins.

Matthew had spent most of the last day's ride in a fruitless attempt to convince the minister there was no reason to pursue the matter. If anything, Leon's death seemed to have made the minister even more determined to set an example of Alex, his voice rising into a rather unbecoming tenor when he insisted this whole debacle was Alex's fault. Had she not attempted to meddle with the wounded slave, he wouldn't have seen himself forced to move her aside, thereby angering her husband. Huh, how convenient for the minister to have someone to blame for Leon's death.

Alex wasn't listening at all by the time Minister Macpherson finished his cataloguing of her crimes. Instead, she was reliving Leon's violent death, wondering who this Clara might be. It left her with a headache, and she resolutely shoved the memories away. Besides, she had other things to worry about, chief amongst them Minister Macpherson's face which was swimming disturbingly close to her own – close enough that she had to wrinkle her nose at his stale breath. She blinked and reared back, almost overbalancing on her little stool.

"I said," the minister repeated with exaggerated patience, "do you admit to helping the slaves abscond?"

"No," Alex replied.

"Daughter..." Minister Walker peered at her from over his spectacles and smiled. "If you admit to it, we will do gently by you."

"I haven't helped anyone abscond." Alex sneaked a look to where Thomas Leslie had come over to sit beside Matthew.

"We have witnesses that say you have," Minister Walker said.

"Then they are wrong," she said, fussing with her skirts.

"The slaves were clothed and fed—" Minister Macpherson began.

"Not by me," Alex interrupted.

"Nay, I did that," Matthew voiced from where he was sitting, "and yet I don't find myself before the bench, do I?"

Minister Macpherson glared at Matthew but composed himself. "To feed and clothe them was not wrong, as it assures they're returned in good condition to their owner," he said, bowing to Mr Farrell who nodded in agreement. The minister paused, adjusted his dark coat and lace collar, and wheeled with impressive elegance to face his fellow ministers. "To hand them a knife, however, was a dastardly deed, allowing them to abscond yet again to wreak terror on innocent people that crossed their way." He slid his piggy eyes in the direction of Alex and sighed. "I'm sure Mrs Graham considered herself motivated by Christian charity, and so it's a lesson we must teach her, no more. But she must learn to respect other people's property."

"A lesson?" Mr Farrell rose out of his seat. "I am two slaves short, and I demand compensation."

"A later matter," Minister Macpherson said.

"Later matter? This amounts to theft, does it not? And thieves we hang! I—" Mr Farrell spluttered.

"Hang?" Matthew rose to his full six feet three, towering over Mr Farrell.

"Now, now," Minister Walker said, "let us get back to the matter at hand. I am sure we will sort the matter of compensation without...err..."

"Two slaves!" Mr Farrell yelled.

"I didn't do it!" Alex's pulse had picked up during Mr Farrell's little outburst, and the look he sent her way only served to increase the loud thumping in her head. "I didn't!"

Minister Macpherson shook his head. "We have witnesses, Mrs Graham. The slave himself pointed you out as the one who handed him the knife, did he not?"

"At your heavy-handed hinting! Besides, does his word count for more than mine?"

"He has no reason to lie," the minister said, "but you do."

Matthew turned the full force of his stare on the minister. "Are you calling my wife a liar?"

Minister Macpherson acquired the hue of a smoked ham but nodded all the same. "She has perjured herself in front of us all."

"No, she hasn't." Thomas Leslie stood up. He removed his hat from his head and smiled at Alex. "At the time in question, Mrs Graham lay sunk in fever at my home."

Minister Walker gave Minister Macpherson a very disappointed look.

"But..." Minister Macpherson began and then came to an abrupt stop, the cogwheels inside his head visibly turning into overdrive. He swivelled to stare at Alex, who was trying very hard not to grin, and then pointed his finger at Matthew. "You did it! You gave them the knife!" He looked around the room and then back at Matthew. "You!"

"I did no such thing!" Matthew said.

"The knife! Look, the knife!" Minister Macpherson brandished the little knife that Alex recognised as belonging to Adam.

"Do you think me a simpleton?" Matthew said. "Would I be daft enough to set a knife with my own mark on it in the hands of a slave?"

"I say you did it! You gave them food and clothes—"

"Which I have never denied!"

"...and then you handed them the knife!"

"Enough!" Minister Walker roared, and as always when that generally mild-mannered man raised his voice, everyone stopped dead. "We won't lower ourselves to further spectacle," he said in his normal tone.

"But..." Minister Macpherson protested, subsiding at the dangerous look in the senior minister's eye.

"No buts." Minister Walker left the room without another word.

"Someone slipped them a knife," Mr Farrell said when they bumped into each other by the door, "and as a consequence two of my slaves are dead."

"And you were planning on welcoming them home with a fatted calf?" Alex asked.

"Oh, no," Mr Farrell said coldly. "I would have had them flogged on consecutive days until they died. But it was my right to do so." He eyed them both in a way that indicated he blamed them for having cheated him of this particular form of entertainment.

"It could have been anyone. They could have picked it up from the ground. It was a rather hectic day," Matthew said. "We'll never know, will we?"

"Huh!" Farrell sounded anything but convinced. He eyed Alex, pursing his mouth. "Minister Macpherson is of the opinion that you knew Noah."

"He is? And on what does he base that conclusion?"

"He says you were most familiar with him at the hour of his death."

"Familiar? How familiar? I held his hand, Mr Farrell – something I would have done for any man facing certain death."

"He was a slave," Mr Farrell said.

"No, he wasn't. He was a free man, and you knew he was, didn't you?" With that, she dropped a half-hearted curtsey and walked off.

"To be fair, Minister Macpherson was but doing his duty," Julian said as they sat down to dinner.

"Duty? So, on top of being a minister, he's some sort of self-proclaimed constable? And wouldn't it have been more in keeping with his religious calling to show the poor men some compassion, rather than drag them back at double pace through the woods?" Alex shook her head at the proffered serving dish of thinly sliced tongue.

"Or he could have ridden straight back here with them, and that would have been that," Matthew put in, "but no, not our Minister Macpherson. He just had to stir up some mischief."

"It would help if Alex didn't goad him so," Julian said.

"Goad him? How do I goad him?"

"You are very well read for a woman," Julian told her, and Alex decided to let the patronising tone pass, "and last time you met him, you left him looking quite the fool."

"That isn't my fault – he does that perfectly well on his own – and he had absolutely no idea what he was talking about anyway." Alex snorted softly as she remembered their heated discussion about alchemy. "The elements are as they are, and only an idiot would believe that lead can be transmuted into gold."

"Quite a few great men actually think it's possible," Julian said stiffly.

"Quite a few great men have problems accepting the earth revolves around the sun," Alex replied, "or that you can't dig your way from here to China."

"You can't?" David looked up from his food with interest.

"No." Alex smiled at her son. "It would get pretty hot. The inner core of the earth is all molten lava."

"How do you know?" Julian asked.

Alex shrugged. "I just do."

Later, Matthew gave her a little speech along the lines that it would be better if she kept all her vast knowledge to herself. Having said that, he insisted she explain a bit more, looking like an eager schoolboy.

"Are you saying we float on all that lava?" Matthew looked down at her sketch and then up at her.

"Yes," she said, "they're called..." she made an effort, "...tectonic plates and they move all the time." She exhaled with pleasure as she freed her feet of shoes and stockings, wiggling the toes against the cool wooden floorboards.

"Move?" Matthew stamped the floor. "This isn't moving."

"Yes, it is. First, you have the world rotating on its axle, which gives us day and night. Then, you have the whole earth orbiting the sun, which gives us the seasons of the year. And then...well then, you have the plates, floating and bumping into each other. That's what causes earthquakes."

"Hmm," Matthew was clearly sceptical.

"I can't prove it to you," she smiled, "so you'll just have to take it on trust."

"Hmm," he repeated, with a twinkle in his eyes.

Next morning, Alex and Matthew were out and about just after breakfast, walking smartly up Main Street.

"No," Alex said, "I won't do it!"

"Aye, you will." Matthew held her elbow in a tight grip. "For my sake and for your own."

"It's him that owes me an apology, so why should I apologise? And for what exactly?"

"We'll go in together," Matthew said, "and I'm sure you'll think of what to say."

It was all Julian's stupid idea, his insistence that they should attempt to patch up their relationship with Gregor Macpherson.

"What relationship?" Alex had asked over breakfast, only to have her ears almost falling off by the end of Julian's long speech regarding the relative status of ministers and members of the congregation, and in particular, female members.

"I'm not sure I want to be a member of his congregation," Alex now said, but that only made Matthew frown at her. To him, being a full member of the Providence Puritan-slash-Presbyterian community was extremely important, for reasons well beyond Alex.

Gregor Macpherson was clearly not in the habit of receiving early morning calls. His jowls sported a lot of grey stubble, there was a spot of egg yolk on his coat, and he was as yet unshod, retracting his bare feet under the table when his servant ushered them in. To Alex, he looked vulnerable – major improvement – even more so when he hastily smoothed down his hair.

"What do you want?" Minister Macpherson snapped, reverting to good old form.

Alex took a big breath, curtsied under Matthew's critical eye, and mumbled something very long and scarcely audible about being sorry for not telling him that she'd been ill.

"You painted me a fool before them all," Macpherson complained.

"I know." Alex kept her eyes on the floor. A very dirty floor, she shuddered, and what was that, growing in the corner? Mould? "I was angry with you."

"With me?" Macpherson had now managed to discreetly remove the egg yolk and was buttoning his coat.

"Well yes. You assumed that I had given them the knife, and you were very glad to have the opportunity to teach me a lesson."

"You need several lessons, Mrs Graham, the main one being in how to behave decorously and modestly among your male betters. I can but sympathise with Mr Graham at times."

"Aye," Matthew sighed, "she's a wee bit headstrong. On account of her being Swedish, I think."

113

Alex seriously considered kicking him, but desisted – for now. Instead, she stood in silence while Minister Macpherson subjected her to a long tirade regarding virtuous womanhood, ending by stating it would appear that at least she had been a fertile wife and a strong helpmeet to her husband in his daily life.

"Thank you," she said, because it seemed to be expected of her, and some minutes later they were back on the street.

"That went well." Matthew gave her a satisfied smile.

"You think?" Alex asked frostily, and set off in the direction of the Hancock home.

"Where are you going?" Matthew grabbed at her, but she evaded his hand.

"Oh, I'm just being my normal headstrong me," she said through her teeth, "and if you don't mind, I prefer being that alone."

Matthew laughed, grabbed at her again, and kissed her cheek. "I like it that you are wild and headstrong, but it didn't hurt to paint a slightly different picture in there, did it?"

"I suppose not," she admitted grudgingly, and took his offered hand.

Esther Hancock was glad to see them, shooed Matthew off to talk with William, and dragged Alex with her to her little parlour to extract every single detail of what happened the day before.

Alex rolled her eyes but gave her a short and succinct account, including the early morning interview with Minister Macpherson.

"That was probably wise." Esther nodded. "He's much respected about town, and a firm friend of Mr Farrell who, I hear, isn't a happy man at present."

"He got three of them back," Alex said.

"Yes, but not the one he wanted to get back, the tall one – Noah, his name was."

"Leon, actually, and he was never a slave to begin with."

Esther cast her a look and went back to her embroidery.

"Where's the baby?" Alex finally asked, having waited for him to appear somehow.

"Duncan?" Esther smiled. "Duncan is off to visit his niece and nephews." Simon's grandchildren, left motherless after Lucy's death more than a year ago, three small children that lived with their father, Henry, and their widowed grandmother, Kate Jones. "He does that quite often," she added, her eyes glittering. "Or rather, Simon goes and takes Duncan with him."

"He does?" Alex leaned forward, intrigued. Kate and Simon?

"Oh yes, several times a week, and quite long visits at that. He comes home quite replete."

"Replete?" Alex stared at her.

Esther waved a hand dismissively. "Not Simon. Duncan. One of the slave girls has a baby, and so, when Duncan is there, she feeds him too."

"Ah." Alex was bursting with an urge to share all of this with Matthew – which she did, the moment they were alone.

"Simon? With Kate?" Matthew seemed to find the idea ludicrous.

"Well, that's what Esther says," Alex said, "and I think she's better informed than you are."

According to Esther's amused and detailed description, Kate and Simon had been spending an increasing amount of time with each other over the last year, at first under the pretext of allowing poor bereaved Simon plenty of time with his grandchildren and lately because Duncan so thrived in the healthy air of the Jones' home.

"Hmm." Matthew sounded very doubtful – as if Simon was not good enough for precious Kate.

"Simon is a very nice man," Alex said seriously, "and he deserves finding someone, don't you think?"

"Oh aye."

Chapter 13

Matthew wasn't quite sure why he'd agreed to accompany Alex to Kate's – mayhap it was just to verify that there was no truth to Esther's gossip about Simon and Kate. It therefore came as something of a revelation to be ushered into the Jones' residence and not only find Simon there, but also find him clasping Kate's fingers to his chest.

Kate was delighted to see them both, if somewhat flustered at being caught holding hands with Simon, and insisted they should settle themselves in the shade. Lemonade appeared at the clap of her hand, with a pitcher of frothing dark ale set down before Matthew.

"Men seem to prefer beer," she said, smiling at him.

In a secluded corner, wee Duncan was fast asleep under a length of sheer linen, and for some minutes Alex busied herself with the wean, at one point lifting the laddie to lie in her arms. Not much to see from where Matthew was sitting – a tuft of dark hair, no more.

"He's very bonny," Simon said with fatherly pride, "strong and lusty." He smiled over at Kate, who gave him an indulgent look, by chance placing a hand on Simon's bare forearm before hastening off to arrange for something to eat. Alex grinned at Simon who grinned back before smoothing his shirtsleeves back down.

"Don't want to incense her too much," he confided. "Women get carried away by the sight of my bare skin."

Matthew snorted into his mug. Kate was experienced enough, he reckoned, not to swoon at the sight of Simon's hairy arm.

"I can imagine," Alex laughed, and Matthew twitched at his sleeve, brushing the dark serge to lie close to his forearm.

He followed Kate with his eyes, surprised by the

conflicting feelings inside of him. An attractive woman, Kate was, and in her soft pink skirts, elegantly offset by a long-waisted bodice in grey and pink, she looked quite striking. The honey-coloured hair was shifting into a lighter shade of blonde, helped along by multiple silver strands, and when she twisted her head, he met a direct, dark gaze that threw him back twenty-five years in time, to feverish nights in a cookhouse, to nights when Kate held him and loved him, and thereby assured him he was still a man, still worth something for all that he lived his days as an indentured slave.

She lowered her eyelashes, a small dimple appearing on her cheek. Yes, she told him silently, there were times when she remembered too. In general, Matthew rarely did, but seeing Kate with Simon opened a sluice gate on memories of long ago nights when she had been the only thing that kept him alive. Her hair, drifting over his chest, her eyes lost in his, her breasts in his hands, and her warmth around his member. To think of those limbs, the still high breasts and the well rounded hips in bed with Simon… He turned his attention to his brother–in–law, engaged in a lively discussion with Alex about the best way to keep heat rash at bay, and let his eyes travel down the short, stout body. No, a ridiculous thought. Friends, no more, assuredly no more than friends.

"He looks just like himself," Simon pronounced, having watched Alex inspect Duncan in detail for the last few minutes.

"Yes, he does, doesn't he?" Alex said with relief, returning the boy to Simon's arms. Something that resembled a smile flitted across the child's face once he caught sight of his father, and the small mouth opened and closed, opened and closed as he tried to communicate, small arms waving erratically. "Blue eyes," she added for Matthew's benefit, who as yet had not held the boy.

"Ah." Matthew took yet another gulp of beer.

Alex threw him a look. What was the matter with him? Barely a word had he uttered since they got here, and why was he staring the way he did at Simon? Matthew caught her eye, gave a little shrug, as if to say, 'What?' Oh. Alex hid her smile in her lemonade. It wasn't Simon he was staring at, was it? No, it was baby Duncan.

Alex moved the chair even further into the shade and took in the splendid gardens: a couple of oaks to offer shade, meandering little paths, rosebushes that were already showing white and pink through their half-open buds, and a frothing sea of oleander, from white all the way to deepest magenta.

"Beautiful," she said to Kate when she returned, preceding a selection of small dishes that the silent slave girl set down on the table.

"Yes, it is, isn't it?" Kate offered Matthew some smoked fish while beckoning for Alex to come and join them at the table.

"Henry's getting married again," Kate suddenly said, glancing at Simon. "It's sixteen months and more since Lucy…" She sounded apologetic, and Simon leaned forward to cover her hand with his.

"It's alright, Kate, life goes on." He smiled when he said it, his blue eyes intent on hers, and a slow blush crawled up Kate's cheeks.

Alex was very amused and turned to share this with a wink at her husband, only to find his eyes locked on Kate's blushing skin in a way that Alex found very offensive. She pulled her brows together as she took in how her husband studied Kate, pulling them together further when those penetrating hazel eyes slid over to rest on Simon with a hostile edge.

"…and I'll be hosting a betrothal party later this week," Kate finished, looking expectantly at Alex.

"This week," Alex repeated, not having heard more than the last part.

Kate gave her an exasperated look. "Will you come? There will be dancing and music."

"Umm," Alex prevaricated, not quite sure what to say.

"Of course we will," Matthew said. "It's a long time since we danced."

★

118

"I don't have anything to wear," Alex confided to Ruth later, "and nor does your father."

"Da can borrow, and you can sew. I can help you," Ruth offered, sitting down to ease the weight off her back. Proudly, she patted her distended stomach. "We're going as well, but I don't think I'll be dancing much."

"Probably not," Alex said with a grin.

"Was the laddie alright then?" Ruth asked.

"Very – spoiled rotten by his new father."

"That's good."

"Better than the alternative," Alex said, making Ruth laugh.

"Is…?" Ruth bit her lip. "Is Sarah better?"

"Yes." Alex sat down and dug around for her fan. "Much better, probably well enough to cope with getting a letter from her pregnant sister." She met her daughter's eyes with a small smile. "That's what you wanted to know, right?"

"Aye, I should have written more, but—"

"Yes, you probably should have and even more, you should have come to see her."

Ruth twisted under the recriminations. "Julian didn't want me upset."

"Julian didn't want you to spend time with your unwed, pregnant sister, however much a victim she was," Alex said, and Ruth averted her eyes.

"You judge me unfairly," Julian reproached Alex later that evening.

"I do?"

"You cast me as a narrow-minded moralist, and that, Alex, is something I'm not."

"Well, no," Alex conceded. "I suppose you're not – not in general. But neither have you been all that supportive of Sarah, have you?"

"Supportive? Once a week, I've written to her," Julian said.

"Yeah. Along the lines that God knows best, and that she must conform and accept and oh, by the way, maybe marry before the baby is born."

Julian looked discomfited. "I still think that would have been for the best."

"And I'm still convinced we did exactly the right thing by her, given the circumstances. When Sarah marries, it will be for love."

Julian shook his head. "Let's hope she falls in love with a man old enough to make his own decisions or a boy very far away from here." He met Alex's angry look and hitched one shoulder in a helpless gesture. "That was the way it is: no good, God-fearing family will wed their son to Sarah – not now."

Alex exhaled and looked down at her mending. He was probably right, and it made her want to cry, because her Sarah deserved to fall in love, be loved, marry, and have wanted children.

"What did you mean about the world's core being molten lava?" Julian asked, no doubt to change the subject.

Alex eyed him warily. Ever since Simon's disloyal and emotional outburst well over a year ago when he screeched time traveller at her, Alex had become far more circumspect in Julian's company, imagining she could see his nose twitch with interest whenever she inadvertently let slip knowledge she had no possibility of proving.

"It's something I read somewhere."

"Ah," Julian nodded, "recently?"

"No, of course not. Way back when I was a child," Alex said airily. With a muttered comment about needing to get on with her dressmaking, she exited the room.

It was like being on a holiday – well, there was no pool, no bar that served drinks with gaudy umbrellas, no evening entertainment, and definitely no partial nudity in the form of bikinis, but to Alex five days to spend only on herself, Matthew, and the preparations for a party was like a two-week all-inclusive. She slept late, coming down for breakfast around seven. She perused the haberdashery and drapers for materials and ribbons, buttons and silk thread, spent several long afternoons with Ruth, cutting, fitting and sewing, and encouraged Matthew to spend time with his friends. She felt like the industrious mice in Cinderella when she set the finishing touches to her new grey silk bodice, offset with panels of soft green that recurred in ribbons and the petticoat that showed through the slashed skirts.

"Wow," she said as she fiddled with the sleeves. "Very wow," she amended when she tried it on.

She was in a buoyant mood when she strolled off with Ruth. Her daughter was a popular person, and their walk was constantly interrupted by one woman after the other who just had to stop the minister's young wife and inquire as to her health.

"You look radiant," Alex grumbled after the sixth stop. "Why don't they just use their eyes?"

"Because then they can't share their gossip with me," Ruth explained, "and if I don't hear it, how on earth is Julian to find out everything that is happening in town?"

Alex suppressed a smile, waved at her daughter when once again she was stopped, and increased her pace up the main street.

She didn't see them at first, concentrated on avoiding the offal in the gutter, but then she heard Simon's unmistakeable voice and looked up to find Simon, Kate and Matthew on the other side of the town square. She started towards them, but slowed successively until she halted halfway.

There was something in the way both men held themselves, very straight, very attentive, that reminded Alex of two dogs circling a bitch in heat. Kate said something and both of them laughed. She appeared to stumble and two hands flew out to steady her. Alex set her shoulders, lifted her chin and walked briskly towards them, slipping in her hand to rest on Matthew's arm.

"Hi," she said, and he looked down at her, eyes hastily adjusting from startled to pleased.

"Hi, yourself." He smiled back.

"I'm off to the apothecary," Alex told him. "Want to come along?" She wasn't about to leave him here, with bloody Kate and Simon.

"Aye, why not?" he answered, and after a quick farewell they walked off together.

"Is it a problem for you that Simon is seeing so much of Kate?"

"Problem? Why should it be a problem?"

"Don't ask me, but it does seem so." And she didn't like it, how he gawked at Kate, always so pampered, so...so... polished. She smoothed at her home-made skirts, irritated with herself for not having worn her new shawl at least.

"I'm glad for him – and her." He smiled down at her. "So where are we headed? The apothecary is that way." He pointed down the way she'd come.

"Later. I passed by the tailor before, and he had a couple of books I asked him to put aside." It still made her grin that the town premier coat maker should also be its bookseller.

"Oh aye?"

"Yes, a rather battered copy of the Canterbury Tales and a very nice bound version on the Greek philosophers."

"The Canterbury Tales?" Matthew looked very interested.

"Probably not adequate reading for a dour Presbyterian, but if you want, I can read it and then tell you the stories."

"I'm not a dour Presbyterian," he protested, "just Presbyterian."

"Same, same," she laughed, and the moment of niggling concern she had experienced when she saw him with Kate faded away.

Chapter 14

Alex gaped as they turned up the drive to the Jones' house at dusk on Friday evening. Kate had spared no expense for her son's betrothal feast, and the wide doors were flung open to receive the guests who walked up a pathway bordered with lanterns, entered the dark panelled hall, alive with candles, and then the main room...

For the first time in her life, Alex was violently envious. She wanted a house like this, with the virginal that stood in pride of place, the silver candelabra, and the three impressive mirrors, each one full-length, that had been fitted into the bottom wall, thereby creating the impression of rooms beyond the room they were presently in. Dotted around stood huge Chinese urns, full of flowers, and equally dotted what to Alex seemed an army of slaves, trays held as immobile as their faces were.

Ruth squealed. "It's beautiful!"

Alex just nodded, stunned into silence by the sheer opulence that surrounded her. She sneaked a look down her dress, and what had in the attic been a wonderful, other-worldly creation lost some of its lustre compared to the clothes that swept by her. There was the elder Mrs Farrell, contemporary in years with Alex but looking about a hundred, and her skirts frothed in grey silk and lace. There was Lionel Smith's new wife, and she had on something in softest blue, the skirts cut back to reveal a petticoat in embroidered silk.

So many plunging necklines, nominally covered by gauzelike lace, so much exposed hair. Jewels that sparkled in intricate hairdos, necklaces, bracelets and ear bobs... Alex felt positively naked in her wedding ring, very grateful that she had followed Ruth's advice and threaded her gold locket on a length of new ribbon.

She held on hard to Matthew, who in her biased eyes looked very nice in his borrowed dark blue coat with sleeves wide enough to show off the lace at the cuffs and an incredible froth of white around his neck. He had tied his mostly grey, thick hair back with a matching dark blue ribbon, exposing the strong lines of his face and highlighting his hazel eyes, and quite a few female heads turned in his direction as he led them across the room to greet their hostess.

Dark blue had been a bad choice. In silk of the same hue as Matthew's coat, a bodice that lifted breasts to stand high and round, and a strand of pearls around her neck, Kate looked exactly what she was: filthy rich. Her hair, her hands that dripped rings, the elegant girdle of chased silver disks that decorated her skirts, all in all Kate looked magnificent, and beside her stood a beaming Simon, proud enough to burst.

"I like the coat," Alex said, eyeing the deep green wool. She nodded at the pretty little bride-to-be, resplendent in light blue, and smiled at Henry Jones who bowed politely.

"I like it too," Simon replied with a grin, "but best of all I like the shoes."

Alex took a step back. "No wonder I thought you'd grown." She laughed. "What's that, a three-inch heel?"

"Almost four, and hell on earth to walk in. But worth it," Simon said, inspecting his silk clad calf with a satisfied smile. "And the buckles do add a certain dash."

"As does the wig," Alex told him, fingering the impressive hairpiece that adorned him. "But maybe you should have chosen another colour, something less—"

"Black," Simon completed for her. "Aye, I know, but there were none others to be had at such short notice."

All the while she'd been conversing with Simon, Matthew had been talking to Kate, and out of the corner of her eye, Alex saw him stretch, thereby making the point that, heels or not, he was still the taller of Simon and himself. He laughed at something Kate said, his eyes lingered on her bosom, and Alex was seriously considering where to pinch him when he finally let go of Kate's hand.

"I have breasts as well, you know," Alex murmured to Matthew when they moved aside to allow others access to Kate. He gave her a confused look. "Well, the way you stared at hers one would have thought you'd never seen any before." She was irritated with herself for having succumbed, yet again, to his wish for decorum, thereby cutting her neckline higher than anyone else's in the room, and having him more or less poke his nose into Kate's exaggerated crease hadn't made things better. Alex smiled sweetly at him, unfolded her fan, and floated off to circulate – alone.

After a round of greeting acquaintances, Alex adjusted her bodice, inspected the flowing sleeves, and returned to the main room, where the fiddlers had now struck up dancing music. Henry and his fiancée led off, twirling in splendid isolation for some minutes before others joined in. Alex wasn't too impressed: the couple-to-be danced competently but without any real spark. She found Matthew standing in a group of laughing men, and made her way towards him. He glanced at her and smiled before returning to his conversation and his beer. Alex stood beside him, watching the dancers.

Tables had been moved aside, and the floor was full of people, all of them involved in a complex dance of turns and twirls and the occasional exchange of kisses. Alex laughed when she saw Simon. In his green coat, his impeccable linen and dark breeches, he danced like a capering faun, elegant and boisterous at the same time. A fantastic dancer, Simon was, and Alex was thrown back to long ago barn dances in Scotland, with Simon lording it on the floor. Now, he was dancing with Kate, as accomplished as he was, and the rest of the dancers gave way to them, applauding when the turns became wilder and wilder.

Alex leaned to the side to whisper a comment to Matthew, but he wasn't there. Instead, he was striding across the floor, and suddenly it was him dancing with Kate, and where Simon was elegant, Matthew was surging power, with strong, flowing lines that complemented Kate in her dark blue silk dress. Alex watched in silence, hating the way they so effortlessly ended the dance, with Matthew flushed and beautiful, but with his eyes on a woman other than her.

The tune changed, and Alex was asked to dance, and she threw herself with enthusiasm into the music, laughing at her partner. Every now and then, she cast her eyes about the room, looking for Matthew, and there he was, swinging Alex easily into an arc high up in the air before planting a kiss on her mouth and dancing away. Kate and Simon whirling by, Simon and Kate coming round again, and then it was Matthew and Kate, and his head was bent towards hers, and Alex smiled at her partner and shook her head, shoving her way through the thronging people to escape to the side.

Julian popped up, and she danced and laughed, pretending not to notice nor care that Matthew was once again dancing with Kate. Bastard, she thought, but led Julian to dance closer and closer, hoping that he'd notice how much fun she was having, how flushed and pretty she looked, and cut in on Julian to dance with her instead. Matthew didn't, and when Julian gasped and mock-fainted she followed him over to the open French doors, agreeing cheerfully that yes, this was a fantastic party.

She stood sipping something she assumed to be a primitive version of rum punch, nodding and smiling at milling acquaintances, all the while tracking her husband's progress on the dance floor. Once, he looked in her direction, and she thought that now he would come and sweep her into the whirlwind, but he just raised his hand and went back to what he was doing, and Alex was both insulted and hurt.

Simon swept by her, kissed her, and dragged her out to dance, made her laugh and left her gasping for air by the open doors. William and Esther stood talking to her for some moments, and then Esther chuckled and nudged William, and all three of them watched Simon lead Kate into yet another wild and exuberant dance.

The fifth time Matthew cut in on Simon to dance with Kate, Alex had had enough. Not once had he asked her to dance, and except for the fleeting kiss when they met on the dance floor, he seemed entirely oblivious to her presence. She retrieved her shawl from Kate's bedroom and, without a backward glance, set out the long, dark way back home.

"Where's your mama?" Matthew collapsed, drenched in sweat, beside his daughter who gave him a very cold look.

"I don't know, but mayhap she had enough of seeing you dance attendance on Widow Jones."

"I wasn't dancing attendance on her, but she's a right good dancer." His head hurt: too much rum and beer – far too much.

"So is Mama, and how many times have you danced with her?"

Matthew mumbled something about not being sure.

"Well, I am, on account of me sitting here with nothing to do but watch. Not once, Da." Ruth stood up, shook off his helping hand, and moved over to join a group of young women on the terrace.

Matthew spent half an hour looking for Alex, and in his belly a little snake of guilt coiled and uncoiled. Eventually, he concluded that she must have left, alone, and the guilt transformed itself into anger that she should be so reckless as to undertake the mile-long walk back to town on her own.

He rushed up the stairs to their room. It was bolted, and he banged on it until she jerked it open so abruptly he fell into the room.

"What?" she demanded, hands on her hips. "What do you want?" She was half-dressed, the underskirt in green hanging unlaced about her middle.

"What do you think you were doing, walking back alone?" he exploded defensively. "You know that road is dangerous after dark!"

"Oh, and you care?" She wiped at her eyes, smudging the kohl even further.

"Of course I care," he spluttered, shamed by the fact that she had been crying.

"Well, now that you've assured yourself I'm safe and sound, you can hurry back to your party, gawk some more at Kate's tits, and see if I care." She turned her back on him, the petticoat landed with a sigh on the floor, and she twisted awkwardly to get at the lacing on her stays.

"I wasn't gawking," he said, and by habit he extended his hand to help her, but she slapped it away.

"Don't touch me! And no, you're right, you weren't gawking. You had your nose stuck between them – more or less. So, why are you still here instead of galloping back to do some more drooling?"

"Ah, but you're a bairn at times."

"A child? Me?" The slap caught him unawares, the force of it strong enough to bring tears to his eyes. "And what were you thinking, Mr Adult? Or should that be thinking *with*?"

"I don't know what you mean," he lied stiffly, touching his flaming cheek.

"Oh yes, you do!" she yelled. "But just to ensure we're on the same page, what the hell do you think you've been doing all night? Blatantly flirting with Kate Jones, dancing with her, swinging her in the air as if she were a feather, and not once, you arsehole, not once did you ask me to dance."

"I was dancing with the hostess!"

"Yeah, right. You were cutting in on Simon because you're jealous of him," she said, and he flushed at her perceptiveness. "And me...well, me you just ignored." She shimmied out of the stays and went to open the little attic window wide.

"Nay, Alex, that isn't fair. I never ignore you." He twisted inside at the look she gave him.

"No? And how many times this evening were you at my side? How many glasses of punch did you get *me*?" It came out very glacial.

"I got a wee bit carried away by the dancing, but then I came looking for you but you had already left," he said, hearing how lame that sounded.

"Ah." She kicked at her discarded finery, sending it flying across the room, and then the shoes went flying as well, landing with two distinct thumps. Just as violently, she tugged at the wooden pins that held her elaborate hairdo in place, and with a shake of her head her hair came tumbling down, in waves of bronze and brown and silver, laced here and there with strands of purest white.

"Don't!" she snapped, when his hand reached out towards that waterfall of hair. "If you do, I'll bite your fingers off." He ignored her, grabbing her by the shoulders.

"You can try," he challenged, and did the only thing he could think of; he kissed her.

Sweet Lord, but she could be a vixen! Every inch of the way she fought him, her nails raked his back, her bare feet swung for his shins. She tried to knee him in the crotch, she hissed and spat, her head whipping back and forth to evade his kisses. He slammed her against the wall, cradled her head with his hands and his lips came down on hers. She spluttered and tried to bite, but he persisted, his mouth moving against hers, his hands holding her still.

He raised his head, gasping for breath, and her blue eyes threw bolts at him, one fist swinging for his head, but this time he was ready for it and deflected it. She scratched him, hard enough to make him curse, and for an instant he came close to hitting her – but he'd never raise his hand against her. Instead, he kissed her again, a forceful vicious kiss. She bit his lip, and he pulled himself free with a hiss.

All of him thudded, all of him quivered. This was his woman, and he was her man, and let her never forget that, goddamn it! When she still fought him, he grabbed at the neckline of her chemise and ripped it apart, shoved her back against the wall and with his hands on her uncovered skin kissed her again, invading her, demanding her. She kissed him back. Ferociously, she kissed him, her fisted hands drumming at his shoulders, his chest. One hand in her hair, she was up on her toes. One arm round her waist, and she was impossibly close, her arms tight round his neck, her body plastered to his. With a grunt, he heaved her up and threw her onto the bed.

"Open your legs," he panted, pinning her down with his body.

"In your dreams," she spat, clamping her legs together. She was heaving with arousal, her pale skin shifting to red on her throat and chest. Her breasts spilled out of the torn chemise, her eyes were wide and dark, and her tongue slid out to wet her lips.

"Open yourself to me," he repeated thickly, sitting on her to keep her still as he stripped off his coat and shirt.

"Fuck off," she told him, and hit him hard enough to make him gasp.

"Oh, I intend to fuck alright," he growled back.

She gave a low howl, she struggled like a fiend, and he couldn't remember when he last had been this aroused, his balls aching and his cock springing through his undone lacings. She tried to shove him off, she pushed against his hold, at the same time grinding her hips against his. Her breath was hot against his skin, and at the last moment he reared back, hearing her teeth snap together where his ear had just been.

He wedged his thigh in between hers, his knees spread her apart, opened her for him. He raised himself on one arm, yanked at his breeches, and his cock rose free and unencumbered. Her fist struck him in the face, but he barely registered it, his blood a loud rushing in his brain, in his member. He gripped at her waist, she heaved, her legs coming up round his hips. Almost there, his cock nudging at her cleft. She bucked, he pushed, and there, finally.

She exclaimed, a soft "oh" that was a white flag of surrender, all of her softening below him, around him. Too late, he hammered home, her surrender came too late, and he drove into her, he plunged deeper and deeper, and every stroke reverberated up his spine to pop like a soap bubble in his head. He had drunk too much, sweat made both of them slick, and still he didn't finish, pushing harder in an attempt to find that elusive release.

He pulled out, dragged her onto the floor, and took her from behind, rearing over her. A male taking his mate, and she met his thrusts with a series of urgent sounds. He twisted his hands into her hair, gentle and rough at the same time, and with a sound somewhere between a sob and a groan, he finally came, pressing his balls as close to her as he could.

The room was suddenly very quiet, the only sound their heavy breathing, and Matthew sank down to rest his thudding head on the floor.

"This doesn't mean I've forgiven you," her voice floated up from where she lay on her front with him half on top.

Right now, he didn't care. All he wanted was to sleep. With a grunt, he pushed himself off the floor and stood swaying for some moments before helping her up.

"Bed," he said.

"Bed." She nodded.

He woke to a clanging hangover and vague but very pleasant memories of last night. When he opened his eyes, she was lying on her side looking at him, her eyes the blue of cornflowers in a sea of barley.

"How many years have we been married?" she asked in a tone that made him look at her warily.

He licked at his cracked lips as he counted in his head. "Twenty-eight come September."

She nodded, studying her wedding ring. "Not once during all those years have I ever looked at another man — not like that."

He groaned. He had hoped he had managed to put this particular discussion to bed last night.

"Kate was different—"

"I know it was different. At times, I even manage to dredge up a modicum of gratitude, because if it hadn't been for her, you might not have been alive. But that doesn't mean I like it, and it definitely doesn't mean that I've forgotten that you broke your vows to me with her — with bloody Kate Jones." He shifted under the weight of her eyes. She fell silent, and the ring went round and round her finger. "So, tell me, what am I supposed to feel when you go green with jealousy at hearing she is walking out with Simon? How am I to take it when you spend an evening fawning over her when I am there as well?"

He regarded her for a long time. "How can you even think...?" He shook his head in exasperation and began again. "Goddamn it, woman, you know I love you, only you, don't you?"

"I do? Let's say I'm not sure about that – at least not right now."

"Ah, Alex! You're just twisting the knife a wee bit deeper."

"And you don't think I deserve to? What would you have done if it had been me dancing with someone else – and a former lover to boot – all night long?"

He looked at her for a long time, his hand coming up to smooth at her hair, her face. His thumb rubbed at the dark smudges round her eyes, thinking they made her look very vulnerable.

"I think I might have killed him – or you." He smiled to show her he wasn't entirely serious.

"Don't be ridiculous!" she said, and he could hear in her voice just how much he had hurt her.

He closed his eyes for an instant. "I would have made you pay," he whispered. "I would have been angry and hurt, and I'd not have wanted you to touch me – or mayhap I'd have wanted you to, but I wouldn't have let you."

She flipped over on her back. "Exactly."

He propped himself up on his elbow, wound a long curl round one of his fingers. "Forgive me, my heart."

She hitched her shoulders.

"Please, Alex. Forgive me, aye?"

"Hmm," she said, but he could see it in her eyes, that she wanted to forgive him, needed to forgive him as much as he needed her to forgive. Just in case, he decided the situation called for a long tender session in bed, and by the time he was done, she was clinging to him, repeating his name in his ear.

They lay close together afterwards, legs still entangled, and he could swear she was purring. He looked down his nose at her. Not a house cat, his wife, more of a catamount. A catamount that raised brilliant blue eyes to his.

"Wow," she said.

"Mmm." He yawned. "Sleep?" he suggested after throwing a look out of the window. She didn't reply. She was already fast asleep.

Chapter 15

It was pure chance that Matthew and Alex were almost down by the port when the shouts went up. From everywhere, people came running, making for the wharves.

"A slaver?" Alex asked, watching Mr Farrell set off, coat flying.

In response, Matthew sniffed the air. She did the same, and her shoulders dropped. Not a slaver, because those boats carried an unmistakeable stench with them, as if all the misery of their unwilling cargo left an olfactory and indelible imprint behind.

"But it has crossed the ocean," Matthew said, studying masts and rigging.

Alex was unimpressed. Anyone could see that, thank you very much.

"There might be a letter for us," she said, before remembering that they had no one left on the other side of the Atlantic to send them a letter.

"We'll pass by the harbourmaster later," Matthew promised, squinting at the sun. He was suffering the consequences of too much alcohol in combination with a very intense night and morning, but Alex felt not one whit of compassion for him. Not today.

There was a letter. In actuality, there were two: one in an unknown hand, and the other with the distinctive lettering of Luke Graham, Matthew's brother.

"From Luke?" There was no love lost between Matthew and his younger brother, in Alex's opinion for very good reasons.

"Apparently." Matthew frowned, took her hand in his, and, without a further word, hurried them back to the privacy of their room.

She hung over his shoulder to read the first letter, a short little thing informing Matthew that Alexander Peden had died January last, in bed. There was a colourful description of how his body had been disinterred by the dragoons to be submitted to the iniquity of hanging after death, but, due to the loud rumblings in the countryside surrounding Cumnock, the powers that be had decided not to follow through.

Matthew sat in silence after finishing the letter, staring towards the east, towards the place she knew he still called home. Sandy Peden had been his friend, his spiritual mentor, and a preacher who attracted a large following during those turbulent years when Covenanters were hunted like animals through Ayrshire. He had also been the person who had convinced Matthew to leave Scotland, prophesising years of terrible unrest for all those that remained behind. And now he was dead – in his bed, as he had also prophesised.

"So he was right after all," Alex said.

"Hmm?" Matthew gave her a dazed look.

"He said, didn't he? How he would die in bed, and how we would bury more than the one child." She looked away, her head full of Jacob and their little Rachel, buried nineteen years ago back home, in Scotland. "I wish he'd been wrong, even if I don't begrudge him a peaceful death.

"And the other?" she said when Matthew made no move to break the heavy seal.

He weighed it in his hand and lobbed it over to her. "You read it."

Alex slipped a finger under the wax, making it crack when she forced the papers apart.

"Dated in December of 1685," she informed him.

Brother, it began, the strong handwriting stark against the heavy paper...

> *It must of course seem to you the ultimate irony that*
> *I, the brother you love not at all, be reduced to turning*
> *to you in this my hour of greatest need. Had there been*
> *any other alternative, rest assured I would not, but I am*
> *rendered incapable of taking action on my own, and can*

but hope that the many years that have transpired since
we last met have served to temper the bitterness between
us — at least enough for you to peruse my letter before
discarding it.

"He's asking you for a favour?"

"Aye, it would seem so." Impatiently, Matthew waved
his hand at her, and she cleared her throat and read on.

I write to you on behalf of my son, my impetuous
Charlie, of an age, I believe, with your Daniel. To
a man experienced in the joys and pitfalls of fatherhood,
there is no need to explain what young men are like
when they hover between manhood proper and the
childish fancies that still at times inhabit their heads, is
there? I can but remind you of Jacob and his devilishly
daring but oh so foolish decision to take ship on his own
for Europe. (I trust he is hale and hearty, for all that
we have not heard from him for nigh on a year, and do
remind him he has a home here whenever he needs it.)

"Oh," Alex said, her eyes misting over, "we never told him
Jacob is dead."

"Why should we?" Matthew said.

"Because Jacob cared for him?"

Matthew threw her a dark look, making her sigh. He
still had problems accepting that his son had developed such
fondness for Luke during his years in London. Alex went
back to the letter.

Enough of procrastinations. I assume that even in your
lost corner of the world, you hear of events here in
England, and surely you are appraised of the fact that
we now have a new king, James the Second, and may
his reign be long and bountiful. Equally, I suppose
you may have heard of Monmouth's failed rebellion
this summer past — a rash and rebellious act against an
anointed king.

I first met Monmouth, plain James as he was then, when he was but ten or so, during the last years of his royal father's exile in the Netherlands. A beautiful and headstrong boy, spoiled and with a dramatic flair that he surely inherited from his mother, for his royal father was a man markedly without airs or pretensions.

Charles heaped this his firstborn natural son with titles and riches, even investing him with a dukedom, no matter that he was bastard born. Ingrate, the son turned out to be, to the extent of plotting against his father's life a couple of summers before Charles' untimely death. Awful, is it not, to contemplate such ingratitude in a child?

"Huh," Alex snorted, "and when Luke killed his own father, that was alright, was it?"

"We don't truly know," Matthew protested, "if it was Luke or Margaret."

"Well, my money's on Luke, just so you know." She had never liked Margaret – bloody gorgeous woman who had first married Matthew then Luke – but she didn't see Margaret as either strong enough or devious enough to lure old Malcolm Graham up to the millpond and push him in.

As a consequence of all that plotting, Monmouth spent the last few years of Charles' life in Holland, dancing attendance on William of Orange while collecting a band of hotheads around him. Unfortunately, one of those hotheads was my son, my only son.

"Oh dear," Alex said.

With an exasperated sigh, Matthew took the letter from her and settled himself on the narrow window bench to continue reading.

I do not understand how Monmouth ever came by the idea that there would be support for a bastard-born son against a legitimate heir. As I am sure you can fully appreciate, the people have no taste for further fratricide after those terrible years of civil war in the forties, and James is well enough liked, despite being a professed Catholic.

It was bound to fail. Monmouth counted on William of Orange's support, conveniently forgetting the fact that William is married to King James' eldest daughter, and on top of that, he allied himself with the Earl of Argyll, that luckless, untalented son of a brilliant father, and well... Did you ever meet the old Earl of Argyll, Matthew? A fox, I hear, although I never had the pleasure myself. But the son, well, the son I knew well, having spent months with Archie Campbell during the Glencairn rising, mediating between him and Middleton.

"He does have quite the cheek, doesn't he?" Alex interrupted. "To chit-chat casually about his own participation in a rising he managed to get you condemned for." Three years in prison, that treachery of his brother had cost him.

"Mhm," Matthew grunted.

Ah well, neither here nor there, although I suspect your temperamental wife is by now spewing vitriolic comments as to my unrepentant nature. For what it's worth, brother, I do have moments of remorse, but it suffices to touch my silver nose to clear my head of such.

"Bastard! So now the fact that you cut his nose off is comparable to him stealing years of your life from you?" It still made her squirm to recall how a wild-eyed and incoherent Matthew had sliced off Luke's nose in payment for years spent in prison, for the child Alex had miscarried due to Luke's beating, but, foremost, for the humiliation of finding Luke with the beautiful but false Margaret – in Matthew's marital bed.

"Do you wish me to read it out loud or not?" Matthew said, sounding irritated. Alex waved for him to go on.

Archie, poor sod, set off for Scotland, there to rouse the Highlands, while Monmouth was to land in the south, and together they would close the pincer round defenceless James' middle. It all went wrong, and well before Monmouth set foot on English soil, Argyll was defeated in the north.

With Monmouth rode my Charlie, no doubt enamoured of himself in armour and sashes, but with no understanding at all of the workings of war and state. It grieves me to admit that my son, while diligent and witty, lacks in comprehension of the mechanics of power. Had he but studied the situation, he would have seen that Monmouth stood no chance to win — not against a crowned king. But Charlie, well, he saw himself set off in the fashion of the dashing Cavaliers, fighting bravely and honourably to place his chosen prince on a throne he had no right to.

There are no honourable wars, as you well know, and fighting battles is a dirty and sordid affair, with little bravery and much knavery. Charlie, I fear, found that out very quickly, but being endowed with very little sense of self- preservation, he stuck with Monmouth to the end.

My son was captured in the aftermath of the battle of Sedgemoor, and carried off to sit in chains in Taunton, where, as well as I can make out, he still lingers. Monmouth was beheaded. I was there to watch, and it was a spectacle: an incompetent executioner that struck the Duke five or six times and yet the wretch remained alive.

My son was condemned to death before the court in Taunton, late in September. It was one of those golden autumn days, a day that began in misty sunrise and dewy grass, a day that should be spent rejoicing in the pleasure of being alive. Instead, I sat at Taunton Castle and watched as a man bearing but a passing resemblance to my strong and vivacious son was brought to stand before the bench. His hair was shorn, his clothes hung ragged and soiled around his decimated frame, and he could barely walk on account of his fetters.

I had tried everything to save him, but this time money had no clout. The King was bent on setting an example, and in Judge Jeffreys he had his man, an ice-cold man with not one whit of compassion in his body. People call him the hanging judge. They whisper his name in revulsion, and justly does he deserve it, for a man more drunk on his own power have I rarely seen. He screamed at witless children, he jeered at the prisoners, accusing them not only of treason, but of dissent and Presbyterianism.

Women were sentenced to burn, mere boys were taken to hang, and in Taunton 500 unlucky souls had their lives gavelled away from them − among them, my lad. It is a strange experience, brother, to bear witness to the passing of your beloved child's life, to sit helpless while a lowly clerk reads out his names and then pronounces his life to be forfeit.

I saw the despair in his eyes, and even more I saw it when Jeffreys announced that Charles Graham wasn't to hang. No, he was to be transported to the West Indies there to serve out his life as a slave. His life! A long, extended death sentence, a slow degeneration from human to beast, from beast to corpse... My lad, Matthew, my bonny red-haired lad to die alone and so far from home!

"The sins of the father," Alex muttered, thinking that maybe there was divine justice after all, even if it seemed somewhat unfair on poor Charlie.

If the King had as his aim to frighten the country into obedience, he has succeeded, but these excesses may come back and haunt him, for people are sickened by the lack of compassion, for the cruelties done. It behoves a king to remember that his subjects are fickle: what

*they love today, they may hate tomorrow, and in
these days of unrest, a king must be possessed of strong
political instincts and a flair for governance. I hope, for
England's sake, that James has this in equal measure as
my mourned and defunct liege.*

*I suppose, brother, that you wonder why I come to
you for help...*

"Too right," Alex agreed, "and what does he expect you to
do, anyway?"

*...and the answer to that is simple: your brother, on
account of his previous relations with the Netherlands,
is no longer in a position of trust. I have been placed
under house arrest while it is ascertained that I have not
in any way been involved in this nefarious rebellion.
I have not, I assure you. I am a loyal subject of the King,
as I was of his brother, and trust matters will soon be
sorted. But, until then... Charlie's ship is to sail in late
March, with destination Jamaica or Barbados – I know
not which – and, assuming he survives the journey, he
will be there in May or June. I fear that in his weakened
state after near on a year in English gaols, he will not
have strength enough left to him that he will live even
another year.*

*I have no one else to ask. I am at my wits' end,
restrained from helping him myself, and I lie awake
at night imagining his sufferings, and cannot truly
bear it. My son, to wither away and die after a short,
stunted life... I beg of you, Matthew, that you show the
compassion for my son I never accorded you. Please help
him, brother. Don't let him die a dog.*

"Very eloquent," Alex said unsteadily. "And how does he
sign off? Your loving brother Luke?"

Matthew just handed her the letter. *Luke*, it said, nothing
more.

Alex watched him turn away, sink his hands into

the window frame and grip it. His shoulders bowed, his back stiffened, and she knew he was reliving his long ago abduction and subsequent slavery – all on account of his brother. What a bloody mess all of this was. In retribution for his disfigured face, Luke had abducted and sold Matthew as indentured labour in Virginia, there to be worked for seven years or until he died, whichever came first.

Damn Luke…a veritable Judas, and now he had the audacity to turn to Matthew for help! Alex's instinctive reaction was to reject it outright, but then she thought of Charlie, the cousin Jacob had grown so fond of, and reluctantly she recalled how good Luke had been to Jacob. In exasperation, she puffed out her cheeks.

"What do we do?" she said, coming over to hug Matthew from behind. She rubbed her face up and down between his shoulder blades, feeling him relax.

"There isn't much choice, is there?" he said. "I have to go down there and attempt to find him."

"Wrong pronoun," Alex told him. "It's 'we', Matthew, not 'I'." No way did she intend to let him face the ghosts of his past alone.

"We," he said and twisted round in her arms to hold her close.

Chapter 16

"Kate? What do you mean we have to talk to Kate?" Alex hated having to run, and when he showed no intention of shortening his stride, she stopped, folding her arms over her chest. "Go ahead," she called after him, "go and talk to Kate on your own, and let's see if I'm still here when you come back, shall we?"

He came to an abrupt halt and stood waiting until she caught up with him.

"Sorry," he muttered. He placed her hand in the crook of his elbow and set off, this time adjusting both pace and stride to hers. "She has boats."

"Aha," Alex replied, having no idea what he was talking about.

"Kate," he explained with a small smile, "she has ships. And most of them trade from here to the Indies."

"Aha," Alex repeated.

They found Simon on Kate's terrace, and from his unchanged clothes, Alex deduced he had spent the night.

"And the wig?" Alex asked, retrieving his coat from where it had slid to the ground.

"Too hot," Simon grumbled, "and I'm not quite sure where it ended up last night." He grinned, his pale blue eyes looking genuinely happy for the first time in very many years. His face broke up even further when the dark nursemaid appeared with Duncan.

"See?" he said. "He recognises me."

Alex gave Duncan a sceptical look. "He has gas," she said, holding out her arms to the child.

"Let me." Matthew slid his big hands under the child to lift him to his chest, escaping to sit on a chair some distance away to acquaint himself with the grandson

142

he had so far scarcely touched.

"Where's Kate?" Alex asked. "Taking a nap?"

"Sleeping? Nay, Kate has been up and about since just after dawn." He nodded to where Kate stepped into sight, a wide-brimmed straw hat shading her face. "Not that she slept much before dawn either," he added with a self-satisfied little smirk.

"Poor her," Alex commiserated.

"Poor her? Nay, Alex, poor me. It's common knowledge, how voracious widows are in bed."

"It is?" Alex eyed Kate with guarded interest.

"Oh aye. Once a woman has discovered the joys a man can give her, well then…"

"Yes, and she of course was very lucky in her husband," Alex said. "I can really see him taking the time to introduce her to the glorious world of sexual completion."

Simon looked at her with interest. "You think he was remiss in those matters? After all, they had seven children."

"I think Dominic Jones was a very self-centred person in bed."

"Ah well, someone has lit her fire," Simon said, "and done a right good job of it."

"Oh," Alex replied, her eyes on her husband and his very pink cheeks.

Simon read Luke's letter in silence and after an inquiring look at Matthew, passed it to Kate who retreated to read it alone. Not a good reader, Alex noted with a spurt of satisfaction, keeping her face blank as they all waited for Kate to work her way through the multiple pages.

"Oh dear," Kate said, and between her and Matthew passed a wordless communication that made Alex seethe inside.

"Yes, you would know," Alex said, earning herself a reproachful look from Matthew. Well, she would, wouldn't she? Rich, successful Kate Jones had, after all, crossed the ocean involuntarily, loaded onto a ship as a convicted criminal.

"I suppose I would, even if it was worse for the men." Kate's mouth tightened, one hand bunching itself round the cotton of her skirts. "They die quickly down there, what with the heat and the toil – and they won't be in the best of health to begin with."

"Nay, not after so many months in gaol." Simon set his elbows on the table and tilted his head at Matthew. "You don't have to do this. You don't owe Luke anything. That brother of yours has cost you dearly. Years in prison, further years of slavery, constant persecution back in Scotland…"

"Nay, but the lad is my nephew." Matthew looked down at Duncan, now fast asleep in his arms, and handed the boy over to Simon. "Jacob would have wanted me to go, and had Jacob been alive, he would have gone too."

"I can arrange passage for you on one of my sloops," Kate said, addressing herself to Matthew. "It will take some weeks, the *Althea* is not due back before the latter part of May, but all in all you'd be down in Jamaica by early July the latest."

"Jamaica, you think?"

"I would start there, a jungle-infested place, I hear. It eats men." Kate shuddered, once again sharing a quick look with Matthew. "I can go with you. I have several contacts that may come in useful."

In your dreams. Alex was very tempted to kick Kate – or Matthew.

"That is kind of you," Matthew said, "and I'll gladly take whatever names you think may come in useful, but Alex and I will manage on our own."

"Alex?" Kate turned to look at her. "Is she coming too?"

"Absolutely." Almost like going on a cruise, Alex was trying to convince herself, hearing Dolly Parton and Kenny Rogers duet their way through *Islands in the Stream* in her head.

"Beware of the ague," Kate said.

"Oh, we will," Alex said. "I'll stock up on Jesuit's bark."

Once the discussion about ships to the Indies had been concluded, Kate insisted on dragging Alex off to inspect her gardens.

"Yesterday…" Kate bent down and studied a patch of garlic, "I…"

"Yes?" Alex prompted when Kate fell silent.

"I had hoped you'd enjoy the evening, and instead you were saddened by it."

"Saddened?" Alex shook her head at Kate's back. "I was insulted and angry."

"Yes, I suppose you would be." Kate straightened up and smiled tentatively at Alex. "I behaved badly. I shouldn't have danced with him more than the once."

"I'm not married to you," Alex reminded her.

"Thank heavens for that," Kate muttered, and they both burst out laughing. They continued their little stroll, stood for some moments looking out over the water.

"Will you marry Simon?" Alex asked.

"Marry Simon?" Kate gave her a very surprised look. "Why would I do that?"

"To stop the whole community from gossiping about you? Or ensure you're not suddenly accused of fornication by Minister Macpherson?"

"Pfff! They can chatter as they wish. I lead a discreet existence, too far away from town for those old busybodies to truly know what happens." Kate unfolded her fan and set it to work as they walked back towards the house. "No, Simon and I are friends, related through our common grandchildren." She fluttered her eyelashes and grinned. "How fortunate that such small children nap frequently during daytime."

"Simon might want to marry you," Alex said.

"Oh, I'm sure he would," Kate answered with a certain asperity. "Widow Jones is quite the catch."

"I don't think that stands foremost in Simon's mind."

"You think not?" Kate sounded bleak. She plucked at a rosebud, breaking it off with a snap. "Widow Jones is not about to remarry. She is far too fond of her independence." She levelled a dark look at Alex. "Maybe you should let him know."

Alex shook her head. "Oh no, that's something you are perfectly capable of doing yourself – independent woman that you are."

★

"Do you think she's right? Will Simon have an eye on her on account of her wealth?" Alex gripped Matthew's hand as they balanced down the rocky shore towards the lapping waters of the bay.

"Of course he does," Matthew replied, "not only, mind, he is foremost taken by her as a woman."

"Hmm," Alex said.

"Alex," Matthew sighed, "you can't deny she is a fine woman."

"Yeah, and we all know she's a formidable dancer," Alex muttered. She stuck her bare foot into the cool water and sneaked him a look.

"Not like you," he said.

"Right," she snorted. "As if you would know, given that you didn't dance even once with me last night."

"Alex…" He looked away. "I've said I'm sorry."

"I know. But that doesn't make it go away, okay? It still hurts."

"I didn't mean to hurt you, lass. You know that, don't you?"

Alex lifted one shoulder, she lifted the other. "But you did – badly."

"I did." He nodded. "I didn't mean to, but I did." He raised their braided hands to his mouth and kissed her fingers. "I love you."

"Good line, given the circumstances," Alex muttered.

"But true," he said, his eyes burning into hers.

"I know."

He looked at her expectantly but she couldn't bring herself to say she loved him, not today, not when she was still angry and humiliated. After some seconds, he exhaled and broke eye contact.

"I suppose I deserve that," he muttered.

Bloody right you do, she thought.

"Kate would be a fool to wed again," Matthew said, reverting to the original subject, "and her son would not approve."

146

"Her son?"

"Anything Kate owns passes to her husband at her marriage, just as you are mine, and all you own or hold is mine to use as I see fit." He laughed at her glower. "He can gamble it away, squander it on other women, and she can't do anything to hinder him. I don't think Henry Jones wants to see his inheritance frittered away by a bounty-hunting wastrel such as Simon."

"Simon to a T," Alex laughed.

They stood hand in hand with the water lapping over their feet. The hot day was misting with evaporating water, creating shimmering veils that hovered above the flat expanse of the bay. An osprey struck a few hundred yards out and rose to soar elegantly with writhing silver in its talons, a sandpiper hurried over the wet tidal flats, and here and there, crabs scurried industriously. To the south, very far away, lay the West Indies, and to the east, in a crammed hold, poor Charlie Graham was being carried across the sea towards them.

"Do you think we'll find him?" Alex asked. At least he'd be distinctive: tall, red-haired and green-eyed like his sire.

"We'll try – if nothing else to bury him."

"You think it's that bad?" Alex looked up at him.

"Aye," Matthew said, "I think Charlie is living through hell, God help him."

It was a slow wade back to town, where they sat on a convenient rock to put on stockings and shoes.

"He has your eyes," Matthew said.

"Who?"

"Duncan. Eyes like the deepest sea on a sunlit day, blue like bluebells in the shade." He kissed her brow and helped her up to stand. "It made me glad to see."

Chapter 17

They arrived on Barbados in May, and it was a humid, hot day. The barred hatch was thrown open, and they were commanded to stand and come up, one by one. As they got on deck, they were forced to their knees, shaved over head and face, doused in vinegar, and then shoved over to the side of the ship where they were lowered into boats.

Charlie Graham could barely stand after two months of constant crouching, and it was even worse when he was landed, the ground tilting under his feet. After weeks in a crammed, airless space, it was a relief to be able to breathe freely again, and he relished the scents of fish and salt, of the rotting fruit that lay beneath a tree the likes of which he had never seen before. A beautiful tree, he mused, staring up at the large pinnate leaves. He edged further into the relative coolness of the shade to wait while the ship was unloaded.

It was a busy harbour, several ships lying at anchor, and a flotilla of small boats were plying back and forth with loads, destined no doubt for England. Charlie tried to recall what day it might be, thinking that in some months he would be twenty. Twenty, and his life was over. Bitterly, he regretted the day he had met Monmouth; even more he berated himself for having been fool enough to go along with this venture, doomed from the start.

He heard a female voice and turned instinctively towards it. He hadn't seen a woman that he could collect in nearly a year, and here came a group of three young girls, all fresh and bright in cotton gowns and straw hats, slaves carrying parasols over their heads. They stopped a distance away and surveyed them, and Charlie was horribly aware of how he must seem to them – emaciated, in chains, recently shorn of hair and beard, he must appear a wild, uncouth man.

He hated it when they laughed, one of them using her fan to point at this one or the other. When they walked off, he attempted to catch the eye of the tallest but she just looked straight through him, as if he wasn't there.

They were led off, well over a hundred men that followed obediently, none of them even considering the idea of escaping. Where to? This was not their land, they were strangers here, and they had heard of venomous snakes and man-eating alligators, and spiders the size of saucers that would bite into your chest and suck you dry, so they hurried on as best they could after their guards, afraid of being left behind to face all these new dangers on their own.

Charlie was rarely hungry anymore, but he was horribly thirsty and swallowed repeatedly in an attempt to lubricate his throat. They arrived in an enclosed yard, were forced to remove whatever remained of their shirts and coats, and one by one they were led up to stand and be sold. At least there was water, and Charlie drank deeply before a sharp jab in the ribs indicated it was his turn to climb the rickety steps and be examined.

Charlie had always been tall, and had for the most part of his life been strong with it as well, but now he was just tall, a reed sapped of strength, of anything but an unquenchable will to survive. He stood swaying on the wooden platform, his eyes focused on the fronds of a palm tree straight ahead, and tried to pretend he was somewhere else, not here, being auctioned off like cattle. The sun was torture on his naked head, on his bared torso and arms. He adjusted his ragged breeches, fingertips grazing cloth that had once been plush, dark blue velvet, and now was sticky and sharp to the touch with encrusted grime.

He was shaken out of his concentration by someone barking his name, and then he was led off, still in chains, towards a waiting group of men. He had hoped their fetters would be struck off them – he had worn his since well before September, could scarcely remember what it was like to not have them, but still he had hoped.

It was a long slow walk in the midday heat, bare feet

stumbling over sharp pebbles and burrs. Charlie could feel the sun scorch his white skin into a painful red on shoulders and the back of his neck, heat pounded relentlessly at his shorn head, and he raised his arms in a feeble attempt to shield his poor brain, but it was too exhausting to walk with his arms like that.

He had never walked in chains before, no more than from the cell to the hall in Taunton Castle or the odd yards across the hold on the ship. But now... The chain dragged heavily over the ground, long enough that he could move, short enough that he be forced to shuffle, and the iron cuffs around his ankles chafed at his skin. Skin blistered, it tore, it blistered again, and still they walked, a silent stumbling line of men. Until one of them decided he'd had enough and sat down, refusing to move a single inch further without food and water.

"Is it steak and eggs you're wanting then?" one of their guards said, using the handle of his whip to poke at the sitting man.

"Bread would do fine," the man said, "and please, some water."

"And a feather bed as well? A horse to ride on?"

The sitting man didn't reply, but the dangerous tone made him get back on his feet. "Water," he whispered and staggered when the whip came down across his mouth. He shut up and resumed his place in the line, shuffling along as unsteadily as the rest of them.

The night was spent huddled close to each other, sweat cooling to an uncomfortable chill on their bodies where they sat wide awake, ears strained to every unfamiliar sound in the oppressive greenery that surrounded them.

It was late afternoon of the next day by the time it seemed they had finally arrived, and one of the men leading them went off to find the overseer, leaving them in the shade. Charlie sat down. His head ached from the sun and lack of water, his feet were throbbing with pain, and his skin... Tentatively, he touched his shaved pate, wincing at how much it hurt.

"What a sorry lot," the overseer said.

"But cheap," his assistant told him.

"Hmm," the overseer said, and went among them to assess their relative health and strength. "Not one of them will last a year." His eyes rested for a moment on the man with the whipped mouth, and then he told all of them to stand.

Wearily, Charlie got to his feet. The overseer nodded at his obedience, and barked at the others to do as he said and get back up. They scrambled, warned by his tone, and he strolled over to the man with the split lip.

"Lick my boots," he said.

Something must have snapped in the man because he just shook his head.

The overseer smiled, almost gently. "I said, lick my boots."

Charlie looked away, swallowing down on what he recognised to be acute fear.

"No," the man said, throwing his life to the wind.

He was still twitching half an hour or so later, his back a bloodied mass.

The overseer beckoned Charlie forward. "Lick my boots," he said, and Charlie knelt and did as he was told.

They all did, and the overseer laughed and told his assistant to make sure they were fed and watered before they were locked away for the night.

"And him?" Charlie asked, pointing at the man hanging from the whipping post.

"He dies there," the assistant said.

It was pitch-black at first, the whole room full of rustlings when the men settled down as well as they could for the night. Other things rustled through the debris on the floor, and Charlie pressed his back closer to the wall when something he was sure was a rat ran across his legs. He shifted his feet, and the length of chain between them clonked hollowly. He was very aware of his near nudity, of all the half-naked bodies around him. The rank scent of dirty, sweaty men rose high around him, and here and there he heard small sounds that were at times suppressed sobs, at times swallowed down gasps of pain.

He blinked, and now he could make out shapes in the dark: humped mounds where men attempted to sleep. It struck him that this was it, this was to be his final home before he eventually died, and he was surprisingly unperturbed by this insight. To die must be easier than to live like this, he reflected, and kicked at the rat as it came back to sniff his toes. It could not, at any rate, get much worse, and with this comforting thought in his head, Charlie fell asleep.

He was wrong. It could get much, much worse, which he realised next morning when they were led out into the sun. He blinked at the sharp light, and shuffled as fast as he could to his place in the line, not about to risk the overseer's wrath after what he'd witnessed yesterday. The ground around the whipping post was still splotched with blood, and he tried to keep his eyes averted from the dark stains.

They were divided up in groups and led off towards the cane fields presently being harvested. Black men were already at work cutting the cane into four-foot sections, and these were then to be bundled and carried over to the mill, immediately. They scurried like rats to avoid the whips as they pulled and dragged at the lengths of cane, tied them together, loaded them onto the mules, and went back to do it all again, an interminable cycle of bending and carrying, more bending and carrying.

By noon, Charlie was sure he was about to die. He collapsed into a panting heap, unable to do more than lift his head when he saw the overseer's boots. Someone grabbed at his right hand, his index finger was gripped and bent backwards until there was a dull snapping sound. He didn't cry out. Pain flew up his arm, constricted his windpipe, and Charlie gulped air like a landed fish, each inhalation accompanied by a high-pitched whistling sound he'd never heard himself make before.

"Get up," the overseer said, and Charlie wasn't sure he could, but managed all the same, cradling his hand to his chest.

"Work," the overseer said, "or I'll do the same to all your fingers."

Charlie had no doubt he meant it, and he dragged and pulled and carried, ignoring the pain that was like gnawing teeth in his rapidly swelling finger.

It was dark when they were led back, and several of them fell asleep over their food, too tired to even eat. Charlie ate. He gulped his food and drank the ale set before him, and, when no one saw, he helped himself to food from the plate of his sleeping neighbour. He had never eaten such before, a roasted vegetable he was told was called yams, beans, something called okra, but no meat. He didn't care. It was food, it was hot, but he was still hungry when they were once again locked in their shed.

Despite his throbbing finger, he fell asleep immediately, woke up to clanging bells and total disorientation, and then it was back on the fields with nothing but thin gruel in their bellies. They worked until they dropped, and then they worked some more, staggering back home through the velvet of the tropical night, and Charlie didn't care about the chains around his feet anymore. All he wanted was food and sleep.

It was quick, this transformation from human to beast. On the ship out, there had been desultory talk, a sharing of stories and hopes that allowed them to hang on to some scrap of basic humanity. Here, there was no talk on the fields, none of them had the breath for it, and at night, they collapsed to sleep as best they could, exhausted beyond the point of rational thought.

Starved already to begin with, the insufficient rations weakened him further, and the gruelling work under a punishing sun left him – all of them – a walking skeleton in less than a month. Charlie stole where he could. He ate anything set before him, he bullied the weaker of his companions into sharing with him, and while the others died, he remained alive. Alive, but a beast, an obedient slave that mumbled *yes, massa, no, massa* like the blacks did, that dragged and carried load after load of heavy cane to the voracious sugar mills from sunrise to well after sunset.

His skin no longer flamed under the sun, having tanned

into a permanent reddish brown decorated with a scattering of uneven white circles where blisters had formed and healed. He was beaten for not being fast enough, he was whipped for standing for a moment in the shade to rest. He had the last remnant of the old Charlie Graham removed when his breeches were ripped off him and replaced by a linen clout, and still he survived, forcing his battered, starved body to work and eat, work and eat.

One of the men tried to escape, in chains an all, and was brought back dragged behind a mule. Charlie barely blinked when the man was branded nor did he much react when the poor sod screamed in pain as he was whipped with canes. He was too tired, too hungry, and too focused on the effort of staying alive. That man died, other men died, several men died, and of the original twelve, there were only four left.

They were moved in to sleep with the blacks, and in a series of silent fights it was made clear to the white slaves that they were lowest of the low. Where before Charlie had been the bully, now he was one of the bullied, and his life shrank even further into a vicious circle of work and food – always too little food. He was uncomfortably aware of the eyes of one of the slaves, a big, hulking man who seemed to have made Charlie his single point of interest.

"You sleep here," the big man said to Charlie and indicated the space beside him, and Charlie didn't dare to say no, because the size of those fists... And so he became Big George's servant, rushing to fetch when George wanted water, or extra food, or fresh straw. Whatever Charlie might find, now belonged to George, and the night he tried to hide away a piece of yams he'd pilfered from the kitchen, George beat him until he crawled at his feet, begging this new master of his for forgiveness. The yams was pounded into the dirty floor and Charlie was commanded to eat it, standing on all four like a dog. The other black slaves laughed. The three remaining whites looked away.

"You's my slave" George snarled when Charlie had finished licking the dirt floor clean of yams. He took hold of Charlie's fetters and pulled, hard, laughing when Charlie fell flat on his face. That night, Charlie slept at George's feet, like the worthless cur he was. The next night, when he made to lie down in his normal place, George just pointed, and Charlie had to crawl to the big man's feet, the chain between his legs dragging at the ground.

It amused George to humiliate Charlie – and he did, repeatedly. A dog; he was lower than a dog, a cringing shadow of his former self. But there were benefits as well, because no one was about to harm Big George's white boy, and at times there was extra food on his plate, a helping hand with his work. Sometimes when he couldn't sleep, fidgeting because his heart raced with the fear of dying, George would sit up and place a big warm hand on him, confirming that somehow he was still here.

Charlie Graham ceased to be. The vague recollections of a former life drifted further and further away from him, and he was nameless, a tall, silent man that did as he was told, always did as he was told. The fetters round his ankles no longer bothered him. It was as if they had always been there.

He was casually whipped, he was ordered around, and at times he was fed and at times he was not, and he was simply a slave, a dispensable resource that would be worked until he died. But deep inside of him, it still burnt: a small flickering flame of life, an insistent heat that wouldn't allow him to give up. Live, his gut screeched, live! The man that used to be Charlie Graham gritted his teeth and did just that, through endless days and never-ending nights.

Chapter 18

Alex sat back on the bench and sighed. The last few weeks had been a flurry of work, the preparations for the upcoming trip coming on top of all the other things that had to be done on a farm their size. She massaged her aching hands, rubbed at a knee, her eyes stuck on the glittering water of the river.

To her far left, she saw Matthew returning from the fields, and by his side walked Mark, gesticulating wildly. Probably trying yet again to convince his father that trips to the unknown were adventures best undertaken by men – like Mark – not women, like her. It wasn't only Mark, it was Ian as well, and even David had lit up like a torch when he heard where they were going, clinging like an enervating burr to Matthew as he pleaded that he may come along. It had been a relief to leave him behind in Providence – at least for Matthew who complained the lad had talked holes through his ears.

The only one with a valid reason for coming along was Ian. As he'd pointed out on several occasions, Charlie was his half-brother, and so it should be him going with Da. Alex smiled to herself. She doubted Ian considered himself Margaret's son, not anymore, not after years and years of being loved so wholeheartedly by her, but it was still an irrefutable fact that it was Margaret, not Alex, who had birthed him. Anyway, no matter their reasons, Matthew was adamant, and by now he'd repeated his responding arguments so often an irritated edge crept into his voice whenever he yet again had to tell them that no, they weren't going, they were staying behind to care for home and family, for their wee bairns and weans.

Alex worried: that she had packed too much, or yet

again too little; that Adam would miss them both too much; that Sarah would feel abandoned; that Mrs Parson might choose this time to die.

"I'll kill you if you do," she threatened, which made Mrs Parson laugh, her black eyes like bright buttons in her wrinkled face.

"I don't plan to, and I'm as hale today as I was a week or so ago, no?"

"Probably more," Alex muttered, looking her over. The totally white hair was neatly bunned and capped, the dark old-fashioned bodice and skirts spotless, and as always, her collar stood stiff with starch. Her hands trembled too much at times for her to thread a needle or perform any precision cutting, her eyesight was gradually becoming weaker, but all in all, Mrs Parson looked the epitome of health, her soft, wrinkled skin pink, her teeth still surprisingly white.

"In particular as she doesn't even clean them regularly," Alex said to Matthew.

"Aye, she does," Matthew said. "I found her with a wee twig just the other day."

"Hmm. Well, she doesn't bathe either, does she?"

Matthew laughed. No, he said, Mrs Parson had as far as he knew never fully immersed herself in any body of water, nor had she ever expressed a wish to do so.

Alex had something of a surprise on the eve of their departure when Mrs Parson told her she was coming with them down to Providence with Sarah.

"Sarah?" Alex said stupidly, looking at her daughter.

"Aye," Sarah said, "we'll be staying with Ruth."

"You will?"

Sarah pulled down her brows into a rather impressive scowl. "I know she's great-bellied, and I dare say I'll cope."

"Oh." Alex tried to catch Matthew's eye. Was this a good idea, to expose Sarah to the whispered censure of the straight-laced Providence worthies?

"Da says I can go," Sarah told her.

"He does, does he?" Alex said, rather irritated with her husband for not discussing this with her. "Then I suppose it's alright. And Julian will make sure you're included in one or two of the Bible groups."

Sarah snorted. "Bible groups? I think not."

"I think aye," Matthew said. "If you're in Providence, you will as a matter of course take part in such."

"Maybe start your own Conversion Narrative," Alex suggested, tongue-in-cheek. Ruth had spent most of last year scribbling a long, tedious description of her evolving spirituality. A must, Alex gathered, for the wife of an ambitious minister.

"There is only one unwed minister in Providence, and that is Minister Macpherson," Sarah pointed out, "and him I don't plan on wedding." She eyed Mrs Parson speculatively. "You should wed him, Mrs Parson. He could do with a wife, and you must be of an age."

Matthew burst out laughing. "Gregor Macpherson isn't forty, and he'll be looking for a fertile wife."

"Not me," Sarah told him.

"Or me," Mrs Parson added.

Adam had been crying, and when the time came to say goodbye, he leeched on to Alex in a way he hadn't done since he was a small child.

"I don't want you to leave me," he whispered. "I want you to stay here, with me."

"It's only for some months," Alex said, kissing his brow.

"Then I can go with you."

"No, honey, you can't." She stroked him over the head. "And what about Hugin and Lovell Our Dog? You can't just leave them, can you? And the wood thrush you saved from the cat – how will it survive if you're not here to nurse it back to health?" The right thing to say, she congratulated herself, feeling how her son squared his shoulder at these his responsibilities. She caressed his downy cheek, smiling down into eyes that shifted in browns and greens before shoving him in the direction of his father. "Say goodbye to your da."

"He'll be alright," Ian said from behind her, and she turned to give this the child of her heart a strong hug. He rested his chin on the top of her head, and they just stood there.

Finally, he released her. "Will you be back in time?" he asked, his eyes drifting over to Betty.

"Of course we will," she said, and he relaxed. "God willing," she added, because travelling in this time and age was not a question of timetables and ETAs. He darkened and she smiled. "I'll be here, even if I have to swim all the way," she told him, which made him laugh.

Just as they were leaving, she took Ian's hand. "I..." She looked off to the north-west, blinked a couple of times. "If he comes, will you tell him that I love him?"

"I will." Ian smiled. He wiped at her wet eyes. "But wee Samuel already knows that."

Some days later, they were finally on the quay, with a sullen David sidling further and further away from them while the *Althea* strained at her moorings. Alex regarded the fifty-foot long single-masted sloop with definite misgivings: very small, in her considered opinion, to be taking them all the way to Jamaica. Around her, a large share of her family bustled, and she had been hugged and kissed so many times she presently just wanted to get on the boat and wave them all goodbye.

Simon and Matthew were talking intently on the further end of the wharf, with Simon nodding repeatedly at whatever Matthew was saying, and in his hands he held the documents he had brought with him for Matthew to sign. His will, Alex knew, and it made her breath hitch. Just as it had made her throat constrict to realise he was travelling armed, not only with both his pistols but with sword and dirk as well.

"Jan will see you safe," Kate said. "He's been sailing these waters for most of his life."

Jan van Verdhoed was a Dutchman – well, his father had been Dutch, while his mother most definitely hadn't, to judge from his skin, a beautiful coppery brown. Surprisingly light brown eyes regarded the world from under straight dark brows, a well-cropped beard in the Spanish style covered his cheeks, and from one ear dangled a golden hoop.

"He looks like a pirate," Alex said, quite taken with this handsome young man.

"Oh, he is," Kate answered, "or rather was."

"Gave it up due to a sore conscience?"

"No," Kate replied with a laugh, "I rather think it was having to witness his father's death at a drowning stake that made him decide to do something else." Kate looked away. "Terrible death, to be tied in place as the tide rises around you."

"Ugh," Alex agreed.

It took exactly twenty minutes for Alex to remember why she didn't like boats. They moved too much, and in the brisk wind *Althea* was bouncing over the waves, making the horizon rise and dip in a very nauseating way.

"Bloody hell." She clung to the smooth, well-worn wood of the railings, leaned out as far as she could go and threw up.

"We're not even out of the bay yet," Matthew said.

Alex glared at him. "Don't you think I know that?" She straightened up, twisted her shawl tighter round her chest and with her eyes fixed on the bowsprit, made it all the way to the front. A mammoth dog raised his head to look at her, thumped the long feathered tail twice against the deck boards and lay back down again, a vividly pink tongue lolling from its heavy lips.

"Poor you," Alex commiserated, taking in the shaggy black and white coat. The dog seemed to grin and then closed its eyes to continue its interrupted nap while Alex went back to concentrating on keeping what remained of her breakfast in her intestinal tracts.

She was thrilled to bits when the *Althea* anchored in the James River just before nightfall – mainly because an anchored ship moved a hell of a lot less than one under sail. Not so her husband, who stood frowning at the outline of Jamestown, a collection of low buildings barely visible in the dusk.

"It will have changed," she said. "After all, most of it burnt down some years ago."

"Still the same: humid and infested with midges." He slapped at his throat as if to underline his statement.

Alex rested her elbows on the railing. "It will have changed," she repeated. She turned to give him a smile. "You definitely have, right? Last time you landed as an indentured servant. This time you're a visiting tourist."

"A what?"

"A man of leisure with money to spend." Not that much money. She sincerely hoped Luke would compensate them for their expenses.

"Hmm." He went back to scowling at the Virginia coast, no doubt recalling with excruciating detail how it had been for him all those years ago when he was offloaded from a ship and sold as a beast — there, in the little harbour they could just make out in the dark.

Early next morning, there was a commotion on deck, with several barks punctuating the captain's angry voice.

"Pirates?" Alex said.

"Don't be daft. Pirates here, in the James? I think not." Matthew tightened his belt, waited while she pulled on skirts and bodice, and ushered her before him onto the deck where most of the crew had gathered round the irate captain and a huddled shape before him.

"Dear Lord," Matthew muttered and shouldered his way through the crew to stare down at their son.

"Yours?" Captain Jan asked.

"For my sins," Matthew said, and his voice was thick with anger.

"David," Alex sighed, "what on earth are you doing here?"

Her son looked up and attempted a smile that wobbled and died away when he saw his father's face. Matthew's brows were pulled down over eyes that were like flint, his mouth settled into a line so firm his lips had all but disappeared.

"Matthew…" Alex placed a hand on his arm only to have it shaken off.

"I have a good mind to toss you in and have you swim all the way back home," Matthew said. "As it is, you won't be sitting much once I'm done with you. Go on." Matthew nodded, undoing his belt.

"Here?" David squeaked, looking about the deck.

"Oh aye, here," Matthew replied, swinging the belt back and forth. Alex felt sorry for her son, but she'd learnt ages ago that in some matters she did best not to meddle, and Matthew in his present state was impossible to reason with. Stupid boy: to so openly disobey his father was a foolish thing to do.

David undid his breeches, dropped them down around his ankles, and bent over, baring a very white rump to the world. Alex closed her eyes. Twelve times the belt came down, twelve times David expelled a whistling sound, and then it was over, David standing up to cover up a bright red bottom.

"A boat," Matthew said. "I need to find a ship that'll take him back."

"Why not let him stay?" the captain suggested.

"Stay?" Matthew spluttered.

Captain Jan grinned at David. "As my deckhand. A lot of work — very hard work. Tends to cure even the wildest lad of the wandering urge. Besides, I don't see any sloops, do you?"

Alex scanned the waters around them and had to agree: very empty, with the exception of two or three fishing ketches.

After a couple of moments of consideration, Matthew nodded his agreement to the captain's suggestion, and David was curtly informed that he was to scrub the entire deck. A look of dismay settled on her son's face, hazel eyes flying to hers in entreaty. Alex made a helpless little gesture.

"And once you've finished with the deck," the captain said, "then we'll set you to cleaning and bailing the bilges."

Captain Jan had business to conduct in Jamestown, and offered Alex and Matthew to accompany him ashore, saying that it would be their last opportunity to properly stretch their legs before they arrived in Jamaica.

"We should have taken David along," Alex said once she was seated in the longboat.

"He has work to do," Matthew said, "a lot of work. That's what you get as a stowaway."

"But he's only thirteen," Alex protested.

"Old enough, apparently, to disobey me. Old enough, therefore, to suffer the consequences." End of discussion, Mrs Graham, his voice told her.

Michael Connor was dawdling at his writing carrel when he saw Matthew Graham leap ashore, and his gut reaction was to flee, run like a hare lest the man should recognise him, but then he laughed, shaking his head. Graham had never seen him. None of them had seen him, and while the Graham men were busy fighting the Burley gang to defeat – and he'd seen his brother, dead – he had crawled all the way back to his horse and escaped.

No word had come back down south as to what fate had befallen the men with whom Philip Burley rode out, and as Michael had no intention of divulging any details, he had kept well away from his home further north – except for one very necessary and clandestine visit to his uncle's cabin. His hand strayed to the heavy pouch he kept safely tucked out of sight on the inside of his breeches – one of three, the other two hidden elsewhere. Courtesy of Uncle Philip, Michael Connor was now if not rich at least no longer destitute – not at all. He went back to his doodling, but where before it had been loops and swirls, now he drew a girl – a girl he'd seen but once and couldn't get out of his head.

It was probably a foolish thing to do, but Michael couldn't help it, drawn to the Grahams as iron filings to a lodestone. He sauntered after them as they walked through the few cobbled streets that comprised Jamestown, and from the way they would at times stop and look, pointing this way or that, he concluded that they'd been here before. He slunk close enough to eavesdrop, was amused to hear how impressed Mrs Graham was with all the businesses and shops, commenting that it was much, much bigger than last time they'd been here – even if it was just as insufferably hot.

"Aye," her husband said, and while the wife seemed well enough at ease, Graham was looking strained, regarding the surroundings with mild dislike.

"Did you know the captain's here to buy silk, not tobacco?" Mrs Graham said.

"Aye well, it doesn't make much sense to buy tobacco here and try and sell it in the Indies. They grow it themselves, down there."

"I remember how proud Sir William was of his homespun silk," she said. "He swore it was going to be one of the pillars of Virginia's future prosperity."

"They have the tobacco. They don't need anything else." Graham's eyes followed a loaded cart that was trundling towards the port: baled tobacco, packed high, with a small boy sitting topmost on the load. The broad shoulders tensed, and Michael recalled that his uncle had mentioned something about Graham having once been indentured down here. No wonder the man was walking about as stiff-legged as a cornered dog.

Michael followed them into the tavern, settled himself at a table beside theirs. The fare was simple enough: cheese and pickles, dark bread, and a stew that Mrs Graham tasted doubtfully.

"Beef? Absolutely not."

Her husband speared a piece of meat with his knife and chewed thoughtfully. "Nor pork."

"Possum," Michael said, "or raccoon."

Mrs Graham shoved the bowl away from her.

Michael laughed at her. "Meat all the same," he said.

She turned to smile at him, and eyes as blue as her daughter's took his breath away. Not like the apparition he had seen step out of the Graham home back in March, but pretty all the same, for all that she was quite old. From under the linen cap peeked a few strands of hair that looked mostly to be brown, here and there a silvered grey. Curly hair. Did she, Sarah, have curly hair? He couldn't recall if she did, had

164

but seen the long fair hair fall like a shimmering curtain down her back.

A stool scraped over the floor. Michael jerked out of his intense scrutiny and found himself eyeballed by Graham, hazel eyes glaring at him from under dark brows.

"My apologies, it was not my intent..." Michael was discomfited by the stare and swept the lock of hair that always fell forward over his eyes to the side. "I'm being most remiss," he said, standing up to bow. "Michael Connor, Mr Graham." As he said it, he would gladly have bitten off his tongue. Fool! To reveal not only his own name, but also that he knew theirs. He sat back down and hid behind his frothing ale, drinking deeply.

"I have no recollection of meeting you before," Graham said, "so how do you know my name?"

Michael gave him a bright smile. "It is my curious nature, I suppose. I was at the harbour when you stepped ashore, and heard the captain address you as Mr Graham." A good enough lie, but those hazel eyes regarded him intently, forcing Michael to suppress the urge to squirm.

"Are you from Jamestown?" Mrs Graham sounded only mildly interested.

Michael shook his head, relieved at the change in subject. "Not as such. I'm from York county, just along York River. My father has a small place there. He's a cooper, and my eldest brother has followed him into that trade."

"Your eldest brother? So you have many?" she asked.

"Three." Of which one had died on the Graham homestead. "It runs in the family, to have many brothers. And you? Do you have many sons?"

"Quite a few," she replied, her face brightening. "Six living and two daughters."

"And you?" Graham interrupted. "What do you do for a living?"

"Not a cooper," Michael said, "although I dare say I could turn out the odd barrel should I have to. No, at present I'm working for the harbourmaster. I have a good hand, and a good head for ciphering."

"A clerk, then," Graham said.

"A bit more than a clerk, I hope," Michael replied. A printer no less, but there was no reason to tell them that. It wasn't as if he had practised this profession since returning from London, but now... He jiggled the pouch, thinking that a printing press was now a possibility instead of an impossible dream. He used the last of his bread to wipe his bowl clean and dug into a small side pocket for some coins with which to pay for his meal.

"I trust you enjoy your stay here." He grabbed his hat and left.

He stood in the shade and watched them leave some minutes later. Distractedly, he wondered if he should perhaps hate this man on account of his brother and uncle, but the thought made him shake his head. Graham had but defended what was his, and the world was in all probability a better place without Philip Burley – and without Joseph, however hard it was to admit it.

Tilting his head, he studied Matthew Graham and his wife, fascinated by how they automatically fell in step, a slight leaning towards each other. Her skirts brushed against his leg, her profile turned towards him, and she said something that made him laugh, bending his head close to hers. Her hand touched his, fingers widened and braided tight together as they continued down the dusty road.

He had never seen anything like it, never seen two bodies come together so effortlessly, so obviously halves of a perfect whole. Welded together, it seemed, and Michael stood where he was, his eyes glued thoughtfully to their backs until they dropped out of sight. In his mind's eye, he kept on seeing a pair of blue, blue eyes and hair gilded by the rising sun. Maybe... Michael slapped his hat against his thigh. Yes, maybe.

Chapter 19

"I didn't like him," Matthew said. "Nor the way he gawked at you and how you responded to it."

"I didn't respond to it!" Alex lied. The young man had eaten her with his eyes, and she had liked it, her back curving to raise her breasts, her stomach held under iron control by a combination of stays and indrawn breath. Quite an attractive man, with thick hair curling in bright chestnut waves to his shoulders, and eyes the colour of a Scottish loch in winter, a mild grey. And strangely familiar: restless fingers drumming at the table, that shock of hair that fell forward over his face... Now why did that particular image make her stomach cramp?

They were back at the harbour, and Matthew led them to sit on a large rock in the shade of a small grove of trees. "I...It's probably fanciful, but no, him I didn't like at all, and neither did I like that he knew my name."

"He explained that, didn't he?"

Matthew frowned. "Michael Connor. It rings a bell."

"Not with me. Besides, it's not as if we'll ever run into him again, is it?" Alex said, watching the longboat making its way from the *Althea*. "Maybe we could find an inn here."

"We lie at anchor," Matthew said. "It's like being rocked in a cradle."

"Not to me."

"You'd best get used to it. We have weeks and weeks ahead of us."

"I know," she sighed.

"Somewhat better today, ma'am?" Captain Jan materialised at Alex's side, joining her where she was staring out across the sea.

"Ugh," Alex replied with a grimace, "it's more a question of there being nothing left to regurgitate. Not even bile." Her stomach lining felt ripped apart after three consecutive days spent hunched over a bucket, but at least today the sun was out and the air on deck was substantially fresher than that of their minute cabin.

"You should eat something," the captain said, and her stomach did a somersault.

"Not quite yet, I think," she replied, looking around for her husband whom she found engrossed in a very thick book.

"What's that?" she asked, sliding down to sit beside him. He handed her the book.

"*The Sceptical Chymist*," she read from the title page. "You understand any of it? Seems pretty heavy to me." She handed the book back to Matthew.

"I try. Robert Boyle is a learned man," he said, "as is our dashing captain. A shelf full of books such as these, he has."

"No romances? No damsels in distress and brave knights riding to their rescue?"

"None, he's a man."

Matthew went back to his reading, and Alex reclined against him, carefully circling the thought that she was hungry – very hungry. And thirsty enough to decide to go and find the cook and beg some cider off him.

She found her son on the deck, looking sullen as he peeled turnips, and decided she wasn't hungry after all. Her stomach rumbled unhappily at this conclusion, and Alex reconsidered. A piece of dry bread perhaps, and a slice of cheese.

"Need some help?"

David squinted up at her and shook his head. "Today's the first day I've been able to sit since Da belted me, and I don't think he would like it much if you did my work for me."

"Probably not." Alex sat down beside him, tucking skirts in neatly beneath her legs. "So, is this something you could consider doing for a living?"

David looked down at the heap of as yet unpeeled turnips. "This? Nay, I don't want to do this."

"I meant the whole sea life thing," Alex said, not too thrilled when the bear that masqueraded as a dog placed his huge head in her lap. She scratched him behind the ears and he settled himself against her, panting in the heat.

David looked off towards the horizon. "I could take to it, and the captain says how I'm a born sailor."

"Oh, he does, does he?" Alex sent a narrow glance in the direction of Captain Jan, who was standing very alone by the prow. "It's a dangerous life, shipwrecks, pirates..."

David shrugged. Such things would not happen to him, he told her, and besides, he could swim – like a fish almost. And as to pirates...his eyes unfocused. "A privateer is none too bad, if you have a Letter of Marque—"

"You're still a pirate," Alex cut in, "and ultimately you may pay for that with your life."

"The captain has such a letter," David informed her.

"He does?" Alex shoved the dog away from her and frowned down at the very wet patch left behind. "Kate says how he has left all that behind, after seeing his father executed for piracy."

"For piracy, aye, not for privateering. And if a Spanish ship comes along..." It was obvious David was hoping this was something that would happen.

Alex looked about the small sloop and shook her head. "Too small, David. And as far as I can see, very unarmed."

David raised his brows in a way that made him look even more like his father than he normally did.

"You think?" He smiled indulgently at her, the effect ruined by the fact that his voice squeaked. "All carry muskets, Mama. Several muskets, even."

"Is he right, do you think?" Alex demanded of Matthew after having recounted her conversation with David. In her head, she was trying to draw a path from Virginia to Jamaica, and however she tried, there was no getting round the fact that any such route would carry them very close to Hispaniola and Cuba – in between them to be precise – and that made it all the more probable that they would encounter a Spanish ship or two.

Matthew's brow creased. "I'll ask him," he said and strolled over to where the captain still stood, eyes intent on the south.

Alex considered joining them, but seeing how Matthew clenched his left hand, resting on his back, she decided not to, and instead studied the ship with new, suspicious eyes. Extremely neat and uncluttered, a man on constant lookout, and a crew that she now realised was larger than the ship needed, with four or five loitering in the sun while the nightwatch was fast asleep below. Her stomach complained again and with a sigh Alex decided to find something to eat. At least her seasickness seemed now to be a thing of the past, obliterated by this new found fear that she might become an unwilling participant in an act of piracy.

"If he sees a ship he can take on, he will, he says," Matthew reported back. "And he very politely told me not to meddle in matters not mine to handle, assuring me he is not about to put us, his cargo or his ship at risk." He glared over at the captain who just grinned, very white teeth flashing in his dark face.

"What a comfort," Alex said.

"Ah well, as long as it's a Spanish ship. It doesn't harm to hinder their dominion over this part of the world."

"Matthew!"

Day after boring day followed. The stuffy cabin became unbearable around six in the morning, remained unbearable until well after ten at night, and in between Alex paced the small deck, sat and stared out at sea, paced some more, sat, paced, sat, paced. She had nothing to do, and with each passing day, she grew increasingly restless, throwing jealous looks at Matthew who read, or helped with the sails, clambering the rigging like a monkey, and in general took to sea life just as well as his son did. Walking about in breeches only, his initial sunburn soon baked into a deep, rich brown against which the old scars on his back stood out in lighter streaks.

"I wish I could undress. I could do with a tan." Alex held her pale arm against his chest and scowled at the contrast. "And it's too hot to walk about in shift and stays and bodice."

"But you will all the same." Matthew adjusted his breeches.

"And if I don't?"

"If you don't, I'll lock you in the cabin," Matthew said, and there was no doubt he meant it. Alex sighed and slouched off to sit in what little shade was afforded by the sails.

"Poor dog," she commented to Captain Jan one day, watching the pile of black and white fur shift as far into the shade as it could.

"Why poor?" the captain asked, snapping his fingers in command. The dog lumbered to his feet and came over to sit at his master's feet, tongue lolling like a pink tie against its chest.

"The heat must be awful."

"Fur insulates both ways, and the men feel safe with him on board." He tugged at a floppy ear.

"Yes," Alex agreed, "quite the impressive watchdog."

"Watchdog?" Captain Jan smiled down at the dog. "No, I think not – too benevolent by far. But he's a strong swimmer and can easily hold a man or two afloat should they have the misfortune to fall overboard."

"What? They don't know how to swim?"

"Most of them don't. Most sailors never learn." Captain Jan patted the dog on his head. "So we have Othello instead." He returned to staring at the horizon, and Alex stood beside him. A blank, empty waste – thank heavens for that!

Matthew noticed it the moment he came out on deck next morning. The ship vibrated with suppressed excitement, and the entire crew was there, flintlocks glinting in the sun. He could taste it, the expectation of a coming fight, and he scanned the waters around them to see their prey.

"Over there." Captain Jan motioned with his sword. "It might be best for your wife to remain below deck."

Matthew wasn't impressed. "It's but a wee ketch," he

said, studying the two-masted little vessel.

"A Spanish ketch, travelling from Cuba to Hispaniola, no doubt," Captain Jan said. "Heavily loaded."

Matthew could see that, and wondered what it carried that Captain Jan might want so badly.

"I want the ship. The cargo will be mostly sugar or such." The captain frowned when Alex appeared. "It would be best if you stay below, ma'am."

"You wish," Alex retorted, making Matthew smile. Should he consider it necessary, he'd carry his wife below himself.

"Where's David?" she asked.

"In the galley with the cook," Captain Jan said, "and if he as much as shows his nose, I'll punish him for disobeying orders."

It was all very devious. A loud, friendly hailing, Captain Jan speaking Spanish as fluently as he spoke English, and the men on the ketch waved back. Captain Jan called out for information about "*los Ingleses*", and the ketch slowed. The surprise on their faces when Captain Jan rammed *Althea* into their boat was total, and even more when sixteen determined men swarmed over their side, armed to the teeth.

Matthew had no intention of joining in unless it was to protect himself and his wife, but he enjoyed the elegance of the operation. The defending crew gave up after nothing more than a token fight, retreating to stand in a small group on the deck while Captain Jan's men methodically went through the ship.

"What will you do with the crew?" Matthew asked, noting out of the corner of his eye that David had snuck out on deck and was watching eagerly.

"Set them in their longboat," the captain said. "It's a long row to Hispaniola, but by no means impossible."

"And with the passengers?" Matthew nodded in the direction of where two men were being dragged out on deck.

"Catholic priests!" Captain Jan spat to the side. "They can swim, for all I care." He said something in Dutch to two of his men, and the black-clad men were grabbed and propelled towards the side of the boat.

"Carlos." Alex blinked. "Oh my God, that's Carlos!" She waved her hand in the direction of the younger priest who was angrily protesting his heavy-handed treatment.

"I don't think—" Matthew began but was interrupted by her shocked yell when the first man was pushed into the water, followed a few seconds later by his companion.

"They can't swim," she barked at Captain Jan. "They'll drown, you idiot."

"I don't care," Captain Jan said, and Alex whirled, making for the railing.

"Alex!" Matthew grabbed for her but it was too late, and to the surprise of both crews, Alex dived in, coming up to swim towards the drowning men.

"Woof." The dog jumped into the water.

"Damn that woman!" Matthew handed his sword to Captain Jan and dived in after her.

"But..." A dripping Alex stood on deck and looked at the retching man.

"I tried to tell you," Matthew said, irritated and wet. "As far as I know, legs don't grow back." He kicked at the two booted feet that stuck out from below the drenched oversized cassock.

Alex crouched down and studied the young man. "It's remarkable, they could be twins." There was a fluttering of the eyelids, and she jabbed at the priest.

"*¿Quien eres?*" she demanded in Spanish.

"I'll do the talking," Matthew said, moving her aside. "So, who are you?"

"Carlos Muñoz," a weak voice replied in English. "I'm Carlos Muñoz, a priest aimed for the Dominican monastery in Santo Domingo."

"Oh aye? I think not. You see, wee Carlos is missing a leg since some time back." He could see the question flare in the man's dark eyes, just as quickly suppressed. Alex was right: the likeness was remarkable – this man was Carlos to the day.

"It's either Raúl or Ángel," Alex put in.

The eyes opened wide at the last name.

"Ah," Matthew said, "so this is Ángel Muñoz, is it?"

"To be quite correct it's Ángel Muñoz de Hojeda, from Seville, no less." She'd gone quite pale, eyes riveted on the man as if she'd seen a ghost.

"How do you know my name?" The young man struggled to sit up.

"Oh, I know a lot of things." Alex eyed the man as if he were a snake.

Captain Jan was studying the man with renewed interest, and in two swift steps crossed towards him, hoisted him to his feet, and tore the cassock off him. A small package wrapped in oilskin flew out of a sleeve. Ángel lunged forward, easily beaten to it by Matthew, who swept it up, out of reach.

Definitely not a priest. Matthew had never seen such grand clothes before. Black rich velvet, piped in red and gold, Brussels lace that presently hung wet and limp from his cuffs and neck, narrow breeches that ended in black boots, the worse for wear after their encounter with salt water. His belt was lavishly decorated, the bar cage of his rapier glinting with inlays of gold.

The Spaniard made as if to pull his sword, retreating towards the railing. With the speed of a hunting hawk, Captain Jan's hand closed on Ángel's sword arm, and after a few moments of struggle, the Spaniard was on his knees, screaming invectives at the captain as his sword, his pistols and a wee dagger secreted in his boot were taken from him.

The man continued his raging as his hands were tied together, at one point spitting the captain in the face. Now that he looked closer, Matthew could see that although incredibly alike, this man was subtly different from Carlos. Colder, harder like, their captive man looked capable of committing one heinous deed after the other, and when Alex shrank back against him, inhaling noisily, he clenched his jaw. Mayhap he should kill him, and then maybe there would be no future descendant to abduct his wife three hundred years from now.

"A hostage, and to judge from this, he's worth a pretty penny." Captain Jan fingered the heavy crucifix in gold that hung around his prisoner's neck.

"Don't touch me! Scum!" Ángel Muñoz snarled.

In response, Captain Jan yanked, and the gold slid into his hands. His booted foot nudged at the other prostrate shape, and with a jerk of his head, he indicated the half-drowned priest was to be lowered into the boat that already included the Spanish crew.

An hour or so later, they were on their way again, two vessels sailing side by side down the Windward Passage. Matthew and Alex were in dry clothes, the prisoner was sitting back against the mast, and Captain Jan beckoned David to come forward.

"Did you do as I said?" he asked in a neutral voice. David lowered his gaze and shook his head. "A stowaway, and on top of that you disobey my orders? I have a good mind to throw you into the sea." David's head jerked up and his eyes flew to Matthew's. "On my ship, it is I that lay down the law, and the men on board follow it or bear the consequences," Captain Jan continued. "You've voluntarily joined my crew, have you not?" David nodded miserably. "And so…" The captain pointed at an empty space on deck, and David fumbled with his breeches. "No," the captain said, "your shirt. Boys are belted on their bare buttocks; men have their backs whipped."

Alex started towards their son, but Matthew took hold of her.

"Leave him be, it won't be too bad."

"He's going to whip him!" Alex hissed. "How can that not be bad?"

"He won't be too heavy-handed, lass. If he is, I will personally feed him to the sharks."

"Bloody brutal," Alex muttered once it was over. "In my time, he would have been reported for that, probably thrown in jail for beating a minor." Not that David seemed all that bothered, grinning rather proudly at the other members of the crew.

"A minor?" Matthew regarded their son. "He's on his way to becoming a man. He did well, the lad did, and it's a lesson he must learn. You don't disobey a given order – ever." He went back to his perusal of the documents they'd taken off Ángel, and handed them to Alex. In Spanish, he sighed, and from what he could make out nothing but a letter and a wee prayer book.

"Give it back!" Ángel yelled. "It's my breviary, and I won't have it sullied by your heretic hands!"

Alex just looked at him. "A breviary? You?"

"Mine, not yours! Give it here! Don't touch it!"

In response, Alex gripped the book and held it aloft. Ángel cursed and yelled, straining at his ropes. She turned her back on him and concentrated on the book. It was old – much older than Ángel – with faded dark red covers and thick paper that crackled at her touch. An initial glance would have her believing it was a breviary, the first few pages containing prayers and readings from the Bible, here and there a brief instruction as to the adequate services for the newborn in peril of dying, for a bereaved mother, or for the daily communion with God.

It took her some time to notice that new pages had been carefully stitched into place between the old ones, pages where the paper was whiter and thinner. These pages were covered in precise handwriting, the ink still standing stark and black. A journal? Alex gave Ángel a long look and went back to reading poetic descriptions of bays and shorelines, of winds and reefs and landmarks that had caught the author's eyes – and a lot of stuff about birds, perched in the oddest formations. Here and there, the odd letter was highlighted and decorated, and at the bottom of each new page was a band of beautifully executed geometric designs, miniature squares and circles, triangles and lines.

"Six gulls?" she read out loud. "Who would bother to count them?" She looked over to where the prisoner sat slumped in his ropes. "I don't think this is quite as innocent as it seems." She studied their captive who scowled back. "He doesn't strike me as an ornithologist – or a devout person."

"Ornithologist?"

"A person who studies birds, you know, what they eat, how they migrate…"

"Whatever for?" Matthew wondered.

"No idea," she admitted and handed him the book. "I like these, though," she said, tapping at the geometric decoration on one page.

"Aye," Matthew nodded, "most pleasing."

Now why did that comment make Ángel smile?

"How do you know my name?" Ángel Muñoz demanded when Alex walked by the mast.

"I just do." She held her skirts so as not to brush them against him. It obviously disturbed him, and she could actually see him dredging through his mind to see if they had ever met before. "No, we haven't met. But once I knew your uncle, a man I very much liked, and I've met the real Carlos Muñoz."

"You knew my uncle? The corrupted priest?"

"A good man!"

"A weak man, a man that made our name a laughing stock, leaving my father lumbered with his bastard, living proof of our shame. But as you seem to know, he is, adequately enough, a priest as well. Last we heard, he was off to spread the word of God among the Indians – probably dead by now." Ángel waited for her to share the more current information she might have about his cousin, but Alex had no intention of telling him anything, disliking this slim, fine-boned man intensely.

Ángel squinted up at her. "You look familiar to me," he muttered. He looked away, shifting on his buttocks. "Yes…" He nodded, looking at her again. "I've dreamt of you, I think."

"Of me?" Alex laughed. "I find that most unbelievable."

"But I have." The Spaniard grinned. "The tables were turned, as I recall. You were the captive, I was the jailer."

Alex paled, clasping her hands hard to stop herself from trembling. Her mind was inundated with images of the future Ángel, his eyes inches from her face as he screamed and threatened her. The crushed knuckle in her little finger began to throb, a physical reminder of her ordeal that rarely bothered her these days, but now it hurt like hell, almost as much as it had done when that damned Ángel had brought the hammer down on it.

The Spaniard chuckled and lifted his tied hands aloft, wiggling his little finger. "I dreamed it," he jeered. "And some dreams come true, they say."

Chapter 20

The coming few days, Alex stayed well away from Ángel. His presence disconcerted her, the way his gaze followed her around sent shivers through her. Whenever he saw her, he'd scream at her, cursing her for bringing him aboard this ship of accursed pirates, for stealing his belongings. The book was clearly of some importance to him, and the only time he went silent was when she sat within sight of him with the old book in her hands.

Alex spent hours poring over the recent entries, trying to figure out just what the hidden message might be. She had no idea what coasts he was describing, where the islets and sandbanks he so carefully noted were to be found, but the more she read, the more she suspected he had been doing some general scouting in the area. And as to the birds... always gulls, always carefully numbered. Was he counting ships in a harbour? Alex had no idea.

Matthew was of no help in trying to decipher this little mystery, neither was Captain Jan who admitted he did not read Spanish. Alex sighed and read, over and over again. And whenever she banged the book closed after yet another day of futile scrutiny, Ángel Muñoz smirked. It irked her and made her even more determined to find out what it was he might be hiding.

One day, as she turned the book this way and that, she noticed that the back cover was much thicker than the front cover. She ran her fingers over the soft leather, and she was sure there was something there, sown into the cover. It made her grin.

"Lend me your dirk," she said to Matthew.

By the mast, Ángel sat up in his bindings. "What now?" he demanded.

"I've found it," she told him.

"Found what?" He strained forward as far as his ropes would let him.

"Your secret." Alex slashed the cover open.

"My secret? I have no idea what you're talking about. And how dare you desecrate my breviary? It's God's words you are slicing in two!"

"As if you care," Alex snorted. "You don't exactly strike me as the most pious of men." She inserted a finger and pulled out some folded papers.

"What is it?" Ángel asked. "That's my book. I demand to know what it is you've found!"

"Oh, and you wouldn't know?" But even as she said that, Alex realised that the sheets of paper in her hand were very, very old. She took her time unfolding them, aware of just how fragile the paper was, the edges disintegrating when she flattened them out.

"That breviary has been in my family for generations. Whatever you've found is mine to read, you hear? Mine!" Ángel struggled and for an instant he succeeded in freeing an arm. Captain Jan clapped him over the head, wrenched Ángel's arm back, and retied the ropes.

Alex stared down at the writing: a faded sepia, it covered the page in a bold, familiar hand – in English. She took a deep breath and closed her eyes. Impossible. Yet another deep breath before opening her eyes.

"Alex?" Matthew knelt beside her. "What is the matter, lass?"

"I…" She bit her lip, swallowed and tried again. "My mother," she whispered. "That's Mercedes' handwriting."

"It can't be!" Matthew reared back.

"But it is." Alex gave him a wobbly smile. "She's the witch, remember?"

"Dearest Lord," Matthew groaned. "Protect me and mine from evil." He threw her a look. "Don't read it. Burn it. Drop it into the sea!"

"I can't." Alex's hand caressed the papers. "I have to."

"What are you whispering about?" Ángel yelled.

"None of your bloody business!" Alex retorted.

"Of course, it's my business! That breviary belonged to my great-grandmother, Juana Sánchez. Cursed be the day she married my ancestor. Cursed may she be for bringing the taint of Jewish blood into my family." He spat to the side. "*Marrano* blood, I tell you. The stigma never fades away."

"Oh, I'm so sorry for you," Alex said sarcastically. "But I'm even sorrier for this Juana Sánchez – I bet marrying into the Muñoz family wasn't her idea. Why did your ancestor marry her, given her dubious bloodline?"

Ángel just looked at her. "For money, of course. Juana Sánchez was a very rich girl. Very rich. And she brought us the house. Too little, in view of all shameful notoriety she brought with her."

"Shameful notoriety?" Alex asked.

Ángel pressed his lips together and refused to say another word.

Alex glanced down at the papers in her hand. A sudden gust of wind caressed her head, and vaguely she heard someone whisper 'Alejandra'. Mercedes had rarely called her Alex, had always preferred to call her by her full given name – in Spanish. Fancies, she thought, and in response she heard her mother's mocking laughter. Shit. It was more than thirty years since Alex had seen her mother last, years in which she had mostly tried to forget Mercedes – or at least avoid thinking of her. Not that it had worked all that well, and now here she was, sitting on a sloop in the middle of the sea, holding several sheets covered with Mercedes' writing. She raised the papers to her nose and inhaled, registering the muted scents of rosemary and cardamom, of saffron and sandalwood.

"If you insist on reading it, let's do it together," Matthew suggested.

Alex nodded and smoothed out the first sheet.

I burn, it began, *I burn and burn, and around me revolve the skies, below me the chasm yawns wide, and I fall like a spinning, burning top. My flesh bursts apart,*

I contort in agony, and I burn, I burn, I burn... And then it is all black, a seeping darkness that drowns my charred remnants, and I know nothing, nothing at all. Not my name, nor my time, nor that once I have been loved and loved. I am: a presence captured in pitch, like a fly that steps into an enticing glob of resin and there remains forever frozen, trapped in hardening amber. And still I burn, but it no longer matters, for what can I do but bear it?

"Oh God," Alex muttered, and she wasn't quite sure if she should continue reading.

Matthew placed a warm hand on her shoulder. "Now that you've started to read it, you'd best finish it."

"Yeah," she replied, regretting not having tossed the sheets away unread. Or not.

I have no concept of how long I lie like this, enclosed in myself, but my dear Juan says it was very many years. And then, one day, I hear the harsh laughter of a magpie outside my window, and I know I am Mercedes. Mercedes? No, first I was Ruth, and then I was Mercedes. For days, I lie pondering my name: Mercedes, the merciful one. But I am not, am I?

Some more days...weeks...months? and I wake one day to the smell of frying fish and am inundated with a sense of loss for him — him, whose name I cannot remember, but whom I can bring forth in my mind. Tall and fair, with eyes like forget-me-nots, and he smiles at me and just like that I recall that he loves me and that his name is Magnus. That is the first word I utter, says Juan. One day, he tells me, one day you sat up and said Magnus Lind. It is appropriate that the first words should be his name. I hope they will be my last ones as well.

At last comes the day when I manage to get out of bed and there, on a small table, lies a bronze looking glass, polished meticulously. I see myself and scream, the door bursts open and there is Juan, but I don't know who he is, this man so eerily reminiscent of someone, and he leads me back to bed and holds my hand and tells me not to worry. He is Juan Sánchez and he will care for me – he and his young granddaughter, Juana. Why? I ask him, and he smiles and tells me I am his abuela, his grandmother. No wonder I look the way I do, because he is very old, and how old must I not be to be his grandmother?

I insist that he bring me the looking glass and stare in horror at the destruction of what was once me. Charred and desiccated, wrinkled to resemble a giant prune, with hair a startling white. Only in my eyes do I recognise myself, in my eyes and in my right hand. I flex my fingers and know I must paint.

"Paint what?" Juan asks.

"My life," I reply, and he agrees to bring me paints and oils and canvases.

I don't truly remember it all. I recall my childhood, our conversion, and the events that befell Dolores and my father. I recall Hector Olivares, and I hiss his name and curse him – everything that happened to my sister and my father is his fault. It was him who accused them, who had the Inquisition drag them away – but Juan opens his eyes wide and says how can I curse him, the poor man lies in agony since decades back, and he has even deeded us this house. This house? It is my father's house, snug in the Judería, but there are no Jews in Seville anymore, we have been driven out – or have converted to the only True Faith.

Juan tells me how it was that Hector Olivares and I disappeared on the same day, very, very many years ago, and how the Archbishop was convinced this was the work of the perfidious Marranos, but no matter how many were tortured, there was nothing they could say as to our whereabouts. I weep as he tells me this, a silent seeping of tears that moisten the linen of my pillowcase. Poor innocents, tortured to death while Hector and I tumbled through time.

In revenge for what he did to my family, I painted Hector out of his time, but when he fell, he dragged me along, and so we spent decades in a complicated cat-and-mouse game, both of us wanting nothing more than to return home. Home. To Seville, to days of baking heat, to the scent of orange blossoms and the muddy Guadalquivir. Home – an elusive dream. So I painted and fell, and Hector came after, promising me he would heap every imaginable pain on my head for doing this to him. I fled and he came after, he fell and I was dragged along, and sometimes it took years before he found me, sometimes he didn't find me at all, but every time I painted a funnel through time to try and find my way back, somehow he was there as well, and his clawing fingers would arrest my journey, leaving me stranded in yet another unknown time.

"What an awful existence," Alex said. Years spent in a desperate attempt to get back home, with that nasty Hector snapping at your heels.

"Aye." Matthew sounded tense.

She glanced at him. "You think she deserved it."

"Aye."

Alex ran a hand over the brittle pages. "She paid, didn't she?"

I tampered with time and was punished, repeatedly was I punished when the ground fell away to leave me flailing as I plummeted through the ages. Sometimes, I managed to forget who I was, and for several years I lived in Glasgow, devoted mother to Margaret, my beautiful little daughter, common-law wife to a horrible, manipulative man whose name I'd prefer to forget. But I remember it anyway. James. What he did to me, what he made me do… No, no, forget it, move on. Think instead of Margarita, my little pearl. I stayed for her sake, but James stole her away – my baby, he stole her, my Margarita – and then, one day they came,

184

screaming I was a witch, and witches must die. My Margarita, I wanted my daughter, but she wasn't there, and there were men in the stairwell, so many men, and in the street they screamed death to the witch, so I fled, diving through yet another time portal. And my little Margarita...¡Dios mío, mi Margarita!

"So she didn't willingly abandon Margaret." Alex shivered. A sister, born three hundred years before her, and even worse, a sister who had been married to Matthew. Some sort of circuitous fate, she supposed, bringing the sisters together.

"Nay, she didn't. Poor woman." Matthew gripped Alex hard. "Poor wee Margaret, to lose her mother and never know why."

"Hmm," Alex said, thinking that Margaret had done relatively well for herself, despite this inauspicious start to life. Given some of her future behaviour, it would seem Margaret had inherited a number of traits from her unknown dastardly father. After all, a woman who betrayed her husband with his brother and then helped fabricate evidence to have her husband condemned as a traitor... She gulped.

"It was long ago, lass." Matthew brushed his mouth over her hair. "And I'm still here while Margaret no longer is." No, Margaret was dead since years back, and Alex felt an unwelcome pang of loss. She'd had a sister, but hadn't known they were sisters until it was too late.

Alex cleared her throat and went back to her reading.

I painted and painted, I fell and I fell, and one day I was in Seville, a Seville vaguely familiar but threateningly different, and that's where I met Magnus, and for him I was willing to forsake the dream of seeing my son Juan again, for him I was willing to live out what life I might have in this strange, foreign world, so different from mine. And I had another daughter, Alejandra, and one day he took her, the damned Hector had her stolen away, and I searched everywhere for her and when

I found her...¡Dios mío! What had the bastard done to her? May you burn in hell, Ángel Muñoz, for the months of abuse you put my Alex through!

Alex had to stop. She gestured in the direction of their captive. "If his great-grandmother is the same Juana as the one mentioned here, then both he and that future Ángel are Mercedes' descendants." Blood relatives. It made her feel sick to the stomach.

"Aye," Matthew said, eyeing Ángel as if he was considering throwing him overboard.

"Bloody impossible," Alex muttered.

I paint, and Juan is worried lest someone should see these little pictures. I paint Margaret and Juanito, I paint Alejandra and her son, the Isaac I have never seen and yet know exactly how he will look – like my Juanito.

I paint time, but there is no magic left in me, and the canvases no longer swirl. They lie dead and flat on the table, and that is as it should be, I suppose. One day, I notice that the time funnels work in some ways. I see Alejandra, and she is no longer in her own time, and I wonder what might have happened to her. Happened to her? In her blood flows my blood, and so it may be that she is more susceptible to the tug of time than others – it is in the Holy Book, how the sins of the fathers will revolve on the sons.

Most of all, I watch Magnus, see him stumble through his days, and I want...oh God, I want to whisper in his ear, let him know how much I love him. At times, I think he hears me, for he will suddenly raise his head and smile, and I swear he sees me as clearly as I see him. But I hope not. I do not wish him to see me thus destroyed.

Juan tells me of the miraculous events of my return: how one day I was found, badly burnt but still alive, in my bedchamber. I shudder as I recall that long fall: a slow-motion dance with Ángel Muñoz immolated in my arms before the eyes of my horrified daughter.

Alex hid her face in her arms. Matthew held her close, not saying anything.

"This is the final proof, isn't it?" Alex cleared her throat. "This just proves, once and for all, that she was a witch, a sorceress."

"Aye, but you've known she was since the day you saw her..." Matthew coughed and looked away. "...burn yon Ángel to death."

Some years later, Juan tells me, Hector Olivares reappeared just as miraculously, but where I was charred when I arrived, sunk into a sleep so deep it was impossible to wake me, Hector woke to agonising pain, to perceived fires that ate away at his flesh. They still do, as I hear it. It should make me glad, but I am too old to feel anything but regret – and fear.

Juan tries to tell me it will all come to nothing, but I can see it in his eyes, that these latest visits from the Inquisition have him worried. It almost makes me laugh. So many years later, and still it seems I may end as Dolores and my father, Benito. And when Juan tells me the Inquisition has dragged Hector off for questioning, I do laugh – out of spite and incredulity.

They will come for me as well, I feel it in my heart that they will. But, until they do, I paint, fields of golden barley with me walking through it, young and supple with my hair as dark as it used to be. I paint squares of blues that shift from palest white to deepest indigo, and this is not time I paint. No, this is the eternal hereafter, a peaceful nothingness where souls commune and meet before their Creator. Juan says those paintings are most pleasing, suffusing him with a sense of well-being, a warmth in his chest. I paint and I paint, but however I try, I cannot commit Magnus to oils. He evades me, and I weep with anger and frustration, because all I truly want and need is him, is Magnus.

I wait to die. Please let me die, please don't let me linger any longer, let me die before the Inquisition comes for me. I yearn for the soothing blues, for the moment when I will once again perceive Magnus' presence by my side. He will be there, I know. Please let me die, please, please let me die.

I am Mercedes Gutiérrez Sánchez, he is Magnus Lind, and we were born five hundred years apart. Magnus Lind, my Magnus. Mi hombre, mi amor, y yo soy tu mujer.

Alex spent a long time refolding the brittle paper. Beside her, Matthew sat in silence, and she could feel his eyes resting on her.

"Mercedes Gutiérrez Sánchez, rest in peace," Alex said out loud, raising her free hand to dash at her wet eyes. My mother.

"Mercedes Sánchez? Who is this Mercedes?" Ángel snarled.

Alex turned to face him and was on the verge of telling him Mercedes was her mother. Matthew's hand closed on her arm, and Alex swallowed back on the words.

"That's the name of the person who wrote this," she said instead. "Was she kin to Juana?" Of course she was, which would mean Alex was related to the angry young Spaniard who glowered at her from under dark brows.

"How would I know? All I know is that Juana came tainted, the descendant of a Jewish witch."

"What happened to her?" Alex asked.

"To Juana?"

"No, to her ancestress."

"To the Jewess? Why should you care? She's been dead for ages."

"Tell me!" Alex said.

"She was dragged to the stake for heresy, she and that wizard lover of hers, the former inquisitor Hector Olivares." Ángel laughed. "Old like the hills the both of them, wizened and ill, and still they held hands when the fires began to lick their feet."

"Held hands?" Alex gripped Matthew's fingers.

"Oh yes, and not one sound did they make as the flames consumed them." Ángel crossed himself as well as he could. "The devil protected his own." He jerked his head in the direction of the papers Alex was holding. "Mine."

"It is?" Alex got to her feet and walked over to the railing. "I don't think so." With that, she let go, and the papers lifted in the breeze, soared upwards for a couple of heartbeats before drifting down to the sea.

"She died at the stake," she said much later, turning to face Matthew, who had squeezed in beside her in the narrow berth. It was too hot to lie crammed like this, but he sensed that she needed him close, no matter that their bodies were covered in a sheen of sweat.

"Aye." Not that it surprised him, and a small part of him considered it right, that a witch should die by fire. But it must be an awful death, and Mercedes did not seem to have been an evil witch – more of an unfortunate one.

"You think she deserved it," Alex said.

"No one deserves to die like that." He stroked her cheek. "It seems she died well."

"Died well?" Alex pulled back from his touch. "How can you die well when you're tied to a post and set on fire? And why was she holding hands with Hector? It was his fault, everything that happened to her family. He denounced her father and her sister. He…" She choked.

"Maybe she forgave him," Matthew said.

"Forgave him? How could she?" Alex subsided against him, pillowing her head on his chest. Matthew tugged at her hair, winding one long curl round his finger. "He didn't deserve her forgiveness," she muttered.

"No, but maybe she needed to forgive." He lay staring out at the dark, praying silently that the good Lord have mercy on this lost soul, that He give her the gift of eternal peace.

Chapter 21

"The moment he comes in through that door, I'll—" Julian shook his head, as he must have done multiple times since the day back in May when they'd discovered David's short letter waiting for them in the parlour.

Ian looked at his brother-in-law and grinned. "I don't think you need to worry on that account. I suspect Da has punished him as it is."

"He was in my care, the little ingrate!" Julian glowered for a while longer but managed to find a smile for Ian's son, Malcolm. "Off you go, Malcolm. Minister Walker is expecting you for your Latin."

The two men watched the boy leave the room in silence.

"He misses his uncle," Julian sighed, "or rather his uncles."

"Aye," Ian said. With no more than a year between them, David and Malcolm were inseparable, and even more so after Samuel had been adopted into the Indian tribe.

"It still tears at Matthew," Julian mused out loud. It took some moments for Ian to understand what Julian was referring to, but once he did he shook his head.

"It tears at both of them, but Da feels the most guilt. It was his promise that led to Samuel going with Qaachow." And also, in Ian's opinion, it was Da that was the most concerned about Samuel's faith, while Mama considered that aspect more or less irrelevant. Ian decided this insight might not be politic to share with Julian, minister that he was, and instead dug into his coat to produce a small wooden rattle. "For the wean, and a right good-looking lad he is."

Julian's face broke up into a smile so wide Ian could see the black, rotting tooth, two teeth back from his right incisor. Instinctively, he ran his tongue over his own healthy teeth, cleaned as thoroughly as always just some hours past.

"The size of him," Julian said, "nigh on nine pounds!"

Ian smiled. The man kept on rushing off on one pretext after the other to peek at his laddie, now all of eleven days old.

"I'm attempting to find him a wet nurse," Julian said.

"A wet nurse?" Ian gave him a concerned look. "Is Ruth poorly, then?"

"No, no, she's thriving. But it isn't seemly, is it? For a woman of a certain standing to nurse her own child."

"It's good for the babe and the mother. It helps the mother recover from the ordeals of birth, and, through her milk, the babe is immunised against disease—" He broke off at Julian's astounded expression.

"How immunised?" Julian asked. Ian didn't rightly know. It was Mama who had explained this to Betty and Naomi: how if a mother had had measles, the wean would not contract them while nursing on account of anti... anti...something in the mother's milk protecting them. Knowledge no woman of this day and age would have, Ian reminded himself with a shudder and therefore looked appropriately vague.

"And it protects the mother from begetting too soon," Ian said instead. From the expression on Julian's face, this was something he was very aware of. "It wears a woman out. Childbirth is heavy work."

"Woman is born to it," Julian said with a slight shrug.

Ian raised his brows.

"I'm almost forty." Julian sounded defensive. "I want sons I can enjoy while still alive."

"And Ruth? Don't you want her alive?" His thoughts flew to Betty, and the constant, nagging worry he was living with these days, not daring to rejoice in the babe for fear of what it might cost him in the end.

Julian made a dismissive sound. "Ruth is young and healthy, the birth was easy, as such things go, and so..."

Ian opened his mouth to say something more but refrained. Ruth was Julian's wife.

Mrs Parson sighed when Ian told her of his conversation with Julian. "He wants her great-bellied as soon as possible again."

"Mama won't like it."

"This is none of her business. This is between husband and wife." She patted Ian's arm. "Ruth is a strong lass – and canny. She'll sort her life out on her own." She slowly got to her feet, and for the first time ever, Ian noted just how ancient she was, her movements careful as she made for the door.

"Will you be able to ride on the morrow?" he asked with open concern. He was in a hurry to return home, this brief trip to Providence undertaken solely to bring Mrs Parson home – he wanted her at hand, for Betty.

"Pfff," Mrs Parson huffed. "Don't worry, laddie. It's my own bed I'm missing, aye?" With a slight creak, her spine straightened up, and her hands busied themselves adjusting her shawl and cap. "It will be a blessing to come home, and I don't think I'll be leaving it again."

Sarah held the wean in her arms as she had never held her own son and studied the sleeping face. Eyelashes so fair as to be almost invisible, the line of future brows dusted in hair just as fair, and a round, bald head.

"Like his father," she said with a giggle, and Ruth giggled back while Patience, Julian's sixteen-year-old daughter, frowned.

"Father isn't bald," she protested.

"Not completely, no," Sarah said.

It would improve his appearance markedly if he shaved off those last remaining strands, but according to Ruth, Julian was prickly when he came to his hair – or rather lack of it.

The babe began to squirm, small head turned towards the warmth of her body, insistent butting motions as he tried to find the teat, and Sarah deposited him with Ruth, retreating to sit on her stool. Patience watched for a while and then left, promising Ruth she would stop by the butcher on her way back home.

"He's found a wet nurse, a slave girl on Farrell's plantation that he'll rent." Ruth caressed the downy head of her soon two-week-old son and sighed.

"Oh." Sarah wasn't sure what to say. She had heard Ruth quarrel repeatedly with Julian over this the last few weeks, but Julian had remained stubborn as a mule, repeating over and over again that his wife would not nurse beyond the baby's first two months.

"It will be a relief, I assume," Ruth went on in a flat voice, "not to find myself constrained by little Edward's needs." She smiled at the head at her breast in a way that belied her words. Ruth shifted the lad to lie at her other breast, and sat in silence for a while. "I don't want to," she said in a strangled voice. "I don't want to let him go into the care of another woman."

"Then don't."

Ruth bit her lip. "He's my husband. I must do as he says."

Julian listened in stony silence before telling Sarah this was a matter in which he forbade her to meddle, and besides, Ruth was wrong to speak of it to Sarah.

"She has to talk to someone," Sarah said.

"To me," Julian replied.

"But you won't listen! You've already arranged matters as they please you, with no consideration for her!"

"I've arranged matters in the best way for us all," he said, sounding irritated.

"Not for her. She loves the wee lad, and wishes to do by him as our mama has done by us. All mothers do."

"They do?" He gave her a sharp look. "And yet I recall you refusing to even touch your son."

His words were like an open-handed slap across her face. "That was different," she croaked, and fled the room.

She had no real notion as to how she came to be so far away from town. She must have walked in a mighty rage, because behind her the Jones' house was nothing but a small square, while before her stretched a rustling sea of reeds, yellowing in the summer sun, here and there interspaced with open bodies of water.

She sat down on the ground, took off her hat, and undid her hair, letting it fall down to lift in the breeze. This was quite a secluded spot, some feet from the meandering dirt track that passed for a road, but still hidden from view as long as she remained sitting. It was hot; hot enough that the air seemed to settle like a wet quilt around her shoulders, mould itself to her body, and drag her down towards the ground.

Sarah undid her cotton bodice, and after a quick look around, drew it off to sit in only her shift and skirts. Longingly, she looked at the water a few yards in front of her. She was filled with a surge of homesickness, a longing to be spending this beautiful June afternoon at home, by the river. She could near on feel it: the initial shock when she submerged her overheated body in the cold, clear river, replaced by the wonderful sensation of swimming naked, the cool water sliding like silk over her skin. Well, she couldn't very well swim naked here, but she could...

Swiftly, she dropped skirts and petticoats, unlaced her stays and in only her linen shift she waded into the water. It was too warm compared to what she had imagined, but it was refreshing, and after one final peek to ensure she was still alone, she lifted her hair out of the way, submerged herself all the way to her neck and then stood, water rushing off her. She made her way back to the shore slowly, kicking at the water to send glittering sprays into the air.

Michael Connor had seen Sarah explode out of the Allerton residence, and had since then trailed her at a distance as she strode across the town, cut towards the river shore and walked off along the water. The path twisted in a series of turns, and for a moment he'd thought he lost her, but he retraced his steps and so he came to be on the track just as she stepped out of the water.

She might as well have been naked, the thin cloth clinging to her breasts and thighs. All of her was revealed. Through her wet shift, he could see the shadow of her bush, the shape of her nipples. He wanted to touch her, had to touch her, and in preparation he wiped his hands against the rough cloth of his breeches. He took a step towards her, a twig snapped under his boot, and she reared her head, threw herself at her skirts, and there, in her hands, flashed a wicked long blade.

"My pardon." Michael held up his hands to show he meant no harm. "I was walking along and then I saw this apparition, this Venus step out from among the reeds and water, and I just had to look closer." Walking along? These last few weeks, he'd followed her whenever he'd seen her, but until today it had only been frustrating glimpses, with no opportunity to initiate conversation.

"Venus?" Sarah looked down her front and blushed, milky skin going a dusky shade of pink. It made her even more enticing, and he couldn't help himself, he took yet another step towards her. She backed away, skirts clutched to her chest. "I fear you have me at a disadvantage, sir."

Michael smiled. "Yes, it would seem I do. Rare are the times a man gets to see a mermaid in the flesh."

"You said Venus just now," Sarah said, and her shoulders dropped somewhat, reassured, no doubt, by his mild bantering. "And now you demote me to a mermaid."

"It's the hair. It flows like golden seaweed round your head." And it did, the sun making it shimmer where it hung loose around her head. Not at all curly, but thick and straight, and so long it grazed the upper slopes of her buttocks.

"Ah." Yet again, she blushed, and blood rushed through his veins to collect in his loins. She retreated a further few steps, keeping a tight grip on her knife.

He waved his hand at the track. "I'll retreat to allow you some privacy," he said, and with a little bow leaped out of sight.

Not too far away, though, close enough that he could watch her dress. She cursed colourfully at the uncooperative lacings on her stays, the buttons on her bodice took her ages to do up, and he liked it that she seemed so agitated, eyes flying every so often in the direction where she thought he was.

He waited until she was busy with her hair before he

reappeared, noting how she moved closer to where she had left her knife. The hat was tied into place, the dagger was picked up in her right hand while shoes and stockings were in her left, and she was ready to go.

"Michael Connor," he said and bowed.

"Sarah Graham," she replied, curtseying. It made him want to laugh. He'd never seen a girl brandishing a knife curtsey before.

"Graham? Matthew Graham's daughter?" He suppressed a smile at her pleased and surprised look.

"You know my father?"

"Not as such," he answered honestly, "but I met him last month in Jamestown." And that was all it took for him to step into her confidence.

They walked slowly along the water on their way back, and all the time she held her knife. She turned to face him at something he said, and he saw just how blue her eyes were. She laughed, and her teeth were very white. She spoke, and her hands floated into the air to underline and emphasise – no matter that they were encumbered with shoes and knife – and Michael looked at the shape of her mouth and wondered what it would be like to kiss her.

Discreetly, he leaned towards her, drawing in her scent. Surprisingly clean, she smelled of water and sundried hay and… He sniffed again, at a loss to find an adequate simile.

They stopped at a point midway between the Jones' house and the town proper, and Sarah sat down to put on stockings and shoes, turning her back on him as she raised her skirts to tie the garters into place.

He was close enough to her that he could brush her back. With a rapid movement, he could have snatched the knife away from her, and then it would have been an easy matter to overpower her. And he wanted to, part of him most certainly did, seeing her on the ground below him, as naked as she'd been when she got out of the water. But he kept on remembering the way her parents walked together, the invisible ties that made them move in perfect synchronisation through the dusty streets of Jamestown, and the image woke a longing in him, a yearning for something he couldn't put into words.

He made his farewells just opposite the meetinghouse, doffing his hat in a deep bow. She curtsied just as deeply and, with a mumbled Godspeed, rushed off down the narrow alley that led to Minister Allerton's house.

Michael stood looking after her for a long time before clapping his hat back on his head and setting off in the direction of Mrs Malone's. He needed a pint or two of the madam's best beer and maybe one of the girls as well. Limes, he decided as he strolled towards the port. Sarah Graham smelled of sliced limes, of rushing water and summer grass.

Chapter 22

"Port Royal, the finest harbour in the whole Caribbean sea," Captain Jan said before going back to calling out orders. The *Althea* was manoeuvred inside the protective sand spit, the Palisadoes, to gently float toward the bustling wharves. "I'm sure to find a buyer for the ketch here, and then, of course, I have the little angel to dispose of." He grinned at Alex, who couldn't help but grin back.

Ángel Muñoz of the seventeenth century was proving to be as obnoxious a person as his future namesake, a diarrhoea of threats streaming from his mouth whenever he was ungagged, which as a consequence wasn't often. After the incident with the breviary, Alex had given the man as wide a berth as possible on a small ship, but every time the Spaniard had seen her, he'd smirked, dark eyes boring into her.

"How dispose of him?" she asked.

"He's an *encomendado,* a rich man by his own accounts, owner of a huge hacienda on Cuba. He will be kept secure until an adequate ransom is paid." He grimaced at the Spaniard. "I have no fondness for the Spanish, and in particular, not for Spanish priests."

"He isn't a priest." She wasn't sure what he was, but she very much doubted he was a plantation owner. More of a royal envoy, a spy perhaps… That little book of his, with all that blather about birds – no, Alex was convinced they were code for something, but think as she might, she hadn't been able to figure out what.

Captain Jan scowled. "No, and if he had been, I would have thrown him back into the sea."

"You would?" She was suddenly very glad that it hadn't been Carlos she pulled from the sea.

Captain Jan hawked and spat into the filmed waters of the harbour and nodded. "They burnt my mother."

"As a witch," Matthew said to Alex once the captain had moved away. "His mother was a native wise woman from somewhere on the mainland. One night, a young woman came to her door and begged for help to rid herself of an unwanted child. The lass died, bled to death, and so... Apparently, it was a Spanish priest that headed the legal proceedings and made sure she was condemned as a heretic witch and not as a murderess. You hang for murder, but you burn for heresy."

"How do you know all this?" Alex asked.

"The crew talks, the cook in particular."

"Oh." She returned her attention to the town crammed onto the narrow tongue of land, taking in the massive forts, the rows of wharves and warehouses and the heavy stone buildings, incongruously English in style, down to half-timbered multi-storey buildings that tottered unsteadily as they reached for the sky. At one end, there were some older buildings, showing clear Spanish influence in whitewashed walls and tiled roofs, and a surprising number of churches dotted the town.

"All faiths, I hear," Alex said, "from Presbyterian to Catholic and anything in between. Very tolerant."

Matthew gave her an amused look. "I don't think the people of Port Royal spend overmuch time in church. It's Sunday, and they are not swarming in the direction of Mass or sermon." Rather the reverse, actually, with most of the inhabitants seemingly gravitating on the port itself. "They don't much look like churchgoers either," he added, sounding disapproving as he took in the gaudily dressed women. Alex wasn't all that interested, mind still stuck on the conundrum that was Ángel.

"I don't think he's a plantation owner," Alex said, nodding in the direction of their captive. She weighed the little notebook in her hand, studying the surrounding ships, the forts with their snout-nosed cannon peeking through the battlements.

"Well, we'll see. But for what it's worth, the captain agrees with you, as do I. That wee Spaniard is up to no good."

"It's in his blood," Alex muttered, "predestined to be evil."

"I thought you didn't hold with determinism," Matthew said with a teasing smile.

"Not in general, but in this particular case…" She hitched her shoulders.

"The captain will turn him over to the authorities, and then it's out of our hands." He looked over to where the Spaniard had been untied, and pursed his mouth. "A soldier," he said as he watched him move across the deck. "I reckon that's what he is. He has the look of a man accustomed to violence." He didn't wait for her to comment on this apparent truth. "Come on then, we must make haste off the ship. I have inquiries to make."

It had taken a long, bitter discussion to convince Alex that entrusting David to Captain Jan was the lesser of two evils, far better than dragging him along to slave markets to see they knew not what state of human misery. Still, she wasn't too thrilled about leaving their son aboard, and nor was David, who looked quite stunned when Matthew told him he wasn't coming along.

"I won't be any trouble," he said, "and I can sleep on the floor."

"Nay," Matthew wasn't about to give an inch. "I have accorded with the captain that you'll remain with him and work your passage home."

"But Da," David whined, "I…" Once again, he looked for support from Alex.

"Hush, lad," Matthew said, "you won't achieve anything by nagging. And I'll have you swear to me that you'll obey the captain in everything, and once back in Providence return immediately to Julian." Sullenly, David promised, his shoulders drooping.

"I thought you wanted to see the world," Alex teased mildly, almost laughing when David muttered something about not seeing very much with his nose a scant six inches from the deck boards. "You're going to Curacao," Alex said to cheer him up. "Captain Jan lives there, I think. And then it's off to Barbados, he said."

David brightened – a bit. "And you?" he asked. "How will you get back?"

"We'll arrange passage once we've found your cousin," Matthew said.

"Do you think you will?" David asked.

"I don't know." Matthew embraced his son. "Godspeed, lad, be bonny and brave, and we'll be seeing you back in Providence."

"Aye." David nodded before hugging Alex hard.

"Wash," Alex said, "and don't forget…"

"…to clean my teeth and eat my greens," David filled in with a faint smile.

Alex kissed him and, for an instant, cupped his face. "I love you."

"I'm not quite sure I like this town," Alex said as she followed Matthew up the wide street that bordered the wharves. She was constantly jostled, her hand slipping out of Matthew's far too often. There was too much exposed flesh, too many raucous men with equally loud women hanging off their arms. Sweaty bodies uncomfortably close, the stale breath of men and women that lived off alcohol rather than food, cloying perfumes, a sharp heel that trod her on the foot, the bleary, unfocused eyes of a scantily dressed woman that barged into her, was righted and towed away by the man by her side… All in all, Alex was not impressed.

"Fleshpot," Alex said once they'd escaped the worst of the throngs. "I never really understood the meaning of that word until now."

"Sodom," Matthew said, "a veritable hotbed of sin."

"And wealth," Alex added, nodding at the large paved thoroughfare a sign proclaimed to be High Street, where the buildings were fine and commodious.

"Oh aye, more rich men here than in the rest of the

New World combined. It's on account of the privateering."

"Are you saying the upright citizens of Port Royal are mostly pirates?"

"Aye, all, more or less, have interests in privateer ships. At least, that is what Captain Jan told me. And quite a few of the distinguished men here in Jamaica are former buccaneers themselves. Like Henry Morgan, pirate turned governor, even if now he's retired, said to be ailing." He indicated they should turn right into a small street, making for a narrow building with a dilapidated sign proclaiming rooms for hire.

"Why this one?" Alex eyed the crumbling plaster of the half-timbered building with misgivings.

"It's run by the sister of the minister of the kirk."

Alex just looked at him. "I don't understand how you do that. We've been here, what? Three hours? And already you've apparently located the minister *and* his sister."

"The minister was easy. I just walked up to the wee kirk while you were packing. The man was delighted to have a congregation of one."

He held the door for her, and they entered a dark panelled hall through which a further door was visible, giving on a small courtyard with a huge cistern and a cookhouse. The tile floor was laid in a pleasing herringbone pattern, the room smelled of mould, of damp that never properly dried, and once they were installed in the very small room, Alex ran a hand over sheets that were clean but distinctly moist. At least the bed frame was hung with mosquito netting, and a thorough inspection of corners and nooks assured Alex there were no spiders or giant cockroaches.

After a quick wash, they were back outside, making for the Customs office, located close to the Chocolata Hole over which Fort Charles loomed, several cannon pointed out across the entry to the harbour. Something niggled at Alex's mind, and she came to an abrupt stop, eyes sweeping the harbour, the protected bay. She counted the cannon, looked across to Fort James, counted the black snouts she could see, and turned to Matthew.

"He's been travelling the islands," she said, holding the

little book aloft. "He isn't counting gulls, he's counting guns, and all that hogwash about bays and rocks, it's fortifications and harbours!"

He gave her a sceptical look.

"Trust me! How many times have I read this?" Alex paged through the breviary. "See?" She waved the open book at him. "Is this not a description of this port?"

Yes, it was, he agreed, listening to her hesitant translation of a poetic description of a sea within the sea, a shimmering lake of turquoise waters banded by green and sand. There was even a detailed description of the shallow banks that protected the entrance to the harbour, disguised as a rather sickening ode to mermaids that played in the shallow seas. And to the south, the little book explained, well, there he saw twelve gulls sitting close together, while to the north, surprise, surprise, he saw but four. Matthew repeated the exercise she had just done.

"Twelve cannon," he said. "Twelve pointing this way, and the rest bristle from the other sides."

"Which he also describes, if somewhat contortedly," Alex said, laughing at poetic lines describing gulls in mid-flight. She tapped at the geometric design that had been so carefully executed at the bottom of the page. "Like a series of miniature compass roses."

They hung over the book. Not compass roses, Matthew ventured after much flipping back and forth. No, this was a code of sorts: the miniature triangles and squares in subtly different combinations on each page. Alex tilted her head. He was probably right, and the embellished letters that dotted the pages contained some sort of key.

"We can look at it further later," he said, straightening up. "But right now, I need to see the harbourmaster."

She tucked the little book away and followed him to the brick Customs House, precariously balanced on stilts to create a storage space beneath.

"Two," the harbourmaster said, "came in a fortnight ago, on the last day of June. Unloaded close to three hundred men and twenty-three women. "

"Very exact," Alex said.

"The women are valuable." The harbourmaster shrugged. "All of them snapped up on the day of their arrival."

"And the men?" Matthew asked. "Are there any name lists?"

The harbourmaster just looked at him. "Of course. The men arrived as property of the Crown, so all documents pertaining to their sale will be archived at King's House."

"Have they all been sold?" Alex asked.

The harbourmaster shook his head. The crossing had taken well over a month longer than expected, and the landed men had been in no fit state to sell — at least not at first.

"The last lot is due up tomorrow. The Crown wants to cover their expense of board and transport, so the lowest asking price is around twenty pounds."

"Is that a lot?" Alex asked naively.

"A good slave sells for seventy up to a hundred or so," the harbourmaster said, "but these wrecks have at most two or three years in them. They're here to die."

Alex swallowed at his callous remark, saw Matthew doing the same.

"Are you expecting more ships?" Matthew inquired as they stood to leave.

"No," the harbourmaster said, "the remaining rebels were destined for Barbados."

They left with instructions as to how to find the slave market, and a caustic comment along the lines that these men were traitors and deserved what they got.

"He's right," Matthew said. "There won't be much sympathy for their plight."

"Twenty pounds…" Alex shook her head. "That's not even what you've paid for our bond servants."

"They don't expect them to live long," Matthew reminded her, "and if they get more than half a year out of them, it is more profit to their owner."

"So, now what do we do?" Alex asked.

"I'll go to the market first, I think, and then it is best we pay a visit to the governor."

"We can give him Ángel Muñoz's book."

"Aye, that we can do," Matthew said. "It might buy us a better reception." They were strolling down what obviously was Port Royal's commercial high end, and he nodded over to a sturdy brick building situated in the intersection of the road they were on with another. "Food? I myself am starving."

Alex sniffed and nodded. "Fish, I think."

They were joined at their table by a Mr Lynch, who explained he had heard from the harbourmaster about their quest, and, although not sympathetic as such, he was willing to extend them what help he could.

"Why?" Matthew asked, burping discreetly after his second helping of fish pie.

"I work for the local government," Mr Lynch explained. "My cousin, Thomas Lynch, was until recently governor."

"And?" Alex said, not at all seeing the connection.

Mr Lynch smiled, took off his magnificent wig and hung it off the back of his chair.

"I must admit to being somewhat curious. It's rare that relatives of indentures cross the sea to search for them."

"Mostly because they can't afford to, and because it takes a bloody long time," Alex said.

"But he must be a most impressive young man to drive you to such actions."

"I have no idea," Alex said. "I've never laid eyes on him."

If anything, that peaked Mr Lynch's curiosity even further, and when he left, his blond wig tucked into the crook of his arm, they had agreed that he would accompany them first to the slave market and then take them to see the Lieutenant Governor.

Chapter 23

The day the sugar harvest was done, Mr Brown decided his slaves were to be allowed an extra ration of food and some cane liquor. He stood watching as the men came shuffling back from the fields, eyes cursorily passing over the few whites, all of them burnt a deep brown and with nothing but thin clouts. Undistinguishable, almost, from the rest of his property, and according to the overseer, good workers the lot of them. Still in chains, all four of them, and in chains they would remain until they died.

His experienced eye roved over them, and in his head he calculated their potential lifespan. Two years? Maybe even three? Enough that they could leave a slave girl or two pregnant, and the babies would be valuable on account of their lighter skin. His fingers drummed against the veranda post, and in his customary low voice he sent the houseboy to find the overseer for him.

The alcohol went directly to Charlie's head, a smooth burning down his gullet, a pool of heat in his belly, and an agreeable numbness in his brain. He was only vaguely aware of the people around him, his entire concentration fixed on the heaped plate in front of him and the miraculously refilled tumbler.

He ate, drank, drank some more, and swayed to his feet, wanting to capitalise on this warm sensation by falling into oblivion on his pallet. Someone shoved at him, and reflexively Charlie shoved back, a fist caught him on the shoulder, and Charlie swung, burying his fist in a face he recognised as being like his – white.

With a muttered curse, he staggered away, and there was another stone bottle of sweet, strong liquor. Warmth flew down his throat to land in his gut, and it was a wonderful feeling. He drained the bottle, sitting by himself in a corner. He sang, a long and convoluted song in Dutch that made him laugh in his loneliness, wishing Peter was here to drink and sing with him.

He sang some more, but now he wept, because this wasn't Holland, and Peter was nowhere near – no, Peter had for almost a year hung in bits and pieces, feeding the crows. A fellow slave tried to wrest the bottle from him, and Charlie roared in drunken rage, kicking until he was left alone with this ticket to total stupor still in his arms. He gulped the remaining liquor and closed his eyes.

He woke to the snuffling of a pig, an inquisitive snout inspecting his face, and initially had no notion of where he was or why. Carefully, he sat up, and his skull had shrunk overnight, banding his protesting brain with horrible pain. He had no recollection of the previous evening, but his gut was tender, and the normally so solid cookhouse seemed to tilt and turn before his eyes. All around lay sleeping, snoring shapes, and he could smell the heavy, sweet cane liquor. It woke a burning thirst in him – and an urge to piss.

Up on one knee, on the other, and Charlie hauled himself up to stand, weaving in the direction of the water barrel. A day of rest, he concluded fuzzily as he took in the silence, the inertia all around. Only the pig seemed its normal scavenging self, busy consuming anything edible it could find. He dipped his head into the barrel, drank, and it dawned on him that he was the only one awake.

Charlie raised his dripping head, squinting at the evil sun. He could...yes, he could, and if he got far enough away, mayhap he could find a stone to break the fetters open. Still no movement in the yard, no sounds but those of snoring men, and so he took a casual step out into the sun, he took another, and another. There was the main lane, a beckoning line of bare red dirt through green fields of tobacco, bordered by trees and huge yellow flowers. He slid his foot across an invisible dividing line, and a heavy blow felled him to the ground.

★

The overseer decided to be lenient – the man was obviously drunk, and a good worker to boot. So he ordered Charlie to be tied to the whipping post and left to consider his sins for some time, and sauntered over to where one of his assistants was already uncurling the flogging whip.

"Thirty, I think," the overseer said.

"Mmm," the assistant grunted.

"And we brand him," the overseer added with a yawn.

"Mmm," the assistant repeated and with a weary exhalation stood to do as he was told.

Charlie's body jerked in pain long after his brain had escaped into unconsciousness, and when his hands were untied, he slid heavily down the post to land in a graceless heap. Someone emptied a bucket of water over him, and he spluttered and coughed. There were hands holding him, lifting him up to stand, and he was glad for their help. Then his chest exploded in pain, and he screamed like a gutted pig when first an S and then a B were burnt into his skin. He fell to his knees, but the overseer told him to stand and he did, of course he did, his teeth chattering in fear that he would be hurt some more if he should totter and fall.

"See?" the overseer said to the silent slaves. "Marked like a beast, will die like a beast." He flicked his riding crop at Charlie. "You won't attempt to run away again, will you?"

Charlie shook his head, tears and snot running down his face.

"Good." The overseer beckoned for George to come over and help Charlie inside.

There was nothing to be done about the burns. The agony when George tried to salve them was such that Charlie folded together, arms cradling himself as well as he could. So instead, George washed the open gashes on his back with salt water, and Charlie wept and sobbed, repeating over and over that he wanted to die, please let him die.

The next day, he was told to stand. His back was inspected and pronounced to be healing well, and the overseer decided he would be allowed one more day of rest. Charlie could barely get to his feet the day after, burning with fever as he was, but obediently he lumbered after his masters and spent the following week working in the blissful cool of the stables. The letters on his chest bubbled and blistered, the lash marks scabbed, and he was back on the fields, back to being yelled at and kicked if he wasn't quick enough.

He and his three remaining companions were put to dig new privies, and then they were told to empty the old ones, standing well up to their naked thighs in human waste. Flies hovered like a veil around him. They settled on his sweating body, in his eyes and his mouth. It was a nightmare, a slow torture of smells and heavy wasting work as the pits were transferred over to barrows, the barrows were rolled out into the harvested field, and the shit was shovelled out and spread before going back for more, and more and more.

They were covered in bites and in festering sores, their backs howled with pain after days of shifting the damp waste, and after each day they stood for what seemed like hours in the creek to wash the stink and filth off themselves. By the time they got to the cookhouse, most of the food was gone, and they'd fight like wild animals for the few remaining things to eat. Charlie usually won, snarling like a rabid wolf at the other three before retreating to eat in the relative safety of a corner.

Occasionally, there were things that reminded Charlie of what it was like to be a man. Like when Mr Brown stepped from his house with a book in his hands, and Charlie recalled that he had once read for pleasure, or when the overseer sat smoking a pipe and drinking beer, and Charlie was transported back to evenings in a Dutch inn, with his friends and his hero, the now dead Duke. And then a sharp word would be thrown at him, and he would remember: he was a slave, a branded man, and his life was no longer his own nor would it ever be again. In such moments, he vehemently wished he could die, that the sky would open and fling a bolt of lightning to obliterate his sorry existence. But every morning he woke to yet another day of drudgery, and his heart was far too strong, his body far too young, to allow him to give up on living.

Chapter 24

Alex had never been to a slave market before. At a distance, she'd seen the holding pens in Providence, too far away to make out more than a mass of humanity, but now she was scant yards away from where silent, apathetic human beings stood waiting their turn as sales lots.

A six-foot wall surrounded the space, killing any hopes of a breeze to relieve the oppressing heat. The stench was overpowering: a heavy carpet of human waste, sweat, vomit and blood, all of it overlaid by the incongruous smell of roasting yams and pork.

In a corner just to the right of the entrance, a food stall was doing fantastic business, three coloured girls scurrying back and forth with heaped plates and brimming wooden cups. A sense of festivity hung over the crowd standing around the open fire while they waited for their food. White men under wide-brimmed hats laughed and talked loudly to one another, here and there with a woman by their side. A gaggle of white children rushed around, dogs barked, umbrellas twirled, and all that was truly missing for this to be the scene of a family picnic were tables with linen tablecloths and quilts thrown onto the ground in the shade of the gigantic breadfruit tree. Until one turned to face the other way.

"Oh Lord," Alex said. Matthew just nodded. One very large group of slaves was being herded forward, and suddenly one of the young women screamed, her arms clutching a child no more than two to her chest.

"No!" she wept. "Please, massa, no." But the child was torn from her, and Matthew's fingers closed tightly around Alex's.

"A healthy maid child," the slave trader said. "The mother

proven fertile, with two live births so far, and already breeding again."

Two? Alex looked at the woman again. She couldn't be more than eighteen.

"Look," the trader continued, setting the child down on a table. "Well proportioned, and with a very nice tone to the skin." The little girl swivelled her head, looking for her mother, but the slave trader forced her to face forward.

Matthew made a sound of absolute disgust. "I don't want to watch this," he muttered.

Alex couldn't agree more, but they were hemmed in by prospective buyers, loud men that pushed them closer and closer to the wooden platform. They watched in stunned silence while the large lot was sold off, one by one, children torn from their mothers, men from their women.

"They do it on purpose," Alex said, crying after seeing a terrified six-year-old being carried off from her family. "At least they could keep the children with their mothers."

"You mustn't allow yourself to become so upset, Mrs Graham," Mr Lynch said in her ear. "They're but slaves."

"They're human beings, and don't tell me you don't think they love each other!" She indicated a man who was hugging a woman desperately, and then he was dragged away in one direction and she in the other.

"The buck will forget her quickly enough," Mr Lynch said, "once he is put among other women. And she'll be breeding again before the end of the year. Good fertile stock." He eyed the woman appraisingly, and Alex was tempted to kick him in the balls, or yank his wig from his head and stomp it into the dirty ground. Instead, she stood mute, clasping her husband's warm, comforting hand.

It took Matthew some time to understand the basic layout, but once he did, he towed Alex over to the furthest corner where a hand-painted sign proudly proclaimed WYTES. Sitting on a chair, a tasselled parasol held over his head, the trader looked half asleep, legs extended before him. In the pen behind him were a group of men, all of them in irons,

211

every movement resulting in dull metallic sounds.

"Restive," the trader said. "Still have preconceived notions about themselves." He laughed and got to his feet. "It irks some of them, to find themselves reduced to this station in life."

"Imagine that," Alex murmured, causing the wee trader to draw himself up as tall as he could – which was not saying much – and glower at her.

"These are rebels, ma'am, punished criminals. It was either this or being hanged – not that it makes much difference, as they'll end up dead anyway." He uncurled his whip and flicked it at the man closest, causing him to yelp and get unsteadily to his feet. "See? Weak and undernourished. Sold cheap and worked until they drop – which is not much longer than a half year or so."

"Wouldn't it help to feed them properly? That way they'd be of more use." Matthew eyed the captives with compassion. In rags, most of them, and after a day or so in the sun, their pale skin was turning the colour of boiled lobster. Several of them had festering sores around their ankles, two coughed constantly, and none of them had red hair or green eyes. He relaxed, at the same time deeply disappointed.

"Men such as these you keep on cut rations. You don't want them regaining too much strength." The trader flicked his whip again, forcing the man who had crouched down back onto his feet. "On cut rations and in irons, until they die," the trader concluded and yawned.

Matthew threw yet another pitying look at the wretches in the pen. If they lasted the year, it would be a miracle, although he suspected these men were ready to die, the light in their eyes permanently dimmed. With a muttered prayer that Charlie still be alive, he led his wife out of the slave market, relieved to leave this melting pot of human despair behind.

"You said Lieutenant Governor," Matthew said as they rode with Mr Lynch back to town. "Do I take it then that the Governor is not in residence?"

"The Governor is not," Mr Lynch said, "nor will he ever

be, I think." He produced a huge handkerchief, mopped his brow, and replaced his hat. "It's a harsh climate, and quite a few of our fellow countrymen find it difficult to live here." He eyed Matthew with slight condescension. "It would seem you yourself, Mr Graham, suffer somewhat from the heat."

"Aye, I don't like it much." Nor did he enjoy riding in a closed carriage on a day as infernally hot as this one, and even less the fact that the interior was so crowded that every bump on the road launched Mr Lynch to squash into Alex.

"And you?" Alex inquired. "Have you lived here long?"

Mr Lynch beamed and nodded. "Since childhood, one could say. And not once have I wished myself back in that accursed rainy corner of the world I should call home. My cousin was among the first to settle here once we wrested this island off the Spanish, back in the fifties, and I myself arrived when Morgan was governor."

"Morgan? The pirate?" Matthew did some discreet dabbing to his face with the loose end of his cravat.

"No," Lynch replied, "his uncle and father-in-law, Edward Morgan." A slight shadow crossed over his face. "We don't go well together, the Morgans and the Lynches," he said, and then changed the subject to a long and enthusiastic description of Jamaica's Blue Mountains.

The carriage bumped its way up High Street and came to a stop just outside King's House. Mr Lynch pointed them in the direction of the door and made his farewells.

"Aren't you coming inside with us?" Matthew asked.

"Best not," Mr Lynch said. "The Lieutenant Governor and I...well...there's a matter of a small debt I owe him, and..." He cleared his throat. "I wish you luck in your quest – but as a good and loyal subject of the King, I must hope you find your nephew dead – traitor that he is." He smiled at Alex. "A body to bury is better than nothing, is it not?"

"Bastard," Alex muttered as they made their way up to the door.

Matthew sighed. "He's right. Charlie is a traitor – condemned as one. And I fear the likelihood of finding him alive diminishes with each day."

They were received in the hall of the King's House by a nondescript man that Matthew at first glance took to be a secretary. He led them to the back of the house and a veranda that gave directly onto the protected bay. The view was spectacular: turquoise waters dotted with ships morphed into hazy greens in the background, lifting slowly towards a misty highland. Thankfully, the area was in the shade of the building, and in one corner was a large wicker cage containing several colourful parrots that seemed delighted at having visitors, squawking loudly in a bid for attention.

"I hear you want to see the Governor," the little man said, throwing a handful of seeds to the birds, "but you'll have a long wait for Christopher Monck."

"Christopher Monck? The second Duke of Albemarle?" Matthew sniffed at the content of the glass set before him. Some sort of fruit drink, a pleasant bright orange that had Alex making a series of enthusiastic sounds.

"You know the man?" A bowl of water had appeared, and their host fastidiously washed his hands.

"I knew of his father," Matthew replied. "Georg Monck was a great leader of men." And more or less single-handedly responsible for the bloodless restoration of Charles the Second, for which Matthew still had problems forgiving him. Monck had been Cromwell's man in Scotland, a confirmed Parliamentarian, and yet it was he that had forged the deal that allowed the king in exile to return safely to his realm.

"Well, unfortunately the son lacks his father's stellar qualities," the man said, "and, although he is the appointed governor, he has as yet to set foot here in Jamaica."

"So who does the actual governing?" Alex asked.

"I do," the wee man said. "I've been doing it for the last few governors, for all that they think it is them that do it."

Matthew laughed, liking this simply dressed man with his ink-stained fingers.

"Hender Molesworth," the man said, bowing to Matthew, "recently acting Governor, presently Lieutenant

Governor, and hopefully soon acting Governor again."

Matthew explained their errand, and Mr Molesworth grew more sombre by the minute, every now and then shaking his head.

"...so if you would be kind enough to allow us to peruse your records, then mayhap we could find the lad," Matthew concluded.

Mr Molesworth gnawed his lip. "In principle, I should not aid you in this matter. The young man has been convicted of treason."

"He's twenty," Alex said. "What foolishness didn't you do at that age?"

"As far as I recall, I never raised my sword against the rightful king – or Protector, as was the case when I was that age." His lips pursed together as if he had bitten into something very sour. "There was very little mercy shown in the rulings made by Jeffreys," he stated neutrally after a lengthy silence.

"Aye, as he had old ladies burnt to death for harbouring fugitives, I would agree with you," Matthew said with an edge.

"The King mercifully commuted her sentence to beheading," Mr Molesworth reminded him.

Alex made a disparaging sound. "How big of him, but what about all the others? The innocent bystanders who lost their lives just at the whim of a bloodthirsty little bureaucrat?"

"Bloodthirsty? I think not. Out to set an example of the cost that lies in defying the King? Definitely." Mr Molesworth nodded gravely, rubbing at one of the larger splotches of ink that decorated his right hand.

"The king for now," Alex said, and Mr Molesworth eyed her with caution.

"For now?" he echoed.

Matthew sighed, rolling his eyes at his wife. Too outspoken, too opinionated, too headstrong, too...too much. He smiled fondly at her, shaking his head.

"What do you think will happen should his wife give

birth to a male heir?" Alex asked. "A boy born not only Prince of Wales but Catholic to boot?"

"The people would rejoice."

Alex laughed out loud. "Come off it. You don't truly believe that, do you?"

Mr Molesworth regarded her for some time, his brow deeply furrowed. "The country would likely go up in flames," he muttered. "Your wife has a fine grasp of politics," he said, directing himself to Matthew, "and pray, sir, what is your opinion?"

"I believe she's right. The people of England won't countenance a line of Catholic kings. It has cost them too much to rid themselves of popery."

"But as yet there is no boy," Mr Molesworth said, "and as yet that nephew of yours is guilty of treason, and has been justly punished for it." Still, he sent off one of the servants, and some minutes later, the man returned with a leather-bound ledger that was placed before them.

Matthew gave a discreet groan. Pages up and down in crabby handwriting, detailing name, price and owner. Not in any kind of order – just a random listing that would have to be read from top to bottom.

They found three Grahams, but one was given as being from Edinburgh, the other was a W Graham, and the third was just plain Graham.

"Well, well," Mr Molesworth said, "bought by Sir Henry, no less." He straightened up and looked at them. "It's a long ride, well over two hours, and it might not be him."

"I must go all the same," Matthew said.

Mr Molesworth chose to ride with them, and they set off at midday, despite the sun and July heat.

"Better the heat than the dark," the Lieutenant Governor explained. "Jamaica can be a dangerous place at times." He indicated their armed escort.

"What? Robbers?" Alex asked.

"Maroons," Mr Molesworth said.

Matthew wasn't overly worried. "Oh aye? We have such in Maryland as well."

"Not like ours. Ours live in the wilds since decades back, strong communities of escaped slaves and natives. They have no liking for white men in general, and English men in particular, no doubt reminiscing nostalgically about their former masters, the Spaniards. Strange race, the Spaniards. They copulate freely with their slaves and the natives, and the children born of such unions are often openly acknowledged and freed."

"Oh, and English men don't? Copulate, I mean?" Alex asked with a bite to her voice. "Or is it the Spaniards' acknowledging of their offspring that you find strange?"

Matthew swallowed back a gust of laughter at Mr Molesworth's flustered expression.

"A child born to a slave is a slave, no matter its sire, that is the law. Anyway, the Maroons are a plague on us, and the roads are unsafe after dark. Men have been killed, women taken captive never to return. An experience, my dear Mrs Graham, I don't think you'd much like."

They rode through endless fields of cane. Man-high and more, it stood like a sea of waving grasses as far as they could see.

"Ready for harvest," Mr Molesworth said, "it will all be cut down within the coming month."

"All?" Matthew stared out across the interminable fields.

"Long hard hours of work," the Lieutenant Governor said, "well into the dark. The harvest is cyclical from January to July, so the slaves move from one field to the other."

They crested a small incline and the fields disappeared behind a screen of trees: huge trees, garlanded with vines that flowered in deep pinks and blues. They rode further into what had become a green tunnel, and the shade was a relief after the previous hour in the sun.

Matthew studied the brilliant greenery with interest, noting ferns as high as he himself was. "A fertile country," he commented.

"Oh, yes," Mr Molesworth nodded. "Most fertile – and vicious with it."

Matthew was very disappointed by the famous buccaneer.

He had expected a vibrant man, imposing of size and voice, and instead, Henry Morgan proved a sickly man, with one foot already in the grave. Not particularly tall, shrivelled due to years, and with a constant racking cough, the erstwhile pirate sat on his veranda, wrapped in a quilt and sipping at a hot beverage which, Matthew concluded after a few inhalations, seemed mostly to consist of rum.

"What?" Morgan said. "Don't I live up to the myth?" He wheezed with laughter, and his dark eyes flashed in a way that made Matthew realise just how charismatic a leader this man must have been. Not anymore, his face swollen by dropsy, his hair receding, and his hands constantly clenching and unclenching, probably to ease the tension of accumulating liquids.

"It's some years ago since you were a permanent scourge on the Spanish," Matthew sidestepped.

"Not that long ago." Morgan coughed. "Not yet twenty years since." He knuckled at his swollen eyes and blinked. "I dare say I'll be remembered for it."

"An infamous buccaneer, that's what you'll go down as, Henry," Molesworth said.

Morgan set his jaw with an audible click of teeth. "I'm not a buccaneer nor yet a pirate. I am, have always been, and remain a servant to the cause of England."

Molesworth laughed out loud, and after a couple of minutes the old renegade joined in.

"You did well out of it, my friend," Molesworth told him. "Very well for a man with no beginnings."

"I did." Morgan studied his home with evident pleasure.

"Not Charlie," Matthew said to Alex once he had seen the unknown Graham. He was shaken by the dismal condition of the man he'd just seen, and eyed Morgan with substantially less admiration than before. "You could consider feeding them."

"Oh, I do," Morgan replied. "Enough to keep them alive."

"You feed your black slaves better!" Matthew exploded.

"Of course, they're far more valuable. Those white

lads, they rarely make it beyond a year, and they whine and complain when they're set to work."

"Then why buy them?" Alex asked.

Morgan looked at her in silence for a few minutes. "It's the King's wish that they die in servitude, and I live to serve my king." Stiffly, he stood and bowed, indicating the visit was over.

Chapter 25

"When can we leave?" Alex asked Matthew next morning, shoving at the eggs on her plate with a marked lack of appetite.

"Well, you're to help Mr Molesworth with the book first." After a questioning look, Matthew switched plates with her.

"I almost regret telling him," she sighed.

Molesworth had twitched all over when Matthew had told him their theory regarding Ángel Muñoz, going on to explain that despite the Treaty of Madrid, there were still occasions when they heard rumours the Spanish were planning to launch an attack on Jamaica from either Cuba or Hispaniola.

"Too late," Matthew said. "So while you sit and talk the officers through that book, I'll find us passage to Barbados."

He came to find her just before dinner, bowing to the commanding officer of Fort Charles, who was leaning back against the wall, arms crossed.

"Under our very noses," Captain Ford said, "the damned Spanish spy has been collecting information about every fort and landing point on the island, and we haven't stopped him!" He was perspiring heavily, mopping at a bright red brow with a sopping handkerchief. With irritation, he regarded the little notebook, now carefully annotated with English comments. "This should bring home to the King how important it is to see this island adequately garrisoned," he said to Molesworth, who nodded in agreement.

"Have you talked to the man?" Molesworth asked him.

"A couple of times, but the man insists he speaks no English." Speculatively, the captain eyed Alex. "You speak remarkable Spanish, ma'am."

"Thank you," Alex replied. It was obvious Captain Ford was waiting for some form of elucidation as to why, but she kept her eyes on her shoes.

"As a good subject of the King, you'll be willing to help us in our interrogations of the prisoner," the officer continued.

"I don't want to see my wife embroiled in such," Matthew cut in. "The man speaks English. Threaten him with the rack, and I dare say he'll become quite vociferous. Besides, there are others on this island that speak Spanish. Half the boat crews I come across seem to know it well enough."

"But only your wife has read the contents of the book." Captain Ford folded his arms over his chest, lifted himself up and down a couple of times on his toes, all the while staring at Matthew. Officers might come in various guises but ultimately they are all the same, Matthew reflected, recognising the pugnacious set to the captain's jaw.

"She doesn't do it without me," Matthew said.

The captain shrugged, informed them to present themselves at the fort around three, and left.

Alex didn't want to do this. She never wanted to lay eyes again on the Spaniard who brought so many restless memories to life, and it didn't help much when Ángel Muñoz was led into the little room.

Dishevelled, in only breeches and shirt, and with a collection of interesting bruises on his face, he kept on repeating in Spanish that he was the victim of a pirate attack and should be allowed to return home.

The captain waited until Ángel was seated before producing the notebook, waving it in the direction of a paling Ángel.

"Spies hang," the captain said.

"*¿Qué dice?*" Ángel asked Alex, who just raised her brows.

"*No te hagas el tonto,*" she said. Don't play the fool.

He spat at her, telling her in Spanish this was all her fault.

"If—" he began, but she interrupted him.

"If I hadn't jumped into the water, you would already be dead!"

"And now I'll die anyway, witch!"

She swallowed at the truth of that. If she'd said nothing about the book, he would at present not be staring a hangman's noose in the eye. They sat and stared at each other in silence while both Matthew and the officer grew restless behind them.

"This won't work," Alex said in English. "He isn't about to talk to me, and I can't say I blame him." She stood up, and on the stool before her, Ángel fell into an epileptic fit.

"No!" Matthew yelled, but Alex was already leaning over the convulsing man. Mere seconds later, she was gasping for breath, throttled by his hold on her neck. Something sharp was digging into the skin below her ear.

"Leave go of her," the officer barked.

"I think not," Ángel said in perfect English. "Not until I am safely out of here."

Alex gargled when he used his forearm to press her windpipe together.

"If you harm her..." Matthew snarled, and Ángel laughed.

"Then what, big man? You kill me?" He waved a piece of bloodied glass in the direction of Matthew, who made as if to rush forward.

"Agh," Alex said when Ángel swiped the glass down the side of her neck.

"See?" Ángel laughed. "She bleeds already. Shall I cut some more?"

"You'll regret it," Matthew growled, unsheathing his dirk.

Alex couldn't help it: she whimpered as she was cut again.

Slowly, the initial shock was receding, and her brain was fast-forwarding through her options. The man was trapped on Jamaica, and cornered men do desperate things. Alex realised with a little knot of fear that he wouldn't hesitate to hurt her, even kill her. The officer was conferring with his men, and from the set of his shoulders, she could see that he was going to let Ángel go, with her his hostage, and God alone knew what he would do to her then. She met Matthew's eyes, blinked once, and slumped in a pretence dead faint.

Ángel staggered with her weight. He cursed, tried to heave her upright, but Alex made herself as heavy as possible, ignoring the stinging pain of the glass cutting into the side of her neck. Matthew's dirk flew through the air, she felt Ángel jerk, his hold on her weakening further. She fell out of his arms and scrambled on all fours towards Matthew, seeing out of the corner of her eye how Ángel slid to the floor. Matthew was on his knees, hands flying over her.

"Is he dead?" Captain Ford snapped.

Matthew looked up from his inspection of Alex's neck. "Nay, I didn't want to rob you of the joy of hanging the wee bastard."

The officer walked over to where Ángel was slumped, and roughly pulled the knife out of his shoulder. In response, Ángel howled, gripped the razor-sharp shard of glass and slashed it viciously across the officer's thigh.

Blood sprayed the entire room. Matthew yanked Alex's shawl off and whipped a tourniquet around Captain Ford's leg. Ángel attempted to stand but Matthew kicked him back down.

"You move and I kick your balls up your throat," he threatened.

The small room was full of people. Ángel was hauled to his feet, still clutching his weapon, the fort surgeon was trying to inspect the damage to Captain Ford's leg, and Alex wondered how on earth it could all have gone so wrong.

She raised a shaking hand to her jawline and stared down at her own blood, smeared across her fingers. The room echoed with shouts and curses. A soldier screamed when the sharp point of glass got him in the face, and then Ángel was far too close.

"Someday, I'll get my own back. In this life or the next,

you hear?" he hissed, spittle flying. *"Algún día te haré pagar."* His eyes were black with hatred, locked on Alex.

"You already have," she whispered, far too low for him to hear, and through her brain fluttered fragmented images of those long months when the future Ángel Muñoz devised one way after the other to scare the daylights out of her.

"An absolute mess," Mr Molesworth said.

"Aye." Matthew's eyes flew to Alex. All he wanted was to be alone with her, gather her onto his lap and hold her close, her heartbeat under his hand. She was sitting with an introverted expression on her face, blood had dried in garish streaks on her neck, and she seemed to be fascinated by her open hands, lying passively in her lap. "The captain?"

Mr Molesworth hitched his shoulders. It was in God's hands, even if the surgeon seemed confident he had managed to get a ligature in.

"And the Spaniard?"

"In irons, as he should have been to begin with."

Matthew was too tired to do more than nod. He was too old for this kind of excitement, and as to Alex... He went over to her and crouched down to take her hands in his. "Alright then?"

She gave him a wobbly smile, and a fat tear slid down her cheek. He caught it with his thumb, wiped it away, and leaned forward to kiss her nose.

"Bath?" he suggested, and her smile gained in sincerity.

"Will you wash my hair?" she asked.

"All of you," he said, closing his hands round her wrists. His thumbs rested over her rapid pulse, and he closed his eyes when her beat surged into him, travelled through his veins and to his heart. Her blood, his blood, one and the same.

Much later, Alex lay naked on their bed, covered by a sheet. She was fast asleep, curled on her side with a hand flung before her and the heavy hair braided back. Matthew stood by the small window, the shutters thrown wide, and looked out on a night of sparkling stars and a timid crescent moon.

He was as naked as she was, and the evening breeze cooled the sheen of sweat into an uncomfortable film of cold, making him shiver. Behind him, he heard Alex stirring from sleep, but he remained where he was.

"Matthew?" Alex asked from the bed. "Why are you standing there?"

He just shook his head. If he closed his eyes, he kept on seeing Ángel digging the glass deeper into her skin, and it was her blood that cascaded like a fountain across the room, not the captain's. One inch further down, one determined slash, and all he could have done was hold her as she died away from him. Irrationally, he was swept with anger that she should put herself at risk like that, and he took a long, steadying breath. It was alright, she was still here, and the Spaniard would hang come the morning.

"I was hot," he said, taking the few paces needed to bring him back to the bed.

"That's why it's called the tropics." Alex yawned, and with a contented little noise she slipped her hand into his.

Matthew lay on his back and listened to her breathing for a very long time.

Chapter 26

Alex had refused to witness Ángel's death, but couldn't very well do the same when Mr Molesworth insisted she read the man's letters home before they were dispatched, to ensure they contained no compromising information.

"It makes me feel like a ghoul, to sit and read letters meant for someone else, and especially when they've been written by a man who was hanged because of me."

"Mmph," Matthew said without much sympathy. He was extremely short-tempered at present, snappish and short in his conversation with her. Alex unfolded the letters: one to his father, the unknown Raúl senior, commending the care of his wife and young son to him, and a very long letter to his wife, Alma.

"I hope he told her all of this while they were together," she said once she was done. She regarded Matthew's back for a while. "Do you know how much—?" She broke off with a rueful shake of her head and concentrated on refolding the letters. He hadn't heard, or at least he pretended he hadn't. "What's the matter?" she asked instead of verbalising the fervent love declaration she had in her head.

"Nothing."

"Right, and I'm a flying pig," Alex said, making his lips curve for an instant. She came over to where he was standing by the window and stood beside him, looking out at the heavy tropical rain.

"You could have died," he said.

"But I didn't."

"If I were to find Charlie, but lose you in the finding, I'd never forgive myself."

"I could get run over by a bus," she said, and at his confused expression, clarified. "What I mean is accidents can happen to you anywhere."

"That wasn't an accident, Alex. That was you being foolhardy. You shouldn't have gone to help him. I even told you 'no', did I not?"

"I don't remember. And how was I to know he was only pretending?"

Matthew emitted a low exasperated sound. "You do foolhardy things all the time. You dive after two unknown men—"

"I thought one of them was Carlos!"

"... and who is to say there wasn't a shark waiting to eat you?"

"Well, you dived after me," she said defensively.

"You're my wife! I can't very well stand by and watch you being chewed to pulp by the nefarious creatures of the sea, can I?" He looked down at her and sighed, his fingers resting for an instant on the scabbed cuts just below her jawline. "Will you attempt to be more careful? Mayhap even listen to what I'm saying at times? Please?"

"I can try."

"I'm not asking for more than that, only that you try." He pulled her close, rested his cheek against the top of her head. "You carry my heart with your own, lass."

Alex rubbed her cheek against him, drew in his particular fragrance and held it in her lungs. "I love you," she said simply.

Next day, Alex stood on the wharf and just stared. This wasn't a seafaring boat, this was a...a...huge barrel?

"It was all I could find," Matthew said, "and it's quite seaworthy – it floats."

Alex did not like the look of the ketch, and said so. Nor did she like the look of the sky and the heaving waves just outside the sandbars.

"I might just as well tie myself to a rope and be dragged along behind," she groaned, "because with these seas, I'll be sick all the way." He gave her a concerned look but she patted his hand. "People don't die of seasickness, they just become weak and cranky and short-tempered."

"A right comfort," he replied, but his mouth twitched as he gallantly helped her on board.

"No cabin?" Alex wasn't sure that was a good or a bad thing, given the size of the boat.

"No. There's a canvas over the foredeck to sleep below. Better in the heat."

"And even better in the rain," Alex muttered. She followed Matthew over to greet the captain, and then bagged herself a seat by the railings. She watched with increasing surprise as more and more passengers came on board, and by the time they sailed, there were ten people to share the cramped space beneath the awning, all but her men. "I'm not sleeping crammed like a sardine under that," she said, waving at the flapping canvas. "Haven't you noticed they all stink?"

The voyage was one miserable blur to Alex. She threw up constantly the first three days, she shivered in driving rain for two, and then she baked, slowly, the last four, sitting by the railing.

Her clothes were stiff with salt, she hadn't washed in well over a week, and her stomach was an echoing cave of hunger that she resolutely ignored – she wasn't about to eat from the cauldron that, as far as she could see, had not been rinsed once since they got on board.

All in all, it was a relief to arrive in Barbados, no matter that they berthed not where she had expected, in Bridgetown, but in a small town further to the north by the name of Holetown.

"Apt," she said to Matthew. "This really is a hole."

At midday, the little place was humming with trapped heat, and Alex looked about curiously, noting an ongoing reconstruction of a church, a collection of well-built houses, the small, but very busy harbour, and a food stall. No, several food stalls, and she made a beeline for the closest, attracted by the scents of frying fish and roasting vegetables. Matthew refused the piece of roasted yams Alex offered him, but tried the slice of pineapple she held out to him.

"We won't find much trace of him here," he said, scratching at his cheeks. Ten days without shaving had left him with a beard.

"No," Alex said through her full mouth. "But we could find ourselves a secluded corner of the beach and lie in the sun for a day or two." And swim…she looked yearningly at the blue waters that lapped at the sands she could see to the south of the town. Matthew shook his head in a firm no.

"A bed, I think," he said, "and tomorrow we must make our way to Bridgetown."

They arrived in Bridgetown late in the afternoon, lulled to a doze by the creaking motion of the ox-drawn cart on which Matthew had secured them a ride. The cart was piled high with fruit, and for the last few hours an increasing amount of flies had converged on the load, buzzing happily as they landed on ripe split fruit the size of a man's head that Alex said were called papaya.

As the cart creaked its way into the town centre, Alex kept on remarking how much it had changed since she'd seen it last.

"More than twenty years ago," Matthew said, taking in this prosperous town. Narrow streets, an imposing church, and all along the careenage shops and warehouses stood jowl to jowl. Alex pointed out the harbourmaster's office, and on the further side he could make out the outlines of some sort of fortification.

"Less depraved than Port Royal," he commented as the cart trundled its way towards the market square. Bridgetown reminded Matthew of a country town, sturdily rooted in commerce and diligence, and he studied the bustling harbour with interest. Well out to sea, a couple of vessels lay moored far apart from the others, but when the wind veered, the smell that floated towards them made him wrinkle his nose. Slavers.

"Or not," Alex said. "After all, there are different types of depravity."

"Aye." For some moments, Matthew stood looking out

at the floating hulks before placing his wife's hand in the crook of his elbow, hefting their few belongings in his other hand, and going to find them lodgings.

"Very nice," Alex said when they were shown their room. One of the housemaids appeared with two pitchers of steaming water, a pot of soap, and towels, and the moment she left, Alex stripped, dropping bodice, stays, chemise, soiled petticoats and skirts to lie in a heap on the floor. Matthew followed this shedding with interest, smiling at the picture she presented in only her stockings. She undid the garters, rolled off the stockings, and sniffed at the feet.

"Euuw!"

"The landlady said how you can give her your clothes to be laundered," Matthew said, adding breeches, shirt and stockings to the pile.

Alex nodded, already sorting through the clothes. She shook out her skirts and his breeches, laid them on a nearby stool. "They'll do – but with a change of linen."

Matthew filled the basin to the brim, dipped his face into it, and scratched at his dripping beard.

"It itches," he said, "and so does my head."

"It does?" Alex motioned for him to sit. "I told you not to sleep so close to them," she sighed a few moments later. "You have lice." She bent to inspect his crotch. "Everywhere."

Once he'd shaved his face, he handed her the razor.

"I don't know…" Alex sounded very doubtful.

"It's only hair. It grows back."

"Yeah, but still."

He met her eyes in the mirror and shrugged.

"It makes you look very harsh, like those marble busts of Julius Caesar," she said once she was done.

"Oh aye? Is that good or bad?"

"I'm not sure…" She cocked her head. "Probably good." She waved his razor in the direction of his crotch. "And there?"

Matthew looked down his flat belly to where his pubic curls sprouted wiry and dark.

"Shave my privates?" He cupped them protectively: the razor was sharp, and he preferred for his balls to remain attached to his body.

"Well, it beats pouring brandy on them and setting it all alight, doesn't it?"

He gave her a very long look, and sat down on the stool, spreading his thighs wide. "If you cut me…" he threatened and then chose to rest back against the wall, eyes firmly closed.

It was strangely arousing, her hands on his member as she scraped off his hair, and he swelled in size as she went about her work, relishing her touch on the inside of his thighs, his balls, and the shaft of his cock. He kept his eyes closed, trying to visualise what she was doing, exhaling when her nail ran slowly up the length of him.

"All done, not an itty bitty louse in sight."

"Where are you going?" he asked when it seemed she was about to stand.

"To wash."

"Later, lass. Not now." His hands rested on her shoulders, the tip of his cock grazing her chest. He bent forward to kiss her, a soft teasing touch of his lips against hers, a flicker of tongue, and she opened to him, and he tasted onions and fish and cider on her breath. He raised her to stand before him, touched her crotch and the soft hair. "And you? Are you sure you have no lice?"

"Quite sure," she answered breathlessly.

"Best make sure." He jerked his head in the direction of the bed.

"But—"

"Shush, wife. Do as I say, aye?" And he loved it that she did, lying down on her back. He motioned for her to spread her legs, kneeling between them with his razor in hand.

"I don't—" she began. Matthew placed a finger over her lips.

He set the razor to her skin and carefully, oh, so carefully began his barbering. She said nothing more. At times, she quivered under his hand; at times, she raised her head to

231

inspect his efforts. Her ribcage rose and fell in short, shallow breaths. Now and then, a guttural sound escaped her. He was done, caressing skin and folds of flesh that he had never seen quite as nude before, and his balls contracted with fiery heat. A finger wiggled into all that moist warmth, and Alex groaned. He did it again, and she made as if to sit, hands reaching out to touch and caress him.

"Nay," he said, and he was hoarse with lust. "Lie still, aye? Lie very, very still, and take what you have coming."

Chapter 27

"The Monmouth rebels?" The harbourmaster scrunched up his face. "Ah, *jaa*. They came in early May or so. All men, and some young boys as well."

"Would there be lists?" Matthew asked.

The harbourmaster yawned but nodded a yes. "The traders were allotted a number each, and most of them will keep records of the sale." His pale blue eyes regarded them with interest, and in particular kept coming back to Matthew's shaved head.

"Lice," Alex said, and Matthew threw her an irritated look.

"Ah." Klaas Hendrijks began to scratch himself. "Vinegar helps."

"And where can we find the traders?" Matthew said, bringing them back to the relevant subject.

The harbourmaster waved across the bridge to the other side of the murky little river. "At the market." He used a stout finger to point in the direction of the three large ships that they had seen already yesterday. "They came a few days ago. Fresh out of Africa, so the traders are busy at the moment." He looked at them thoughtfully. "It may serve you to wait some days."

"Some days? We don't have some days! The lad has been here three months. He may already be dead!"

"In which case, he won't be less dead in a week," the harbourmaster said with some logic. He had a surprisingly full lower lip, and at this he now pulled, releasing it to flap back against his teeth with a dull plop. "In general, there will be little sympathy for his fate. The colonists here hold firmly to whoever sits on the throne – the growth of their own personal fortunes depend entirely on the goodwill of England."

"He doesn't deserve to die a slave," Matthew said. "No man deserves to die like that."

"Hm," the harbourmaster said, "now that is a sentiment I wouldn't repeat here on Barbados. After all, the majority of the population here are slaves, will live and die like slaves." He stroked his exuberant moustache and shrugged.

Any further discussion was interrupted by the arrival of Mr Hendrijks' daughter, a lass of about seventeen. Matthew gawked. The girl before him was no lilywhite copy of her father. No, this was a lass with skin the colour of a dusky rose, eyes of sloe, and hair so black it shone blue in the sunlight. An elbow dug into his side, and Matthew retook his eyes, turning an affronted face on his wife.

"Marijke." The lass curtsied, lowered her eyelashes, and peeked at Matthew.

He bowed back and introduced his wife.

"I suggest you join us for luncheon," Mr Hendrijks said, "and afterwards I will point you in the direction of the markets. At present, you won't find the traders there. They avoid the midday sun."

Klaas Hendrijks was most delighted to hear they knew Captain Jan, and over chicken and wine, he regaled them with one story after the other of the adventures he had shared with Jan's father.

"We came here as young men, and once here, none of us ever wanted to go back." He smiled wistfully. "It was a heady life it was: buccaneering all across the Spanish Main."

"You're a pirate?" Alex asked.

Klaas grinned. "Among the best, and wise enough to stop before I got too old – or was caught."

"Not like Jan's poor father, then," Alex said.

"No, Pieter left it too late." Klaas sighed. "They say it took a long time for him to die. The tides aren't high enough to drown you outright, but high enough to let all kinds of creatures come close."

"Not a death to aspire to." Matthew's toes curled at the thought of being fed on by fish and whatnot.

"Very few types of death are," Klaas said, "unless it is

to die sated and happy in your own bed."

After dinner, Klaas suggested that mayhap it was best if Mrs Graham remained here, with his daughter, while he accompanied Matthew to the slave market.

"It's…" Klaas cleared his throat. "Well, it's not a place for tender-hearted women like yourself."

"Are you sure? I'll come if you want me to," Alex said to Matthew, but he could see in her face that this was an experience she would rather do without.

"Aye, I'll be fine on my own. I don't want you to see this."

He fervently wished he didn't have to see it either, because this was worse than anything he'd ever seen before. Free men, albeit black, many of them bellowing like maddened bulls as they tried to wrest themselves free from the chains that held them. Men that shrieked in rage and pain when red-hot irons were held to their skin; men that were dragged along behind their laughing new owners, still protesting, still calling for… Matthew had no idea, but he recognised the timbre of despair in their voices, the stubborn refusal to accept this new station in life, and he wept inside for them.

Worst of all were the women. As naked as the men, they were thronged by eager male buyers, their legs spread apart, their privates prodded while loud comments were made as to their potential fertility and virginity.

"Animals." Matthew wanted to smash his fist into someone's face.

Klaas put a restraining hand on his sleeve. "Come away. Let us commence this searching for your nephew instead."

Matthew followed him to the long row of stalls that housed the traders, and repeated his errand in one booth after the other. The harbourmaster had been right: in general, his inquiries were met by a cold and disinterested look, but Hendrijks was respected and well liked, and at his insistent wheedling, trader after trader reluctantly agreed to peruse their records to see if they recalled a Charles Graham.

"Tall, you say?" the penultimate trader said.

Matthew nodded, using his hat as a primitive fan. He

had a notion that Charlie would be as tall as he and Luke at least. "And with red hair."

"No hair on them when they were brought here," the trader laughed. "All of them shaved on account of the lice." His eyes rested for an instant on Matthew's shorn head. He shrugged and commanded his slave to fetch him his book, flipping through it with exaggerated slowness.

"Hmm," he said, "yes… Arrived May seven. Will be well broken in by now – or dead."

Matthew stiffened at the casual tone but let the remark pass.

"I sold him to Brown," the trader said to Hendrijks, who obviously knew who this Brown was. "He'll be working cane, your nephew. Brown owns one of the bigger sugar plantations on the island."

"Is that good or bad?" Matthew asked Hendrijks as they made their way back across the bridge that gave the town its name.

"Sugar is a heavy crop, but Sassafras Brown is a good enough man. Born here, recently inherited his plantation from his father. Very rich, and as yet unwed. He has been in contact with me regarding Marijke."

"Ah," Matthew replied, "and is the lass willing?"

"The lass will do as her father tells her, but yes, Marijke is not averse. It will be a pleasing twist of fate for someone of her background."

"Her background?"

Hendrijks studied him suspiciously before commenting that surely Mr Graham had noticed that Marijke was not pure white?

"Nay, I didn't. Mostly, I noticed that she's right pretty – but don't tell my wife that."

Klaas burst out laughing. "I won't," he promised and went on to explain that Marijke's mother had been born a slave, the daughter of a Spanish *encomendado* and a Carib woman. "She was aboard one of the ships we boarded, sold from her birthplace to a man on Hispaniola. I kept her as my share of the loot."

"Ah," Matthew nodded, "and did you free her?"

"Free her? I never owned her, did I? Canela, her name was, and her skin was indeed the colour of cinnamon. She died when Marijke was born." A shadow drifted over his broad face.

"I'm sorry," Matthew said, disconcerted by the fact that Klaas' eyes were overflowing with tears.

Klaas produced a gigantic handkerchief and blew his nose thoroughly, wiped his eyes, his moustache and his mouth, and by the time he was done, he was back to his composed self, suggesting he give Matthew a guided tour of the town itself.

After a long but entertaining afternoon with this new friend of his, Matthew politely declined Klaas' offer to stay for supper, steering Alex through dark and empty streets back to their lodgings.

"Sassafras?" Alex chuckled, sitting down on the bed. "A man?"

"He can't very well help what his parents named him," Matthew said, chuckling as well. "According to Klaas, he's not a bad man – cultured and well read. Spends most of his time on his plantation, coming down once or twice a month to Bridgetown to woo wee Marijke." He was most relieved. Surely, an educated person such as this Brown would be a compassionate man, and so it was but a matter of days before this quest for his nephew was happily concluded – assuming, of course, that wee Charlie hadn't sickened and died.

"Wouldn't that be somewhat unorthodox?" Alex asked. "The daughter of a slave to wed a slave owner?"

Matthew hitched his shoulders. The lass was exquisite, and any red-blooded male would not see much beyond that.

"No, of course not," Alex agreed a bit too sharply. "Men are ruled by their cocks, not their brains, right?"

"Oh aye," Matthew said, "had I been thinking when I met you—" The rest of what he planned to say was lost in a squawk when she walloped him over the head with one of the pillows.

★

"How long will it take?" Matthew asked next day. He was restless, had been up since before dawn, and now it was well after eight, and they should make haste.

"A day and a half," Mr Hendrijks said, "on foot, that is. Riding will be somewhat quicker – you can easily cover the distance within a day."

He helped them rent a couple of mounts and wished them a hasty Godspeed before hurrying back to the harbour. Two new Dutch slavers, he threw over his shoulder, and then there was the English ship, arrived with merchandise of all kinds: wines, tea, silks and linens, furniture and books. Alex waved to him and went back to inspecting the horse she was supposed to ride.

"I don't like her," she said, "and look at how she rolls her eyes. She doesn't like me either."

"I can take you on a leading rein," Matthew suggested, irritated by this unnecessary delay.

Alex gave him a glacial look. "That won't be necessary," she told him, and swung unaided into the saddle.

For the first few miles, they rode through smallholdings, dusty little places where former bond servants and indentures attempted to scrape a living out of soil that stood like red clouds around them when they worked the ground. Small neat gardens, scraggly fields of barley and tobacco, here and there a rose that wilted in the fierce heat...houses that reminded Matthew of Scottish crofts – small, dark and probably insufferably hot in the tropical heat. Most of the little farms seemed to be populated by the sum total of one very lonely white male, and Matthew made sure his pistol was on prominent display as they passed man after man that devoured Alex with their eyes.

Since some hours, the small farms had been left behind. They seemed to be in some sort of forest, with far too many tall trees and too much exuberant greenery around them. Matthew's skin itched. The path twisted and turned, and he couldn't see much more than a couple of yards ahead. Even here, in the shade, the heat was such it plastered his shirt to

238

his skin. The bark of the trees bristled with evil-looking thorns, creepers hung like giant cobwebs over the path, and only in glimpses could he see the sky.

"I don't like this. What if a giant python just drops off a tree to strangle us to death? Or a panther." Alex threw a nervous look at their surroundings.

"They don't have snakes here, as I hear it, and as to big cats, I find it most unlikely. Too swampy." The air reeked of stagnant water and dark mud.

"Crocodiles?" Alex said.

"Alex," Matthew sighed, exasperated. "You worry—" He never got to finish, wheeling towards the sound of breaking branches. Something the size of a small catamount rushed across the road. Alex's horse decided this was quite enough and bucked one, twice, thrice. Alex landed with a grunt on the ground, and the skittish mare took off, back the way they'd come. By the time Matthew had verified Alex was alright, the horse was long gone, forcing them to share a mount for the rest of the way.

Chapter 28

"In all probability, a feral pig," Mr Sassafras Brown said once they had made it up his lane – a beautiful lane bordered on the one side by cedars, as yet very young, and on the other by sunflowers, their yellow heads dipping under their weight. "The half-grown pigs escape now and then – quite the nuisance they are."

He regarded them with open curiosity, eyes resting for a bit too long on Alex's chest. "I hope you weren't seriously hurt, ma'am," he said, motioning at the dirt stains on Alex's skirts. For a few seconds, his eyes lingered on Matthew's sword, his pistol.

"No," Alex said with a stiff smile. Her hip was hurting like hell, and she longed for hot water and soap, but for now it could wait. When he inquired if he could perhaps offer them a cool drink, something to calm Mrs Graham's ruffled nerves, she smiled her acceptance and followed him as he led the way to the veranda.

Alex sipped at what she took to be guava juice, liberally spiked with cane liquor, and smiled yet again in the direction of Mr Brown. She wasn't quite sure how to behave around this exceedingly polite young man with his elegant clothes and inquisitive eyes. It was obvious he was waiting for them to explain the reason for their visit, equally apparent that Matthew was uncertain how to broach the subject, choosing instead to submit Mr Brown to a series of questions about his plantation and its yield, every now and then making adequately impressed noises.

The subject broached itself when the slaves returned from the field, just as dusk was gathering along the fringe of untamed jungle that bordered the further end of the yard. Alex's gaze flew to the men, and unerringly locked on the tallest of them, undeniably white despite the dark tone of his skin. She couldn't rightly make out either hair or eyes, but she could see her own sons, her man, in the set of the shoulders, and was convinced this was him: this was Charlie Graham. Beside her, she heard Matthew's indrawn breath, near on a moan, and in his chair Mr Brown tensed, dark eyes boring into Matthew before flying over to the slaves.

Alex held the subject at bay for some further minutes, inquiring how Mr Brown had come to have such an unusual name. Not that she was at all interested, but she wanted to give Matthew some minutes to collect himself, and also it seemed polite to show some interest in their host.

"My father," Mr Brown said with something of a pout on his well-formed lips. "He was very fond of trees – and anything that grew." He waved his hand in the direction of the sunflowers – a product of his father's eager plant collecting, he explained.

"Like mine." Alex nodded sympathetically. "I was dragged off to look at flowers far more often than I wanted to."

Mr Brown smiled at her, and used one finger to loosen his cravat from his skin. Quite dirty skin, and despite a pervasive scent of lavender, the ripe undertones of sweat, urine and sheer grime wafted in drifting waves from the planter, making Alex suppress an urge to wrinkle her nose.

"But he didn't name you for his darling plants. While I am Sassafras, my brother is Cedar and my sister was Magnolia."

A heavy silence fell. Alex finished her drink and massaged her swollen ankle. She had landed awkwardly with her foot beneath her, and she worried it might be sprained. With a mumbled excuse she stood, making for their satchel that Matthew had left at the doorway to the veranda.

Matthew noted Alex's slight limp as she crossed the few yards, and even more he registered Mr Brown's near on rude inspection of his wife's posterior as she bent over. He was on the verge of reprimanding their young host when Mr Brown abruptly turned to face him.

"It's not that I wish to seem inhospitable, but rarely do I have people riding up from Bridgetown to see me, and even more rarely people I don't know. So, if you don't mind me asking, sir, what exactly is your business?"

Matthew took a big breath and downed the last of his drink. "It's a matter concerning one of your indentures." Matthew spoke at length, ensuring he underlined repeatedly how young Charlie was, a lad no more. From Mr Brown's bored expression, this made no major impression, and once Matthew was done, Mr Brown sat back, spending several minutes rearranging the folds of lace that flowed down the front of his brocade waistcoat, fiddling further with his lavish cuffs. He gave Alex a fleeting smile when she rejoined them before returning his attention to Matthew.

"I'm not sure I want to sell him. I'll get a couple of years of work out of him before he sickens and dies. Nor am I sure I should sell him – at least not to you. You're his uncle."

Matthew nodded that aye, he was.

"He's here on account of being a traitor to his king. His sentence was one of servitude until death. To allow you to buy him is to subvert the course of justice."

"I told you, he's a lad," Matthew said, trying to keep the agitation out of his voice. "A youngster led astray by his seniors."

"Ah." The planter looked him up and down, let his eyes drop over to Alex, shifted them back to Matthew, and there was a gleam in them, a lurking amusement. "Besides, it'll make Big George unhappy to have him go."

"George?" Matthew wasn't quite sure he had heard correctly.

The planter nodded in the direction of a large, solidly built black man, well over six feet four and with hands the size of frying pans presently crossing the yard.

"My best slave; enjoys having his personal servant – and white at that." Mr Brown chuckled and waggled his brows.

Matthew clenched his hands around the need to hurt the popinjay before him.

Mr Brown got to his feet and edged away, as if aware

of the explosive anger surging through Matthew. "Let us repair inside," he said, "before we're eaten alive by the mosquitoes."

He led them into a library that made Alex exclaim. Matthew was not quite as impressed, for all that there were more books here than he had ever seen before. No, instead he smelled mildew and dust, and he suspected most of the tomes would be filmed by a green fuzz should he take them down from their shelves. In pride of place stood a small gaming table on which stood a chessboard.

"I'll play you for him," Mr Brown said, a strong square nail tapping at the chessboard.

"You'll play me?" Matthew echoed.

The planter scratched himself on his chest and nodded, yawning hugely. "Hot, isn't it," he commented, "and hotter it will be before the summer is done." He twisted a pawn in his hand. "So what say you?"

"What are the stakes?" Matthew asked, not at all liking the way those dark eyes lingered on Alex.

"What? Oh yes, well, I suppose there must be an element of risk in it." Mr Brown grinned and jerked his head at Alex. "If you lose, she stays here overnight." He scratched himself again and tilted his head, waiting.

"She stays here overnight?" Matthew felt the weight of his sword against his leg, and calculated how many strokes it would take to lop Mr Brown's head from his neck.

The planter nodded and threw a speculative look at Matthew. "It all depends on how you rate your nephew's life. If you win, he is free. If you lose, she stays the night, and we play yet another game tomorrow." He grinned like a jack-o'-lantern and sat back.

Matthew threw a desperate look at Alex. "How do I know it is truly him? I but glimpsed the man."

Mr Brown nodded sagely. "A good question, Mr Graham, a very good question." He beckoned them to follow him out on the veranda and called for the overseer to come over, conferring in whispers with him for some minutes.

The overseer muttered something, threw a guarded look in the direction of Matthew, but inclined his head before striding off.

There was a yelp, a scuffling sound, and a man was hauled to stand on the opposite side of the yard. A tall, skeletal man, red hair standing like a fiery fuzz around his head, his normal long stride hampered by the fetters round his legs. The man blinked in the light of the lantern held above his head, and even if Matthew couldn't make out if his eyes were green, he recognised the features – his own features – almost caricatured in his gaunt face. Then he saw the brand, and his fingers stiffened with a violent need to hurt this cultured, oh so elegant bastard of a man.

"You've branded him?"

"I brand all my blacks – and the whites when they try to escape. It has a very deterring effect." Brown nodded to the overseer who barked something to Charlie which made him cringe and bow before he hurried off as fast as he could.

"I'll pay you double for him," Matthew tried again. Lord! It was like seeing an image of what he himself would have become had not Alex found him all those years ago.

"I think not. I'll have you play for him or I keep him." Mr Brown rubbed at his nose and called for more drink, a shadow of a girl appearing immediately with a brimming pitcher.

"Do it," Alex whispered to Matthew.

"I can't risk you!"

"You have to! He'll be dead within weeks if we don't get him out of here! Besides, you'll win," she whispered, "and if you don't..." Quickly, she pulled his hand to rest against the concealed handle of her knife.

"Oh dear, oh dear," Mr Brown said and moved his knight. "Check, I fear." He peered down at the board. "Mate," he added with a smirk. Matthew was unable to meet Alex's eyes. He had great respect for her capacity to defend herself, but to leave her alone here... No, he wouldn't do it, he decided, squaring his shoulders, and his fingers crept down to rest on the hilt of his sword.

"So, Mrs Graham, I shall have you escorted to your room. Supper is promptly at eight." Mr Brown clapped his hands together in a gesture of delight. "It's a long time since I had the pleasure of a female guest, and, if I may say so, one as ravishing as yourself."

Matthew flew to his feet. Mr Brown backed away.

"Don't get your hopes up," Alex snapped, and Mr Brown gurgled with amusement.

"The bed I hope will be to your liking. It is newly acquired and is comfortably wide — wide enough to accommodate both yourself and your husband." Brown laughed at their confusion. "Really, Mr Graham! What can you think of me?" He looked Alex up and down and smiled at Matthew. "You have an attractive wife, but my preferences are for women younger than myself, not old enough to be my mother."

"Bastard!" Alex exclaimed.

Mr Brown laughed again. "Come, come, Mrs Graham. Tonight you are my guest, and I hope we'll pass a most entertaining evening together."

It was an indication of how upset Alex was that she threw but a cursory look at the hot water and expensive French soap waiting for them in their room. Instead, she crawled into Matthew's arms, and Matthew wasn't quite sure who was comforting who, but supposed they needed it both, this proximity to one another.

"What an absolute creep," Alex said, drenching one of the towels to wipe at the dirt stains on her skirts.

"Aye," Matthew agreed. The man behaved most erratically, shifting from conscientious host to cold-hearted slave owner in the blink of an eye, and this whole charade with the chess game… No, he did not intend to remain here longer than necessary, and in his head he was busy reviewing the lost game, trying to find the draw that had shifted the board in Mr Brown's favour. An excellent utilisation of his rooks, and then the way he had used his knight… Matthew shook his head at how easily he had fallen into that trap.

★

Alex would have preferred a tray in their room, but things being as they were, Matthew and she were summoned at eight. The dining room was as opulent as the library, the lit beeswax candles making the room stifling. Once again that lingering smell of damp and rot, and that in combination with the red walls and dark floors gave Alex the impression of a carefully maintained mausoleum – nothing in this room seemed to have been changed since the death of the older Mr Brown.

"Did your father come here as a bond servant?" Alex asked, sipping at the spicy soup.

Mr Brown gave her an insulted look. "Certainly not! He was a gentleman through and through – well educated as well." He threw a dark glare at the serving girl, indicating with his head that she had forgotten to replenish their glasses. The girl looked distressed, whispered a "Sorry, massa" and topped them up too high, which made Mr Brown's brows lower threateningly.

"Oh," Alex replied, "our nephew is also a gentleman and even has a degree from Oxford. It hasn't saved him from ending up here." That struck home, she could see, concentrating on blowing on her soup.

Mr Brown made a dismissive sound. "Those fanciful stories you sometimes hear about men overcoming their dismal servitude are mostly lies. Indentures rarely live through their sentence, and if they do, they rarely become men of property. We make sure they don't," he smirked. He changed the subject to the wine, and went on to describe his recent trip to Paris, entirely oblivious to the silence of his guests.

"Do you speak or read French?" he asked Alex, having given up on drawing a stony Matthew into the conversation.

"No," Alex said. She wasn't about to share with him the single French phrase she could remember – *Voulez-vous coucher avec moi* seemed very inappropriate given the recent chess game.

"Ah," Mr Brown replied, and it was clear this was a major drawback in his opinion.

Matthew shoved his plate away from him and glared at their host. "It sticks in my craw that we sit here, partaking of good wines and food, while only a stone's throw away my nephew is lying in filth."

"You lost," Brown reminded him, "and until you win that's where he stays." He smiled broadly. "It's such an unusual pleasure to have guests – I hope your stay will be a long one."

Alex clamped a hand on Matthew's thigh. Killing Brown would not help.

Sassafras Brown was a man clearly starved for company – even unrequested company. Over the coming days, he talked incessantly, a verbal flow that leapt from the political situation in England, through long ruminating reminiscences of his long dead mother – French, of course – to an attempted discussion on a play he had seen by Racine. He waited eagerly for their reaction. There was none, and with a condescending little sigh, Brown left the subject of French playwrights, and instead shifted to describe the crops grown on his plantation.

"Very profitable," he said, after having shown them the hogheads packed full of sugar. He waved his hands at the tobacco fields, commented that the quality here was never as good as in Virginia, but good enough nonetheless, and then slyly added that both these crops depended on heavy labour, so it was fortunate, was it not, that he had slaves of all colours at his disposal? He grinned at the deep red that suffused Matthew's face and after tipping his hat, sauntered off to discuss something with his overseer.

Every afternoon culminated with the daily chess game – at times played indoors, just as often on the veranda. With each passing day, Alex could see the tension build in Matthew. Brown humiliated him. No matter Matthew's considerable skills in the game, Brown was always a step ahead, those dark eyes of his glittering with amusement when Matthew yet again fell into Brown's elegantly executed trap.

"Oh dear." Mr Brown beamed at Matthew, who looked

as if he was about to explode. "Checkmate again." He rose and bowed, humming to himself as he left the room.

Matthew slumped dejectedly by the board. "He is a right canny player," he muttered. "I don't quite know how to beat him."

"Let him win a couple of times," Alex said, "and study how he plays. He'll probably grow careless."

"A couple of times?" Matthew gave her a despairing look. "This is the fifth consecutive loss, and while I dabble in the gentlemanly pursuit of chess, wee Charlie slaves another day in the field." He swept the board and its pieces to the floor, and stalked outside.

Chapter 29

"Who was that?" Ruth threw a long look after Michael, who was already halfway round the closest corner.

"A man," Sarah said, forcing herself to look away from where Michael had disappeared. She hugged her secret close, and felt it glow inside of her. Forty-six days she had known him, and every one of those days she had contrived to see him, short stolen moments discreetly out of sight from the nosy busybodies of Providence. Until today, that is, when she'd lost track of time, thereby causing Ruth to come looking for her.

"I can see that." Ruth shifted her baby closer to her, and pursed her lips into a narrow funnel. "So who?"

Sarah pretended not to hear.

"Sarah! You can't walk out alone with unknown men! It's unseemly. And you, in particular, must at all times behave with utmost modesty – you know that."

"I do? Why?" Sarah knew, of course. A constant whispering surrounded her, lads would hurl the odd insulting comment after her, and all she could do was pretend not to hear. Lasses her age would at most bid her a good day before scurrying off to whisper and point, while their mothers would cluck and simper to Sarah's face, only to shake their heads and mutter behind her back that where there was smoke there was fire – look at her, so vibrant and inviting.

"Your reputation," Ruth hissed. "It must remain untarnished."

"Too late for that," Sarah said bitterly. "But not through any fault of mine."

Ruth sighed, hefting precious Edward close enough that she could brush her lips along his wee lace cap. "I know, but please, Sarah—"

"I haven't done anything!" At most, her hand had grazed Michael's in passing, and while Sarah longed for every glimpse of him, every moment spent in his company, envisioning anything more made her insides shrivel. "We'd best get going," she added, extending her stride.

"It was you, not me, that was late," Ruth retorted, puffing in her efforts to keep up. "And don't run!"

"Sorry." Sarah dropped her pace somewhat. They were on their way to visit Kate Jones, hoping she might have news of their parents that had as yet not reached them. Already into August, and so far there had been but one letter, from Jamaica, in Da's bold hand.

"So, did Julian agree?" Sarah asked, mostly to break the lengthy silence.

Ruth gave her a brilliant smile, and for the coming minutes Sarah was submitted to a long and detailed account of just what Ruth had said to convince her husband that wee Edward would thrive best at his mother's breasts. Sarah listened distractedly, made the right noises at the right time, and by the time they'd reached Kate's house, Sarah was quite convinced Ruth had forgotten all about Michael.

Sarah liked Kate Jones: no condemning looks, no snide remarks, just a woman who greeted her cheerfully whenever they met, and who had no compunction in strolling through Providence with Sarah at her side.

Kate invited them to join her in the shade, but shook her head when Ruth asked if she had any news about Mama and Da.

"No, I haven't heard more myself, except that Captain Jan is planning to go to Curacao and then back up through Barbados to load sugar." Kate smiled down at Edward and complimented Ruth on her son, saying that with each day the boy grew more and more like his father. Most unfortunate, in Sarah's opinion, because whatever other attributes Julian might have – and she'd be hard-pressed to list them – good looks was not one of them. Aye, he had bonny eyes, a darker grey than Michael's, and aye, he had right nice hands, but beyond that…

A sound from the opposite side of the shaded courtyard made Sarah turn. A baby basket stood in the shade. A small chubby fist waved in the air, the gauze covering held in a tight grip. Some minutes more, and a very demanding sound came from the basket's depths. Sarah jerked and got to her feet.

"Have you ever seen him?" Kate said.

Sarah shook her head. She had seen her uncle about town on several occasions since she got here, and they had talked about anything and everything but the fact that the child she had birthed now lived with Simon.

The few times she'd seen Simon with what she assumed to be the lad in his arms, she had fled, ducking into convenient shops or alleys. Once, she had followed them all the way to the meetinghouse, and when Simon had hefted the boy up higher on his shoulder, Sarah had seen eyes as blue as her own stare back at her.

"Maybe you should," Kate suggested.

Sarah swallowed, and all she could hear was the loud rushing sound of her blood through her head.

"He has the strangest hair," Kate went on. "It's growing out fair at the roots, but the ends remain the same black they were when he was born." She smiled at Sarah. "He's a very sweet boy, and he looks just like you, only you."

"She stiffened up when Kate suggested she might hold him," Ruth told Julian later that night, "and then she wheeled and just ran off." She sat down by the small table and proceeded to brush her hair. It spilled like rippling copper down her back, and Julian lay propped on one elbow and watched as all that hair was captured and braided into a loose night plait – unnecessary as very soon he would undo it, spread it out to lie fanned around her head.

"I felt so sad for her," Ruth said, and Julian grunted an agreement: a sorry business, in truth. He fidgeted when she began washing, making small sounds of increased irritation when she insisted on rubbing hands and face with scented oils and lotions. After her skin, she turned her attention to her teeth. An obsession, in his mind, this constant teeth cleaning, and now he was expected to do it as well, even to the point of masticating a couple of leaves of mint every night.

Julian groaned silently. His entire domestic life danced to the tune set by Alex Graham, and he didn't like it, frowning at the surprising amount of vegetables he was expected to eat, at the cost related to weekly baths, at the insistence that he change his shirt at least once a week, and that he wash not only face and hands but also his member twice a day.

"Mama says," Ruth would begin, and Julian stopped listening. For the last few weeks, this had been the constant preamble as he had been bombarded with one reason after the other for why Edward should be fed by his mother, not some stranger, and eventually he had succumbed with ill grace, snapping at Ruth that she was being disobedient and opinionated but that, for the sake of his own peace, he would reconsider.

She was finally ready for bed, and floated towards him across the bare wooden boards. She giggled when he tickled her flank, squirmed when his fingers drifted over her mound, and then he rolled himself on top of her, savouring the fact that he had a young, fertile wife. Her thighs were strong and smooth, her arms warm around his back, and he settled himself inside of her for a long, slow ride towards completion. A son, she had given him a son, and God willing she would give him many more.

Next morning, Ruth told Julian of the man she'd seen speaking to Sarah.

"A man?"

"I have eyes," Ruth replied, "and it was not a woman nor yet a lad."

"But she can't be talking to unknown men on her own!" Julian frowned at the floor. Sarah was as headstrong as her mother, and deep down Julian would now and then reflect that had Sarah not been disobedient, she would never have been abducted. He pulled on his right stocking and retrieved the left one from where he had dropped it to the floor the previous evening, gartering them both just above the knee before pulling on his dark grey breeches. His coat...now, where had he put his coat?

"Here," Ruth said, holding it out to him.

"I'll talk to her," Julian said and hunted about for his shoes.

"There." Ruth pointed to where she had placed them, neatly side by side just beside the door. "Yes, I think it may be wise to point out the importance of decorous behaviour. Otherwise, Da will never see her married."

No sooner did Sarah come down the stairs but Julian led her off to his study.

"What?" Sarah said, yanking her arm free from his hand.

Julian cleared his throat and went on to tell her that he would not tolerate any indecent behaviour, not while she was under his care.

"Indecent behaviour?" Sarah's low alto climbed to a piercing soprano. "What are you insinuating?" She glared at her sister, making Ruth blush.

"I saw you," Ruth muttered, "talking to that unknown man."

"Oh aye? And what precisely did you see?"

"Just that you talked," Ruth said, "for no more than a moment, but still."

Sarah huffed. "I exchanged some words with a man wishing for directions, and you accuse me of fornication?"

Julian didn't like her tone, and even less the way she was scowling. "Now, now, Sarah, Ruth hasn't done anything of the kind. We are but pointing out that—"

"—you would be discredited if I behave like a wanton," Sarah bit him off, and her blue eyes spoke of a serious intent to do them both bodily harm. "I have no intention of doing that, and as far as I know, I've never behaved in a way that merits such concern." With that, she left them standing in the study and with impressive dignity exited the room.

"But it's only out of concern for you," Michael said an hour or so later when they met where they usually did, in the small copse of trees that bordered the graveyard.

"I don't think that's entirely true." She looked down at her hands, busy with a long, uneven grass braid. "He's far more concerned about his reputation, what with him being a minister. I don't understand how Ruth can be so besotted by him."

"She is?" Michael pillowed his head on his coat, and looked up at the few splotches of blue that were visible through the foliage. Sarah made a disgusted sound, and Michael laughed. "It's a good thing for a wife to be besotted with her husband. It would help in the bedding." He snuck a look at her. "To be bedded by force can't be a pleasurable experience, can it?" She flinched, and he closed his eyes before she could catch his look.

"No," she whispered, and the desolation in her voice made Michael want to take her hand. He didn't. Instead, he pretended to sleep, relaxing into an agreeable doze.

The August heat was constant and cloying, and the little garret room he rented had enough air to see him through at most two hours before he began to twist and turn, sweating like a pig despite his nude state. Here, there was a breeze, and he felt himself begin to slip into real sleep, dreams lining up along the outer edges of his subconscious.

A soft, recurring sound disrupted his rest: a steady click, click, click that he recognised but couldn't fully place. Drowsily, he opened an eye and just as quickly closed it again. Sarah Graham was a Presbyterian, and... No, he must have seen wrong. Yet another peek, and he raised himself on his elbow.

"A rosary?" His voice made her drop her beads, and he picked them up and handed them back to her. She was embarrassed, stuffing them back out of sight.

"Are you a Catholic?" Michael knew she wasn't — or at least that her father wasn't — and her sister was married to one of the ministers.

"No, but it helps at times." She clearly didn't want to talk about it, but Michael pushed on.

"So, how?"

"A friend — a priest — gave them to me."

"You count a Catholic priest among your friends?"

She nodded once.

Michael sat up. "Don't your parents...err...don't they object to such a friendship?"

Sarah gave him a flashing smile, followed by a hitched shoulder. "Mama no, Da isn't entirely comfortable with it."

"No, I can imagine not," Michael murmured.

"Carlos helped me through my moment of dire need." Sarah looked away at absolutely nothing, a softness to her lips that made Michael jealous.

"Aren't you too young to have lived through a time of dire need?" he asked unnecessarily. After all, he knew of her ordeal, or at least Uncle Philip's bald – and probably not entirely truthful – version of it.

"No," she answered in a voice he could barely hear.

His hand rested for a moment on her arm. "Tell me."

Sarah shook her head. "I don't think I can – or want to."

He decided to let it lie for now. Instead. he dug into his shirt and produced his own rosary, a beautiful set of beads he had inherited from his devout mother. He couldn't quite remember the last time he had said a decade, nor when he last went to confession, and given the present religious rumblings here in Maryland, being Catholic was something best not shouted out loud.

"I'm a Catholic." He smiled teasingly. "Next time we meet, we can sit in silence and tell a decade or two – most decorous."

Sarah laughed. "I don't think it would do my reputation much good," she said, getting to her feet. "Tomorrow?" she asked, and he liked it that her blue eyes were bright with need.

"Tomorrow," he promised, and watched her walk sure-footed down the rocky slope.

"I saw you!" Ruth challenged, stepping out from the shadow of the meetinghouse. "You *are* seeing a man on the sly, and that you mustn't do!" She was bright with righteous indignation.

"I'll see whoever I wish," Sarah snapped back, "and if

255

I have one friend, one single friend, then how can you be-grudge me a few hours in his company?"

"It's not appropriate. You're the sister-in-law of a minister, and mustn't expose yourself to gossip of any kind."

"Oh aye? For my sake or yours?"

"For your sake, of course," Ruth said, sounding offended.

"I think not. I think you're so puffed with pride at being the minister's wife that you won't have me risk any kind of slur on you."

"I'll tell Julian," Ruth threatened.

"You do that and I'll never speak to you again." Sarah left her older sister speechless as she hurtled down towards the sea.

Chapter 30

It was an exquisite dress, a beautiful thing in pink silk that consisted of a tight little bodice, skirts that were pleated and ruffled. Every afternoon, it was hung out to air on the back porch; every afternoon, Brown would come out at five, lift down the dress and hand it to one of the slave women. And, as Alex understood early on, the woman who was handed the dress had the dubious pleasure of joining her master in bed.

"He hits them," Alex said to Matthew, nodding as discreetly as she could in the direction of one of the housemaids. The poor woman looked as if she'd run into a door.

"Aye, I can see that."

"We must do something," Alex said.

"What?" Matthew asked testily. "There's nothing we can do."

Unfortunately, he was right, so Alex bit her tongue and tried to be as supportive as she could when her husband night after night was humiliated at the chessboard by Brown. Every time, Matthew begged that he be allowed to buy Charlie free, and every time, Brown refused.

At times, Brown would lead them on long walks across his lands, and just by chance – huh – they'd happen upon where Charlie and his fellow slaves were worked like beasts, whips flying, insults hailing. Alex would hang like a leech round Matthew's arm while that damned Sassafras Brown just grinned before leading them off on yet another excursion of the surrounding forests.

He pointed out kapok trees and gumbos; he spoke of music and plays, of poetry and science, enticing even Matthew into a long discussion about the properties of comets. But he refused to allow Matthew or Alex to talk to Charlie, telling them both that if they did, he'd have Charlie flogged.

"Once you win, not before, and at this rate, perhaps he'll die before you do," he said with obvious glee, and Matthew raged in private, suggesting one more preposterous scheme after the other to save his nephew from this slow death.

"We can't," Alex said, "and you know that. There are five white men here including Mr Brown, and two of them constantly carry muskets. We'd not get beyond the lane before they caught up with us."

After yet another massive supper, they were sitting in the library, Matthew and Alex hostages to their host's bonhomie. The little serving girl entered with a tray laden with teapot and mugs made of china so fine it was almost transparent, and set it down before Alex with a curtsey. Alex did a double take: the child was wearing the pink silk dress. It was far too big for her, the bodice gaped over a narrow chest that had nothing to fill it with, and the hem dragged on the floor.

"...don't you agree, Mrs Graham?" Mr Brown was saying.

"Hmm?" Alex hid her face by busying herself with pouring tea. There had to be something she could do to help the girl. Inspired, she held out a brimming cup to Mr Brown and upended it right over his crotch, scalding her own fingers in the process.

"Oh God!" she exclaimed. "How clumsy of me!"

Mr Brown was doing a little dance, his dark eyes narrowed with anger. Curtly, he excused himself and stalked off in the direction of his bedroom.

"You! Hetty! Bring me cold water, a lot of water," he called over his shoulder, and the girl ran to do his bidding.

It was just before dawn when Alex stumbled over Hetty, lying on the veranda. No longer in the dress, the girl was shivering in a stained linen shift, arms hugged protectively round her waist. When Alex tried to touch her, she shied away.

"I'm sorry, missus, sorry, so sorry," the girl mumbled through a badly swollen mouth, and struggled to stand.

"Jesus," Alex said, and once again tried to touch her.

Hetty backed away. "It was me own fault. The massa be right angry wi' me for not doin' as he says." She gulped back on a sob. "I…" Agilely, she got round Alex and made for the safety of the cookhouse.

"It is none of your concern," Mr Brown snapped when Alex confronted him over breakfast. At least he was limping – too bad she hadn't scalded his penis.

"She's a child!"

"She's my property," Mr Brown said, "and I'll do with her as I see fit—"

"Bastard!"

"…just as I will with your precious nephew." He bowed and left her to consider that particular little threat alone.

After supper that evening, it was as if their previous conversation had never taken place. Instead, Mr Brown went on about how difficult it was to live so far away from what little cultured society was to be found in Barbados.

"Shortly, I hope to install a wife here with me," he said, smiling in the direction of Hetty – yet again in the pink dress – who tried to smile back. "I'm of an age to wish for sons to carry on my line."

"No major loss to humanity if that doesn't happen," Alex muttered in an undertone. He gave her the creeps, this strange man, one moment all cultivation and polish, the next a cruel boor.

"I hope for a wife with whom I can share my passion for everything French," Mr Brown went on, smiling dreamily into the smoke that hovered round him. He drew heavily on his pipe for some moments. "Yes. It would be most pleasing should she speak French, like my sainted mother did."

"Marijke Hendrijks doesn't speak French," Matthew said, still seated by the chessboard.

"Marijke Hendrijks?" Mr Brown lowered his pipe to look at him. "How do you know her?"

"I've met her," Matthew said, "and her father."

259

"Oh yes…well, you would, wouldn't you? Klaas being the harbourmaster and all that," Mr Brown said.

"A very nice girl," Alex put in. "She deserves a nice, loving husband." Not like you, she thought, throwing Brown a challenging glance.

For an instant, Sassafras Brown met her eyes, brows lowered threateningly. But he didn't reply. Instead, he sucked at his pipe, sending up a veil of smoke between him and his guests.

"I think he's insane," Alex confided to Matthew once they were back in their room. "He's too erratic. One moment he's the perfect, courteous gentleman, the next he's a beast who abuses a child of twelve or so. She doesn't even have breasts yet!"

"Mmm," Matthew replied, throwing himself to lie flat on the bed. "He didn't like it, did he, that we know Klaas and Marijke."

"No," Alex said, "and he's quite right to be worried. Since we've been here, it's been the same every night: he takes a woman to bed, and they stumble out hurt in the morning. Of course I'll tell Klaas!" She pummelled at her pillows and slid down to lie beside him. "God, I hate this place!"

"Aye." Matthew frowned up at the ceiling and rolled out of bed, returning with his dirk and one of his pistols that he slid in under the pillow.

In the middle of the night, Alex woke to a draught, and saw the door close quietly. Beside her, Matthew was wide awake, a cautionary hand on her arm. Oh God, the planter had been standing there, looking in on them! Alex sat up, shivering in bed. Neither of them slept any more that night.

Matthew won the chess game the next day. For a moment, he just sat, staring at the board, before looking at Alex.

"Pack," he said. "We leave within the hour."

"Surely you don't mean to set out now, this late in the day?" Mr Brown asked, surprisingly unperturbed by his loss.

"Aye, we do," Matthew said.

"Ah," Mr Brown said, and there was a ghost of a smile

on his face as he moved over to his desk where the document transferring Charlie's contract was already drawn up. Brown set his name to it, gestured for Matthew to sign it, and wrote out a receipt for the twenty pounds Matthew paid over. "I'll have the overseer bring your nephew," he said, and left the room.

Charlie didn't understand. He'd been woken at dawn and led to work, and no matter what he did, he did it wrong. The ditch was too shallow, it was too crooked, he was digging too slow, and the whip came down time and time again on his bare back. He was set to dig yet another ditch, and he made an effort to dig straight and neat, and still the overseer yelled at him, and he was beaten yet again. He begged for them to stop, and when they started him on a third ditch, he made an even greater effort, and he dug and dug, and the ditch was very straight. But not quite, as the overseer pointed out, and Charlie squealed when they used a cane instead of a whip.

"Please," he bawled, "please don't hurt me anymore." Mercifully, they stopped, leading him off in the direction of the yard. He could scarcely walk, but he managed to stand when he was told to, and he blinked because someone was calling him Charlie, and no one had done that since the day last September when his father had called after him in Taunton.

He had no idea who the big man before him might be, but the woman beside him, she looked familiar, and with a jolt he realised she looked like his mam – brown-haired where Mam had hair like black silk, but eyes as blue, if a few shades darker.

"Mam?" he quavered, even if he knew she wasn't – not unless he was dead and this was a heavenly angel.

"No," the woman replied, and put a hand on his forearm. "I'm your aunt."

Charlie licked his lips. Aunt? Why were they here? He swayed with the effort of keeping upright, and could vaguely make out that the tall man that he supposed must be his uncle was yelling at Mr Brown. Charlie cringed at Brown's angry reply. Please, don't hurt me, he thought, and closed his eyes in expectation of a new blow. Someone was kneeling by his feet, and he screamed when the chisel skinned the inner side of his foot, and then the fetters were off, and Charlie Graham suddenly realised he was still alive.

The woman helped him into a clean shirt, but said she had no breeches for him. "This stays here," she said, and he was hugely embarrassed at having her hands on him as she undid the grimy clout and dropped it to the ground.

"I haven't washed..." he said in a weak explanation at the stink of himself.

"Well, we forgot to tell you we were coming, didn't we?" she said and Charlie managed a weak twitching of the lips. His uncle came over and without a word carried Charlie over to the horse.

"You ride," he said, and Charlie smiled at his accent. It reminded him of Jacob, the towheaded cousin that he'd met six years ago. He didn't protest at his uncle's suggestion because his foot hurt something awful, and he didn't think he'd make it down the lane unaided. He was leaving! The ground was moving beneath the horse's hooves, and his head was spinning with hunger, fear and incomprehension, but this much he grasped: he would die somewhere else, not here.

"Kill them," Brown told the overseer. "Hunt them down and kill them and throw their remains into the wilderness or the sea." He almost giggled at the elegance of it all. Graham probably thought he had outplayed him, when in fact he, Sassafras Brown, had outwitted the tall Scot. And now it was all happening just as he'd planned. Yes, he would say, wrinkling his brow in concern, yes, he had met the Grahams. He had even sold them their nephew and waved them off on their return trip to Bridgetown. He watched the odd little cavalcade drop out of sight and turned to his man.

"Wait until dark," he said, "and if you want to have the woman first..." He felt a slight tightening of his balls and looked around to where Hetty was waiting. Goddamn the Graham woman for sticking her long nose into what was no concern of hers! And he could only imagine what would happen to his prospective wedding should she get the opportunity to tell Hendrijks what she'd seen. No, he couldn't let that happen. Marijke Hendrijks would make him a perfect wife, young enough to mould to his tastes and so very, very pretty. And, on top of that, rich. If half of what the rumours said was true, she was easily the richest girl on the island. Oh yes, little Marijke was meant to be his, and if the Grahams had to die for that to happen, so be it. He jerked his head in the direction of the house, and Hetty obediently hurried inside. "I'll be waiting to hear how things went when you come back."

The overseer just nodded.

"He's done that on purpose," Alex said, indicating the faint lines of blood that had seeped through Charlie's shirt. "And that," she added, indicating the lacerated ankle. "It smells of a trap, somehow."

Matthew frowned, tightening his grip on the reins. "He let me win, he wanted me to win. That's why he had the contract ready." He patted at the front of his shirt where the legal document transferring ownership of Charlie rested against his chest. Alex stumbled, and he grabbed her hand. "They'll find us ready, not unsuspecting and asleep."

"And they have flintlocks and we have..." She waited for him to fill in.

"...a sword, two loaded pistols and two dirks."

"Whoopee." At least it would be dark, and that would make the muskets pretty useless. "Retirement," she sighed and dabbed at her sweaty face, "and you know what? Definitely not in bloody Florida or somewhere hot."

"Retirement," he smiled, "but not yet."

"No," she said. "So, all for one—"

"—and one for all," Charlie filled in weakly, and the three Grahams actually laughed. Probably due to a well-developed appreciation of the macabre, Alex reflected as she shoved the fear that was clawing its way up her throat back to lie grumbling in her gut.

Chapter 31

By the time Matthew found a campsite he felt adequate, it was well into the night, their slow progress lit by a heavy yellow moon and the rustic torch Alex was holding.

"Good." Matthew inspected thorny thickets that stood like a castle wall behind them before helping the semi-conscious Charlie off the horse. The poor boy was so weak it had been all he could do to remain astride, propped by Matthew or Alex. He needed a rest, and so, truth be told, did Alex after well over six hours of walking in this suffocating heat. She grimaced: and how coincidental that Mr bloody Brown had no horses to lend them – or so he said – thereby forcing them to walk.

"Only one direction of attack," Matthew said, and Alex felt her mouth go dry. She threw a look at Charlie who had collapsed into himself, wrapped in both her and Matthew's cloaks to stop him from shivering. No help at all from there, and what on earth could she and Matthew do against a determined band of four or five men?

"Why?" she asked. "Why do you think he'll send his men after us?"

"Marijke," Matthew said. "Too fat a catch to risk losing."

Matthew built a small fire, they heaved Charlie even further into the protective circle of thorns, and Alex helped Matthew fashion two humps out of branches and leaves just to the side of the fire.

"They'll call that bluff soon enough," Alex said.

"Aye, but by the time they do…" Matthew levelled his pistol and mimed pressing the trigger. He tried to hand one of the pistols to Alex but she shook her head.

"I'm a lousy shot, and I suspect an even worse one in the pitch-dark." She crouched down beside him, leaning into his comforting warmth. "I'm scared."

"So am I," Matthew said into her hair. All around them, the unfamiliar jungle rustled, small things scurried into the circle of weak light that surrounded their fire and were swallowed up on the other side, and Alex shifted even closer.

They came when the moon had sunk well below the fringe of trees. The horse whickered, and Matthew was on his feet in one fluid motion, helping Alex up.

"Where?" she whispered in his ear. "I can't see a thing!"

"Listen," he replied in a murmur, and tilted his head to the north, just off the path they'd walked down on a few hours earlier. A rustling, a snapping twig, the regular sound of controlled breathing...

Alex stood on tiptoe, straining her eyes in an effort to see. There! Something lighter than the surrounding woods floated disconcertingly through the trees. A face – several faces, and they were at least five.

The men approached the fire cautiously. The leader shoved his sword into one of the little humps and cursed. Matthew fired his pistol. One of the men hollered and clutched at his backside before taking off the way he'd come. Someone raised an axe as if to bring it down on Charlie's defenceless head, and Matthew fired his second pistol. The man with the axe fell in slow motion into the fire, sending showers of sparks into the air. He screamed, someone pulled him free, and a bleary-eyed Charlie struggled to sit, his face skeletal in the faint light.

A torch was lit, and in the sudden flare of light, Alex saw that behind the white men were two blacks, making the total seven. Two were out of commission, and now Matthew was out in the clearing, wielding his sword to force the overseer back. A shot went off, whizzed by Alex's head to bury itself in the tree behind her, and then the overseer was using his musket as a club in a furious attempt to keep Matthew at bay.

Alex heard strange high-pitched noises, and, with surprise, realised they came from her as she rushed across the clearing to defend the helpless and bemused Charlie from yet another attack. One of the men had pinned him to the ground, his hands round Charlie's neck. Charlie gargled and kicked, his arms flailing weakly.

"Shit!" Alex sank her knife into the shoulder of the man. Jesus, it hurt! The shock of blade on bone made her fingers tingle, but at least the man before her folded together. She rolled him off Charlie and wheeled, trying to find her man in the dark.

Matthew was having problems. The overseer and one of his assistants were slowly forcing him back, calling loudly for someone called Tom to come and help them. Tom, it seemed, was the man who had Alex's knife firmly embedded in his back, so all he did was groan. But out of the corner of her eye, Alex saw another man close in on Matthew from his side.

"Watch out!" Alex launched herself at this new assailant, grunting when her foot connected with something soft. She swung again, and karate skills she hadn't used actively for very many years came back to her, flowing from the brainstem down her spine and out into her limbs. She bunched up her skirts and whirled, her foot coming up to hit the man squarely in the chest. He sort of melted to the ground, a boneless heap of flesh that landed with a soft moan, and she turned, panting, back to her husband.

A torch held high glinted on the dull steel of Matthew's sword as he lunged, swiping viciously at the legs of his opponents. The overseer hopped away, cursing loudly. Someone levelled a gun, Matthew's blade whistled through the air, and the pistol spun away, a scream echoing through the heavy black night. Something flew through the darkness, hit Matthew, and down he went.

"No!" Alex rushed towards him, and for a few minutes she couldn't see more than a flurry of limbs. Matthew swore, and he was up again, still with his sword in hand, still alive. The overseer grabbed at Alex, and instinctively she chopped at his arm, following up with an elbow in the direction of his face. It made him howl, the bastard. She yanked herself free and retreated to stand over Charlie's prostrate body while Matthew drove the last of them off. One last lunge and he had the torch, holding it aloft for a second before dousing it against the damp ground.

It was eerily silent. They found each other by touch, his left hand groped for hers, and they stood still in the tropical night. The cicadas resumed their chirping, bushes began to rustle, and with a small sound Matthew sat down, having first assured himself that the man that had toppled into the fire was dead. To the far right, the man called Tom was crawling feebly in the direction he had come.

"Are you alright, lass?"

"I think so. Well, my bladder is about to burst." She shifted a bit closer to him. "And you?"

"Ah," he groaned, "I won't be able to raise my arm tomorrow. It's a long time since I had to engage in swordplay such as this."

"Tell me about it. I think I've sprained my hip."

"Your hip?" Matthew laughed softly. "How is that?"

"I kicked one of them. He's still here, somewhere." She squinted into the dark, now not as absolute as before, and made out a huddled shape some yards away. "I hope he isn't dead." In response, the heap uttered a guttural sound. "Oh, good." She just had to pee, and stood up on shaking legs. "I'll be right back."

"Stay close."

Alex clambered over Charlie, and squatted where she still could see the pale square of Matthew's shirt.

"At least we're still in possession of a full-bodied white slave," she said.

"Aye," Matthew replied morosely, "but the horse is gone." He reloaded his pistols and helped Charlie to stand. "We must get started. We must be out of here before they come back."

"Come back?" Alex was too tired for this.

"Aye, come back. They haven't finished, have they?"

"But..." She pointed at the dead man and his two wounded companions.

"There's more where they came from," Matthew said.

Great, absolutely fabulous. Black hairy things with a lot

of legs settled themselves in her gut and her knees.

"And him?" She eyed his nephew with concern. How on earth was he to walk?

"I'll manage," Charlie said, and to her surprise he got to his feet unaided, setting first one foot, then the other forward in a shuffling, unsteady walk.

In the shifting greys of receding night, the narrow dirt road looked like a silver band through total blackness, and slowly they made their way south, Alex jumping at any sound that might indicate pursuit. They found the horse a half mile or so down the road, and the creature was delighted to see them, its coat shining with panicked sweat. Charlie half lay, half sat on the horse, and Matthew hurried them on, muttering that they had to leave this morass of trees and wildly growing things behind as soon as possible. He limped, at times his breath caught, but when Alex asked, he just waved her away.

"Nothing," he said, "I but twisted my ankle." He increased their pace, making Alex jog.

Alex had a stitch in her side, the taste of her blood in her mouth, and her heels were burning with blisters inside her shoes, and still Matthew wouldn't let up on the pace, for all that it was almost dawn and they were out of the woods, hastening through a flat expanse of tobacco fields.

"I…" She gasped. "I need a break." She stopped, bracing her hands against her knees. "A breather, please, Matthew."

"Not here," he said, trying to tug her back into motion. "Later, Alex, but not now."

"My feet," she moaned. Her hip, her knee, her right arm – but mostly her feet.

"Take your shoes off," he said, and down he went on his knees, tugging off her shoes. Just then, the woods behind them erupted with the sounds of men and horses.

"Run!" Matthew yelled, dragging at Alex. He slapped the surprised horse hard over its rump, sending it careening out on the open fields towards a group of men already busy among the rows of tobacco. Charlie fell off halfway there, landing with a squelching sound. Alex ran. Mouth open, hair flying, she ran with her hand held hard in Matthew's, not daring to look back, not daring to think of anything but of reaching the men who had now stopped their work to stare at them.

Their pursuers were almost upon them. Any moment, Alex expected to be trampled to the ground, to die from a shot in her back. With a whimper, she tried to increase her speed, and now it was her dragging Matthew along because he was limping badly, at times hopping on one leg. Something whined through the air; a burning sensation flew up her arm. A shot? A peek down the sleeve, and she was bleeding, a shallow graze no more. Matthew's leg gave way below him, throwing them both to the ground. Oh God, oh God. Alex tightened her hold on Matthew's hand, and squished her eyes shut. One heartbeat, two heartbeats. Nothing. Three heartbeats, four heartbeats. Oh, bloody hell! If you're going to shoot me, do it now! Still nothing, so Alex drew a long breath, raising her head enough to see their assailants were nowhere close.

"Ugh!" Alex groaned, spitting gravel and dirt.

"Alright?" Matthew helped her to stand.

"They just left?" she asked, looking over to where Charlie had succeeded in getting back on his feet.

"Aye, they didn't much care for having witnesses." He nodded to where the field hands were approaching them at a jog, some with hoes held high, their white foremen with muskets.

"Lucky us," Alex said.

"Very," he said, looking exhausted. He found his hat and helped Alex adjust her dirty and torn clothes. "Come on then, lass, it's a long way back."

By the time they staggered into Bridgetown, it was well into the afternoon, and people stopped to gawk at the dishevelled threesome that made their way towards the water: Charlie in only a shirt, Alex barefoot, with a torn bodice and no hat, and Matthew in a shirt dark with blood as were his breeches. The horse was the only one looking reasonably normal, if somewhat tired, and it was on shaking knees that Alex at last came to a stop before the harbourmaster's house. She smiled with relief at the sight of Klaas, bounding up from the wharves towards them.

"My dear!" Klaas' eyes rushed up and down Alex. "You look most bedraggled."

"Why, thank you, that was just what I needed to hear." Alex lunged forward to grab at Charlie who had somehow grasped that they were at their destination and so proceeded to slide off the horse, landing in an unsteady heap on the ground.

"Go inside." Klaas moved Alex aside. "I'll take care of the lad. Go and see to yourselves."

She nodded and made for the inviting coolness of the house, shadowed by Matthew.

Charlie was whisked away by Klaas and Marijke to be taken care of. Klaas was clearly shocked by the state of Charlie, muttering a loud stream of what Alex supposed to be colourful Dutch invectives, at least to judge from the impressed expression on Marijke's face.

A bath was just what Alex needed, and she smiled her thanks when the maid poured in the last buckets of water into the hip bath. She shed her dirty, sweaty clothes, and stepped into the lukewarm water. She scrubbed and scrubbed. She split lemons into halves and squeezed the juice into a handful of sugar and used the resulting mixture to do a deep peeling of legs and arms, elbows and heels. She washed her hair, she rinsed it repeatedly, and when she finally got out, the water was scummy with dirt.

"Your turn," she said to Matthew, but he seemed reluctant to undress. The bath was refilled, and with a commanding gesture she told him to get out of his clothes – now. "Why didn't you tell me?" she asked, ignoring the twinge in her hip and knee when she knelt down to inspect the bruised and bleeding wound to his thigh.

"I didn't notice," he replied with a shrug, "not at first." A wooden spear of a sort, he said.

She prodded. There was something stuck beneath his skin, deeply embedded.

270

He inhaled.

Alex sat back on her heels with a sigh. "I hate having to do this. I absolutely abhor having to cut into you."

"That makes two of us. I don't much fancy it myself, to lie on my back while you dig into me only inches from my balls."

She insisted on washing him first, scrubbing all of him a bright pink before motioning for him to lie down, calling for Klaas to come and help. Matthew was pale by the time she was done, the borrowed shirt clinging to his chest and arms. Klaas gave Alex an admiring look, helped Matthew to sit, and set a glass of whisky in his shaking hand.

"Thank you," Matthew said, and downed it all in one gulp. He managed to smile at Alex, nodding when Klaas suggested he might want to lie down. With a grunt, Matthew got to his feet, leaning heavily on Klaas as he made for the stairs and the promised bed.

"I'll be right up," she promised. "I'll just clean myself up a bit first."

Matthew was naked under the fluttering mosquito netting, and in the dusk of the closed shutters, he looked very vulnerable. He slept heavily, so heavily that he didn't wake when she rolled towards him to pillow her head on his chest. He just grunted and draped his arm along her back. He made a very dissatisfied sound when her thigh nudged his bandaged leg, a sliver of green showing beneath his eyelashes before he sank back into his dreams.

Alex shifted closer towards him, not caring that it was too hot to have his skin this close to hers. Dead tired and she couldn't sleep. Restless and needy, she pressed herself even closer, a slight undulating movement to her hips. She stroked his chest, his stomach. She rose on her elbow to properly see him, and bent her head to kiss his nose, his cheek, the corner of his mouth. He didn't wake; he didn't even stir. Alex dipped her head to his neck and inhaled, absorbing his scent, of man, of soap, of burbling, ice-cold water.

With her tongue, she traced the outline of his mouth, and his lips twitched in response. She flexed her hips, somewhat more demanding, because she wanted him, God, how she wanted him, how else to fill this throbbing void inside of her? Her hand drifted lower to where his pubic hair was beginning to sprout and softly touched his sex. He slept on, but his legs widened under her touch. The skin on his scrotum shifted and tightened, his cock stiffened, and Matthew opened one eye to look at her, somewhere midway between arousal and irritation.

"I'm injured," he remonstrated in a cracked voice. "Recently operated on."

"I can't sleep. I need you," she said, dropping a light kiss on his mouth.

"Do you now?" His hand sank into her hair to hold her still as he kissed her back. A long kiss — a kiss that began as a whisper and ended in surging heat, his tongue, his lips, claiming hers, moulding her mouth to his. She broke away with a gasp.

"We could have died," she said, and her arousal was tinged with fear, with relief that they were still here.

"But we didn't." He kissed her again. A hot kiss, a rough kiss, that left her lips somewhat bruised.

"No, we didn't. We whipped their arses," she said, making him laugh.

"Aye, that we did." He gripped her backside and lifted her closer, urging her on top. Carefully, she settled herself on him so as not to jar his bandaged leg. His hands came up to cup her breasts, and she moved rhythmically up and down, impaling herself on him over and over again. His hands drifted down to her waist, and he was demanding and urgent in his hold. Alex followed his lead, riding him at an increased pace until he came, a guttural "nnngh" exploding from his lips.

"A very good bed," he said drowsily as he settled himself afterwards, his long body lying like a protective shell around her. "It didn't creak, not once."

Chapter 32

Charlie woke after several consecutive days of dream-ridden sleep, and for an instant he was convinced he was dead, and that somehow the Lord had seen him for a good man and welcomed him to heaven instead of banishing him to hell.

He fingered the sheet with its broad band of Brussels lace and studied the heavy wood of the bedposts. Just beside the bed, there was a little table that held ewer and basin, and hanging on the opposite whitewashed wall was a small painting, a Dutch still life.

He sank back onto his pillow. It had all been a terrible dream, all of it, from the moment he boarded the ship at Antwerp to the confusing images he had of a fight in the darkness of a jungle night. This was Holland, and soon Cornelia would call up to him that breakfast was ready and that the young gentleman had visitors waiting for him in the parlour.

He rolled over to stretch and muffled a gasp when his weight pressed his lacerated back against the sheets. He perused his surroundings again. No, this wasn't Holland. For a start, it was far too warm, and through the window he could see a pawpaw tree. He squinted down his body to where his feet stuck up, each ankle neatly wrapped in linen bandages. God's truth! All of it had happened. Every single detail of what he hoped had been a nightmare had actually been done to him. Charlie wanted to die. His bladder wanted to pee, and with a groan he rolled out of bed, making for the chamber pot.

He pissed, shook himself, and took a deep breath before pulling off his shirt. He stared at his skin. He was covered in a patchwork of bruises, of gashes and half-healed wounds.

"There's not very much we can do about those," someone

273

said from behind him, making Charlie whirl so fast he nearly fainted. He hadn't heard her come in, immersed in his inspection of the two letters that decorated his chest. "The rest of you is healing well enough," she continued.

He grabbed for his shirt, hastily covering himself, and regarded her warily. He thought he might have met her before, but who was this woman who had the temerity to enter unannounced into his room?

She set down the tray she was carrying and smiled. "I'm Alex Graham, your aunt by marriage."

"Oh." Charlie's attention was distracted by the smell of hot food from the tray. Eggs… Milk toast with cinnamon, even some fried ham. His stomach gurgled with joy.

"Slowly," Alex said when he threw himself at the food.

Charlie didn't listen. He had to eat as much as he could. You never knew, did you, if there'd be food tomorrow.

"He's still a condemned man," Klaas said to Matthew. The two men had taken a morning walk around the harbour with Matthew attempting to find berths back home.

"Aye, and legally bound to live out his life like a slave."

"And if we're going to be precise, those years are to be lived out here, in Barbados." Klaas did his lip thing again, pulling at it before releasing it. "Some would argue it's my duty to stop you from taking him off the island – or at least inform the Governor."

"Aye, although at present getting off the island seems a difficult venture." Matthew regarded the anchored ships with irritation. None of them had destination Virginia or Maryland. This was the third day running he had limped down to make inquiries, all of him itching with the need to get back home – and place a safe distance between himself and Sassafras Brown.

"He's too well respected," Klaas had sighed when Matthew had voiced his intent to accuse the planter for attempted murder. "And how will you be able to prove anything against him? Your wife's word carries no clout, and as to your nephew…well, best he not speak at all, I think."

And no matter how frustrated this made him, Matthew had to concede Klaas was right: his word would count for nothing here.

Alex came to meet them when they entered the house. "He's awake and lucid. Unfortunately."

"Unfortunately?" Matthew said.

"It all came back to him, I think." Alex bit her lip, brows pulled together in a worried frown. "He keeps on fingering the brands."

"Ah." Matthew looked away, stopping himself from scratching at the brand on his buttock. Alex rested a hand on his arm.

"Yours is healed and small. His are huge and infected, what with his constant picking at them."

Matthew glanced down at her, met a concerned, bright blue look. "Aye," he said, forcing himself to smile. "Mine is nothing but a faded memory." Not true, not at all true, and from the way she raised her brows, his wife didn't quite believe him. "I'll go and talk to the lad." With a swift kiss, he left her in the dark hallway.

Charlie was standing at the window when Matthew entered, large hands gripping the sill as support. All bones, Matthew sighed, thinking it would be a small matter to count each bone in Charlie's tall frame. His nephew gave him a careful smile.

"Better, then?" Matthew said.

"Alive at least, and strong enough to travel." A hungry look flashed over Charlie's face. "When can we leave this accursed place?"

"Well…" Matthew explained the situation in a couple of sentences.

"I'm still a slave?" Charlie sat down on the bed, stupefied.

"An indenture, not a slave," Matthew hastened to clarify, "but you could still hang should you return to England."

Charlie's hand went to his neck. "I saw my best friend hang, there in Taunton," he said in a small voice. "The judge, Jeffreys his name was, well, he made sure the poor unfortunates saw all the implements before they were led up to the noose." Charlie sucked in air. "They hanged him, cut him down alive, and…" Violent tremors rippled through him, his nostrils dilated. "They…" He wet his lips. "…he lived, they made sure he lived while they…" He covered his crotch with his hands. "They cut it off," he whispered, "his member. And then…"

"Shush, lad. It does you no good to remember such, does it?" Matthew interrupted.

Charlie laughed, a raspy, coughing sound. "I can't forget."

"With time, it fades." Matthew clasped the bony shoulder for a brief moment. "Stay away from England, at least for two or three years."

"We were twelve that went to Mr Brown," Charlie told Alex next morning, sitting very still while she washed the nasty wound on the inside of his foot.

"Twelve?" Alex looked up at him. "There were only four of you when we got there."

Charlie jerked at the stinging sensation when she applied the garlic poultice. "The other eight died in the first month." He couldn't even recall their names – had he even know their names? One had been young, younger than himself, and he thought he might have been named Jack, but the others were just anonymous blurs, weaklings he had stolen food from whenever he could. His gut tightened in shame – but what was he supposed to do?

"George…" He gave her a guarded look to see if she reacted to the name, but all he could see was the top of her head, her hands busy bandaging the blistered rings around his ankles. "George said that was always the case, how most died within a few weeks, and the few who remained on their feet after that could survive at least for some years."

"That must have been comforting." Alex used the bedpost to lever herself upright. For some moments, she rubbed at her hip, her lower back, muttering something about being too old for all this.

"Not really." He took off his shirt and rolled over on his

belly, gritting his teeth at the discomfort it was to lie naked under her eyes. She covered his arse with a towel, and he relaxed. Her hands busied themselves with his back, and the whole room smelled of lavender and lemon balm.

"So who was George? The overseer?"

"The overseer? I don't know what his name was. No, George was one of the slaves." Charlie closed his eyes, and he could see himself grovelling like a dog at the big man's feet, the lowest of the low, a slave to a slave.

"Oh." Alex drew the thin sheet up over his shoulders. "Stay like that for some time. Take a nap or something, okay?"

"Okay," he mumbled, half asleep. It made him smile, that expression – it reminded him of Jacob.

The next time he saw Matthew, Charlie asked him what Jacob might be doing. Was he still in the colonies or had he moved back to London?

His uncle studied his hands. "Jacob's dead."

"He's dead?" Charlie blinked. Not Jacob, not his tall, strong cousin.

"Aye. He was shot well over a year ago. He…well… we had a spot of trouble with a band of renegades, and Jacob took it badly when they abducted his sister and so…" Matthew hitched a shoulder and exhaled.

"But he…" Charlie counted in his head, "he was not yet two and twenty."

"Youth in itself is no protection against death, is it?"

Charlie agreed. If his uncle hadn't come to find him… He was flooded by a wave of gratitude, and shifted closer to Matthew on the bench they were sharing.

"Why?" he asked.

"Hmm?"

"Why did you come to find me?"

"Well, I didn't do it on account of the love between me and my brother," Matthew said with an edge. He lifted his face to the sky, sitting with his eyes closed. His thick lashes glistened with moisture, and with a start Charlie realised his uncle was weeping.

"I did it for Jacob. I did it because he would have wanted me to. He loved you." Abruptly, Matthew stood and walked off.

Klaas was becoming something of a burr, Alex reflected, but smiled all the same as her host popped up from behind a rose bush, clearly delighted to see her. She had hoped for some hours alone in the cool dusk, but she couldn't very well berate the man for enjoying his own garden.

Matthew she had left inside, struggling over the letter he had decided to write to Luke, and his mood had been so frayed by the time she made her fourth suggestion that she had decided it was best he was left alone to his creative endeavours.

"Charlie can write," she had suggested as she left the room.

"Nay, he can't. Haven't you seen his finger?"

"His finger?" Mentally, Alex rushed through the various wounds and cuts and scrapes she had seen on Charlie's body. She couldn't remember anything wrong with his hands.

"They broke one of them," Matthew had informed her, and scowled at the as yet blank piece of paper before shooing her out to leave him alone.

"Still no boats?" she asked when Klaas came over to sit beside her.

"No, but they'll come."

"I'm in a bit of a hurry. I have a baby to deliver." She hoped their family had received the letter they had sent from Jamaica, and wondered how they were all coping without them. Probably very well: both Ian and Mark were grown men with competent wives.

Klaas gave her a surprised look, and allowed his eyes to wander down to her waist.

"Not mine! My son's."

"Ah." Klaas nodded, still staring at her — eyes drifting from her face to her breast, from her chest to her legs, back to her breasts.

"You're gawking," Alex said, amused by the wave of

red that flew up Klaas' face. She nodded in the direction of where Matthew was coming towards them. "And he's a very jealous man."

Klaas was suddenly on his feet, and with an apologetic little bow said something about having to review his ledgers before taking off up the path.

"That man looks at you as if you were a bone and he a dog," Matthew remarked when he sat down in the spot Klaas had vacated.

"Mmm?" Alex said.

"You know exactly what I mean." Matthew followed the harbourmaster out of sight before extending the paper he held in his hand to her.

> Brother;
> I have found him. As I write, Charlie sleeps in a room close by and he is nowt but a bag of bones, but alive. I dare say he will carry the ghosts of his ordeal with him to his dying days – something I am in a better position to fully comprehend than you – but hopefully he will heal, even if it takes years.

"Is it too harsh?" Matthew asked.

"Harsh? You're just telling the truth." She went on with her reading, scanning the brief description of their travels and adventures before they found Charlie, and dropped her eyes to the last paragraphs.

> Don't ever think I set out on this quest on your behalf. Nor did I do it for your son, my nephew, who to me bears an uncanny resemblance to his sire. I did this on account of Jacob, my lad, who spoke always warmly of you and your son. He would have rushed to the aid of his cousin, and seeing as Jacob is dead, I went in his stead. Had it not been for him, I wouldn't have found it in me to help you, for no matter how I have tried, I haven't forgiven you for the iniquities you put me through.
> Seeing Charlie a destroyed man brought it all back:

the constant hunger, the humiliation, the slow destruction
of my inner core, and the rage that surges through me
even today threatens at times to eat me alive. That is
perhaps the greatest of the wrongs you've done to me.
I live constantly in the shades of that long ago, unable
to forget, and therefore to forgive. It diminishes me as a
man. It leaves my soul corroded, and all because of you.

Alex folded the paper together with shaking hands. "Is that the way it is? Do you live in constant shadow of the long ago?" She felt strangely insufficient.

"Nay," Matthew said with a crooked smile. "But, now and then, the darkness still rises inside of me."

"And you never tell me," she said, terribly hurt.

"No, I handle it on my own." His hand came down to grasp hers. "It soils me, and I don't want you soiled as well." He raised her hand to his mouth, and kissed her palm. "I need you to be my beacon of light when my fire flickers and fails. I can't have you tarred with the pitch that at times wells inside of me."

She rested her head against his chest, listening to the reassuring sound of his heart and his breathing. "It was so very long ago, Matthew, a lifetime ago. Isn't it time to just let it all go?"

"I can't, and these last few weeks... Don't you realise this is how my dear brother wanted me to live out my last years? In chains and constant despair, far from you and my home?"

Alex dragged her face back and forth across the cotton of his borrowed shirt. "But you didn't."

He tightened his arm around her. "Nay, I didn't, on account of having a most miraculous wife who came and found me."

"Best decision of my life," she said, kissing him softly on the cheek.

"Brown is in town," Klaas said some days later, stuffing his pipe with slow, measured movements. They were sitting outside, savouring the cool evening breeze.

"Och aye?" Matthew straightened out of his slouch.

Klaas lit a taper from the lantern and sucked with concentration until the tobacco began to glow before sitting back with a soft grunt.

"Whatever for?" Alex asked.

Klaas blew some smoke her way. "Business, I imagine. And he'll be coming here, I think, to ask for Marijke's hand."

"Oh," Alex said, thinking that should she ever see the planter again, she'd be seriously tempted to ram a poker up his arse.

Klaas sighed noisily. "I'm not looking forward to it. He'll not take it well when I refuse him, and Brown..." he cleared his throat, "...well, he makes a most uncomfortable enemy."

"So do I," Matthew said quietly.

They didn't say anything for a while, the only sound Klaas' sucking at his pipe.

Matthew rose. "I'd best see to my weapons." Without waiting for Alex, he strode inside.

Chapter 33

"Calumny!" Mr Brown insisted, "She's a viper, that woman, pure venom drips off her tongue with every word she utters."

"A what?" Matthew wasn't about to allow this preening peacock of a man to insult his wife, and stepped up close, glad of his inordinate height that had him looming over Brown.

"You heard! A gossipmonger, a scold, a…" Brown seemed to choke on his anger; his fine brown eyes flamed when he looked at Alex who just looked back. "Ingrate, to partake of my bountiful generosity for days on end, and then to repay by spreading unsubstantiated stories of my abuse." He laughed jarringly, and shook his scented dark curls.

"As I recall it, your hospitality was more or less forced on us," Alex said. "It was your hare-brained idea to play chess with Matthew for Charlie's release."

"Release?" Brown spluttered. "How release? The man is convicted of treason! Are you now saying you intend to set him free?" He turned to one of his companions, making an agitated motion of his head. "No respect for the king's justice, and now they will set a rebel loose!"

"I bought him off you," Matthew said, "and you knew all the while that he's my nephew."

The elder of the two men accompanying Mr Brown fixed pale eyes on Matthew. "Your nephew?"

"Aye," Matthew replied.

"And is it then your intent, sir, to set him free?"

"Nay, of course not. I aim to put him to work like a beast in my fields, abused and mistreated as he was here."

Mr Brown flushed a bright red. "A slave – he's to live out his life as a slave." He pointed at Charlie who was doing his best to remain invisible – difficult for someone as tall and as fiery of hair as he was. "And look at him! In shirt and coat as if he were a gentleman, and no longer in chains!"

"Hmm," the elder companion said, frowning. "I'm afraid I must insist he is shackled. That is the way the sentence was laid out." He motioned to the younger man. "Take him to the smith, and have him fitted into chains."

Charlie mewled, pressed himself flat against the wall.

"No," Matthew said, blocking any access to his nephew.

"No?" The elder man gave him an incredulous look. "That is not for you to say."

"I say it all the same. No." He stared the other man down, and turned to nail his gaze into Mr Brown. "Did you tell them that you sent men after us to kill us?"

"I did no such thing!" Mr Brown protested, but his eyes flew all over the place, giving lie to his statement.

"Mr Brown!" the elder man gasped, and Matthew nodded.

"Seven, they were," Matthew said, addressing Brown's companions. "Twice they came, and yet they didn't succeed."

"He's lying," Mr Brown insisted. "Really, gentlemen, how can you even listen to him? You know me well enough to know I don't condone violence – at least, not among free men." His younger companion snickered, a glance flying between him and Brown.

"And yet that's what happened," Matthew said, "and I dare say your overseer is still in a bad way. I recall slicing up most of his side." As if by chance, his hand came down to rest on his sword.

Mr Brown found the moment opportune to leave, throwing over his shoulders that the Governor would be informed, and what would Matthew Graham do when they came to chain his nephew? "And forget about him leaving the island," he added with a sneer. "The Governor won't allow it."

Matthew sank down to sit beside Charlie who was still shaking with fear.

"It'll be alright," he said, even if at present he couldn't envision quite how they'd get out of this corner. Mayhap they could dump Charlie into a barrel and smuggle him aboard a ship? "Can you swim?"

"No." Charlie wound long arms round long legs, and hid his face against his knees. "They'll come for me, and not even you, Uncle, will be able to stop them." Matthew didn't reply, sharing a helpless look with Alex over Charlie's bent head.

The Governor sent Matthew a curt note, informing him that Charles Graham had been sentenced to death and had his sentence commuted to a life of servitude, in chains, on Barbados.

"I will not countenance the man to be carried off the island, thereby subverting the course of justice, and he will, no matter that he is now under your ownership, be fitted with chains within the week."

Matthew crumpled the paper and sent it sailing into the hearth. "Damn Sassafras Brown! Now what do I do?"

Klaas plopped his lip a couple of times before giving a dejected shake of his head. "Mr Brown stands high in the confidence of the Governor, no doubt helped along by the fact that the Governor is severely in Mr Brown's debt."

"He is?" Alex asked, looking up from where she was mending one of Matthew's shirts.

"A betting man, the Governor, and as you yourself have cause to know, Mr Brown is an adept player, not only at chess but also at dice in general." Klaas sucked at his pipe. "A boat, a swift boat. You must pray for one to come in within the coming days."

"Apparently you have a hotline to God," Alex said to Matthew two mornings later.

"Hotline?" Matthew asked, his eyes stuck on the welcome sight of the *Althea* entering the Bridgetown harbour.

"You know, you call, He listens." Alex smiled.

Matthew gave her a displeased look. "Such levity isn't appropriate when talking about God."

Alex shrugged. "Let's just say that you've been praying much more than I have these last two nights."

"Aye, that I have." He draped an arm around her shoulders, and gave her a little squeeze. "But you, my little heathen, you don't do much praying."

284

"Yes, I do, but mostly in silence and without any fixed form."

Matthew kissed her cheek. "Plenty of time for us to study the Bible together on our way home," he promised, laughing at the way her face squished together at the thought.

Captain Jan listened to the whole sorry tale, eyed Charlie with some compassion, and assured them that he would do what he could to help. "But I have cargo to take on, and that will take some days."

"Some days?" Matthew said. "How many days?"

"Three?" Captain Jan replied with a shrug. "We sail on Saturday."

"Three!" Matthew's eyes flew to Charlie. The Governor was sending men around on Thursday to ensure the dangerous rebel was once again appropriately shackled.

Captain Jan made an unconcerned sound. "A day or two in chains has never killed a man. And once on board, we'll get them off him."

Charlie stood up and left the room, his large fist crashing into the wall.

Next morning, a pale Charlie followed Matthew to the local smith, his eyes glazing over as his ankles were once again fitted with fetters. It was a long walk back to the harbourmaster's house, with Matthew having to shorten his stride substantially to pace himself to Charlie's careful shuffling. His nephew was in pain: the unhealed skin around his ankles had broken open, blood staining the linen bandages. Men and women stopped to study his progress, suppressed giggles and whispered comments following in Charlie's wake. Halfway back stood Brown himself, arms crossed over his chest and a smirk on his face.

"Ignore him," Matthew said to Charlie in a low voice. "Don't look at him, just keep on moving." And Charlie did, a slow walk that left him covered in sweat by the time they made it back to the relative safety of Klaas' home.

Captain Jan joined them for supper that same evening. Once the table had been cleared, Klaas ushered his male guests into his little study, making Matthew bite back a little smile at the offended look on Alex's face. Well, that was how things were mostly ordained, he tried to convey with a little shrug. In reply, he got a loud snort.

"We'll be done loading late tomorrow," Captain Jan said, "and I suggest we bring you aboard that night and set sail immediately." He held out his pewter cup for a refill, and said something in Dutch to Klaas who replied with a biting edge.

"What?" Matthew asked.

"I was just pointing out that the Governor is no fool," Captain Jan said, "and so we must be discreet."

"We'll use the jetty at the bottom of my garden," Klaas suggested. "We'll have to pole the boat for some yards, but at least we're not in open view."

On Friday evening, they stood on the jetty and waited, all three of them straining towards the regular sound of oars coming towards them. They had said their farewells well over an hour before, and now Klaas was standing some feet away, a blinded lantern in his hand to guide the boat in. He muttered in irritation.

"The tide is beginning to turn," he whispered. "Why did it take them so long?" He exhaled when the prow of the boat became visible, blinked once, twice, and raised the lantern in surprise.

"The dog?" he said. "Why has he brought his dog?"

"Probably because Charlie can't swim." Alex gave the Dutchman a hug and kissed him on both cheeks. "Thank you," she whispered, and stepped into the boat.

Charlie was helped to sit, and Matthew was last, using his legs to shove the boat off before leaping aboard, making the whole little boat careen disconcertingly.

"Show-off," Alex muttered, her knuckles cramping on the thwart. Matthew's teeth shone white in the night.

They had all begun to relax when they were hailed loudly from the side. Two boats floated out of the gloom in their direction. Captain Jan cursed viciously and told his rowers to hold, snapping his fingers to Othello. The dog lumbered to his feet, and once again the little boat tilted. Charlie squeaked and grabbed on to Alex who sat closest. Sassafras Brown held a lantern aloft, and grinned.

"Oh dear, oh dear," he said. "What have we here?" Anything else he had planned to say was lost when Othello at a whispered command from his master jumped, flying like a hairy, extremely heavy bullet towards the surprised Mr Brown. Othello landed on the starboard planking, and his additional hundred-odd pounds overturned the boat, and suddenly the dark was filled with frightened voices and the frantic thrashing of men in the water. Unfortunately, their own boat was rocked as well, and with an oath Alex fell overboard, dragging a hapless Charlie with her.

She broke the surface, spitting like a drowning cat. "Charlie?" Oh my God! With his chains, he must have sunk like a stone, and now he was dead, and it was all her fault. She dived, trying to peer into the gloom. No Charlie. "Charlie?" she gargled, before diving yet again.

"Here, Alex," Matthew called from several yards away. "We have him here."

She heard him say something soothing to Charlie, and swam on the spot, trying to get her bearings. There, she could make out the longboat thirty yards or so from her, with Captain Jan at its prow, lantern held high. Her skirts dragged at her legs as she began to swim. Halfway there, something else got hold of her, and with a surprised little 'eh' she was pulled underwater.

"Alex?" Matthew swam in circles. "Alex, where are you? Alex?" Where was the woman? Matthew did a frantic full turn, trying to see anything, something in the dark. To his far left, he could still hear the men from the overturned boat, but Alex seemed swallowed by the sea.

"We have to go," Captain Jan hissed.

"I can't!" Matthew said. "I can't leave Alex."

"She might be dead," the captain said. "She may have drowned."

"Not Alex." Matthew filled his lungs and yelled. "Alex! Where are you?"

In the far distance, he heard a muffled reply, cut abruptly short.

"He's taken her," Matthew gasped. "Goddamn that worm of a man, he's taken my wife!"

Chapter 34

It had taken Alex at most a second to understand who it was that had pushed her underwater. Up she came, gasped for air, and before she could scream or fight, she was submerged again, dragged towards the far-off shore. Brown was a strong swimmer. Actually, he was a bloody strong man, as Alex realised when she tried repeatedly to kick herself free from him out there in the water. At one point, she thought she heard Matthew call her name, and she filled her lungs and yelled for him, tried to do so again but had her head brutally pushed into the sea.

Now they were almost on land, Brown wading through the shallows with Alex spluttering behind him.

"Let go of me!" Alex yanked, succeeded in freeing one of her hands, and dealt Brown a hard punch to the side of his head. The planter grunted, grabbed at her flailing hand and when she kept on struggling, hit her back, punching her so hard in the gut she collapsed to the ground, all air knocked out of her. He tore at her shawl, used it to tie her hands together and heaved her back to her feet.

"Walk," he said. No way. Alex had no intention of making this easy for him, shrieking like a cornered rat when he dragged her over the pebbled beach in the direction of one of the warehouses. "I told you to walk," he hissed, slapping her in the face.

In reply, Alex rose on her toes, kneed him so hard in his crotch he stumbled back, and for a few seconds, Alex was free, running hell for leather in the general direction of Klaas' house.

Brown brought her down roughly. Pebbles and grit scraped her skin, she had sand in her mouth and her nose, and her jaw ached with the impact. He rolled her over, his knife in one hand. "Now, Mrs Graham, no more of this. Either you walk, or I cut your throat, here and now."

Alex swallowed, was back on her feet, and walked meekly in front of him, the tip of his knife an uncomfortable, constant prickle in her nape.

He pushed her inside one of the warehouses, lit a lantern, and studied her for a couple of minutes. He sauntered close, and she spat him in the face, making him laugh.

"Should I want to, I would," he said, "but you're not much to look at in your present state, are you, Mrs Graham?" He reached out to tweak at her breast. She reared back so quickly she overbalanced and crashed into the wall behind her.

"Nor are you," she snapped back, "and once I get out of here, I'll—"

"Get out of here? What makes you think you ever will?" Mr Brown kicked at one of the solid walls, jerked his head at the barred window. "No. Mrs Graham, this is where you die. Tonight, I'd wager, and as we both know, I'm an accomplished gambler. Frightened?" he jeered.

Alex just shook her head.

"Oh yes, you are, but that's what you get when you meddle in affairs you should best leave alone."

"I have no idea what you're talking about," she said stiffly.

"Marijke Hendrijks — she was supposed to be mine, she was meant to be mine, and then you ruined it all, you witch." He straightened up, looked down at her. "Have you got any idea how rich she is? And now it all slips through my fingers, all on account of you and your slanderous mouth."

In the weak light from the moon outside, she couldn't make out more than the general shape of him — that and his eyes, gleaming wetly. She took a deep breath, crouched and launched herself at him, tied hands held like a battering ram before her. She took him unawares, and sent him flying to land against the opposite wall. She kicked him, heard him grunt before collapsing on the floor.

Her hands...she had to get her hands free. She used her

teeth to worry at the knot, felt the material give. There! One hand free, the other, and she rushed for the door. He'd bolted it upon their entrance, and she couldn't budge the damn thing, no matter that she tore at it with both hands.

"Think! Think, think!" Right, she needed some kind of tool, looked about desperately in the dark. A stool, a piece of sacking, some rope...nothing she could use as a crowbar, and Brown was groaning, already moving.

"Shit!" She grabbed yet again at the bolt, tugged, and it gave a half-inch. "Yes!" Another tug, another half-inch. She threw a worried look in the direction of Brown. He wasn't there. She ducked, forewarned by the rush of air, and the stool crashed into the door. Alex yelped, darted away from the planter who swung for her, roaring that she was going to pay, he was going to punch her, kick her, and then, well then, he'd tie her up and set the warehouse on fire, and how would she like that?

"Uhhh!" The stool caught her on her right shoulder, but she was still standing, still capable of moving. Brown was forcing her into a corner, laughing as she attempted to break free. She was getting tired. All of her hurt, and her right arm hung useless. Alex backed away, trying to find enough space to use her martial arts skills, but the shed was too small, there were uprights everywhere, and she stumbled over discarded sacks, over broken crates. Instead, Alex opened her mouth and screamed for her husband.

"No one will hear you," Brown sneered, lunged and pinned her down.

"No!" she shrieked when he dragged her towards one of the supporting uprights. "No!" she gasped when he clapped her over the head, bringing her to her knees. Her hands – he tied them to the upright, laughing at how she struggled to free herself.

"Apt, Mrs Graham, you'll burn, like the accursed witch you are." She shook her head: she was no witch. That just made him laugh, his mouth an inch or so from her. "Not so cocky now, hey?" he said, and his hand did whatever exploring it wanted to do, no matter that Alex twisted like an eel. "Too old," he said, pinching her hard. "Well, time is flying, so best get our little bonfire started." He giggled, looking about the little space. "It will go up like a torch, I think."

"Please," she said, "please…" She yanked, she pulled, and her wrists protested at the pain. The shawl ripped, but Brown had used twine as well this time, and her tugging only resulted in the thin rope sinking into her rapidly swelling hands.

Brown ignored her, humming to himself as he concentrated on lighting a couple of lanterns. It took him an awful long time to do so, and all the time, Alex screamed. At the top of her voice, she called for help, for Matthew, for anyone. So hoarse, so dry – her voice barely carried at times.

"There," Brown said, satisfied with his lighting. "And now…" He placed one of the lanterns on the rickety stool, nudging it until it slid to stand precariously on the edge. "Oh dear, I wonder how long it will take for it to fall over."

"No," Alex groaned, unable to tear her eyes away from where he was arranging rubbish in a neat pile below the stool.

"Very nice," he said before reclining one of the lanterns against the back wall. "The wood is quite dry," he said over his shoulder. "Look, it's already beginning to smoulder." Once again, that high-pitched giggle.

"Help! Oh God, please help me!" She renewed her efforts, tugging wildly at her ties.

"I don't think He'll hear you," he snickered, making for the door.

"No," she shrieked, one long panicked note that reverberated in the enclosed space.

Mr Brown stopped in the doorway and swept her a bow. "A pleasure, Mrs Graham, but now, I fear, I must go." With that, he sent the lantern still in his hand sailing through the air, and disappeared.

"There!" Matthew froze. "That's Alex." Except that he'd never heard his wife scream like this before.

"She's in one of the warehouses," Captain Jan said, pointing to where faint light leaked out from a small window. Yet another scream, a loud anguished 'Matthew', a high-pitched repeated 'please'.

Matthew set off at a run, with the captain and the dog at his side. He saw a shape emerge from the warehouse, heard Alex scream, heard the door slam closed. Matthew didn't quite understand why Alex was screaming as she was, unless there was more than one man. Smoke – why could he smell smoke? He heard Jan gasp beside him, the younger man rushing off in a sprint with the dog at his heels.

Sweetest Lord! Matthew increased his speed, forcing himself to fly over the rocky ground, despite his bandaged thigh. The shed was alight. Alex shrieked, calling for him, a high wailing that tore at him, made him sob with fear as he ran. Captain Jan was at the door, struggling to lift the crossbar.

"Help me," Jan gasped, and together they lifted it off. The door was hot to the touch, part of it was on fire, and, God, where was Alex? Jan kicked the door open. Smoke welled, thick and black. Fire was everywhere, tongues of bright light that danced all over the further wall, the ceiling. Matthew rushed inside, making for the terrified, gibbering woman that was his wife, tied to one of the posts.

Jan cut through her bindings, the ceiling behind her gave, and burning spars fell all around them. Together, they dragged her towards the door, a distance of two or three yards no more, that seemed interminable, the warehouse crackling with fire, the smoke making it near on impossible to breathe.

"Hurry!" Jan gasped, and just as they reached the doorway, it began to fold, half of the doorframe on fire. The dog barked, whined, barked. Jan and Matthew staggered outside, with Alex hanging in their combined arms.

"It's alright," Matthew crooned. "You're safe, Alex."

She breathed in heavy, rasping gulps; she coughed and retched, coughed and coughed. Remarkably unscathed, Matthew concluded after a swift inspection: no broken limbs, no major burns – at least, not that he could see.

"We have to go," the captain said. "That Brown will raise the alarm, and I have to get the *Althea* out of here before the Governor gets his boats into the water – or, even worse, trains the cannon of the fort on us."

"And how do we get out there?" Matthew estimated the distance to a furlong, no more, and had Alex been her normal self, he'd have suggested they swim. But now… he steadied her to stand, and all she did was drag in one wheezing breath after the other.

"We steal a boat," the captain said. "Here, let me help you."

"I can walk," Alex croaked. "Of course I can."

"Are you sure?" Matthew asked.

In reply, she just nodded, stumbling after Captain Jan.

In less than five minutes, they were making their way across the harbour towards the *Althea*.

"Charlie?" Alex asked.

"On board, I hope," the captain said, eyes on the distant shoreline. "Torches. We'd best pick up pace." He threw himself into his oars; Matthew did the same.

"He was going to burn me to death." Alex couldn't help it: her hold on Othello tightened, her face buried in his warm, wet fur.

"Well, he didn't, did he?" Captain Jan gasped between his rowing.

"No thanks to him," Alex muttered. "I hope he dies a horrible, painful death, preferably with his cock in his mouth."

"Alex!" Matthew said.

"Well, I do! Men like him deserve to." It helped to get angry. Ranting at Sassafras Brown made it possible to shove away the events of the last hour or so, eternal minutes when she'd been sure she would die, roasted like a trussed chicken.

Only once they were on board did Matthew have an opportunity to take in the full damage done to her. His mouth tightened into a long, displeased line.

"He hit you?" Matthew asked.

"Only a couple of times. He was too excited about the prospect of lighting his little bonfire." She shuddered at that, just had to crawl into his arms, a few minutes of gulping in his reassuring scent, of assuring herself she was still here, with him, not a burning corpse in the little warehouse that at present stood like a beacon against the black of the night.

He rested his head against hers, stood silent, and held her.

"I…" Alex snuck her hands in under his damp shirt, had to touch his warm skin.

"I know," he whispered into her hair, tightening his hold on her.

She fidgeted in his embrace, and he released his hold. Her shoulder was too tender, her face was a collection of swellings and scrapes, even if nothing seemed to be seriously damaged. She lifted her shoulder up and down a couple of times, and gave him a shaky smile.

"No big deal. All I need is a good night's sleep. A bath would be nice, but that's not on the cards, is it?"

"I think not." Matthew stroked her cheek. Around them, the ship creaked into life, and Alex took his hand, making for the railings.

"At last," Matthew said. Behind them, Barbados was nothing more than a large, dark lump against a slightly lighter sea, and above them the sky spread itself in an endless field of stars. The night was warm, so warm that Alex was glad her clothes were wet, and by the mast Charlie was sitting half asleep, long spindly legs stretched out before him.

Matthew went to help with the sails, and Alex remained by the railings, watching Barbados drop out of sight. The swells increased, the *Althea* dipped and rose, and Alex felt the contents of her belly come surging up her throat.

"Bloody hell, what is it with boats and me?" She leaned over the railing and retched.

"Mint helps," a young voice informed her, and Alex turned to look at her son turned experienced sailor.

"No, it doesn't. At least it doesn't work on me."

David came to stand very close, eyes scanning her face. His mouth set in a line as displeased as his father's, and he gave her an awkward hug. "Are you alright then?" he asked, handing her a bucket.

"Yes, I am." A new wave of bile and vomit flew up her throat. "All things being relative, of course."

David laughed. "I must go. I'm on the nightwatch."

"Good, please make sure the damned boat stops bucking about."

"Bucking about?" David laughed again. "The sea is calm tonight, Mama."

"No, it isn't," Alex grumbled.

"You're an awful sailor," David said before scurrying off to where the first mate was calling for him.

Alex groaned, took a firm hold of a bucket, and crawled off to lie down somewhere out of the way. She should probably change her clothes, she yawned, but knew that she wouldn't, far too tired to even make the effort. She pillowed her head against a coil of rope, and stared up at the flying stars, winking like diamonds at her. She yawned again and fell asleep, one hand on the bucket, the other on the dog that had draped himself along her legs.

Matthew found her in the wee hours, and undid her hand from the bucket. He rinsed it out and replaced it, shooed the dog away, and, with a grunt, stretched out beside her, pulling her cloak over them both. His hand found its way inside her clothes to cup a warm and soft breast, and in her sleep Alex pressed her arse towards him. He chuckled in her nape, and kissed her just behind her ear.

"I think not," he whispered, "not on the open deck of a boat."

"Just hold me," she replied, and pressed herself even closer. So he did, rocking them gently back and forth, shrouded by her heavy cloak.

Chapter 35

Alex wasn't sure whether to laugh or cry when a bedraggled Carlos was dragged into the light early next morning. Carlos had no such compunction, his face breaking out into a smile of such sweetness it made Alex's breath hitch.

"How on earth—?" she began, and then threw a worried look at Captain Jan. "You know he's a Catholic priest, right?"

Captain Jan nodded, looking askance at Carlos. "It would be difficult to miss, and this one carries no hidden weapons under his cassock."

"But I thought—" Alex said.

"Oh, I was planning to," Captain Jan told her. "I had already thrown him in the water, but your son started bleating about this being a friend of the Graham family, and the stupid boy dived in after him and then—"

"—Othello jumped in after," Alex said. Now that she looked closer, Carlos bore clear signs of a recent beating. "You hit him?"

Captain Jan shrugged. "Not me, but yes, someone did." He leaned forward to touch Alex's bruised cheek. "Just as someone hit you."

"It's not too bad," Alex said, having given Carlos a brief recapitulation of the events last night.

"Not too bad? The man was going to murder you!"

"I know," she said, swept by a wave of remembered fear. Carlos gave her a careful hug, rearing back when she yelped. "My shoulder, it's a bit sore."

"As is your face, I imagine." Carlos' brows pulled together in a ferocious scowl. "Men like him should be hanged." He threw an angry look in the direction of the captain. "And so should he. That man's a pirate, a sea wolf."

"A privateer," Alex corrected.

"Nomenclature," Carlos snorted, "and your son is a pirate too."

"David? He's just a boy."

"Precisely," Carlos nodded, "and that's why they got close enough to board us."

Alex could feel her brows travel higher and higher up her sore forehead as Carlos told the story of how *Althea* had lain apparently deserted, a young boy crying piteously for help, because his shipmates were all dead or dying, and so the Spanish ship had nudged cautiously closer.

"And you didn't recognise him?" Alex asked.

"No. He was dirty and covered in what we presumed to be blood. But we weren't about to board her, not until we knew how the crew had sickened and died."

David had played out a credible act of vomiting and stomach clutching, moaning that his head hurt, it hurt to breathe and, God, how his armpits ached, and he had wept and asked them to please take him aboard because he was scared to sit here among his dead companions. "Our captain refused, but took the sloop in tow, and so we lumbered on, slowed considerably."

In the middle of the night, Captain Jan and his crew had used the towline to get themselves aboard the *Santa Teresa*, and come morning, the ship was under Captain Jan's control, with most of the Spanish sailors set adrift in boats.

"How set adrift?" Alex asked.

"Adrift," Carlos said, "several days of hard rowing from the closest island." The Spanish captain, two ladies travelling with the ship, and Carlos himself had been carried along to Curacao, where Captain Jan had deposited his three hostages, considered selling Carlos as a slave – "What?" Alex squeaked – but had thought better of it at David's pleading and taken Carlos along.

"What for?" Alex asked.

Carlos shrugged. He had no idea, but so far he had been kept hard at work in the galley.

"And you?" he asked. "What other adventures have you lived through since we last met?"

Alex looked at him for a long time, not knowing quite where to begin. "Well, for a start, we've met your cousin, Ángel."

"My cousin?" Carlos' mouth fell wide open. "Is he here?"

"Not anymore," Alex said, and settled down to tell him the full tale. "I'm sorry," she ended, "that he's dead."

Carlos gave her a quick look. "I'm sorry too."

"Oh." She gnawed her lip. Twice, she had indirectly robbed the priest of his relatives, and from the expression on his face he was grief-stricken. "I...well, I didn't have the impression you cared so much for him."

"Cared for him?" Carlos just looked at her. "Oh no, Alex, I didn't care for him at all. I'm just sorry that his passing should leave me so unperturbed." He tugged at his dirty cassock and gave her a wavering smile. "It makes me less of a priest, I fear, that I'm actually glad to hear he's dead." With a little bow, he excused himself, muttering something about needing to pray – it was the least he could do for his cousin.

"Why?" Matthew asked Captain Jan. "Why not just leave him in Curacao?"

"I'm not quite sure." Jan eyed the priest with obvious disfavour. "Your son begged me to take him along, and he might come in useful. If nothing else, I can use him as a distraction should I need it. I can always throw him in the water."

"If you do, my wife will dive after him – she is right fond of the wee man."

"Hmm," Captain Jan said.

"And so am I, for all that he's a papist and therefore eternally damned."

Captain Jan laughed. "You truly think God cares?"

"It used to be I thought that aye, He did. Now...well now, I don't know." Matthew rubbed a finger over his healing thigh. "At times, I think God looks down on us and sighs at our infinite capacity to kill and harm each other – all in His name."

"My mother's people were wiped out because of God, forced to baptism and a life in a *misión* well to the south of Cumaná, the men dying in the fields, the women taken over by the Spanish invaders." Captain Jan spat into the water, and gave Matthew a dark look. "A good God would not allow such things to happen. So I believe God is fickle and cruel, a despot who sets us out like pieces on a gigantic chessboard, and when He grows bored by the slowness of the game, He just upends it and watches as we drown or sink."

Matthew stared at him. "Nay, He wouldn't do that."

Captain Jan snorted. "I thought you were a Presbyterian. Isn't that in line with what you believe? That randomly God gives out grace to some and withholds it from the masses – and the few chosen for salvation are not in any way more deserving than the others, they were just in luck the day when God made up His mind."

"It isn't quite that simple," Matthew said.

"Of course not," Captain Jan agreed. "Nothing is ever simple about God." He smiled crookedly and with a little bow left Matthew on his own.

Captain Jan heard Alex out, and then he simply smiled and told her it would be best if she didn't meddle in matters not her concern, and he, as captain of this ship, would do as he pleased to earn his living.

"A pirate!" Alex said. "And you've made one of my son as well."

Captain Jan shrugged and with a rather steely voice reminded her that neither she nor her husband, and even less their unfortunate nephew, would be on their way from Barbados if it hadn't been for him.

"In fact," he said, "you might have been dead." Alex took a step back, and something in her face made the captain relent. "I'm very glad that isn't the case, but what I do with my ship is not for you to voice an opinion on." He moved off, and Alex decided to vent her anger on her son instead, cornering him by the bow.

"Mama," David tried, exaggerating a yawn, "I'm right tired."

"I don't give a shit."

"I didn't have a choice. The captain told me what to do, and you told me I was to obey him."

Alex was unimpressed. "You helped him steal a ship, and on top of that, God knows how many men died!"

"We didn't kill any," he protested. "Well, not that I saw."

"You left them to row across an empty sea!"

"I didn't. The captain did. And I did save the wee priest."

"Huh," Alex said, and decided it was time to check on Charlie again. "Come and meet your cousin."

David shone up, saying he had so many questions he wanted to ask this unknown relative about his adventures.

"No, you won't. I don't think he wants to talk about it." She studied Charlie, sitting by the mast, long legs crossed, eyes fixed vacantly on the horizon. When they got closer, she saw his ankles were oozing, a mixture of pus and blood and clear liquids that left runnels down his skin, and Alex bent down with a frown. "You've been tearing the scabs off again."

Charlie hitched a shoulder. "I don't do it consciously. I just pick at them." He studied the ring of irritated skin around his right ankle. "I'll always have the marks on me."

"They'll fade," Alex said – just as the marks around Matthew's wrists were now almost invisible unless you knew where to look.

"But they'll always be there," Charlie ran his thumb over the scabs. She could almost see how he shook himself free of these thoughts before smiling up at her son. "David, right?" he said, and patted the deck beside him.

David beamed and slid down beside him, and in no time at all, he was talking about this new exciting life of his aboard the *Althea*. Alex tousled his dark hair, and decided to go off in search of something to eat. A crisp apple, she thought, or a nice slice of cheese. Her stomach happily agreed, assuring her it would do its best to keep whatever she gave it down.

★

Carlos was alone in the galley when Alex came in search of food. Sadly, there were no apples, but he did find her some cheese and a heel of bread. After ensuring the cook was nowhere in sight, Carlos followed her up on deck.

"How is Sarah?" Carlos asked. Just saying the name out loud filled him with ringing joy, bringing forth an image in his head of Sarah in the maple woods surrounding Graham's Garden, drifting leaves clinging to her skirts as she walked by his side, her fair head leaning towards him.

"Better. We left her staying with Ruth."

Carlos nodded. That would seem a wise thing to do, and no doubt Minister Allerton would take the opportunity to strengthen Sarah's faith.

"Probably," Alex said unenthusiastically. "At least she'll be well supervised, and maybe it will do her good to socialise with girls her own age, for all that it will only be over Bible discussions."

"And the child?"

"Little Duncan? Oh, he thrives!" Alex smiled, brushing crumbs off her skirts.

"Duncan?" Carlos frowned. "His name is Jerome."

"Not anymore. Now it's Duncan, and he's been baptised into the Presbyterian Church."

Carlos smiled to himself. The sacrament of baptism was indelible, and little Jerome was therefore forever a Catholic. He wondered if Sarah still carried the rosary beads with her, but this was not something he could ask her mother. Sarah, he whispered mutely, and in his head she turned towards him. No, don't think of her, do not wish for her, and never, never imagine her undressed before you. He would burn in everlasting hell unless he truly repented, and he swallowed at the thought. I'm a priest, I have pledged myself, body and soul, to the Holy Church, and the Holy Church will never let me go. That much his confessor had made very clear: to break his vows would be to become an apostate, eternally damned to hellfire.

"And you? Have you decided what to do next?" Alex asked.

"I don't decide, but I was on my way to the mainland when this accursed pirate fell upon us." He glared at Captain Jan who was standing on the opposite side of the ship. "I'm meant for Caracas," he said with a deep sigh. "A backwater, a city struck by earthquakes and pirate attacks."

"So maybe this is an opportunity, maybe you can find a ship going back to Spain instead, and once there, well, they won't send you back, will they?"

Carlos laughed hollowly. "The Holy Church can be most persistent at times." But to be back in Spain... He could retreat into a monastery and live a tranquil life surrounded by books and the reassuring rituals of prayer and monastic rule. A most pleasing little daydream, however impossible. "I'd best get back to my tasks." Captain Jan was eyeing him with mild irritation, and Carlos didn't doubt for a second that the captain would overrule both Matthew and Alex and punish him should he be sufficiently provoked.

"Turnips?" Alex asked.

Carlos grimaced. No, today it was yams and plantains, and salted fish that had to be rinsed repeatedly before the cook could fry it.

"Sounds nice," Alex said.

Carlos huffed and moved away, his eyes on the deck to ensure his wooden peg did not catch on something and send him sprawling. He hated yams, but he suspected his opinion would not count at all.

Chapter 36

Julian listened in astounded silence to Ruth's whispered confession, his wife admitting to having seen Sarah sneak off on several occasions, and just the other day, Emily Farrell had remarked that she'd seen Sarah with a strange man, and... Under his eyes, Ruth wilted, apologising for not having told him sooner, but she hadn't truly known, and it was only when Charlotte Wells had told Ruth that Sarah was often to be seen with a man just off the graveyard, that Ruth had realised she had to tell him. Well, his wife he would chastise later, but his sister-in-law needed to be firmly dealt with immediately.

"You will not – I repeat, you will not – act in a way that risks your reputation." Julian stood tall and straight by his desk.

"I haven't done anything improper!" Sarah said. "And you have no right to order my life."

"I have every right! I'm your brother-in-law and your minister! And you'll do as I say, understood?"

Sarah shook her head, jaw setting stubbornly.

"I'm entrusted with your spiritual welfare!" Julian yelled. "You won't see that man again, and you'll tell me his name."

"What man?" Sarah said. "I don't know what you're talking about." She swivelled and left the room, pushing her sister rudely against the doorframe, and made for the front door, reaching it only seconds before Julian.

His hand clamped down around her arm. "You go outside with your sister or not at all," Julian said and dragged her back inside. In an act of inspiration, he pushed her to the floor and forced shoes and stockings off her, handing them to Ruth. "She may only leave the house in your company."

After one last sinister glare at his sister-in-law, he left for his meeting with the other ministers.

"Don't touch me!" Sarah spat when Ruth bent down to help her up.

"Sarah," Ruth said, "you know it's out of concern for you."

"Nay, it isn't! It's out of concern for the gossiping ladies of Providence – you set higher store on them than on me."

"That isn't true! But I won't have you acting the hoyden."

"Hoyden? When have I acted the hoyden?" Sarah was on her feet, and, with a swift movement, reclaimed her shoes.

"You sit and talk with a man, alone! Don't you see how it reflects on Julian, that you act so indecently while under his roof and care?"

"I don't care how it reflects on Julian!" Sarah wrenched the door open and left. She was already late for her meeting with Michael, and she flew up the back alleys, ignoring displeased looks and comments as she hastened up towards the meetinghouse and the graveyard beyond.

He wasn't there, and all of Sarah shrivelled together, a silent crumpling to the ground. She withdrew into the deeper shade of a large pine, and settled herself to wait. He would come, he always came, she assured herself, and her hand slid into her petticoat pocket to close around the comfort of her rosary. A gust of laughter escaped her. If Julian was truly concerned about her spiritual welfare, the prayer beads were by far a greater issue than Michael.

She caressed the first bead and whispered the Lord's Prayer, closing her eyes to stop herself from staring in the direction he would come from. She said one Hail Mary, she said two, three, four – a whole decade, and still he didn't come.

Sarah sat in the shade, and told another and another decade, and slowly she was submerged in the meditative peace of prayer. In the pit of her, a little flower bloomed, a whispered assurance ringing in her head that things would be alright. Sarah opened her eyes and there, crouched before her, sat Michael, his chestnut hair aflame with the sun that backlit him. Like an angel he was, and without further conscious thought, she leaned forward and kissed him.

Michael almost overbalanced, but righted himself at the last moment, his lips still touching hers. A very chaste little kiss, he thought when she sat back, her face a warm shade of pink. Her cap had come askew, long tendrils of blond hair escaping her braid to float around her face in a most enticing manner, and her mouth was soft and moist, the tip of her tongue visible between her lips.

He had no idea what he wanted with her anymore. Ever since he'd first seen her, that day in March, she'd been like a constant, chafing itch, a need to further explore, to touch, to bed. But what had begun as an interesting little challenge was becoming something entirely different, filling him with feelings he had difficulties putting words to. He still at times considered whether to throw her on her back, shove the skirts out of the way, and take her. There were days when all of him throbbed with want, with sheer lust, but he shied away at the thought of forcing her, because how would he bear the look in her eyes if he did such to her?

Once again, he recalled how unconsciously Matthew Graham and his wife had adjusted rhythm and stride as they walked down that dusty street in Jamestown and with sudden insight he understood that was what he wanted as well. He wanted Sarah to mould herself to him the way her mother fitted into her father, hands wound tight around each other. He fell to his knees, cradled her face, and kissed her back. Not at all chaste this kiss, but a careful exploring of her, a gentle prodding until she opened her mouth to him, and he realised with a satisfied start that he was the first man she had ever kissed.

"I have to go!" Sarah was on her feet, discomfited and hot, strangely moist in places she had never been quite as aware of before. She gave him a hesitant smile, swallowed her thundering heart back into place, and left him sitting alone in the shade. She licked her lips as she walked, trying to recapture all those strange sensations his mouth and tongue had woken in her. Bubbles of exuberance surged through her, small pinpricks of joy that made her want to sing or laugh – an exuberance that was wiped away when she entered through the back door to be met by an angry Julian and an equally upset Ruth.

"I told you, didn't I?" Julian was livid, eyes black with anger. Swiftly, he lunged, and in a matter of seconds, he was dragging her up the stairs to the little room she shared with Patience.

"I'll not have you shaming me and mine in this way," he said, panting with exertion.

"Let go of me!" She tugged at her hand. "Ruth! Tell him!" Sarah threw a look at her sister, who refused to meet her eyes.

She struggled wildly when Julian shoved her in the direction of the bed. Panic was shrinking her windpipe, because he was hurting her, and the last time a man had manhandled her like this... She gulped down air, and hit him squarely across the face with her free hand.

"Leave me be!" she screeched, and yet again threw a pleading look at her sister. "Ruth! Help me!"

Julian's lip burst open, and with an exclamation he slapped Sarah. She yanked at her hand. Frantically, she attempted to wrest herself free, but with a grunt Julian threw her across the bed.

"Hold her," he said to Ruth, struggling with his belt.

"Julian..." Ruth's face appeared hovering at the side of the bed, and Sarah tried to smile at her, because her sister would help her, wouldn't she?

"I said hold her. I'll not have my authority flaunted in my own home, nor will I allow a girl to raise her hand to me!" He pulled at Sarah's skirts.

Sarah screamed, because there was no bed below her. No, she was back to that awful afternoon in the woods when two men had shoved her skirts out of the way, and laughed as they hurt her and ravaged her.

"Julian, no!" she heard Ruth say. The belt came down with a stinging thwack across the back of her thighs, and Sarah pushed and heaved, gripped the bedpost to try and drag herself free.

"Hold her still!" Julian yelled. Ruth's hands came down on Sarah's arms, pinning her flat to the bed.

"You'll do as I say in the future," Julian said once he was done.

Sarah didn't hear him. She had scurried away to hide in the inner reaches of her soul.

"But surely, Julian," Ruth was close to tears, "you don't need to lock her in!"

"She can meditate on her behaviour for some time. It will do her good," Julian said, and pocketed the key before retiring to his little study. From somewhere in the house came the high, wailing cry of an abandoned Edward, and Julian popped his head back out through the door. "Your son," he snapped. "Take care of our son, wife!"

Ruth was already on her way, damp patches on her bodice. From the little room behind her came an absolute silence, and Ruth thought that was even worse than the screaming that had come before.

It was equally quiet some hours later, when Ruth unlocked the door.

"Here." Ruth placed a tray beside the bed. Sarah lay curled on her side, her face to the wall. "You have to eat." Ruth stretched out her hand to touch her sister. The reaction was spectacular. Sarah rose off the bed in one fluid moment, backing away into a corner with her knife in her hand.

"Don't touch me!"

"Sarah, it's me, Ruth."

"I know who you are," Sarah said icily, "and I won't have your hands on me ever again. You helped him hurt me."

"You hit him! And you disobeyed him. He was within his rights to punish you!" And he was. Of course Julian had to punish Sarah when she had so brazenly flaunted his

308

authority, but Ruth felt somewhat queasy at how he had gone about it.

"He has no rights over me!"

"Aye, he does! He is in Da's place while you stay with us."

"Da won't like it that he belted me, and neither will Mama." A triumphant gleam appeared in Sarah's eyes at Ruth's obvious discomfort. "Get out." She motioned towards the door. "Take your food with you. I won't eat anything you've touched."

She threw herself in rage at the door when Ruth turned the key, she yelled and screamed and kicked, and Ruth had no idea what to do, standing there with her carefully prepared peace offering in her hands.

"I'll unlock the door tomorrow morning," Julian said. After well over an hour of constant sounds, Sarah had quieted again, and the Allerton household was getting ready for bed after a far too exciting day. Malcolm, who adored his young aunt, had refused to eat either dinner or supper in silent solidarity with Sarah. Patience had complained about being locked out of her room, but was now settled in bed with Mercy, and Ruth had finally managed to soothe a fretful Edward back to sleep. It was probably her own agitation that made the babe so restless, she reflected, and her hands knotted themselves tight around the material of her shift. She shouldn't have let him hit her.

"She hit me first," Julian said, "and I didn't hit her very hard, did I?"

Ruth hitched a shoulder. To her, it seemed he had. Sarah was right: neither Mama nor Da would be pleased to hear of this. Since last spring, they had become exceedingly protective of their youngest daughter, and to hit her, to slap her like Julian had done, and then throw her on her front and belt her – it must have been a far too tangible reminder of that awful experience.

Julian squirmed in bed when she said this out loud. "You're exaggerating."

Ruth shook her head. "She was terrified, and I don't think she'll ever forgive me." A single tear rolled down her cheek.

★

Julian unlocked the door in the morning, and told Sarah she was welcome to join them for breakfast. She didn't, and Ruth was torn with worry.

"She'll eat when she's hungry enough," Julian said, and held out his bowl for more porridge, adding a generous knob of butter and molasses. Malcolm was ushered off to school, Patience was sent to do errands with Mercy in tow, and with a brief kiss on Ruth's brow, Julian stood to go to the meetinghouse and yet another meeting.

Ruth sat in the silence of her kitchen and nursed Edward. Still no sounds from upstairs, and Ruth was at one level relieved, not knowing quite how to meet her sister's eyes, and at another concerned, because mayhap Sarah was poorly. With a small sigh, she adjusted her clothes, took Edward in her arms, and climbed the stairs to see her sister.

Sarah wheeled when the door opened. Her shoulders relaxed at the sight of Ruth, and she continued folding away the last of her few items of clothing.

"What are you doing?" Ruth asked.

Sarah closed the canvas bag. "I'm leaving."

"You can't leave!" Ruth took hold of Sarah's arm, but was brusquely shrugged off.

"Aye, I can, and I don't think you can stop me." Sarah shouldered by Ruth and made for the stairs.

"Where will you go? I have to know, I am your sister!" Ruth could hear her own voice breaking.

"My sister? I don't have a sister. I have but six brothers." Sarah fixed Ruth with a cold look. "As to where I will go, I don't rightly know. I may go down to Mrs Malone's and earn my living on my back, in keeping with the wanton you seem to think I am." The door slammed, and Ruth sank down to cry on the stairs, her babe cradled in her arms.

By nightfall, Ruth was sick with worry, as was Julian. He had looked everywhere for her, even going to Mrs Malone's to ensure she wasn't there, but it was as if Sarah Graham had been swallowed by the earth. No one had seen her apart from the odd sighting just after she left the house in the morning, and now they sat facing each other over the kitchen table, and Ruth had no idea what to do.

"How do we explain this to Da and Mama?"

"She left," Julian replied. "Inconsiderate little wench that she is, she just walked out."

"You shouldn't have punished her."

"She should have obeyed me. And it was you who told me in the first place."

Ruth hid her face in her hands. If only she'd overlooked Sarah's two-hour disappearance yesterday, none of this would ever have happened. Instead, she had been filled with indignation at the way Sarah openly disregarded Julian's instructions.

"Mayhap she's ridden home." Yes, of course, that was it. How foolish of her not to think of that immediately. Even Julian seemed slightly relieved.

"Where would she get a horse?" he asked.

Ruth made a dismissive gesture. Sarah could have borrowed one.

"I'll ask around on the morrow." With a firm hand, Julian led her to bed.

No one had lent Sarah a horse. No one had seen her. No one had any idea where she had gone.

"Sweetest Lord," Ruth whispered when Julian told her this, "what have we done?" She hiccupped with agitation as she turned to face her husband. "Da...oh God, Julian, Da will never forgive us if anything has happened to her!"

"She brought it down upon herself," Julian said, but Ruth could hear how worried he was.

"I don't think Da will care," Ruth groaned.

Chapter 37

Alex was dozing in the shade when the warning cry went up, and the previously somnolent ship transformed into a beehive of activity, with a cursing captain berating the lookout for his late warning.

"What?" Alex snuck her hand into Matthew's.

"I don't know." He frowned at a small speck that was growing into an impressive ship under full sail.

"A Spanish galleon," the cook told them, "and from the looks of it, headed directly towards us." He sighed theatrically. "By tonight, we will all be prisoners of the Spanish King."

"No, we won't!" Captain Jan snapped, but he looked as pale as it was possible for him to look, his normal copper hue shifting into a yellowish tan. He swept his deck, instructed the first mate to hold the *Althea* steady on a north-northwest course, and had Carlos brought before him.

"God must have had a reason for me to spare your sorry life after all." He grinned down at the little priest.

"I won't do anything to help you!" Carlos said. "I'll gladly see you swing from the mizzenmast – you and all your crew!"

Alex croaked a 'no', eyes flying to her son.

"But we both know that isn't what will happen, don't we?" the captain said. "I might be hanged, but the crew and the Graham boy, and most certainly both Matthew and Charlie Graham will be carried away as enslaved sailors." Captain Jan beckoned Charlie over and ripped his shirt open, baring the branded letters. "This one is already marked a slave, and soon the others will be too."

Carlos stared at the bubbling, dark S and B. The priest's narrow shoulders slumped in defeat, throwing Alex and Matthew a look. "What will you have me do?" he said in an emotionless voice.

"We found you, we saved you, and we're on our way to Florida where you aim to find a ship back home." Captain Jan nodded to himself, and spent the coming fifteen minutes embellishing the story until both he and Carlos had it down pat. After that, he called to the lookout to hail the galleon, and the *Althea* was slowed to lie nearly still in the water.

"We can't outsail her," Captain Jan explained to Matthew and Alex. "She carries far too much sail. Look, two mizzenmasts and two lanteen sails." Alex counted four masts in total, and an impressive amount of billowing canvas. Equally impressive were the cannon ports. Thankfully, most of them were closed, but two in the uppermost level stood wide open, and Alex moved even closer to Matthew when the snouts of two cannon appeared.

"Will they fire?"

"No," Captain Jan said, "we're not attempting flight, are we?"

Carlos hailed the Spanish captain in a carrying voice that made Alex look at him in admiration. She'd never heard the priest speak in anything but the softest of tones, and this baritone voice, ringing with authority, made her view him in a very different light.

"The mouse that roared," she giggled nervously, watching Captain Jan walk over to stand beside the little priest.

"What is he saying?" Matthew wondered.

"A terrible story," Alex said. "How his ship was attacked by pirates, how the crew was set into boats, and he, being a priest, was thrown to drown in the sea."

"Hmm." Matthew eyed Captain Jan's stiff back. "A wee bit too close to home for comfort. And then what?" Matthew said, watching Carlos wave his arms and hands around, his voice still pitched at a level that would carry through a cathedral.

"Well, there he was, struggling in the seas, clinging for days to a wooden spar. He had given up hope, was using what strength remained to him to pray for a quick and merciful death when he saw the unmistakeable dorsal fin of a shark come towards him." Alex had to crane her head back to make out the galleon's captain, several storeys higher up in the air than they were, standing among the sailors that thronged the railing of the Spanish ship.

The masts were now bare, the sails had been taken down to allow the warship to float along at pace with *Althea*. From the stern fluttered the Cross of Burgundy, red on white with the Spanish royal arms superimposed on it.

"Shit," she muttered, "they can just drop down on us."

"Aye, but they're far too close to use the cannon," Matthew said.

"Given that they seem to outnumber us ten to one, I don't find that much of a comfort," Alex replied.

"So what happened with the shark?" Matthew prompted.

"Nothing," Alex snorted, "you know that!" Still, she translated as Carlos described his abject fear and then, lo and behold, this man – here he clapped Captain Jan so hard on his back the captain actually winced – had appeared in the water beside him, and with no concern for his own life, dragged them both to safety.

"Ah," Matthew said, "a very slow shark."

"Geriatric," Alex said, "and I'm not sure the Spanish captain is entirely convinced."

Out of nowhere, the air filled with men, Spanish men, dropping down via ropes to land on the deck of the *Althea*. Captain Jan looked increasingly more nervous, sinking his hand into Othello's hairy ruff, but he didn't move nor as much as blink when the Spanish captain landed before him, sword drawn.

"Permission to board?" the Spanish captain asked with an edge of irony.

"By all means," Captain Jan replied.

The Spanish captain nodded, sheathed his sword, and turned his attention to Carlos. A huge grin appeared on his bearded face. "Ángel! My dear, dear friend! At last!" He enveloped Carlos in a hug, all the while repeating how glad he was to find him alive. "I thought I recognised you from above, but thought it best to make sure." He released Carlos who gave him a weak smile and shook his head.

"I'm not—"

"And this, I presume, is the English dog who sequestered you," the captain said, pointing at Jan. "Well, him we'll dispose of quickly."

A snap of his fingers, Captain Jan was on his knees, his nape bared. One of the Spanish soldiers raised his sword, and any moment now poor Captain Jan's head would be severed. The dog went into protective mode, growling as he threw himself at the men holding his master. David yelled, jumped, and landed on the man with the sword, and suddenly Matthew was no longer at her side but shouldering his way through the Spanish soldiers, sword held aloft, his eyes on their son who was screaming, rolling away from a booted foot.

"Enough!" The Spanish captain discharged his pistol in the air. "Tie them up," he said, indicating Matthew and David. Matthew shoved his son behind him, sword held at the ready. The Spanish soldiers eyed him with some respect, but no matter that Matthew was tall and strong, he was one and they were eight.

"No!" Alex pushed her way towards the Spanish captain, "Don't harm them. *Por favor, no.*"

The captain swivelled on his toes. "You speak Spanish?"

"I am Spanish." Well, not quite, but no need to explain that at present. "My husband and I are passengers, no more."

The captain shrugged. "He shouldn't have interfered. He dies."

"*Por Dios*, no!" Carlos threw himself forward, caught his peg on something, and fell to the deck. With surprising speed, he was back on his feet. "These are my friends, all of them. And I'm not Ángel Muñoz. I am Carlos, a priest."

The captain squinted at him. "Not Ángel?"

"His cousin," Carlos replied, "an envoy of the Holy Church who would have died if it hadn't been for the captain of this sloop. Look." He held up his peg leg. "I would have died in the sea, eaten bit by bit, if it hadn't been for Captain Jan. A true hero."

The Spanish captain stared at the wooden peg, at Carlos.

Alex sidled over to stand beside Matthew. Captain Jan remained prostrate with Othello standing over him.

"Is he dead?" she whispered.

"Nay. But best remain where he is at present. Yon dog has these papist bastards frightened out of their skins." Constant tremors rippled through him, his sword still brandished before him. "If..." He pressed her arm against hers.

"No ifs," she told him sternly.

"No ifs," he said, the faintest of smiles on his face.

Carlos and the Spanish captain were at present involved in a low-key discussion involving a lot of hand gesturing, many glances thrown their way, and a repeated inspection of Carlos' peg leg. The Spanish commander barked an order, his men took a few paces back, and Captain Jan slowly got to his feet, adjusting his clothes as he went over to join Carlos and the Spaniard.

"Let's just hope he never asks to see the stump," Alex said to Matthew, "because even a total incompetent would see that is no new wound."

"He won't, will he?" Matthew said comfortably, far more relaxed now that the two captains were talking to each other. "Carlos is a priest and therefore allowed a certain modicum of privacy."

Matters were swiftly concluded after this. The Spanish captain apologised profusely, and Captain Jan bowed, shaking his head in a deprecating gesture. But his hand kept returning to his nape, and Alex suspected their dashing captain was far more affected than he let on by this sudden brush with death. If it hadn't been for the dog – and David – Captain Jan's head would by now have been bobbing in the sea like a coconut.

A few minutes later, Alex was escorted forward by Matthew to where Carlos was preparing for imminent departure by way of a rope.

"God works in mysterious ways," Alex said and hugged Carlos, to the amused jeers of the Spanish seamen. "You were not meant to remain here in obscurity, despite your uncle's best efforts. So, go back to Spain and wrest a life for yourself – you'd look good in cardinal red, I think." Carlos' lip wobbled, his dark eyes bright with tears.

"*Que Dios te proteja,*" she said and kissed him on both cheeks. "God be with you, Carlos Muñoz."

"*Y a ti – siempre a ti.* I'll remember you for the rest of my life, Alex Graham."

"Of course you will." She smiled, wiping at her wet eyes. "It's difficult to forget someone who's cut your foot off."

Carlos just nodded, was swept into a bear hug by Matthew which made him squawk and nearly overbalance, and then up he went, dangling like a puppet on a string as he was pulled aboard the Spanish vessel.

Alex stood for a long time with her eyes locked on the galleon. For as long as she could see it, she remained by the railing, and she was convinced Carlos was standing on the poop deck, staring back at the *Althea* as she was staring after him.

Matthew came with her cloak and draped it round her shoulders, wrapping his arms around her for extra warmth. They stood in the shimmering September dusk, pressed together. To the east, it was already night, darkness staining upwards across the sky, and the evening star appeared, a solitary twinkle in the dark.

"He'll be alright," he said.

"He loves her," Alex sighed, "and he will never forget her." Venus, she reflected, the evening star isn't a star, it's a planet, named after the goddess of love.

"He wouldn't have made our Sarah a good husband – and not only on account of him being a priest," Matthew said, and his hands came down to her hips.

"No." He was right: Sarah would have eaten Carlos for breakfast. She turned to Matthew and rubbed her cheek against his chest. "Love me," she whispered. "Please lay me down and love me until I fall asleep in your arms."

"Gladly," he said, steering her towards their little cabin.

After the lingering dusk outside, it was very dark inside, but Matthew had no time for lanterns, for fumbling with flint and steel. He spread first his cloak, then hers into a makeshift bed on the cabin floor onto which he dropped the pillows. Alex made as if to undress, but he stilled her hands. "Let me."

He took his time. The buttons on her bodice he undid one by one, fingers lingering on her chest, mouth pressed softly to her throat. She swayed and leaned into him, head thrown back as he kissed his way from one shoulder to the other. The cotton fabric of the undone bodice slid down her arms to fall to the floor. Her skirts and petticoats, the recalcitrant lacings on her stays – it was like peeling an onion.

"Lie down." He held her eyes as she complied, gracefully sinking to her knees before reclining backwards. He undid his breeches, no more, before kneeling beside her. The embroidered shift was new, with an interesting and decorative lacing all the way to her navel. One eyelet at the time, and for every inch of her skin he bared, he had to stoop and kiss it. It made her twist and squirm, her hands coming up to touch him, to tug at his shirt. Matthew took hold of her wrists and held her captive, his mouth travelling slowly over her breasts.

He could feel her pulse through his fingertips, and when he kissed her, she moaned into his mouth, and he marvelled that it should still be like this between them. He released her hands, his mouth still covering hers, and undid her hair. She shook it free of braids and coils, a ticklish, dark cloud that framed her pale face. He combed his fingers through it, draping curls to adorn her shoulders, her chest.

She was by now entirely naked, while he remained mostly dressed. It was strangely alluring, her so vulnerable in only her hair, while he, fully clothed, held her in place with his weight and his strength. She was all soft skin and rounded curves, from the slope of her hip to the silky texture of her inner thigh. Warm and welcoming, round and rosy, and when he nuzzled her throat, she sighed, widening her legs. He entered her, still in shirt and breeches, and held still. She stared up at him, eyes dark smudges, no more.

"For all that I am six and fifty, I come to you like a callow lad. Should it be like this, that it takes but a graze of your fingers, a flicker of your tongue, to rouse me?"

"I don't know, but I think it's a gift." Her hands floated up to grab at his head, and she raised her back off the floor to kiss him breathless. His cock strove deeper and deeper inside of her, nudging at her core. He came with a muffled groan, and for a fleeting instant regretted they were now too old for there to ever be a bairn again.

Afterwards, she pulled off his shirt and massaged his back, and he was surrounded by the scents of mint and lemon, the sound of her wordless humming. He was nearly asleep by the time she was done, noting through half-closed eyes how she slipped into her shift and stepped into her petticoats. His hand closed on her ankle.

"Where are you going?" he said drowsily.

"Hungry," she said, patting her stomach.

"I'll go. You stay here and wait. I don't want you filling the crew with indecent thoughts."

"I was planning on dressing first," she said.

"No doubt, but any man with eyes in his head can see you come directly from your lover's arms." He sniffed, grinning when she blushed. "You smell of it as well."

He was still laughing when he closed the cabin door behind him, walking over to the leeward side to relieve himself. A strange, breathless sound came from the direction of the mast, and Matthew turned, stuffing his member into his breeches.

"Charlie? What's the matter, lad?"

His nephew raised a contorted face and used a fisted hand to beat himself on the chest. "The matter? These are the matter, these, you hear?" He opened his torn shirt, baring the unsightly brands. "I want them gone. How can I walk straight and free when on my skin I carry the constant reminder of my erstwhile owner, Mr Sassafras Brown?"

"Unless someone knows you have them, they won't see them," Matthew said, which made Charlie look at him with such dislike Matthew retreated a foot or so.

"I must get them off."

"Impossible. There is no way to purge your skin of yon letters – well, unless you take a knife to yourself. Nay," he continued at the hopeful expression that flew over Charlie's face, "to do so would be too dangerous. You might die in the attempt."

Charlie ducked his head.

"Charlie!" Matthew shook him, hard. "I haven't travelled for months to buy you free only to have you die on account of vanity."

"Vanity?" Charlie spluttered. "How can you say such? Look at me! Branded like a beast!"

"But alive, aye? Alive and strong, and with your life before you." Matthew gave him yet another little shake. "Promise me, lad, that you'll not do anything daft."

For a long time, Charlie studied his hands. "I promise," he finally said. "I'll not do something foolish."

Chapter 38

Michael had heard the hue and cry for Sarah Graham – it was inevitable that he would in a town as small as Providence – and in his chest his heart flipped. She hadn't been waiting for him beyond the graveyard, and he racked his brain trying to think where she might have gone, spent several hours searching for her, before deciding that she would of course return home, however reckless it was to brave the wilds alone.

He set off that same afternoon, riding at a steady pace due north-west. He found her at dawn, a sad little huddled shape under an oak, and urged his horse towards her, overwhelmed by a need to wrap his cloak around her and take her in his arms to comfort her.

"What happened?" he asked once he was close enough for her to see him. He dismounted and walked over to her, Pegasus trailing him like an obedient dog.

"He raised his hand against me. He called me wanton and punished me for it." She was trembling, he could see, but the September morning, if chilly, was not uncomfortably cold, and she was warmly dressed. She looked up at him, and in returning light, she was bleached of colour, just a varied selections of greys. "I'll never let a man hurt me again."

"Surely, he wasn't that harsh," Michael said, sitting down beside her. He knew what she was referring to, but as the subject had never been broached between them, he couldn't very well pretend he did.

Sarah kept her eyes on her hands and the rosary beads she was twisting round and round. "Carlos always said you had to forgive to be able to go on, but there are some things you can never forgive, never, however hard you try." She slipped the beads back into their keeping place but still refused to meet his eyes.

"And now you will never forgive Minister Allerton."

"Julian?" Sarah laughed. "What do I care about him? He is mostly a nice man, even if he's old like the hills." She shifted on her backside, a sibilant intake of breath accompanying her movement. Michael studied her and frowned. Had the minister belted her? A wave of protective anger rushed through him, and he moved closer to her.

"I've never told anyone before," she said in a voice that was strangely colourless, "well, with the exception of Carlos, of course." Michael didn't at all like how her voice softened when she said the priest's name, nor how something of regret washed across her face. She took a big breath, she took two, and turned to face him, and his windpipe clogged at the panic in her eyes.

"You don't have to tell me anything," Michael said, and he meant it.

"Aye, I do," she answered, and he shook his head hard enough that his hair should fall, as it tended to do, like a heavy curtain over one of his eyes. Sarah's brow wrinkled, eyes on his irritating forelock.

"What?" he asked, shoving the curls out of the way.

"Nothing," she said, but her gaze remained glued to his hair.

For well over an hour, she talked, and Michael twisted inside as her slow, dispassionate voice retold every detail of what had happened to her well over a year ago. Her hands strayed to her ears when she told him of how she was forced to use her mouth, and Michael clapped his hands over his own ears, begging her to stop. He knew enough now, didn't he? She didn't hear. She was talking just as much to herself as she was to him, and she just couldn't stop. Finally, her voice wound down, and she sat in abject silence waiting for his condemnation.

Michael didn't know what to say or do. She described an act of violence, a permanent rending of someone's soul, while Philip had retold the taming of a young wench, an inexperienced girl that had been taught quickly to offer up and be quiet. Anger and shame, disgust and pity warred inside of him. Philip had died too easily. A shot through his heart and he was gone, when he should have wept and begged for mercy, when he should have crawled and howled as everything that was done to her, to Sarah, was done to him. Michael swallowed and knew he had to tell her the truth, and maybe she would stand and spit him in the face, and how was he to bear it if she did?

"I shot him," he said.

"Who?" Sarah rose on her knees. "You shot Julian?"

Michael shook his head, and once again his hair fell over his eye. Rays of sun were filtering down through the canopy of trees by now, touching her face into gold, and he shifted that much closer to her, close enough that his fingers met hers.

"Philip," he said, and she threw herself backwards, scrambling in her haste to get away from him.

"You were there?" she croaked, and he nodded, explaining how he had been hidden in the blackberry brambles when Philip entered the kitchen garden. And when Philip raised his knife, well, there was no choice, so he just levelled the pistol and shot him.

"Why?" she asked.

"Why? I just couldn't let him kill you." He watched her warily, tilting his head to see her now that she was on her feet. His answer was clearly not the one she wanted.

"Why were you there to begin with?" she asked, eyes stuck on the unruly lock that covered half his face. She whimpered, and without waiting for an answer, turned and fled.

He caught up with her and tried to wrap an arm round her waist so as to bring her to a halt. Christ and all His Saints! The heel of her hand crashed into his face. He reeled back. Sarah pivoted, grabbed at his left arm. Aah! Her hip slammed into him, she twisted and wrenched, and he was airborne, tossed high like a doll. His head burst into thousands of pieces — or so it felt — when he hit the tree, sliding down to land on his knees. He tried to stand, but his legs wouldn't obey him, and instead he fell flat on his face.

He wanted to open his eyes, he wanted to ask her how she had done what she did, but his brain was one long howl of pain, and so he stayed where he was.

"Michael?" He could hear the quaver in her voice, and he wanted to reassure her that he was alright – but he wasn't, not really, and was that blood that he felt trickling down his forehead? With an effort, he opened his eye to find her kneeling beside him. His arm...his sleeve was dark with blood, his left forearm badly gashed.

"Michael?" She tried to close the wide gash with her trembling fingers, and he gasped, making her fly away from him. He struggled up into a sitting position and blinked at her. There were two – no, three – of her, and Jesus, his arm hurt, and his head... His mouth was full of blood, and he spat, tried to lick his lips clean.

"How?" he asked, gesturing at his arm, his head.

"Mama taught me," she said, her eyes very close to his. "She taught me to defend myself. Not that it helped when..." She closed her eyes for an instant. "I didn't mean to hurt you."

"But you did," he wheezed.

"May I...is it alright if I...?" There were her hands again, fingers touching his aching head, his lips, his limbs. He just nodded, dizzy with pain.

His arm throbbed. She had torn her petticoat to shreds for bandages, and if he raised his arm to his nose, it smelled of her, of her secret places, and it made him even more light-headed than he already was. His head was examined and the shallow gash washed but pronounced unimportant, while the bump... Her fingers were light but insistent, lingering a bit longer than necessary on his nape. He smiled when, in passing, she washed his bruised face, dabbed at the swollen lip and brushed at his hair, forcing that mischievous lock away from his brow.

"He's my uncle," Michael said, "or rather he was my uncle, and my brother died at Graham's Garden as well." He was uncomfortable on the damp ground, but she insisted he had to rest, at least some hours more, and so she had fetched his horse and her few things, and they were now several hundred yards from the main path. "He told us of how your father had sold him and Uncle Walter as slaves to the Indians, and he insisted he wanted revenge."

"Da didn't sell them. They were planning on selling him." Very briefly, she described how they had tortured Matthew, and Michael winced. Would Graham ever allow his daughter to wed Burley kin? The thought startled him so much he opened his eyes, if only for a second, and there she was, her braid having come undone from cap and coil.

The sunlight danced over her head, her face, her shoulders. It glinted on the mother-of-pearl that decorated her hairpin. She was close enough that he could feel the warmth of her exhalations against his skin, see the dried tear tracks on her cheeks. He closed his eyes again at the blue of her gaze, and attempted to bring some control into his jumbled brain. Wed her? He tasted the words 'my wife' in his mouth, and saw that they suited her. His wife... His head was thudding with pain, and he was so tired, so very tired. He groaned and rested back against the trunk.

"Does it hurt?" she asked in a worried tone.

"Yes." He peeked at her, groped for her hand. "I'm not like them, I—" The following words were lost in a violent bout of vomiting, leaving him shivering. Sarah helped him clean himself off, held the water skin for him, and sat down very close to him.

"Here," she said. He opened one eye to see her patting at her thighs in invitation, her skin shifting into a pink hue.

Michael subsided against her with a grunt, winced as he lowered himself to pillow his head on her lap. His breeches were wet where he'd been sitting for too long on the mossy ground, and she managed to cover him with his cloak without jarring his arm.

"I'm so sorry," he yawned, the words woolly in his mouth.

"Sorry? For what?"

"That I didn't shoot him before he did all that to you." His eyelids kept on dropping down, heavy as lead, they seemed, and as she didn't say anything, he didn't either, content to lie like this, half asleep with his aching head in her lap.

A finger tickled over his ear, brushed over his nose, his eyebrow. Michael's lips twitched when her fingers danced over his mouth; he exhaled when she caressed his aching head. He had been riding in only shirt and coat, no cravat at the throat, and suddenly a warm hand snuck down the neckline, rested for a moment over his heart. Such a warm hand, such gentle fingers, and when she found his nipple, he gasped, making her retract her hand as if he'd been red-hot.

A few minutes and her hand was back, this time to once again travel over his head, his face. Gingerly, Michael twisted so that he lay on his back, opening his eyes to see hers hanging over him. He raised his hand, cupped her cheek, and ran a finger over her mouth. Sarah closed her eyes but sat still as his hand dropped down to her neck, her shoulder.

All of her trembled – a human aspen leaf – when he traced her neckline, and he reminded himself he had to be careful, so careful and gentle with her. Her thighs bunched under him when the back of his hand grazed her breasts, so Michael took her hand instead.

"I want you for my wife," he said, and with a huge effort managed to sit up. His vision blurred, his head throbbed with pain.

Her tongue flickered nervously over her lips. "Your wife?" she echoed.

Michael nodded, brushed at a tendril of fair hair. His wife, mother of all his future children. "I don't think your father will approve, and not only because of my kin, but also on account of my faith." He leaned towards her and kissed her, and he could taste his blood on her lips.

It was dark by the time they set off. She boosted him up onto Pegasus and clambered up behind him, her arms closing around his waist. She rested her face against his back, and sighed.

"What?" he asked, using his thighs to manoeuvre the horse towards the south.

"Nothing," she replied.

He set his hand on her leg and gave it a little squeeze. His wife to be... He suspected Matthew Graham would be less than happy when he returned from foreign lands to find his daughter not only wed but a Catholic to boot. He had no idea why he'd insisted she should convert before they wed – maybe it was a gesture to his devout mother – but he had been agreeably surprised to find her willing.

Her arms tightened round him, he felt her shiver against him, and wondered if it was out of fear or exhilaration. A bit of both, he supposed. Well, she had nothing to fear, not anymore. Michael Connor would let no man harm her again – so help him God.

Chapter 39

Matthew woke to a heaving ship and the sound of wind and rain. Alex's berth gaped empty, and after a few initial moments of concern, he calmed down, supposing the movements of the boat had brought back the greensickness. He was still dressed, and his head reminded him the previous evening had been far too long and far too wet as Captain Jan and he had sat sunk over an interminable game of chess. He had won, Matthew recalled with some satisfaction before the ship keeled to starboard, throwing him hard against the wall.

As he suspected, Alex was clinging to the railings, so white around the mouth it would have been hilarious if it hadn't been for the look of absolute misery in her eyes. She smelled of vomit and fear, and from the state of her hands, it was evident she'd been out here for quite some time, holding on for dear life.

"Why didn't you come and wake me?" he said, using his hand to smooth back her hair. The ship rolled, and he was almost pitched out to sea, laughing shakily as he righted himself.

"That's why," she croaked. "I don't dare to let go."

"The captain says it will blow over quickly." Charlie came to stand on her other side.

"I'll believe it when I see it," Alex muttered, scowling at the sea.

"He would know." Matthew tried to sound encouraging.

The water was a forbidding black, capped with angry white froth, the sky a compact mass of grey. Waves the size of the *Althea* rose and fell, at times slapping into the sloop with such force the timbers creaked in protest.

"How long do you think you'd survive in that?" she asked.

"Not long at all," Matthew answered, and took a firmer hold of her.

"They say it's a good death. To drown is apparently quite pleasant."

"How can anyone know that?" Matthew asked, irritated with her for this very morbid turn of conversation.

"They talk to people who nearly drowned, but I don't want to drown."

"Me neither," Matthew said, "and nor does our captain."

The storm passed just as quickly as Captain Jan had predicted, and Alex found herself looking down at water the colour of storybook seas: a light greenish blue that was transparent all the way to the sandy bottom.

"We'll run aground!" she said, and Matthew made an exasperated sound, pointing to where one of the seamen was reeling in the lode line.

"Well over ten fathoms," the sailor called out.

"Sixty feet? It looks much closer." Alex leaned over the railing the better to see. The water teemed with life: schools of fish, huge, nasty-looking jellyfish, and, suddenly, a swift dark shape that ploughed through the water.

"Where are we?" Matthew asked Captain Jan who was staring out across the becalmed sea.

Captain Jan squinted at the sun, brought out his quadrant, and stood for some moments deep in thought. "Just off Bermuda," he concluded, "not too far off course." He frowned at the surrounding waters. "I don't like it: too close to the main route to Spain. We'd best hope for wind lest we suddenly find ourselves in the company of more Spanish ships."

"Here?" Alex looked about.

"Ships are mostly found at sea," the captain said with a little smile. He scanned the limp sails and sighed. "With this heat, in these shallow waters…" He shook his head. "It can at times cause hallucinations. No, best repair to the shade before our brains get cooked." He flashed them some teeth, and hastened over to discuss something with his first mate.

"He's right, this whole place…" Alex waved her hand at the surreal blue of the water, flat and shimmering around them. "…I don't like it. And it's bloody hot, and all of me stinks, and it isn't as if I can take a swim or something, is it?"

"Absolutely not." Matthew steered her in the direction of the little shade accorded by the sails.

Very quickly, tempers frayed. Men played dice and fought each other, they played cards and quarrelled, they queued for water and came to blows, and it was fortunate that the captain had but to show himself for his men to calm down, loud invectives becoming mutters, punches becoming shoves.

One of the most affected was Charlie. He sighed and groaned, he stood for hours in the sun, and stared up at the sails as if willing them to suddenly fill with winds. He drank too much beer, he picked constant arguments with Alex or Matthew, and spent more and more time on his own.

"Like a truculent three-year-old," Alex said to Matthew after yet another altercation with Charlie. She frowned over to where he was standing, very alone in the bow. "You don't think he'll do anything stupid?"

"Like what? Leap into the sea?" Matthew gave his nephew an irritated glance. "At present, I wouldn't much mind."

"Me neither. He could sleep with the fishes for all I care." But she didn't mean it, feeling mostly sorry for Charlie who seemed to be reliving far too many memories of his last two years. And all the time he fingered his brands, long fingers travelling up and down the S and the B through his shirt.

David was entirely unaffected by the heat, and was therefore the best company available. Now, he crowed with pride, and landed yet another gleaming fat fish to the pile by his feet. "Snapper," he said, "and the cook will fry them fresh for us tonight."

That sounded very nice, and Alex made appropriate enthusiastic sounds, studying her son. He had filled out over the last few months, the lanky boy replaced by a tall adolescent, arms and legs full of muscle.

"Looking forward to coming home?" she asked, and he stiffened perceptibly. Alex swallowed back a sigh. Matthew would not countenance his son becoming a sailor – at least not until he had finished one more year of school – and David was as stubborn as his father, fully capable of taking matters in his own hands as he had proved by stowing himself away to begin with. "You're too young to go to sea, and your father won't allow it. You know that."

"I'm well over thirteen, and I don't want to go back to school. Whatever for? It isn't as if Da will be sending me to Boston to study, is it?"

Alex didn't like the envious tone in his voice. "Would you want to? You could live with Daniel for a while." Their minister son would be more than happy to have his brother staying with him.

David hitched his shoulders. "I don't want to be a minister," he said, and son and mother shared a little grin of relief. In Alex's opinion, one man of God in the family was quite enough, and at times she had problems keeping a straight face when Matthew read Daniel's letters out loud. To his credit, so did Matthew, commenting that young newly made ministers had a lot of edges to grind down.

"So what then? Because I don't believe you really want to spend your life on a boat either, do you?"

"I'd like to be a lawyer." He went on to explain how Uncle Simon had said he could clerk for him, and then he could go to Glasgow as Uncle Simon had done to study. "He says how he can set me up like," David went on in a rush, "that he has friends in Glasgow for whom I can clerk while I study – it wouldn't cost you much." His eyes begged for her approval, and she leaned forward to cup his cheek.

"It's very far away," she said.

"Aye, I know that."

Alex smiled at him. "Go and tell your da. He'll be thrilled to bits."

"You think?" David asked.

Alex nodded adamantly and shoved him off in the direction of his father. It made her smile, to see her son and husband stand side by side, deep in conversation. It made her grin when Matthew whooped and clapped David on the back before enveloping him in a bear hug.

"Da," David protested, "I must get the fish to the cook." Matthew released him, helped him pick up his spilled catch, and watched him out of sight before turning to smile at Alex. She gave him a thumbs–up and went back to studying the sea, fascinated by the teeming life below them.

She wasn't quite sure how it all happened. One moment, she was leaning over the railing, the next, she heard loud screams, and swivelled to see Charlie and Matthew locked in a fight. A knife. Charlie was holding a knife, and from where she was standing, it seemed Matthew had a grip on his wrist, trying to make him drop the blade. She frowned. Why was Charlie bare-chested? Her skirts were in her hands, feet moving rapidly towards them. Charlie shrieked, turned so that she could see his front. Blood, so much blood, and in a flash she understood what he'd been trying to do.

"Stupid idiot!" She flew over the deck, worried that Charlie might somehow harm Matthew, because her gangly nephew was roaring with incoherent anger, attempting to wrest the knife free. Blood dripped from Charlie to spatter the deck, he was swaying on his feet, and still he fought, screaming at Matthew that it was his knife, his skin, and if he wanted to cut the damn brands out then it was not for Matthew to stop him.

"It'll kill you," Matthew panted.

"I don't care!" Charlie yelled. "I want them gone!" He lunged, closed his hands round a belaying pin, and yanked it loose.

"Charlie! Don't!" Alex screamed, but he didn't hear her – or he didn't care. The first blow caught Matthew in the arm. The second in his head – so hard Matthew staggered back, still holding on to Charlie's right arm.

"Let me go!" Charlie screeched, and the third blow hit Matthew full in the face. Matthew fell backwards, crashing into the railing. "Ha!" Charlie pulled his arm free and shoved his uncle to fall into the sea.

Matthew landed with a splash.

"Matthew!" Alex hung over the railing. Arms and legs moved feebly, he turned a bemused face upwards before he sank.

"No! Matthew, no!" Wildly, she looked about for help, and there was Captain Jan running towards her. "Here!" She handed him the end of a rope, and threw the rest of the rope coil and herself overboard.

She sank like a stone, and the water was deliciously cool, and strangely luminescent, and she couldn't see Matthew. Nowhere was Matthew, and she swam as gracelessly as a floundering dog, hampered by her skirts, and then she saw the white of his shirt, and she dived to where he floated several feet underwater. His hands were splayed like starfish, his shirt billowed elegantly around him, a human stingray flapping his way towards the bottom.

She grabbed for his wrist, and he slid through her grasp. She thought her lungs would burst. She grabbed again, and the rope she held in her hand slipped away from her. She screamed in the water, bubbles spurting from her nose and mouth, and Matthew seemed to hear, turning slowly in her direction. She got hold of his shirt, she kicked towards the surface, and there, thank heavens, was the rope, and somehow she got hold of it. Someone pulled on the rope, and Alex gripped her husband hard, crying underwater.

She gulped down air when they broke the surface, and Matthew hung limp in her arms, water streaming out of nose and mouth. Othello swam circles around them, Captain Jan came splashing towards them, and together they managed to tie the rope around Matthew. At the captain's command, Matthew was hoisted into the air, as lifeless as a sack of barley.

"Oh God," Alex sobbed. "Please, God, no!" Yet another rope snaked down, and moments later, she was back on board.

Alex barely touched deck before she threw herself over him. She breathed into his mouth, she forced air into his lungs, and in between she did CPR, grunting with the effort of making his ribs and heart move. At last, he coughed, coughed again, drawing in a rasping breath of air that made him spew up masses of sea water. Alex helped him sit, and his eyes stared at her without any recognition.

"Matthew?" She had to touch him, cradling his bruised head, running fingers down his neck to feel the reassuring thud of his pulse. "Matthew?"

He closed his eyes with exaggerated slowness, and after what seemed to Alex an interminable amount of time, opened them again to look at her. "Alex?" He sounded very confused.

"Let's get him inside," Captain Jan said.

The captain helped her get Matthew out of his sodden clothes and into his berth, and left, assuring her he'd be close should she need it. Matthew's eyes were glued to her but unfocused, staring straight through her. His hand, however, was tightly braided round hers, and suddenly a shudder ran through him, and his eyes returned to normal. With a strangled sound, he curled together, still holding on to her hand.

Alex slumped on the floor beside him, shivering in her damp clothes, but she wasn't about to let him go. One-handed, she managed to strip off her skirts and undo her bodice. She crawled into his berth, and somehow they made room for each other.

She woke with a crick in her neck, pins and needles up her left leg, and a tongue that was like sandpaper in her mouth. Some idiot was shining her in the face with a torch, and it was only after a couple of minutes that she realised it was afternoon sunlight, streaming in through the porthole. She disentangled herself, and landed with a painful thump on the floor. Matthew made the most of her sudden disappearance from the berth, grunting in his sleep as he shifted to lie more comfortably. She had to drink and then she had to pee...no, she had to pee first, and blearily she hunted around for the chamber pot. It all came back to her as she crouched over it, and she bit back a sob. He had almost drowned – and it was all Charlie's fault.

"He wasn't himself," Matthew said without opening his eyes. "He was drunk."

"He hit you! He shoved you off the ship!" Alex closed her eyes at the memory, at all the blood on Charlie's chest.

"He…" With a muttered curse, Matthew rolled over on his side, fingers flying to his swollen face, his head. "He was out of his mind. This heat, too much beer, and, on top of it, the pain."

"Self-inflicted," Alex said, finding it very difficult to feel any compassion whatsoever for Charlie.

"Aye. But all the same…" Matthew moved his head this way and that. "He'll need you."

"No way!"

"He's gouged a sizeable hole in his chest. You need to sew it." He extended his right arm, looked at his hand and flexed it a couple of times. "I have no idea how he could do such." To Alex's huge irritation, there was an element of admiration in his voice. "It must take a lot of courage – or desperation."

"Or he's just an incredibly stupid person," Alex said, but promised she'd go and check on Charlie if Matthew promised to remain in bed until she returned.

She returned an hour later, sinking down to sit in her berth.

"What was he thinking of?" she said. "And his aim was off, way off. Anyway, he sleeps – he'll probably sleep well into tomorrow given how much laudanum the captain gave him." She gave him a long look. "He could have died – idiot."

And Matthew heard it in her voice that it would take her a long time to forgive Charlie, however much she pitied him. Not that it surprised him, because this wife of his was as protective and ferocious as a lioness when it came to her own, and especially when it came to him. He smiled – somewhat crookedly. She had saved his life, and he shifted in his berth, had to feel his body move as he willed it. Such a strange sensation, to float downwards, helpless and bemused. He had vague recollections of bright green water, of light that reflected upwards from the sandy bottom, of fish – so many fish.

"You could have died," she said in a small voice, and came over to sit beside him. In the sunlight, she looked worn, the fine lines he generally never thought about clearly visible. Her hair was full of tangles, the skin under her wet eyes was puffy, and he could see she was making an effort not to cry. Never had she looked lovelier to him than she did right now, and he stretched out his hand to touch her cheek.

"You know, don't you?" he whispered. "You know that I would have died thinking of you – only of you."

"I know." She smiled tremulously, and used both her hands to anchor his to her face.

Chapter 40

"I never thought the sight of Providence would make me so happy." Alex regarded the tidal marshes that flowed by on both sides of the *Althea*. The tide was out, and on the mudflats flocks of terns gathered only to rise in a flapping white cloud when the ship sailed too close. The last two weeks had been relaxingly uneventful. No priests, no Spanish galleons, just a small ship making its way back home.

"Aye," Matthew said, drawing in deep breaths of the briny, cool October air. "It's good to be back."

From the stern came Charlie, and with a muttered little curse, Matthew took off for their cabin, saying he had things to pack. Alex sighed. Since Matthew's near drowning, Charlie had become a walking apology, a fawning red-haired shadow that drove Matthew – and Alex – to the brink of despair.

Charlie followed his uncle out of sight with the sorrowful eyes of a hound, and came over to Alex. "He hates me."

God! Men, and in particular young men, had the most annoying tendency to wallow.

"You know he doesn't, if anyone's pissed off at you, it's me, not him."

"You hate me too." He nodded morosely.

"Charlie! Had Matthew died, I would personally have hefted you overboard to end up as a shark's dinner. But he didn't, okay? So will you please stop moping before it drives me crazy enough to ram a knitting needle up your arse?" Charlie's face set in a frown – in Alex's opinion a major improvement on the last weeks of abject misery. "Grow up," she said, and decided to do some last-minute packing of her own.

There was no one to meet them, and Alex was disappointed, even if rationally she realised they wouldn't know they were coming on this specific boat. But still, it was not much more than a ten-minute walk from the harbour to Julian's house, and by the time the sloop was safely moored, the whole town would have known about the new arrival – and its passengers.

Ruth looked more shocked than pleased when she opened the door – at least to begin with. Then she was in Matthew's arms, in Alex's arms, hugged David, and curtsied to Charlie who was staring openly at her. Well, not to wonder: the same dark red hair, light eyes, and a general similarity in features made them look like twins.

"We could be siblings!" Charlie blurted, grinning at Ruth.

"We could," she said, "but we're not – we're cousins." But she seemed as entranced as he was, eyes returning repeatedly to his eyes and his hair.

Alex was led over to admire little Edward, fast asleep in his basket, and she wondered at her daughter's interminable flow of words. Ruth never prattled. She was concise and to the point, witty and quick in her replies, but now she was gushing, exclaiming over how well Mama looked, and wasn't that a right pretty bodice, had Mama bought it in the Indies, and why was Da's hair so short, and was it true then, what they said that in the Indies, white lasses were always accompanied by slaves that held parasols over their head, and... Alex raised her hand to stop this torrent. Ruth fell quiet, her eyes sliding to the side, long fingers fidgeting with her apron.

"What is it?" Alex asked at precisely the same time as Matthew turned to Julian and asked for Sarah.

"How do you mean, gone?" Matthew towered over their son-in-law who, for all that he was a minister and an important man to boot, cringed.

"She left several weeks ago," Julian said, backing away from Matthew.

"Left?" Alex repeated. "Just like that? Why would she do that?"

"She was seeing men on the sly," Julian said in a condemning tone. "That was not behaviour I could condone, so I punished her for it."

"Men?" Alex asked. "She was seeing men as in plural?"

Julian shuffled on the spot, cleared his throat. "Well, no, but Ruth saw her on two or three occasions with a man. And I can't have that, can I? How does it reflect on me if my own sister-in-law lacks in modesty? And—"

"What man?" Matthew interrupted, directing himself to Ruth.

"We don't know. I just saw her with him, but I fear she's been seeing him since June. Unacceptable, isn't it?" Ruth looked at her father, at Alex, as if hoping to see them nod in agreement.

"And you didn't think to ask her nicely about it?" Alex asked. "Before condemning her as a potential harlot?"

Ruth went an unbecoming deep pink.

"We were very clear," Julian said. "Both Ruth and I told her she had to stop seeing him."

"People were beginning to talk," Ruth filled in, "and we were worried."

"Very worried." Julian nodded.

"Worried about what? Her well-being or your reputation?" Alex said, snorting in disbelief when Ruth opened her eyes very wide and told her that of course it was Sarah they worried about.

"How did you punish her?" Matthew asked. "What did you do to make her run away?"

Looks flashed between Ruth and Julian — several looks.

"I belted her," Julian said. "No more than a dozen strokes or so."

Alex clutched at Matthew, who closed his eyes and drew in one very long breath.

"You belted a lass who was forced to her knees and raped? Didn't she fight you?"

"As a matter of fact, she did," Julian replied, fingering his lower lip. "Ruth helped me hold her."

"What?" Matthew and Alex said in unison.

Alex sank her eyes into Ruth. "Is this true? You held her while he beat her?"

Ruth whispered an abject yes.

Alex closed her fists around an urgent need to slap her daughter, slap her until she screamed. Instead, she wheeled on Julian. "Ruth is too young to know any better," she said, thereby relegating her daughter back into inane and inconsiderate childhood, "but you, surely you're experienced enough to temper judgemental thinking with compassion." His skin flared. He opened his mouth to say something, but Alex turned away from him, from them both. "We have to find horses," she said to Matthew, "and if we hurry, we'll be in Graham's Garden in two and a half days."

"She isn't there," Ruth whispered. "We don't know where she is." And then she burst out crying.

Alex very much wanted to leave her like that. Stupid, inconsiderate girl – what had she done? Matthew shoved her towards Ruth, and no matter that Alex kept her arms firmly crossed, Ruth clearly saw this as an invitation, throwing herself around Alex's neck. Alex stood stiffly, incapable of doing more than patting Ruth on her back. Ruth sagged against her, the shiny head burrowed into Alex's shoulder as she repeated brokenly that she was so sorry, that she hadn't meant for Sarah to be hurt, that...

"It's okay," Alex lied. "Your father will find her." She was sick with worry, and when she met Matthew's eyes, she could see that he was as well, face pale beneath his tan.

"Aye, of course I will. Have you any idea where she might have gone?"

"Simon might know," Julian said. "I saw him ride in but an hour ago."

"Simon?" Matthew asked.

"He's been looking for her," Julian explained. "Him and Mark, riding hither and thither for the last weeks."

"In your stead?" Matthew said coldly.

Julian muttered something about not being certain Sarah would be much pleased should he find her.

"No, probably not, she'd turn and run – totally

understandable, if you ask me." With that parting shot, Alex bid daughter and son-in-law farewell and hurried after Matthew, already hastening off in search of Simon with David and Charlie at his heels

They found him with his feet in a tub and a tired set to his mouth. Still, he brightened at the sight of them, clasped Matthew's hand, and waved Alex to sit, telling them both to calm down. After some moments of gawking at Charlie, Simon drily informed him that he was remarkably like his father in looks.

"Not that I'll hold it against you," he added. "Assuming, of course, that you're less of a viper than he is." Charlie flushed, eyes going very green. The situation was diffused by Esther, who popped her head in and suggested that Charlie and David accompany her to the kitchen – and the large fish-pie just out of the baking oven.

Once they were alone, Simon turned the subject to Sarah. Through a huge yawn, he said that he was recently back from St Mary's City – and a right fine place it was – and that he had news to share.

"There were two possibilities. Either the man dishonoured her and sold her off down south—" Simon broke off, assuring them that he was sure this was not what had happened.

"How can you be sure of that?" Matthew demanded.

"Because I have proof of the other possibility – that he wed her."

"Married?" Alex squeaked. "But she's not even eighteen!"

Matthew gestured for her to be silent, and motioned for his brother-in-law to continue.

"I have a business acquaintance in St Mary's," Simon said. "Mr Nuthead – a printer."

"Nuthead?" Despite everything, Alex had to laugh. "Is that his real name?"

Assuredly, Simon informed her with a grin, pointing out that this was the first printing establishment in the colony of any note. With Nuthead's help, Simon had located the two town lawyers, and after several hours of wheedling, had managed to extract the information from one of them that yes, he had drawn up a marriage contract in the past weeks for a Sarah Graham.

Simon asked Matthew to hand him his satchel, and after some rooting about, extracted a folded document. "A copy of the deed," he said.

"Michael Connor?" Alex looked down at the unfamiliar name. "Who the hell is Michael Connor?"

"Not from here at any rate," Simon said, raising his hand to hide yet another huge yawn.

"Nay, it says here how he's from York County in Virginia." Matthew looked at Alex. "What was the name of the lad you made eyes at in Jamestown?"

"I did no such thing!" Alex was swimming in relief at seeing her daughter's signature on the contract. No abduction, no further humiliation, but an elopement. Quite romantic, in fact, not at all in keeping with Sarah's hard-nosed take on life, and that made her frown. "I think his name was Michael, but wouldn't that be quite the coincidence?"

Simon cleared his throat to indicate he had more to say. "I found the priest."

"The priest?" Matthew sounded confused.

"Aye, the Catholic priest that wed them."

"Catholic?" Matthew spluttered. "Has she wed a papist?"

"Worse than that, I fear," Simon sighed. "She was baptised a papist before he wed them."

The explosion was formidable, and even if Alex could understand that a lot of what Matthew said – no, yelled – was a reaction to the fear he'd felt for his Sarah, she still considered it all a bit overboard.

"Oh, for God's sake, Matthew," she finally snapped, "let's get our priorities right here, shall we? The most important thing is to ensure that she's okay."

"Okay? How can you say such? She has lost her faith!"

"Don't be such an idiot! God is still God in whatever guise we pray to him, and by now you're old enough to know that there are just as many good and deserving Catholics as Presbyterians."

Matthew scrubbed at his face and sat down. "Aye, but it doesn't help, does it? If you're a papist, you're bound for hell everlasting."

"Bullshit!" Alex snorted, making Matthew smile – if somewhat crookedly.

"I don't think Calvin would agree with you," he said.

"Calvin probably never got properly laid in his life," Alex retorted, "and as a consequence, a lot of what he says is full of testosterone-driven drivel. I bet you he had a crush on a Catholic girl who refused him, and so he set off to do his own little religious thing, and while he was at it got his own back on both Catholics and women."

Simon burst out in loud laughter. "Calvin will be very displeased to hear you disparage him so."

"See if I care," Alex muttered. "It's not as if I'll ever meet him, is it? As far as I know, he's dead." And once she made it up to heaven, she didn't plan on spending her valuable eternal time conversing with a narrow-minded bigot, but she decided to keep that to herself.

Chapter 41

It took Matthew an afternoon to make the necessary arrangements. Kate lent him horses, Simon promised to take care of David, grinning as he ensured he'd keep the lad very busy, and next morning they were ready to go, with Charlie insisting he should accompany them – more, Alex suspected, out of a desire to spend as little time as possible with Simon than any genuine concern for Sarah. Not that Alex felt any need of telling Ruth or Julian their news, but Matthew insisted they deserved to be told, so the trip started with a little detour to Julian's house.

"A Catholic?" Julian swayed where he stood. He regarded Alex blankly for some moments before exhaling loudly. "This just proves, doesn't it, how weak women are spiritually."

"You think?" Alex asked.

"For the sake of a man," Julian grimaced. "For that, she gives up any hope of salvation."

"I would say she ups her odds substantially. After all, as a Catholic, it's her actions and her penitence that give her a place before God, not some predetermined lottery ticket."

Julian's eyes flashed with reproach. "Shame on you, Alexandra!" he said, and looked to Matthew for support. "You tread dangerously close to heresy at times."

"At least I always keep in mind the most important teaching of the Bible," she said primly.

"Oh, you do? And what, pray, is that?"

"Do unto others. Ultimately, Jesus is all about love and compassion." That struck home, she could see – and now for the *coup de grace*. "I would have thought a minister would have known that too – Carlos definitely did, for all that he was a Catholic priest."

"You're at times somewhat too straightforward," Matthew chided once they were on their way. From behind them came the strangled sound of Charlie swallowing back on a gust of laughter.

"And he's at times horribly patronising," Alex said, looking about with interest. They had never ridden from Providence to St Mary's City before, and the path hugged close to the shores of the bay, bordered by stands of reeds and wild grasses that grew in impressive tufts. Now, well into autumn, it was all a soft dun colour, shifting through browns and greys.

"Do you think we'll find her?" Alex asked and nudged the mare she was riding closer to Matthew.

"Aye," he replied, "and then…" He swallowed, looked away. "To do this to me, to marry without my consent!"

Alex made a discreet face. Who cared about his consent? "At least you saved on the dowry."

From the look he gave her, Alex deduced this was no help at all, and at his continued sulking, she opted for riding with Charlie instead.

Matthew was an efficient and tenacious sleuth, and after less than two days in St Mary's City, he came back to the inn feeling very pleased.

"I found them. They're staying on a small plantation just north-west of here." He studied his wife's purchases with resignation. Cocoa beans that in his opinion were horribly overpriced – but Alex was overjoyed at having found such, going on and on about chocolate – cinnamon bark, cardamom pods, ginger, nutmeg, and a further assortment of herbs and spices. "Did you not think you could buy this in Providence?" he asked, inspecting the bolts of broadcloth she had also purchased.

"I had to keep busy while you were out doing your Sherlock Holmes thing. Besides, the apothecary here is excellent."

"And Charlie?" Matthew asked.

Alex winked. "I suspect he's making up for lost time.

345

Not that I hold with whores but in this specific case, it seems to help. He comes back slightly lighter of mind after each bout in bed."

"Different standards?" Matthew inquired. Had it been him setting off to carouse in a whorehouse, she would have flayed him alive.

"He's not mine. Not like you or our boys are. Someone else has brought him up, and I don't think Luke has any moral qualms whatsoever about visiting a whore."

"Mmm." Matthew wondered if Jacob had ever told her of the night in London when Luke had taken him to the best brothel in town. Probably not. "Do you think it's easier to be a Catholic whore than a Protestant one?"

"A Catholic?" Alex spluttered. "Why on earth would it be that?"

"On account of being able to confess and gain absolution for their sinful ways – and I don't know any Presbyterian whores."

"Oh, you don't? And just out of curiosity, how many whores do you know, Mr Graham?" Her eyes narrowed into shards of angry bright blue.

Matthew hitched a shoulder. "The lasses at Mrs Malone's are all Catholic – or Anglican."

"Well, that's a relief for your sensitive male souls, only depraved women in sight. And you didn't answer my question. "

"I know them all by sight, and it happens I talk to them through the evening, buy them a beer." He grinned at her and backed away. "I may whet my appetite outside, Mrs Graham, but I always eat at home." Her brush struck him squarely between the eyes. He picked it up and chased her round the bed.

On the walk out to the plantation, Matthew was sunk in silence, listening with half an ear no more as Alex nattered on about this and that.

He cast her a look. His wife was nervous, hands smoothing at her skirts, her cap. So was he, uncertain as to what etiquette applied when one cornered the man who had eloped with one's daughter. A small vociferous part of him was urging for drawn swords while the saner part suggested a calmer approach – mayhap a punch or two, no more. He laughed at himself, making Alex give him a startled look.

"What?"

"Nothing." He drew in a long, steadying breath. His lass would not take it kindly should he harm the man she had chosen, and given how much she resembled her mother, Matthew decided the prudent approach would be to clasp his hands behind his back and adopt a benign, if somewhat displeased, countenance.

"There." Alex laid a restraining hand on Matthew's sleeve. They were just on the edge of a small stand of wind-battered trees, and to their left, a little creek flowed sluggishly towards the bay.

It was a bright, blustery autumn day, the air filled with golden and red leaves that floated haphazardly this way and that. The meadow before them was dotted with grazing cows and the odd horse, and in the midst of all this was Sarah. Her head was thrown back, and she was laughing, a bubbling sound that he hadn't heard for well over a year.

The man with his head in her lap said something more, and Sarah bent her face towards him. A hand floated up, a finger traced her ear, and drifted slowly down her cheek, and the tenderness in the gesture made his wife turn towards him with a teary smile.

"She's happy," she whispered.

Matthew took off his hat and strode out into the sunlit meadow, sinking down to his ankles in the muddy ground.

His lass: she was laughing and smiling, said something to her man that was cut off when she saw him, squelching towards them. Sarah's mouth fell open, she scrambled to her feet, and her man – his son-in-law – stood up as well. Matthew's chest tightened with pride at the sight of his bonny lass – pride and loss, because she was no longer exclusively his, not anymore.

Without a word, he opened his arms, and Sarah flung herself at him, her cap flying off behind her. Matthew grunted when she collided with him, but managed to steady them both and stood holding her to his heart while over her head he locked eyes with the interloper, the man who had stolen his daughter away without his say-so. He had been right: it was the young man from Jamestown.

Connor bent down to retrieve Sarah's cap, and came forward slowly. Sarah disengaged herself from Matthew's arms, and went to stand beside her husband.

"Your cap, wife," Connor said, and she blushed and covered her head. Connor's arm came round Sarah's waist, drawing her very close to him. His chin went up, his eyes met Matthew's, and in absolute silence they stared each other down.

"Men!" Alex said from where she was coming towards them. She glared at Matthew. "You could have helped me, instead of just barging off!" She raised her muddied hem at him. "Not all of us have boots." She swept by him, and to his annoyance kissed not only their daughter but also a most surprised Michael Connor.

"That was very irresponsible of you," she admonished. "You've had both Julian and Simon in a total fit trying to find you."

"I didn't want them to, and as to Julian…" Sarah's eyes darkened.

"Hmm, yes. And now I hear you've converted as well?" Alex sounded entirely unconcerned, as if this was but a minor matter. Matthew muffled a groan, and Sarah gave him a wary look.

"Aye," she said, sounding defiant. "My husband wished it so."

Her husband wished it so…it near on made Matthew choke. His lass, a lost soul. Silently, he prayed, begging the dear Lord not to be too harsh on her. He stood to the side as his wife conversed with their daughter and new son-in-law, asking them about everything from how they got here to what the wedding had been like. Not, Matthew knew, out of any true interest, but more to give him time to collect himself. Now and then, her eyes flashed to his, a concerned wrinkle on her brow at his continued immobility, his silence.

"I need to talk to you, lass." Matthew took hold of Sarah's arm. "Alone," he added, when Michael made as if to come along. "This is between father and daughter." Two grey eyes met his, Michael's mouth set into a stubborn line, and the young man squared his shoulders, looking at Sarah.

"It'll be fine," Sarah said, smiling at her husband as she followed Matthew towards the nearby stand of trees.

Matthew came to a halt and turned to face her. "How could you?"

"I...well, I love him."

"Not that! I have eyes of my own. But to renounce your faith, lass, how could you do such?"

"Mama says—"

"Mama! You know well enough how important this is to me. And now – you're foresworn."

"Not according to Carlos – or Mama." Defiant blue eyes burned into his, the long, generous mouth, so like his own, set in a displeased line as impressive as his.

"You've done wrong," he sighed.

"Nay, that I have not. I have found my own way to God."

"Your own..." Matthew stuttered, but after a couple of heartbeats of further glaring decided this was not going to help – besides, it was too late, dear Lord it was too late. He pulled her close and hugged her, telling her that no matter how angry he was – and he was – mostly he was relieved to find her hale. Sarah smiled, wept, smiled again, before launching herself into a panegyric over her new husband.

"He what?" Matthew looked in disbelief at his daughter and then back at his wife, who was talking to their new son-in-law some twenty-odd yards away.

"You heard me," Sarah said. "He shot Philip Burley."

Matthew's brain scrambled with the effort of assimilating this. The name, the piebald horse! The man his daughter had wed was at best a brigand, at worst a murderer, a black-hearted rapist.

"Oh aye? And why was he there in the first place? To pillage and burn, to wreak havoc on our family, and

349

you have gone and married him?" Matthew's hand closed around the hilt of his sword.

"But he didn't. Instead, he saw me and shot his uncle."

"His uncle?" Matthew turned towards Connor. Sweetest Lord! Burley blood wed to his lass! No, this was too much, he had to… Matthew staggered, eyes on the lock of chestnut hair that fell across Connor's brow, just like that accursed Philip Burley's hair used to do, albeit that his hair was as pitch-black as his soul.

"He's his own man, Da. He isn't his uncle," Sarah said, putting a hand on his sleeve.

He tore himself free, shoved her away from him. "He's a Burley! He is kin to the men who—" He closed his eyes. "How could you? How can you stand his hands on you?" How could she do this to him, to the memory of her dead brother?

"Da," Sarah was close to tears, "please, Da. He's not like them, he's kind and—"

"I don't want to hear it! He has Burley blood – tainted, evil blood." Matthew spat at her feet and walked off.

He stood leaning against a tree when he heard Alex come up behind him.

"Matthew? Are you alright?"

Alright? "She's wed to a Burley," he said in a lifeless voice.

"No, she isn't, he's a Connor. And you can't blame him for his uncles, can you?" But he could hear it in her voice, that she was disconcerted too.

"So you don't care?" he demanded. "It is no matter to you that she's married to Burley kin?"

"I…" Alex hesitated. "Of course it matters. But—"

"He rode with Philip Burley! I slew his brother on my land!" He closed his eyes at the memory of his honed sword blade slicing through the younger man's flesh.

"I'm sure he doesn't hold that against you."

"Hold it against me? The man should be hanged and instead I find him my son-in-law!" Matthew knotted his fist and stuffed it in his mouth to stop himself from screaming the invectives that thronged his throat. His daughter wed to scum. His daughter a papist.

When Alex placed a hand on his shoulder, he shrugged it off. He didn't want her touch, he wanted to be alone with his rage. Besides, if Alex had not encouraged Carlos' and Sarah's friendship, none of this would have happened. He should have married her off the moment he found out she was pregnant, he thought angrily, but knew even as he thought it that he never would have done so – not when his lass was as fragile as a cracked egg. He sighed deeply.

"Matthew?" Alex sounded tentative, her fingers brushing at his cheek. He sighed again, and slid down to sit. She crouched before him. He scrubbed at his hair, at his unshaven cheeks.

"How can she bear him to touch her?" He gave her an anguished look.

"She knew him as Michael first. By the time he told her who he was, she was already in love with him. But apparently, she did have something of a shock."

That caught Matthew's interest, and he laughed when Alex described how Sarah had sent Michael flying.

Alex nestled up close and rested her cheek against his shoulder. "You see it too, don't you?" she said. "That's why you're so angry."

"See what?"

"How they dance around each other, like moths round a candle flame – like you and me," she said, rubbing her face against his shirt.

Aye, he did, and it made him sick to the gut that his lass should find such magic with a man that should be her sworn enemy. Matthew made a small sound, conveying with fine precision just how disgusting he found the entire matter.

"Give him a chance. He can't help his beginnings – none of us can."

"Hmph," Matthew said, but put his arms round her.

Chapter 42

It was fortunate, Matthew reflected, that neither Sarah nor Michael were with them when they met Minister Macpherson a day's ride or so north of Providence. The minister was riding with several armed servants, looked Charlie up and down a couple of times, and expressed a warm welcome to the colony.

"We need men like you," the minister said. "Young men who don't hesitate to take up arms against the evil papists – king or not." Charlie shifted in his saddle and muttered a thank you. The minister went on to offer Matthew the loan of a couple of his men, seeing as at present there was much unrest.

"Unrest?" Matthew asked.

"Oh yes, the Indians are out in force, and even worse, we have papists attacking good Protestant homes." The minister shook his head. "All papists should be driven off, don't you agree, Brother Matthew?" From the gleam in the minister's eyes, it was apparent he knew about Sarah, was but taking the opportunity to twist the blade deeper.

"As long as they live peaceably with us, I think not," Matthew replied in a calm voice. As he heard it, the aggressors were his own brethren, the papists acting mostly out of self-defence.

"Ah, but they don't. And then what?" The minister rode his horse closer. "No, Brother Matthew, mark my words, it is time this colony is cleansed, once and for all. Throw them all into the sea, I say."

"In keeping with your general character," Alex muttered – fortunately too low for the minister to hear. Matthew sent her a warning look. He had no desire for further altercations with the ministers of his kirk, this whole matter with Sarah would be difficult to live down as it was. He near on squirmed inside as he collected the pitying looks of the other elders he'd met in Providence. To his relief, Alex took heed, angry blue eyes shielded by lowered lashes.

"Mmm?" Matthew had not caught the minister's latest remark.

"I said," the minister repeated, "that it is a calamity, this matter with your lass. However, she's been raised in the kirk, and I dare say we will find it in us to forgive her and welcome her back – once she's admitted to her grievous fault and done adequate penance for it, of course."

"Ah," Matthew said, thinking this mountain of a man had more subtlety in him than he'd imagined – a most graceful turning of the screw, this was.

"Yes," the minister continued, nodding so enthusiastically his chins, his jowls, wobbled. "What she needs is a husband of the right faith, a man who will take it upon himself to lead her back, to spare neither rod nor tongue in his efforts to make her see the light." Minister Macpherson straightened up in his saddle, a motion accompanied by a creaking sound that had Matthew wondering whether the fat man wore some sort of corset. "Someone like me," the minister clarified with a little smile. "A sacrifice, of course, but one I'd gladly undertake to bring this lost lamb back to the fold."

"Sure you would," Alex said – yet again in an undertone. "Pervert."

Matthew had but the vaguest idea what this word might mean, but he suspected it was an adequate label to stick on the eager minister. Not much of a man of God at present, more of a man inflamed by twisted lust.

"That is most kind of you," Matthew replied, "but I am sure you're aware Sarah is recently wed." From the surprised look on the minister's face, it would seem Julian had chosen not to share this information with his fellow ministers.

"Oh." The minister arranged his features into a grave mask. "I am sorry for your loss, Brother. It must grieve you to have lost your lass and know her bound for hell everlasting."

"Aye," Matthew said through gritted teeth. The minister wasn't done.

"Ah well, lax mothers raise lax daughters."

It was a miracle, in Matthew's opinion, that Alex chose to do nothing but raise her face to look at the minister – for a very long time. With the softest of snorts, she set heels to her horse and rode off, with Charlie falling in behind.

"Bastard," Alex said once Matthew had caught up with them.

"Aye, he enjoyed that. Still, he is but voicing the opinion of the majority of our fellow colonists."

Alex looked quite drawn, the corners of her mouth drooping slightly. "Will they be alright?"

"Who? Sarah and Michael? Aye, of course they will." At least for now, he amended silently, and St Mary's City was mostly papist. "I am more concerned about how he will keep her."

"You know how. He's a printer, and that Mr Nuthead has offered him a partnership."

"Aye." Matthew looked away.

"What?" Alex rode close enough that their knees touched.

"I don't like it. Yon Michael is the youngest son of a cooper, and yet he has the gold to set himself up as a partner. Blood money – Burley money."

"You don't know that," she said.

He didn't deign to answer. Instead, he urged his horse into a trot.

A few hours after dawn two days later, they turned into their lane. Alex stood in the stirrups, craning her neck for that first glimpse of her home, and there it was, the smoke rising straight from the chimneys of the big house. The lane dipped and turned on its way to their yard, the huge oak that stood at its centre was still in leaf, and just beyond the barn she could make out the river, glittering like silver in the early morning sun. Home: she sat back down with a thud, ridiculously glad to be back.

A gaggle of children rushed to surround them when they were sighted, and Alex stood for a very long time with Adam in her arms. Hugin cawed Alex in the ear, tenderly plucked at her hair before spreading his winds to fly over to perch on Lovell Our Dog. Adam took Alex by the hand, and led her down to the smoking shed where they together counted to seven pigs in bits and pieces.

"And a further three Ian sold at the Michaelmas market," Adam said, "and it was me that helped him with the slaughtering."

"You?" Alex asked – her youngest preferred healing animals to butchering them.

"Mark was off looking for Sarah, and Agnes was sick at the time, and Betty is great-bellied as is Naomi, and Mrs Parson is a wee bit too old, she says, to slaughter and salt all on her own."

"Naomi is with child?" Alex asked, latching on to the single piece of truly important news. She had as yet to see either of her daughter-in-laws – or her elder sons – as Adam had effectively monopolised her from the moment he saw her.

"Aye, well into her fifth month by now." Adam sighed theatrically. He lived surrounded by bairns and weans, he informed her. Soon, there would be nine small Grahams – excluding himself, of course.

Before she could properly greet her eldest sons, Matthew strode off to inspect his fields with Mark and Ian at his heels. After a quick hello to Naomi, a hug for Betty – who was the size of a beer cask – Alex went to find Mrs Parson, who was sitting on the small bench by the kitchen door, face raised to the October sun. They didn't hug, they just held hands – for a long, long time. A gust of wind rattled through the long, thorny branches of the rambling rose just by the door, showering them with white petals from the tenacious roses still in bloom.

"So, you're too old to help with the pigs, I hear." Alex cleared her throat of a wad of emotion.

The old woman fixed her with a sharp eye and informed

her she had been busy as it was. "Thomas Leslie was took poorly so I spent some time at Leslie's Crossing nursing him, and then Agnes trod into a hornet's nest and she was right ill for some days, and then we have wee Lettie, no?" She smiled fondly at the child in question who was leaping about on crutches as a consequence of trying to ride the bull.

"For our sins," Alex muttered, just as fondly. "Was he that ill?"

"Hmm? Oh, Thomas, you mean. Aye, he was. Fortunate that I was there." It came out very casual. Instead, Mrs Parson nodded in the direction of Charlie, standing quite alone by the stables. "A chip of the old block, that one. Bonny lad, if somewhat thin. So, was he worth the effort?"

"Well, I don't think he deserved to die," Alex prevaricated.

"But?" Mrs Parson asked, studying Charlie who was doing a slow turn, taking in the Graham homestead with an expression of awe on his face.

"Saving him could have cost us our lives." Alex glanced at Mrs Parson. "And if I have to choose between him and Matthew, well…"

Mrs Parson snorted – loudly. "No one is worth as much to you as Matthew, so that isn't saying much does it?" She threw Charlie yet another look. "If he starts behaving like his father, I'll serve him hemlock for dinner. The world would not cope with another Luke Graham."

Alex laughed. "Oh no, Charlie is nothing like Luke – he's too naïve."

"Strange, isn't it," Alex said to Matthew a few hours later, "no sooner do we set foot on our lane but we're inundated by visitors."

"Inundated? It's just the one." Matthew laughed, raising his hand in greeting to Thomas Leslie.

"Yeah, and we've just waved goodbye to John Ingram." Alex rolled her eyes at Ian – still no opportunity for a nice long chat – and with a little sigh, went inside to advise

Agnes there would be one more for their late dinner.

Thomas Leslie waved away their concern at his shrunken frame.

"I was sick to the gut for over a week," he explained, "and I have as yet to fully recover." He beamed at Mrs Parson, who beamed back, and Alex raised her brows in surprise. She studied them both with increased curiosity over dinner, biting back on laughter that threatened to choke her when she saw Mrs Parson fuss with her hair, Thomas' eyes hanging off her hands as the starched cap was discarded, the hair smoothed into place and covered once again.

"She did that on purpose," she said to Matthew in an aside. "There was absolutely nothing wrong with her hair."

"He didn't seem to mind." Matthew winked, and went off in search of Charlie with Thomas in tow.

"You're flirting with him," Alex said to Mrs Parson. "He's too young for you." That was probably an exaggeration, given the mere decade in age difference between them.

"We're old enough the two of us to choose for ourselves," Mrs Parson retorted, "and you of all should approve, no? All that free love you blather on about."

"Free love?" Mark stretched for another slice of pie, giving her an interested look. Alex sighed. With the exception of Mrs Parson and Simon, only Ian and Mark knew of her unorthodox background, but while Ian, just like Matthew, preferred not to talk about it, Mark loved hearing titbits from her future life.

"I was a product of all that free love, more or less, but I didn't practise it much." She resigned herself to explaining what she meant, seeing Mark's eyes widen at the titillating concept of sex without babies.

"It can be done now as well," Alex said with some irritation. "Not one hundred per cent foolproof, but still…" She broke off at the amused look in Mark's eyes.

"Oh aye?" He sounded just like Matthew when he said that. "Is that why you gave Da nine bairns?"

"Well, it doesn't always work," Alex mumbled, making her son break out in laughter.

It was almost dusk before Alex had the opportunity for her longed-for talk with Ian.

"Finally!" Alex smiled at her eldest son and patted the graveyard bench beside her.

Ian lowered himself to sit. "Are you alright? You look a wee bit thinner."

"That's because I throw up continuously when we're at sea," Alex said.

They settled back, and she told him most of their adventures, including the terrible night when she'd almost died at the hands of a pyromaniac.

"I have these pretty awful dreams," she admitted, rather embarrassed.

Ian placed a reassuring arm around her. "You're still here."

"Yes, I am." Alex rested against his solid frame. "So, what do you think of your brother?"

Ian's face clouded. Charlie was just as he remembered him, he said: red-haired and green-eyed. He sighed, admitting that he could still recall how utterly miserable he had been at finding himself so totally replaced in Luke's affections by newborn Charlie, his status in Luke's household changing overnight from Beloved Only Son to Tolerated Cuckoo.

"But that wasn't Charlie's fault," Alex pointed out.

"Nay, of course not. But seeing him, well, it brings it all back. And he's uncomfortably like his father."

"Very, but only on the outside. However contradictory it seems, Luke – viper that he is – has managed to raise a fine son." Apart from when he'd clobbered Matthew over the head and thereby almost killed him. Alex gnawed her lip and decided this was an incident best not shared with Ian – and anyway, Charlie had done enough penance as it was.

Ian shifted on the bench, and nodded over to the gravestones that Alex had swept clean and decorated with one white rose each: one for Jacob and one for Magnus. "Did you miss them?"

"Miss them?" Alex looked over at the stones. "I always

miss them." She stood, ostensibly to rearrange the flower on Jacob's headstone. Her eyes locked on the serrated silhouette of the north-western forests, now at dusk a dark, jagged line against a lighter sky. Him she missed the most: her Samuel, her little Indian son. Alive and well, she hoped, but lost to her.

"You're hurting," she stated as they made their way down.

Ian didn't try to argue, he just nodded. "Betty hasn't been able to help me as much as she usually does, what with her being the size of a dray horse." Alex cracked her knuckles ominously, and used her head to indicate his cabin. He grinned down at her. "You don't frighten me, Mama."

"That's because it's far too long since I massaged you," she growled, and he laughed, leading the way.

He really was in a bad way, but as the oil and the steady rubbing heated his skin, he relaxed, falling into a heavy slumber while Alex prodded and worked her way through layers of stiff muscles.

"I've tried." Betty attempted to kneel beside Alex.

"I'm sure you have, and please get up, before you get permanently stuck down here."

Betty laughed and swayed back to her feet.

"He's right." Alex took in Betty's gigantic size. "You're positively huge."

Betty grimaced and moved over to where she was brewing raspberry tea. "I hope she comes soon."

"She?" Alex chuckled. "No, Betty Graham, that's a he!"

A long day ended with a chilly bath in the river – far too cold for more than a hasty dip – and after spending hours over supper, surrounded by their family, Alex and Matthew retired to their bedchamber.

"…alternatively, Betty is carrying two, but Mrs Parson insists it's only one." Alex sighed and shook out her hair. "It seems very big."

"Aye," Matthew replied, taking her brush. He met her eyes in the looking glass, and worked his way through tangles and curls, brushing until her hair lay crackling down her back. "She'll be fine," he said with a quiet certainty Alex found very reassuring. "You can see it. The lass isn't afraid."

"No," Alex agreed, recalling Betty's face. Lit from within she was, her eyes glowing like dark amber in the sun.

She opened one of her many stone jars, sniffed at the content to ensure it hadn't gone rancid, and rubbed hands and face and neck with this her home-made concoction of grease, herbs and roses. She took his hands in hers and worked some balm into them, twining fingers round and round his until they were both slippery-handed.

"Bed?" she suggested with heavy innuendo, sliding his thumb in and out between her well-oiled fingers.

The rope-frame creaked under their combined weight. Matthew had lit the headboard candle, throwing the room into a pleasant golden light. The linen rustled below them, smelling faintly of sun and hay. It was good to be home, to lie close to each other and say nothing at all. He caressed her face, her neck. She leaned towards him to place a kiss on his mouth. He tasted of beer and smoked trout, of butter and bread. When he rolled her over, she hooked her legs around his. It was good to be home, to feel his weight on her body, the heat of his skin. Her shift was shoved out of the way, his hot breath tickled her neck, her ear. They moved slowly together, joined from groin to sternum, hands tightly braided.

"Home," she whispered.

"Aye, home," he replied, dipping his head to brush her nose with his.

Chapter 43

"I need a new pair of breeches," Matthew informed Alex a week or so later, holding up a well patched pair that had decided to give up on life.

She looked at the new tear and frowned. "I'm seriously behind in my sewing, and Adam has shot up like a leek over summer, so he needs both shirt and breeches."

She went over to inspect her two winter skirts that hung neatly from their pegs. She'd have to sacrifice one of them to sew up breeches for her son, and then she'd make herself new skirts out of the dark green she'd bought in St Mary's City. Luckily, Mrs Parson was taking up any slack in the knitting department, turning out woollen stockings at a horrifying speed for all of them.

"Aye, well," Mrs Parson said drily, "seeing as I was remiss in helping with the hogs, I'm making up for it like this, no?" Her eyes twinkled, taking the edge off the reprimand, and she went on to suggest that maybe Alex could bake yet another of those cocoa cakes as Thomas Leslie would be stopping by for dinner.

"He is?" Alex asked.

"Aye," Matthew replied from behind her. "Not to pay court to Cinderella here, but to have words with me and the Chisholms about the Indians."

Alex swallowed back a laugh. Her family loved her stories, and the one about Cinderella was a particular favourite with Mrs Parson.

"Cinderella," Mrs Parson muttered and extended one stoutly shod foot. "And how do you see me fitting into a glass slipper?" She wagged a finger at him, and threatened she'd knit him pink stockings if he wasn't careful.

★

Thomas Leslie sat back, replete, and beamed at the table in general and Mrs Parson in particular. Robert Chisholm gave him a surprised look, followed his adoring gaze across the table, and looked even more surprised, but forgot all this when Alex asked him if he wanted seconds.

"Most tasty," he complimented, and served himself some of the cake.

"So, Indians," Matthew said, shoving his plate away.

"I somehow suspect these aren't local Indians," Thomas concluded after bringing Matthew up to date on the latest spate of homestead attacks.

Robert and Martin nodded in agreement.

"Oh aye? Why not?" Matthew asked.

"Too violent." Thomas offered his tobacco pouch to Martin, and the two men spent some minutes preparing their pipes. "There is an element of desperation, and the violence is such that any local tribe would know we will raise the militia and come after them." Thomas shrugged and nodded to the south. "I think they are foreigners, dispossessed of their own lands, and, if so, the Iroquois will do away with them quickly."

"Iroquois?" Alex said, thinking of her Samuel.

"Yes, this is their land – well, what isn't ours, of course." Thomas smiled reassuringly at Alex. "It's no great matter, Alex. A few bands of desperate braves, no more. Easily vanquished, I'd reckon."

"But for now, we must watch out for our own," Martin said, and the six men nodded and began to plan guard duty for the coming weeks. Alex kept careful eyes on them, but from their relaxed positions and their occasional laugh, she gathered none of them were particularly worried – not even Matthew seemed unduly concerned. She listened for some time longer but was soon bored out of her mind by the long rambling discussions and decided instead to go and check on the expectant mother, dragging Mrs Parson along with her.

"How are you feeling?" Alex asked Betty who turned tired eyes in her direction.

"I don't get much sleep, and my back…"

Mrs Parson patted her reassuringly on her thigh. "It'll be any day now, lass."

Betty managed a faint smile and smoothed down her skirts. "I can't wait," she said, sounding as if she meant it. She patted at her head and frowned. Her hair stood like a red brown cloud around her face, curling wildly this way and that, and with an irritated sound, she clapped her linen cap over it. "Let's hope she gets her father's hair," she said before waddling off.

"It's a big child," Mrs Parson said, her cheerful tone wiped away. "And it hasn't turned."

"And three weeks late." They shared a concerned look: a huge child and a breech birth. "She'll do fine," Alex said brightly, "right?"

"It's in God's hands, lass. I don't think it will come amiss to pray."

The waters broke in the middle of the night, and Maggie came rushing to bang at the door. Alex and Mrs Parson ran to help, Matthew efficiently bundled Ian and his three children out of the cabin, stopped by Betty's bedside to give her an encouraging smile, and then left the women to it.

"I'm so sorry," Betty said, shifting on the drenched mattress. Alex told her not to be silly and helped her up to stand, holding her while Agnes dragged the sodden, heavy material off the bed.

"Walk her," Mrs Parson said to Alex, busy warming oil rich with herbs by the fire.

"What are you doing?" Betty asked, highly embarrassed when she was told to lie down, her thighs spread apart so that Mrs Parson could apply the oil.

"Lubrication," Alex said, and then Betty was back on her feet to walk. All that night and the whole following day, Betty walked, her stomach hardening into a huge orb at regular intervals. She drank the herbal teas Mrs Parson steeped, she allowed herself to be oiled, and she walked and walked, her breath whistling in and out of her nose during the contractions. And then, finally, the contractions changed, and Mrs Parson made odd noises as she examined Betty, lying once again on her back.

Four hours later, they were all drenched in sweat. The room was out of necessity hot, Betty had torn off her shift to twist about in only her damp and reddened skin, and she no longer even tried to smile – she just concentrated on breathing as the pain seemed to tear her apart. Blood trickled out from between her legs, and Mrs Parson called for more oil.

"It's stuck," Mrs Parson whispered to Alex, "and I can't even get a finger in to help."

"Ian!" Betty screamed. "I want Ian!" She looked around wildly. "Please," she croaked, "Ian, I…"

Agnes was already on her way, braids flying behind her as she rushed across the yard.

It was a testament of how worried Mrs Parson was that she didn't even try to remonstrate when Ian rushed through the door.

"Sit behind her and hold her," Mrs Parson said to a white-faced Ian, "and help her push, aye?"

"Help her push?" Ian had his wife in his arms, eyes fixed on her bloody thighs.

"You'll see," Mrs Parson assured him, and he did, his wrists raked by Betty's nails when she bore down time after time again. Nothing happened. The baby's legs and pelvis had effectively corked the passage.

"We have to cut her!" Alex hissed. "Otherwise, we'll never get it out."

"Cut her?" Ian's hands came down protectively over Betty's belly.

"Not there, you idiot!" Alex snapped, frazzled into impatience through a combination of fear and exhaustion. Betty twisted in pain, complaining that someone was driving knives into her, and could they please stop. Ian cried into her hair, begging that they do something.

Mrs Parson palpated the distended belly and frowned. "The afterbirth," she said in a low voice to Alex.

"Oh shit," Alex replied, and handed the knife to Mrs

Parson, who just as promptly handed it back, indicating her shaking fingers.

Ian stared at them and clutched his wife even harder. "What mean you to do?"

"We have to give the baby passage," Alex explained. "If it comes to the crunch," she said as steadily as she could, "will you have us save the mother or the child?" For an instant, her arm shook wildly. Saving the mother might mean dismembering the child.

"Betty," Ian replied immediately, "save my wife." His eyes looked huge in the dim light of the cabin, hanging off Alex's face in search of reassurance. Alex nodded once.

At the next contraction, Alex cut according to Mrs Parson's instructions, two swift incisions in the perineum. Betty barely reacted. She was more or less unconscious by now, a swollen weight in Ian's arms. Alex took a big breath, and timing it with Betty's violent contractions, managed to insert her fingers into the birth canal. The pain had Betty sitting upright, shrieking like a flayed cat, and Alex had to grit her teeth not to scream when the smooth musculature closed around her hand and imprisoned it.

A leg, two small legs, knees pressing into the vaginal wall and hindering the baby's passage. She had hold of something – a foot – and with a quick prayer to God that He please not let it slip away or somehow come off, she pulled at the next contraction and one little leg was out, dangling grotesquely. One more contraction and both legs were out. There was blood, very much blood. Betty writhed and kicked, screamed and roared, and then the baby was outside, more or less tugged free by Alex's panicked hands. The afterbirth descended in a rush of even more blood, drenching the bed.

"Here!" Alex handed the blue and limp baby girl to Agnes.

"She'll bleed to death!" Ian wept. "Oh God, Mama, do something, please do something!"

Alex didn't reply. Together with Mrs Parson, she was trying to locate the bleeding, and, with a relieved sigh, she

365

saw that most of it came from a deep tear up the vaginal wall.

"For a moment, I thought I might have cut too deep," she whispered to Mrs Parson, and without thinking too much, placed the red–hot blade of the knife against the welling blood. Betty moaned but didn't wake, and the room was filled with the unpleasant stench of frying human flesh.

"You did well," Mrs Parson said, looking so haggard Alex told her to sit down by the fire while she finished with this.

"Let's just hope I don't sew the wrong bits together by mistake," she muttered, wincing every time she sank the curved needle into the pink flesh. No one heard her. Betty was in a deep faint, Ian was kissing the top of her head between repeating her name, Mrs Parson had leaned back against the wall with closed eyes, and Agnes was busy with the baby, massaging the little girl to breathe.

"Will she live?" Alex asked over her shoulder.

"She will," Agnes replied, sounding determined. Some moments later, the baby mewled. "She'll live. God be praised, she'll live," Agnes said, bursting into tears.

"She'll never heal entirely, I'm afraid," Alex said to Ian once a cleaned and changed Betty had been put to bed. Her daughter–in–law looked like a shrunk wraith, all colour bleached out of her. "I think it will be painful for her to… err…well, to make love. At least for quite some time." Ian just nodded and went back to stroking his wife's face. "And no more children, Ian, no matter how she begs, never again."

"No more, I'll never put my Betty through this ordeal again." He gave her a despairing look. "She will live, won't she?"

"She will," Alex said.

Ian nodded and went back to staring at his sleeping wife. As yet, he hadn't asked about the baby.

"A girl," Betty said weakly a couple of hours later. Despite Ian's irritation, Alex had insisted on waking her regularly throughout the night, forcing her on her feet and even at one point insisting she had to use the chamber pot.

"Yes," Alex smiled at her daughter-in-law. "A gigantic girl. Ten pounds and counting."

Betty's lashes fluttered close, but her mouth turned up in a proud smile. Alex shook her gently and handed her a mug of rosehip soup, laced with the last of the cream for the season. Poor Betty could barely sit, but struggled bravely all the same, using her hands to lever herself sufficiently upright to drink.

"What will you name her?" Alex asked Ian who was sitting on the bed with his newborn daughter in his arms. For an instant, she rested her finger on the fontanel and felt for the reassuring thrumming of the rapid pulse. Still tinged with blue, still somewhat flaccid, but definitely alive.

"Grace," Ian said, "for it's through the grace of God that she lives, and her mother too." His hand gripped tight around Betty's wrist, he tipped towards her, rested his head on her shoulder, and cried. Betty lifted her arms to hold him, and over his dark head she met Alex's eyes. It was time to leave, Alex decided, blowing Betty a kiss before stepping outside.

Alex stood for a while on Ian's doorstoop. Every limb, every square inch of skin on her was tired. She was dirty and smelled of blood and other fluids, and at present the walk over the yard to her own bed was like contemplating crossing the Sahara desert. Her knees gave way, and she sat, legs extended before her, head resting against the cabin wall. It was cold. Dawn was still nothing but a lighter band of grey along the eastern horizon, and she really should get back on her feet. Later. She closed her eyes.

"Bath?" Matthew materialised out of the darkness. Gently, he helped her to stand, took her hand, and in the breaking November morning, they walked over to the laundry shed. The little space was agreeably warm — Matthew must have lit the fire some while ago — and Alex creaked down to sit on one of the long benches and began to undress. He helped her with knots and lacings, her fingers gone numb, her eyes blurred with tears.

"She almost died."

"But she didn't, did she?" He lit candles, filled the tub with water from the cauldron and the rainwater barrels until it was an adequate temperature, hot enough to make her dance when she got in, bearable enough that she could force her buttocks through the surface to sit on the bottom.

"Oooo!" she gasped. Matthew got in as well, lowering himself inch by inch into the hot water.

They didn't talk as they washed each other. They came together for a kiss and a caress, and then slid apart to lie drowsily facing each other with water well up to their shoulders. Alex used her toes to tickle him, and he smiled and returned the favour. They added more hot water, they argued over the pumice stone, and by the time they regretfully decided they had to get up, their fingertips had shrivelled into raisins, and Alex's hair had corkscrewed round her head, making Matthew grin and tell her she looked like the Medusa.

He slapped her hands away and sternly told her to lie still while he spread the fragrant oil across her skin. Together, they examined the new scar on his thigh, and he rolled her closest nipple between his thumb and finger. She commented that his groin was once again well covered in hair, pretended mock horror and plucked a single hair she insisted was entirely white, and he yelped and growled that how would she like it if he plucked her? And the hair wasn't white – it was her eyesight going, as anyone could see that if anything the hair in her hand was fair.

"Fair?" she chortled, and he kissed her hungrily until she stopped laughing and wound her arms around his neck instead.

Chapter 44

Matthew was cleaning his musket and instructing Adam in the fine art of gun maintenance when the troop of six unfamiliar men came trotting down his lane. Matthew regarded them with caution, eyeing their uniform clothing, their sashes and hats, the swords that hung at their sides, and the muskets that were carried with casual ease. Soldiers of sorts, he concluded, and a little tremor flew up his spine. Matthew Graham had no fond memories of the English soldiers in Cumnock.

"Master Graham?" the apparent leader said once the horses had been halted.

"Aye." He shoved Adam in the direction of the house. "Tell your mama we have guests."

"We are here on account of one Charles Graham."

"Charlie? What would you want with him?" Out of the corner of his eye, Matthew saw a bright red head appear in the stable door, just as quickly retracted.

"So, he is here, is he?" The man dismounted, beckoned for his companions to follow suit.

"I didn't say that, did I? I just asked what business you might have with him."

"Charles Graham is a convicted rebel. We are here to ensure justice is carried out as it was laid out."

"Oh aye? On what authority?"

The man produced a deed and handed it over. "Lord Calvert will not have it, a traitor here, in the colony."

Matthew finished reading the document, a tersely worded document instructing him to surrender his traitorous nephew to these men so that he could be shipped back to Barbados and live out his sentence.

"Who told you he'd be here?" Matthew asked, handing back the deed.

"Lord Calvert was informed by the Governor of Barbados that you took it upon yourself to steal him away."

"I didn't steal him. I bought him."

"You attempted to pervert the course of justice," the man flared, "and that, Master Graham, we cannot condone."

By now, Matthew had been joined by Mark and Ian, both of them carrying guns. The troop of six shuffled on their feet, their leader giving Matthew's sons but a cursory nod.

"So," the man said, "where is he?"

"Not here. Wee Charlie has seen fit to leave. He yearned for home, I reckon."

"You'll not mind us verifying that he's not in residence, I trust."

"As a matter of fact, I do," Matthew said, "but I'll not stop you."

The leader sent off his men to search the farm, commenting that Charles Graham should be easy enough to spot, what with his uncommon height and red hair, and to Matthew all of this brought back uncomfortable memories of those repeated, humiliating searches of Hillview in Scotland. However, these men were far more polite, and when they came back empty-handed, Matthew's shoulders eased down from their uncomfortable stiffness. He had no idea where Charlie was hiding, but it would seem the lad had chosen wisely.

"We might be back," the spokesman said once the troop was horsed again.

"Aye, you might," Matthew muttered to his back as the horses ambled out of sight.

"They didn't believe you, did they?" Mark said.

"Nay, lad, I think not." Matthew sighed. He had no desire to end up in an altercation with the colonial administration, but neither could he give up Charlie.

Adam came back just before supper after a walk in the woods, and told Matthew that their previous visitors had made camp a mere mile or so from the house. "And I saw two or three of them slinking through the woods, like."

"Ah," Matthew said, throwing a worried look at where Charlie was sitting huddled together and with his hat on, despite being indoors.

"We'll have to dye his hair," Naomi said.

"Dye my hair?" Charlie straightened up from his slouch.

"Black or such," Naomi said.

"Black?" Alex sounded doubtful. She pulled off Charlie's hat, tugged her fingers through the bright red hair. "You know how to do this?"

Naomi assured them that she did, and a few minutes later, the women had placed Charlie on a stool, busy with his hair.

"Hmm." Matthew inclined his head this way and that as he studied the end result.

"What?" Charlie's hands flew to his hair, now an impressive…purple? Aye, Matthew sighed, the lad's hair was now an unfortunate deep purple rather than black.

"At least it's not red," Alex said, laughter bubbling through her voice.

"Nay, that it's not. A nice colour," Mrs Parson put in, "if somewhat unusual."

"Unusual? How unusual?" Charlie glared at Naomi.

"I didn't know, did I?" Naomi said. "I thought it would be the same to dye hair as to dye wool – and Mother always used red maple bark to make wool black."

"But it's not." Alex laughed, and Charlie flew up, demanding that someone bring him a looking glass.

Come morning, the purple notes had faded somewhat, leaving Charlie with hair that at a distance could pass for dark grey. Fortunately, as it turned out, because all day the troop remained close, silent shadows that made no attempt to hide their presence as they studied the comings and goings on the Graham farm.

"It's not as I can ask him to leave, is it?" Matthew said when Alex complained about all this. "Where would the lad go?" He speared yet another baked onion, crunching through it before speaking again. "They'll grow bored soon enough. Let's hope it rains – that will drive them back home even sooner."

That night, they were woken in the small hours by frantic knocking on their front door.

"Let me in, let me in! For the love of God, please let me in!"

Matthew bounded down the stairs in only his shirt, grabbed his musket, and opened the door. One of the troop fell inside, breeches undone, barefoot and unarmed. He was covered in blood, an arrow protruded from his back, and every breath was accompanied by a rattle.

"Indians," he said through bloodied lips, "dear Lord, so many Indians!"

"Where?" Matthew closed the door with a bang, handed Alex a pistol, and waved for Charlie to secure the back door.

"Up there..." A long digit pointed up the lane. Matthew cursed, told Adam to fetch his breeches and the extra pistol.

"No." Alex stood before the door. "No way. You're not going out there."

"I have to," Matthew said. "They need help."

"Help?" Their guest began to laugh – nay, wail. "There's nothing you can do to help them. Oh God, oh God, please..." There was a gurgle, a long wheeze and just like that, the poor man died.

The carnage was such that Matthew gagged. The air buzzed with blowflies, lengths of gut hung from the disembowelled men, mouths had frozen into silent screams, baring teeth, mutilated tongues, and, in one case, a severed cock that had been rammed down the unfortunate's gullet. All five had been scalped – while alive, Matthew suspected.

"Christ have mercy!" Mark's eyes slid this way and that, as if attempting to find something to rest his gaze on that was not spattered with blood.

"Wolves," a voice said from the shadow of the trees, and Qaachow came out to stand beside them. "Twice they have raided our villages, leaving a trail of blood and tears behind."

"Wolves? Rabid wolves, I'd say." Matthew clenched his hand round the stock of his musket.

"Cornered wolves," Qaachow corrected with a slight stretching of his lips. "Soon."

"How many?" Matthew asked, seeing before his mind's eye how his home was overrun by these savages. As of tonight, they'd sleep in the big house, all of them.

"Here?" Qaachow shrugged, called out something in his own tongue. Matthew took a step back when Samuel appeared with his bow in hand. The lad gave him a brief smile before going over to stand by Qaachow.

"Eight, I count it to," Samuel replied in English, studying the gruesome scene with far more dispassion than Matthew liked.

"You shouldn't be seeing such. Your mama would not like it."

"My son must see," Qaachow said. "A man must learn everything he can about his enemies before he sets out to hunt them."

"Hunt them?" Matthew had to clear his throat. "You mean to take an untried lad with you?"

"Untried?" Qaachow shook his head, placing a hand on Samuel's shoulder. "White Bear is blooded. Two nights back, he killed his first man, did you not?"

Samuel nodded, a wide smile on his face that had very little to do with the darkness in his eyes.

"He's but a lad!" Matthew exploded.

"You keep on saying that, and I keep on reminding you that to us he is almost a man." In a low voice, Qaachow said something to Samuel that had him melting back into the shadows. "I don't risk my sons needlessly," he added before following the lad out of sight.

"Not a word to your mama," Matthew told Mark as they made their way back home, "about wee Samuel, I mean."

Mark was still green about the mouth, but inclined his head to show he'd heard.

"...so as of today, I want us all to sleep here," Matthew said, shoving his half-eaten breakfast away from him. Mark and Naomi nodded, Agnes was sent off by Alex to arrange for pallet beds, and Charlie was looking animated for the first time in weeks, loudly insisting that he should be included in the riding sentry.

"Hmm," Matthew said, looking about for paper and ink. He had to write to the Governor and to the elders in Providence. These Indian savages could suddenly decide to move south.

"I can handle both gun and sword – I'm a gentleman."

"Hmm," Matthew repeated, which only served to inflame Charlie further, long fingers raking through his dyed hair as he repeated that he was a man, he'd seen battle and blood, had he not? Matthew raised a brow, dipped his quill in the ink, and concentrated on his letters.

Charlie would not let the subject go, and once the letters were written, sanded, folded and sealed, he accompanied Matthew and Mark out into the yard.

"I'm quite the marksman," he insisted.

"Oh aye?" Mark sounded unimpressed. He handed Charlie a flintlock, called for Adam to set up some targets. Matthew and Mark shared a grin. A flushed Charlie returned the flintlock some minutes later, muttering about not being used to rifled barrels, and the target had been hit.

"Notched," Mark corrected, reloaded, raised the gun, and blasted a hole straight through the middle of the wooden block.

"I still want to ride. You need me," Charlie said. With a little sigh, Matthew acquiesced, and suggested Charlie grab some sleep before setting out after supper with Mark. He left them to their target practice, and followed the promising scent of baking buns to the kitchen.

"I'm not sure I follow you," Alex said to Matthew, and slapped his hand away when he reached for a third bun. "You don't like Charlie riding out because he might be hurt?"

"That band of renegade Indians is ruthless." Beyond ruthless, Matthew shivered, more like maddened beasts.

"And just so that I understand, you allow our sons to

ride sentry duty, you ride it yourself, but your nephew must somehow be protected?"

"It isn't his land, is it?" Matthew replied, matter-of-factly.

"No," Alex said, "but one could argue he's living here, for free. We've given him clothes and a place to sleep, we feed him, and you've even advanced him spending money — not that there's much to spend it on here."

"I've gone to very much trouble to see him safe. It would be a trifle unnecessary to have him come to harm here." Matthew edged closer to the workbench and pretended a great interest in the four large trout presently being stuffed with fennel and parsley, one arm stretching out behind Alex's back to grope for another bun.

"If you don't put it back, you'll go without supper," Alex said without turning around. "I don't want you to go fat on me."

"Fat?" Matthew hastily returned the bun. "I don't have a pound of fat on me." He grabbed at her arse and squeezed a bit too hard. "You on the other hand..."

"Huh!" Alex shoved him out of the way to place the fish to cook on the hearth, and gave him a basket of buns to take down to Betty and Ian. "And tell Ian he'd best move Betty up now — I've already made up the bed in Sarah's room."

Matthew cursed when he cracked his head against the lintel of the cabin door, ducked exaggeratedly, and stepped into a small circle of light from the single candle burning on the table. The rest of the cabin was sunk in gloom, weak daylight filtering in from the one unshuttered window. Ian placed a finger to his mouth in a hushing gesture, and stood to draw the bed hangings closed round his sleeping wife and child.

"She's so tired. She always is." Ian shook his head at the proffered basket.

"Give her time, son." Matthew counted back in his head. Little Grace was not quite a fortnight old, and while the wean had recovered from the ordeal of birth, her mother was constantly wan, shuffling as she performed the few chores Ian and Alex would let her do.

Ian poured them both some beer and regarded his mug morosely. "Will she ever recover?"

Matthew didn't know what to say. Alex had privately voiced to him that it would be ages before Betty was back to normal — if ever.

Ian studied him silently and turned away. "I was a right daftie."

"The two of you."

"And now she will never want to again, will she? And it will be like Simon and Joan, she in constant pain, unable to take him into her, and he, well, he had to find release elsewhere." Ian dug his fingers into his scalp and moaned. "Except that I don't want to. I want only her, Da."

"Give her time," Matthew repeated, "and it isn't like with Joan, is it? My sister had a canker gnawing at her insides, an evil growth that slowly sapped her life away." His son didn't reply. He just buried his face in his hands. "It'll be fine, lad."

"I'm no mindless bairn, Da."

Ian poured them both some more beer, listening with a distracted expression while Matthew told him about the Indians and his decision to have them all sleep in the big house for now. Ian promised he'd bring Betty over once she was awake, and after a second or two of silence, Matthew got to his feet, clasped Ian's shoulder, and left.

Ian remained where he was. The little cabin was agreeably quiet, a drowsy peace sinking over him as he sat and stared into the embers in the hearth. He could hear the wean's soft snuffling, how Betty said something to their daughter, and he straightened up, squaring his shoulders and arranging his face into an expression of unperturbed calm.

A long-fingered hand touched his cheek, wild fuzzy hair tickled his face, and Betty sat herself carefully down in his lap, arms coming round him to press his face against her swollen breasts.

"I want you too," Betty breathed, and her fingers combed their way through his hair.

Ian groaned and wrapped his arms around her.

"It will be fine," Betty said, echoing his father.

And Ian believed her – he had to. Before he could reply, the door banged open, and the cabin was full of children, high voices laughing and demanding food. Betty ignored all three of them, gripped Ian's face hard between her hands and kissed him – a soft, warm promise of future nights, a kiss that tasted of milk and honey, and faintly of cheese.

"You haven't cleaned your teeth," he reproached once she let him go.

"And did you care?"

"No," he whispered, and kissed her again.

Next morning, Charlie and Mark rode in well after dawn, the latter grim, the former looking as if he'd had his heart scared right out of his chest. Charlie gripped the musket so hard his fingers had whitened, and nearly fell off the horse when Mark told him they were home.

"What happened?" Matthew asked, eyes flying up and down his son to ensure he was safe and sound.

"A skirmish just to the west of the Ingram place," Mark answered, still in the saddle. Matthew knew his son. For all his light words, Mark was much affected, hands spread wide on his thighs to stop them from trembling.

"A skirmish?" Charlie croaked. "They must have been twenty – no, thirty at least!"

"Fifteen or thereabouts, I would say," Mark said, "but it was difficult to see in the dark." He dismounted, nodded a thank you at Adam who had appeared to take the horses, and smiled in the direction of Naomi. "They'd been up by the Peterson farm," he explained, and Charlie's face took on a pasty look when Mark described the total destruction of the primitive homestead.

"All of them?" Alex asked, coming to join them. "Even the children?"

"All," Mark confirmed, and his normally light eyes were dark with recollection. "We wouldn't be here if it hadn't been for Qaachow." Naomi snuck up to stand in his arms. Mark kissed the top of her head, tightened his grip on her, and nodded for Charlie to continue.

"They were all around us," Charlie said. "Martin Chisholm was riding first, and we saw his horse rear and he flew off, and I was sure he was dead." He cleared his throat and looked with admiration at Mark. "You rode your way through them to get to him, and then Robert was there, and I managed to kill one of them, I think." He had never killed a man before, he said in a thread of a voice, at least not to see him fall before his eyes. Charlie clutched the musket to him, took a deep breath, and continued with his story. "I suppose it was but a matter of minutes, age long seconds when we were thronged by the Indians, and I...well, I was certain we would die, no matter that Mark and Robert were standing back to back and giving as good as they got."

"You did your part, cousin," Mark interrupted.

"Not much," Charlie said, "and when that arrow struck Robert in the leg..." He closed his eyes. "A certain death, until that Indian you call Qaachow came down the hillside with his men at his back. It evened the odds, one might say."

"Samuel was there," Mark blurted. "It's wrong, Da, to take him along! A lad, no more, to go raiding in the dark."

"Samuel? Was he alright?" Alex asked Mark, grabbing at his sleeve.

"Well enough, not harmed as far as I could see." Mark turned to face Matthew. "It's war, aye? Qaachow means to avenge himself for the raids on his villages, for the stolen bairns, the killed men. And he will go after them with all the men he has – all, no matter age."

There was a hissed intake of breath from Alex, no more. She stumbled, steadied herself.

"Qaachow will prevail," Matthew said, taking her hand.

"But men will die and be hurt – on both sides," Alex said.

Matthew opened his mouth to assure her Samuel would be kept safe, away from strife, but shut it again, slowly.

"Oh God," Alex groaned, and wrenched herself free from Matthew's hand, running off in the rain.

Matthew caught up with her just before the entrance to

the graveyard. "You can't think Qaachow would risk him."

"He did last night. To them, he's a man," Alex stated in a colourless voice. "But to me, he's still a child – my child."

"To me as well, lass." On the shelf in the room Samuel once had shared with David and Adam stood twelve horses, one for each of his birthdays, carved to spring alive out of the wood by Matthew. Twelve – and already burdened with weapons and the necessity of killing.

Alex wiped her eyes with her sleeve and stuck her hand into his. It was surprisingly cold, like holding a handful of water, and instinctively, his fingers began to knead, bringing blood back down to her icy digits.

"He's due home in three weeks," Matthew said, "and if the fighting still rages, he stays."

"Three weeks?" Alex shook her head at him. "Anything can happen in three weeks!"

"Aye, I know that. But I don't know where he is, do I?" Exasperated, he swept his arm across the deep blue green of the western forests. "Where do you want me to look? How can I find him in all that?"

He had known for a long time that Alex held him to blame for the loss of Samuel, but never had it stood plainer to read in her face. It tore at him, it savaged his innards, curdled his blood, to have his wife look at him as she now did, all of her reproaching him for the promise he once gave, for not having done as she said and send Samuel away before Qaachow could claim him.

She retook her hand and gave him a singularly blue look. "Let's hope he isn't killed before he's due back."

She might as well have skewered him with a red-hot poker. He had to wheel away from her to hide his face, stood for some seconds holding his breath as he willed the tears back. The dried leaves rustled underfoot as she came close enough to touch him, a hesitant hand on his back.

"I'm sorry, that was very much under the belt."

"I'll leave tomorrow," he said and strode off.

"No, Matthew! Matthew, wait!"

He just increased his pace.

★

He rose while still dark and dressed in silence, not wanting to wake her. They had patched up as well as they could last night, but her unspoken accusation was like a thorn in his heart, a chafing irritation that had him sleepless most of the night, and by now he was too restless to remain any longer in bed. He was being unnecessarily foolish, he knew, and his rational mind was telling him to remain here, at home, as she had begged him to do last night, insisting that the woods were too dark and too cold, far too wild and dangerous for him to set out on his own – his own arguments, more or less. But their discussion had woken a fear in him, a driving need to ensure his son was alive, and so he felt he had no choice – not now, not after what she'd said yesterday.

He stood for a moment looking down at her, curled as always on her side, and wanted very much to kiss her but was too angry inside, and so he opened the door, padded down the stairs and out to the stables. He had his foot in the stirrup when he heard her open the kitchen door.

"Matthew?" she called. "Matthew? Please don't…"

He sat up and rode off, without a backward glance.

He was back three days later, worn out from long days of riding, and equally long nights huddling under pines and hemlocks, doing without a fire so as not to attract undue attention from other wanderers. He had found his way back to Qaachow's village and gaped at the destruction. The longhouses were burnt to the ground, the smaller buildings seemed to have been uprooted, and of the busy, comfortable place Alex and he had visited back in February there was absolutely no trace.

Trodden into the moss, he found a small doll, and where the longhouse used to stand he found the charred remains of a Bible – his Bible, the one he had given Samuel. For some hours he scoured the area round the village looking for something, anything, that would indicate where the former inhabitants had gone, but they had not wished to be followed or found, and so the forest told him nothing at all, unbroken branches swaying in the wind, thick moss hiding any sign of human feet. In his frustration, he stood in the clearing, arms spread out, and called his son's name.

"Samuel!" he had yelled. "My Samuel!" The air reverberated with his voice, a raven cawed at this disturbance of the peace, and Matthew stood with his face upturned to the weak sun filtering through heavy clouds, and tried to will his heart into silence as he listened for a returning call.

"Nothing," Matthew said as he dismounted.

Ian nodded. What had Da expected?

"And you were right," Matthew continued, nodding in the direction of Mark. "The village is no more." He looked about for Alex, but she was nowhere in sight. "Your mama?"

"Inside," Mark replied a trifle too coolly.

Matthew lowered his brows for an instant.

"She isn't very happy with you," Ian said. "She hasn't slept at all since you rode off, and she's right, isn't she? It was a daft thing to do."

"I had to," Matthew said curtly, irritated at being told off by his son. He coughed into the crook of his arm.

Ian regarded him through narrowed eyes. "Aye, mayhap. But you could have taken someone with you, and not left Mama to fear all kinds of untoward endings to you – alone in the wild."

Matthew felt a twinge of shame, quickly suppressed. "She wished me to go."

"Not like you did, not slinking off in the dark without telling her farewell." Mark clucked at Aaron to lead him off into the stables, and Ian went with them, leaving Matthew to face his wife alone.

Alex frowned down at the result of her efforts. It didn't look like the cabbage dish she recalled from long weeks spent with her Swedish grandmother, and it didn't smell all that appetizing either. Not that she was all that interested in cooking, not now when her back was prickling with his presence, her nostrils widening in an effort to catch his scent, that lingering mixture of wood smoke, fresh water and newly turned earth.

She could hear him moving behind her, how the cloth of his breeches rustled when he shifted on his feet, the slight squeak of one of his boots, but obstinately she kept her face on the food, adding more butter and syrup to the layered cabbage and finely chopped meat before returning the closed pot to sit in the coals of the hearth. His breathing was loud and constricted, she could hear him swallow back on a cough, clear his throat, but still she kept her back to him. She was aware of his eyes on her nape, and then he was right behind her, close enough that his exhalations should warm her skin.

She had lived off her rage these last few days: anger at him for subjecting her to day after day of abject fear, anger at herself for having taunted him the way she did. She had imagined him dead in multiple ways: scalped, drowned, shot through the head, decapitated… And now he was back, safe and sound, and without a word she turned to bury her face against his damp coat, noting in passing that he had lost one button and that his lapel had an ugly stain – blackberry, she thought.

On the hearth, something hissed, and the smell of burnt syrup filled the air. Alex didn't care. He was back, with her, his arms holding her to his beating heart.

Chapter 45

Samuel came home six days later on a makeshift stretcher, and Thomas was the first to see, exclaiming and rising to his feet from where he sat chatting with Mrs Parson in the warm, sun-drenched kitchen.

"What?" Mrs Parson who was surprisingly limber both for age and size was on her toes beside him, processing the scene before her in a matter of seconds. "Samuel, it's wee Samuel!"

Alex was halfway to the door, alerted by Mrs Parson's tone, and by the time she reached her son, the farm was in an uproar, people spilling out from cabins, storing sheds and stables. The Indians set the stretcher down and retreated, uncomfortable with all these white people, and only Qaachow remained, kneeling by Samuel's side. Alex dropped to her knees, and a second later, Matthew skidded to a stop beside her, red and out of breath after his sprint from the barn.

Her son moaned. "Mama," he slurred, "Mama." Someone had bandaged his head, strips of rawhide holding a soft square of buckskin over his right ear and side. His shoulder...his right arm... Alex folded back the heavy pelt and gasped at the damage done to his son.

"A tomahawk," Qaachow explained almost inaudibly, dark eyes never leaving his adopted son's pinched face.

"How?" Matthew asked.

"We came upon them five nights ago, and we did them battle. They are all dead." Qaachow brushed at the hair that fell over Samuel's forehead. "He was a warrior among warriors, and I didn't see, at first, that he was down. And when I did—"

"You swore you'd keep him safe, and you return him

to me like this?" Alex didn't dare to uncover his head, her hand hovering a scant inch over where his ear should be.

Qaachow made a helpless sound. "There was nothing I could do, and I brought him here as quickly as I could."

"Five nights ago, you said," Alex bit him off. "Where were you? In Virginia?" She motioned for Charlie and Mark to lift the stretcher and carry Samuel inside, placing the back of her hand against her son's heated skin. "He stays. White Bear is no more."

Qaachow bowed his head at the finality of her tone and rose to his full length, only a couple of inches shorter than Matthew. His face was etched with grief, his normally so erect stance curved under the weight of guilt. As far as Alex was concerned, she hoped he was drowning in it.

Alex hurried inside after the stretcher, and left outside were Matthew and Qaachow. Never had Matthew seen the Indian chief so distraught as he was today, and yet it was not enough.

"Was Little Bear unharmed?" Matthew asked, going unerringly for the jugular, and Qaachow shrank yet another inch or two.

"He remained with his mother."

Matthew nodded thoughtfully. "But my son you considered old enough to risk."

"He's my son too," Qaachow said.

"Nay, he isn't. You chose when you left one behind and took the other with you to fight, and him not yet thirteen." Matthew spat with precision between Qaachow's feet. "You'll excuse me," he said with exaggerated politeness, "but I have a son to tend to."

The kitchen was converted into a sickroom, a disturbingly small shape laid out on the broad oak planks of the kitchen table. Thomas was snipping through the bindings, talking all the while to Samuel who had opened his eyes but otherwise appeared unconscious. Ian returned with bottles of brandy and cane liquor, Mark was busy by the hearth, murmuring to Mrs Parson. And Alex stood immobile before her son, not wanting to see, yet knowing she had to.

Matthew gripped her hand for an instant, a warm, comforting touch, and pointed her in the direction of the basin full of steaming water and the lye soap. Alex almost smiled. In her family, cleanliness was firmly ingrained, and in particular when dealing with the sick or wounded.

Mrs Parson inspected the long slashing cut that began at the shoulder and opened the back of Samuel's arm. Even Alex could see it had been cleaned and closed expertly, packed into fragrant herbs.

"Hmm," Mrs Parson said, studying how the skin rippled in places. "Now, that I haven't seen since I was a wee lass, and my fool of an uncle near on chopped off his foot. Right rare, even then to have a healer do such, but old Annie Campbell came from a family of healers, from mother to daughter since the first stone of Scotland rose from the sea, and she had insisted it would work. Which it did, aye?"

"What would work?" Alex asked, bending even closer. Oh my God! Her son's wound was crawling with maggots!

"Leave it be," Mrs Parson said when Alex looked round for her knife.

"Leave it? But they'll eat him!"

"Only the sick parts, the dead flesh," Mrs Parson said.

Thomas Leslie bent to peer. "I've seen that once or twice, and as I recall, it works." He sniffed. "No smell of rot, no warning stripes of red on his skin."

The arm was one thing. At least it was still there. The ear, however, was gone. Once again, Mrs Parson was of the opinion that the resulting wound had been well cleaned and that there was no need to disturb the lad by fussing further with it.

"And it's no great loss, is it?" she said, giving Alex's hand a reassuring pat. "He will still have most of his hearing, and once his hair grows out, you won't even see it." Alex gave her a long look. Samuel had big ears, and on the other side, the ear showed through the hair. But she was relieved all the same: two inches to the side and the tomahawk would have buried itself in Samuel's skull.

★

Samuel slept for two full days, waking at intervals to eat and drink, use the chamber pot with Da's or his brothers' help, before being dragged back under to a world of whites and blues, safely anchored to life by his mama's hand, so strong and warm around his own.

When he finally opened his eyes, the first thing he saw were his horses, prancing on the shelf above his head. The second thing was Da, asleep on the bed beside him, and Samuel turned on his good side to face him. He sniffed at the clean sheets and looked down at his shirt. Not his... it was too big, and when he lifted the sleeve to his nose, it smelled faintly of Jacob.

Samuel stretched his arm. It strained and hurt, and when he moved it backwards his shoulder protested. He opened and closed his fist, he straightened one finger at a time, and they all worked. He lowered his lashes and tried to remember what had happened. He'd had his bow in hand, an arrow on the string, and pain had exploded behind his ear, down his shoulder and arm. He must have gasped because suddenly Da's eyes were wide open and close to his.

"You'll live," Da assured him, and Samuel nodded, dry-mouthed. One part of him was dead, and his Indian family would mourn the passing of White Bear, but he, Samuel, he was still alive. His tongue quivered with the need to say something in Indian speech and to hear Little Bear laugh in his ear in response. His gut closed in on itself in loss, and he curled himself around the pain. Da propped himself up on an elbow and looked down at him, and Samuel looked back, knowing that his eyes were the same shape and colour as those gazing down at him.

"Hungry?" Da asked, smiling down at him. Samuel nodded, wondering if he'd ever again sit beside Thistledown and help her turn corn over the open hearth.

It was a relief when David came home, riding with Julian, Ruth and Malcolm, because to him Samuel could talk unhindered, and they would lie close together in the bed once Adam had fallen asleep while Samuel tried to explain just how much it hurt. Not his ear, nor yet his arm, but something in his chest was hollow, a constant ache for his other people.

"But you're back with us," David said.

"Aye." He was, and he was glad, but also sad, because one part of him would always be White Bear, just as one part was Samuel. "I...how can I choose?" he asked his brother, although truth be told he no longer had a choice, did he? With his damaged arm, he would never have a place among the Indian men.

David gave him a brief hug. "I don't understand, but I don't like it that you hurt so much. Is there no way for you to be both?"

"No." Samuel rolled away from him and held his breath to stop himself from weeping. Men do not weep, Qaachow always used to say, and for all that Samuel was wounded, he was still a man – man enough to have killed, man enough to have survived combat.

"Maybe Da—"

"No!" Samuel shook his head vehemently. "Da can't help – no one can."

Apparently, David didn't agree. Three days before Christmas, Da came to find him, and suggested they take a wee walk. They walked in comfortable silence through the woods closest to the farm, and so deep in thought was Samuel that he didn't notice when Da came to a halt until he bumped into him.

"There," Da said, pointing to the further end of the clearing they were in. Samuel's chest tightened, his throat swelled. "Go on, lad, it's alright." He gave Samuel a light shove. "Be home for supper, or else your mama will flay me." With that, he left, and Samuel flew over the ground to where Qaachow and Thistledown, Little Bear and wee Hawk Tail stood.

One whole day being White Bear; one full day in which his Indian family showed him just how much they loved him and missed him.

"You've always got a place at my hearth," Qaachow said

as they made their farewells. "You're my son too, White Bear, a most beloved son."

"And you're my father – you always will be," White Bear said with a smile. "But for now, I stay here, with Da and with Mama. I think I must." Ruefully, he indicated his arm.

"Maybe it's for the best." Qaachow sighed, and for the first time ever White Bear saw something akin to tears in his Indian father's eyes. "For now, at least."

"For now," White Bear said, before turning to hug Thistledown.

Da was waiting in the yard when Samuel came back home. The setting sun patterned the slopes in elongated shadows, there was a crust of frost on the grass, and the air smelled of snow. The white oak stood in stark outline against the eastern horizon, its denuded branches raised towards the skies. Da was sitting on the bench below the oak, legs extended before him, two of the dogs at his feet.

He smiled when he saw Samuel. "Alright, then?"

Samuel joined him, sitting down as close to him as he could. "Thank you," he said, scrubbing his head against Da's shoulder. A big hand came up to ruffle his hair.

"You're welcome, son."

If having David back home was a pleasure, Samuel was not quite as enthused by the presence of Ruth and Julian. He had quickly gathered that Mama was somehow displeased with them – it showed in how she talked to them and, more importantly, in how little she talked to them.

When he asked David, all he got was a shrug, saying that it all had to do with Julian belting Sarah – so hard, in fact, that she had gone and baptised herself a Catholic. Whatever the truth in all this, Ruth spent far too much time coddling him, and even worse, in Samuel's opinion, was when Julian decided they might as well make up for time lost and together review the Bible.

Hours of religious instruction were made somewhat less boring when Julian decided Charlie should join them. Samuel gaped at Charlie's horrifically non-existent biblical knowledge, as did Julian.

"I don't want to do this," Charlie said. "I'm convinced, Minister Allerton, that I have the knowledge I need for my spiritual well-being. After all, I've studied at Oxford."

"Ha," Julian snorted. "Classics and Humanities! No, my dear boy, you're sorely in need of spiritual guidance – has no one properly instructed you in the Holy Book?"

"Umm," Charlie mumbled, grimacing behind Julian's back, and Samuel stuffed his hand in his mouth to stop himself from laughing.

"He's lost one soul to Catholicism, now he's about to pry one soul from Anglicanism to Presbyterianism," Alex commented to Matthew, still laughing after having listened to Charlie's loud groans at having been set the book of Job to study during the week.

Matthew made an amused sound. "Anglican? Nay, Alex, Charlie is woefully ignorant about the Christian faith in whatever guise you may present it. We're doing him a favour by ensuring he gets such good tutelage."

"Probably beats the hell out of doing Humanities in Oxford," Alex laughed.

"It seems to me he mainly caroused." Matthew nabbed a piece of warm saffron bread behind Alex's back.

"I saw that!" she warned, but he was already at the door, innocently holding two empty hands aloft, his mouth full. "Men…" she muttered, and Lettie nodded seriously from where she was standing on a stool to help. "Not all, of course," she amended with a smile, adjusting the blanket in Edward's basket.

From outside came loud calls and shrill laughter, and Alex propped her chin up in her hand to watch her three youngest boys and Malcolm play a heated game of football. Her eyes stuck on Samuel, still bandaged around head and arm, but here, with her. She exhaled, content just to look at him, and turned back to her granddaughter, alerted by the sudden and suspicious silence.

"Lettie!" Alex flew after the child who was sprinting out

of the kitchen at full speed with a sizeable piece of saffron bread clutched to her chest. Too late, and Alex glowered, but laughed when Lettie pranced like an Indian chief with her prize in her hands. "That child is a throwback to Rachel."

"She is?" Ruth said, sitting down to feed Edward.

"All through," Alex smiled. Well, except that this little imp had eyes as blue as her own, while Rachel's had been hazel. She busied herself making some chamomile tea, lost in memories of little Rachel, dead since almost twenty years.

"Have you heard from Sarah?" Ruth said, recalling Alex to the here and now.

"One letter. It seems Michael is doing well for himself as a printer's assistant." Sarah had sounded lonely, left a bit too much to her own devices in a town she didn't know, and on top of that pregnant.

"She's carrying?" Ruth made big eyes at this. "But they're but recently wed!"

"Oh, don't worry, the child is definitely conceived in wedlock."

Ruth blushed. "I didn't mean it like that."

Alex sighed and came over to sit beside her, tugging at the heavy dark red braid. "I know you didn't, but it comes out sounding as if you did." Ruth mumbled something indistinct about not being able to help if other people valued her words at other but face value.

"Will she be staying down south, then?" she asked.

Alex nodded, inspected the dried apple ring she had found in her apron pocket, and popped it into her mouth.

"You could go down and visit her," she suggested.

Ruth shook her head, smoothed down Edward's hair before carefully replacing his woollen cap. "Julian wouldn't approve," she said and left the room.

"Julian wouldn't approve," Alex mimicked in an undertone, and Mrs Parson laughed.

"Wee Sarah is an apostate. You can't have a minister's wife consorting with such."

"Huh," Alex snorted, draped her shawl over her shoulders, and went to find the Christmas ham.

★

After Christmas came Hogmanay, and the men carried trestles back and forth while the women prepared one dish after the other in the increasingly stuffy kitchen. Even Betty was there, insisting loudly that she was the only one who knew how to make a good honey cake, and what was New Year without one of those?

"One?" Alex shook her head at her. "Try five or six. What with the Chisholms and the Leslies and the Ingrams..." Mentally, she counted through their guests, and threw a despairing look at the prepared food. "This will never be enough. We all know old Mrs Chisholm eats like a horse."

"So do her sons," Mrs Parson said, "and Thomas is no mean eater either, is he?" This said with a possessive pride that made Alex grin at her.

"Oh, I'm sure you've got something squirrelled away for him to nibble on should he go hungry from the table," she teased, and Mrs Parson raised her brows before going back to minding the beef stew that was simmering over the hearth.

There was no time for her hoped-for bath. Instead, Alex had to do with a hasty wash in their room before donning her finery. She brushed an imaginary speck of dust off Matthew's coat, and took a step back to inspect him.

"Quite the laird," she teased, and twitched the lace at his cuff to lie better. He looked very pleased with his appearance, and twisted this way and that with the small looking glass in his hand. He had cut himself while shaving, and blotted the scratch with a linen towel one more time before turning to look at his wife.

She liked it that he ate her with his eyes, all the way from her dark red bodice, her breasts swelling against the embroidered cotton of her long-sleeved chemise, to her intricately braided and coiled hair. With a flirty look at him, she raised her skirts to garter her stockings with ribbons as dark red as her bodice.

"Let me," he said, and tied one neat bow around each leg, smoothing down her petticoats and skirts afterwards. He drew her into his arms and kissed her cheek. "Dance?" he murmured, and slipped his hands round her waist, crooning softly under his breath. Alex smiled and closed her eyes, recognising the song as one of the many she had taught him through the years, all about too much honesty, too much love, and holding on to each other until we died.

Matthew broke off to smile down at her. "True, isn't it?" he said, the back of his hand resting for an instant against her cheek.

"True," she breathed, and turned slowly in his arms. Oh yes, she intended to hold on to this man of hers. Every day that remained of her life, she planned on holding on to him.

Chapter 46

Charlie returned from Providence's harbourmaster with several letters – three for him and one for Matthew – and Matthew took one look at the handwriting and tucked it into his coat pocket, saying he would read it later. Charlie nodded, mumbled an excuse, and set off in the direction of Kate Jones' warehouse. There had been no further visits from the militia, so apparently Matthew's letter had convinced Lord Calvert Charlie was no longer in his colony, but just in case, their nephew kept his head shaved and covered by a stylish dark wig.

"Nice of Kate to take him in," Alex commented, watching him walk off. A very different Charlie to the wreck they had found on Barbados, self-confident and boisterous, even if at times given to long hours of brooding introspection.

"Aye," Matthew agreed, "and she'll keep him gainfully employed for a year or so."

Kate had developed quite a fondness for Charlie, and suggested that such a worldly young man might find it less irksome to work for her than act the farmer at Graham's Garden. They were all relieved by this arrangement, and so Charlie rode through Maryland on Kate's behalf and was to take ship to Jamestown and Charles Towne in some weeks there to conduct some further business.

Alex settled herself more comfortably on the low stone wall that ran the perimeter of the Customs House. The April sun was agreeably warm, and a recent shower had cleared the air of any dust, leaving it crisp and fresh. David and Samuel were playing an intense but low-voiced game of marbles in the protective shadow of a tree, keeping a watchful eye out for any approaching minister. Her gaze lingered on Samuel. He could no longer raise his arm above shoulder level, and his ear wasn't about to ever grow back, but it didn't seem to bother him unduly.

They had tried to have him stay with Ruth and Julian, but Samuel got restless behind doors. So, after a couple of attempts, they had arrived at a compromise: Samuel spent a month at a time with Julian, studying for long, long days, and then he had a month back home, a month with extended visits to his Indian family.

Alex set her mouth. Had it been up to her, Samuel would never have been allowed close to Qaachow again, but Matthew had overruled her, stating that the lad had need of them. And he did, Alex admitted reluctantly. No matter that her son was now mostly Samuel, White Bear was still very much alive.

"What are you thinking?" Matthew asked, coming to stand beside her. He extended a rosebud to her, plucked from the nearby bush.

"Nothing, really," she said, accepting his gift. She tilted her head back to look at him. "She seemed happy, don't you think?"

"Quite," Matthew said.

Their short visit to St Mary's City had reassured them as to their daughter's well-being, and Matthew had even admitted to Alex that he found Michael a good enough sort, industrious and serious for all that he was a papist – and with Burley blood.

"Ready?" He extended his hand to her, helped her up to stand. They strolled along the shoreline, making for Kate's house and waiting dinner. Halfway there, they were hailed, and stood waiting while Simon came jogging towards them, coat tails flying behind him.

"And Duncan?" Alex asked.

"Duncan?" Simon groaned and shook his head. "I had no idea that a lad that small could run you so ragged."

"What did you expect?" Matthew said. "We told you."

"And he talks, incessantly that wee lad prattles." Simon threw Alex a dark look. "From his grandmother, no doubt."

"Nay," Matthew said, "she still has her tongue."

"I'm not talking to you – either of you." Alex increased her pace so that the two men could fall in step behind her. Alex wasn't really listening to their conversation, far more interested in a pair of curlews that ran back and forth over the mudflats bared by the receding tide.

"...and by now most of them are dead," she caught, and turned to Matthew.

"Who?" she asked.

"I thought you weren't talking to me," he said, but became serious as he explained how Captain Jan had told him most of the Monmouth rebels carried over to Barbados were dead.

"And him? Brown?" Alex asked. "Has Jan heard anything about him?"

"Hale and hearty," Matthew replied with a crooked smile. "A constant companion to the Governor."

"Too bad," Alex muttered. "I'd sort of hoped he's been swallowed whole by a crocodile." She threw her husband an oblique look. "It's strange how often the bad guys thrive and prosper, and the good guys dwindle and die."

"Aye," Simon said, "but ultimately it catches up – at least we must hope it does."

"Not much of a comfort," Alex said.

"He'll get what's coming to him in the afterlife," Matthew said.

"Whoopee," Alex muttered, making Simon grin.

It was late afternoon, nearly evening, by the time they made their farewells and set off back to town, hand in hand through the spring green grasses that bordered the waters. Dusk rose like smoke from the damp ground, hovered at first round their legs, and then shot up towards the violet sky, and suddenly it was almost night, whatever little light remaining trapped in a hovering line of white and green on the western horizon.

As always, Alex felt short-changed: light passed too quickly into dark, and the witching hour, the time when the world hung perfectly balanced between night and day, was far too short at these latitudes. She longed for interminable twilights that shifted gradually from blue through purple to grey, evenings spent sitting by an unlit window watching how night folded itself over the land.

"My grandmother loved April evenings," she said. "She'd make us a cup of tea, and then we'd sit by the kitchen table and not say a word while her apple orchard sank slowly into the night."

Matthew tightened his hold on her hand but didn't reply.

"I miss them," Alex went on, "the northern nights." She shook herself out of her maudlin state and picked up her skirts. "Last one to the watering post is a rotten egg," she challenged, and shoved him hard before flying off.

Supper was soup and rye bread, followed by an hour or so in Julian's little parlour, Ruth and Alex sitting to one side while the men locked horns over the chessboard.

"She's marrying Macpherson?" Alex couldn't keep the surprise out of her voice, eyeing Patience with pity.

"It's a good match," Ruth said.

A good match? Patience might not be the prettiest of girls, but she was young and healthy, had a very nice smile, and to burden her with a man like Gregor Macpherson... Alex grimaced in disgust.

"He's a minister," Ruth said, "an educated man."

"Educated? The man's a boor."

Ruth gave her a severe look. "He's a minister," she repeated, "and Patience is eighteen come September, so it's time she's wed."

"Minister Macpherson is positively ancient," Alex hissed, not wanting either Julian or Patience to hear. She shook out Matthew's spare shirt and threaded a needle to stitch the undone hem back up.

"He's two years younger than Julian," Ruth said.

"No! Really?" Alex sneaked a look at her son-in-law who looked at least ten years Minister Macpherson's junior. Ruth nodded and rested her eyes affectionately on her husband.

"He's a good-looking man," she whispered with pride, leaning against her mother.

"Mmm," Alex replied, thinking that her daughter must be blind to consider Julian handsome in the company of her Matthew. She liked how he kept his hair short these days, letting it hug the shape of his skull, and right now, with a two-day beard sprouting salt and pepper on his cheeks, he looked decidedly rakish – almost dangerous.

He looked up and caught her frank look, returned it in kind before dropping his eyes to the chessboard, leaving her short of breath and very warm. Alex pricked herself in the finger and swore. Matthew smiled, moved his knight, and declared Julian checkmate.

"Aren't you going to read it?" she asked Matthew much later, resting back against the pillows in their bed. He stood silhouetted against the open window, a dark shape against the somewhat lighter dark beyond. Rain pattered on the sill and the shingles of the roof, and from very far away came the single bark of a dog. When Matthew turned, the whites of his eyes gleamed for an instant, and then all she saw was a blob of white crossing the few yards towards her. His shirt rustled when he lay down beside her. She scooted close, using her toes to caress his hairy shins.

"Tomorrow," he said. "I don't intend to go and find a taper now." He turned her over, fitted her into the curve of his body, and slid his hand in to cup her breast. "I'm in no hurry to read it. I've done my brother a favour, but damned if I want to be the recipient of fawning gratitude from a man I hold in such low regard."

Alex stretched languorously in the early dawn and sat up in bed. An insistent bird had been chirping good morning for the last hour or so, and Alex was in two minds about whether to kill it or enjoy its cheerful greeting.

She padded over to the window, and the bird flew off in a flurry of brown and bright orange, cheeping saucily that it would be back the moment she moved away. She watched its dipping flight to the neighbouring roof, and dropped her eyes to where Luke's letter lay on top of Matthew's belt and knife.

"Bring it here," Matthew said from the bed, pummel-ling their combined pillows into a comfortable backrest. She did, curling up beside him to rest her cheek against his chest. She yawned and slid her hands in under his shirt, letting her fingers travel in a desultory fashion over his chest, down to his navel and up again, tugging every now and then at his hair. He shifted in protest when she tugged too hard, but was otherwise silent, the papers that crackled in his hands the only sound. After a very long time, he folded the papers together, and Alex noticed his hands were shaking – shaking badly.

"Matthew?" Alex sat up.

He was stunned, eyes glazed, and mutely he handed her the letter. Not only a letter, but a formal document of some sort, and Alex frowned at official seals and signatures, trying to make sense of what she was reading.

"Oh my God!" She had to put some distance between them to see his face. "He's bought back Hillview!" She smoothed the deed, staring at the name Matthew Graham '*hereby confirmed as sole owner of said property*' and unclenched her hand from the letter and quickly scanned it through.

I could think of no other way to express my eternal gratitude for what you did for my son than to buy for you the place that I suspect still holds your heart. I don't know if you wish to return yourself, or if perhaps Ian would, or Mark... But at least you have a home in Scotland again – our home. Mayhap there will even be a day when we can sit together under the orchard trees and converse with no other intent than to share the memories we have of a time before it all went sour and warped between us.

"Wow," Alex said, very impressed.

"Wow, indeed," Matthew nodded, one long finger tracing the name Hillview over and over again.

"Retirement," Alex said in an effort to break the emo-tional mood. It worked, Matthew giving her a quick smile.

"Retirement? I don't think taking Hillview back will be a restful proposition."

"So what will you do?" she asked, and felt her stomach turn inside out. How was she to stand it, being separated from her children?

"I have no idea," he replied, but she could see the yearning in his eyes, how it twisted through his face.

"Once you know, be sure to tell me," she said and patted his thigh. "After all, where you go, I go, right?" She managed to keep her voice steady while inside of her it was all turmoil. A double-edged gift this, a gift she already wished he had never been given. Damn Luke! Why couldn't he just have refunded Matthew for his expenses? She was quite convinced he knew exactly the upheaval and heartbreak his generous gesture would cause, no doubt chuckling as he drafted the letter. No, that was probably unfair, but still… She blinked, keeping her eyes hidden.

"Alex?" Matthew drew her close. "I won't go anywhere without you," he promised, and kissed her ear. In a gesture similar to a benediction, his hand came down on her head, stroking softly at her hair. "My wife, my Alexandra Ruth, a gift from the Lord himself, a helpmeet and companion to see me through every one of my worldly days and well beyond – no matter where I choose to go."

"Huh," Alex said, touched to the heart by his tone. "I bet you say that to all the girls."

"Nay, only to the ones I want to bed."

That made Alex laugh, and for a little while the cramp in her stomach abated – a little while, no more.

The Graham Saga continues in

To Catch a Falling Star

Isaac Lind should not have drunk quite as much as he did that evening, but flushed by the success of his latest exhibition, he allowed himself to be dragged along, to be toasted in pint after pint of lager.

By the time he left the pub, he was unsteady on his feet, but in a very mellow mood. He stood for some moments by a high brick wall, sniffing at the lilacs that hung over it into the narrow little street. Late April was a nice time of the year, and even here in London it was difficult to miss the advent of spring, the heady scents of flowering shrubs competing with the permanent smells of stone, exhausts, and muddy tidal waters.

Isaac continued on his way, strolling towards the river. It was going to be a long walk home to Notting Hill, but the night was warm, and Isaac was in no particular hurry. Veronica and Isabelle would be asleep anyway, and knowing Veronica, it might make sense to walk off some of this agreeable buzz before showing up back at their little apartment.

He stood for a moment with elbows on the stone parapet and decided that someday he would paint this – a silhouetted London lapped by the returning waters of the Thames. He yawned and looked at the swirling waters below: multiple little maelstroms, murky waves slapping in irritation at each other as they jostled for space. He yawned again, his mind drifting over to his latest piece. An urge built in him to hurry to his studio, not his bed, and look at it again. So, instead of continuing on his way home, he turned to the right, making for the attic space he rented for his painting.

The eye-scanner at the main gate let him through with a loud peep. He shrugged off his leather jacket as he took the stairs, making for the top floor. Yet more security, and when he swiped his thumb on the keypad, the door swung open on well-oiled hinges. Yet another swipe and the space came alive with lights, a soft whirring informing him his computer was back online. His fingers flew over the screen, and music flowed out of the two narrow speakers, a slow monotonous Gregorian chant.

Paintings leaned against the walls, bursts of vivid colours that implacably drew the beholder's eyes into whatever little detail was hidden in the depth of the heaving colours. One was a study in reds and oranges, and in their midst, one could vaguely make out a burning twisting figure, mouth wide as it screamed out its anguish to the world. Isaac extended a finger to touch it and laughed nervously. He could feel his skin blistering with the heat.

"How can you do this?" his agent had said, shaking his head in admiration. "How on earth do you make it so vibrant? Hell, I can even smell the stench of roasting flesh!"

Isaac wasn't sure how he did it. His fingers worked, and he slipped into a subconscious state where colours flowed together on the canvas, and all according to an inner voice. It scared the hell out of him, but that wasn't something he was about to admit – not even to himself.

He flicked off the old sheet that covered his latest work, a painting that was very different from anything else in the room. Just looking at his depicted somnolent courtyard filled him with unwelcome sensations of vertigo, a niggling feeling that he was walking a tightrope over forbidden zones – like he'd done all those years ago when, as a boy, he had painted the picture that allowed his grandfather, Magnus Lind, to dive from this time to another. Impossible, of course, and yet it had happened.

He caressed the wooden frame of the picture, a depiction of an empty, stone-flagged space, surrounded by arched walkways in whitewashed stone. In the middle, a fountain, a constant welling of water, and Isaac knew exactly what the water would taste like and how cool it would feel to his fingers. In olive greens and muted browns, with the odd dash of whites and startling blues, the water spilled over the fountain's edge to fall in transparent drops towards the ground.

Isaac reared back, and in his head he heard a mocking little laugh. *Too afraid to look deep into your own work?* Well, yes, he was. Sweat broke out across his forehead, beaded his upper lip, and made him wipe his damp hands against his jeans. He tried to break eye contact with the falling water, but now he heard it as well, the pitter-patter of drops on wet stone, the trickling sound of water running through a narrow channel, and there, just where he had painted it, a minute point of white beckoned and promised, entrapping his eyes in a shaft of dazzling light.

Carlos Muñoz was walking back to his room when he saw the stranger lying sprawled half in, half out of the fountain. With a soft exclamation, he hurried as well as he could to the groaning heap of a man. Carlos wrinkled his nose. The man was drunk, but how on earth had he ended up here in the monastery's secluded courtyard? He swept the cloister walks but they were empty, most of the monks hastening back to their beds from matins for a few more hours of sleep.

Carlos kneeled clumsily on account of his peg leg, and turned the stranger over. He yelped and dropped the man back onto the cobbles, scrambling back a few feet. Ángel? Here? But no, it couldn't be – his cousin had died two years ago on Jamaica, hanged by the neck for spying on behalf of his royal Spanish majesty.

"Fucking hell," the stranger groaned, and Carlos scooted backwards, got back to his feet.

"¿*Inglés?*" He hadn't spoken English since he returned from the New World. "¿*Es Usted inglés?*"

"No," the stranger moaned and sat up, "if anything, I'm Scots." He spoke passable Spanish, understandable but heavily accented, and looked about himself with trepidation. "Bloody fucking hell," he cursed in English, and Carlos thought the young man reminded him of someone – apart from being a disconcerting copy of himself.

He extended his hand to help the man stand, and they were nose to nose, of identical build – albeit that the stranger was a couple of inches taller – both with a soaring quiff of dark hair over the right brow, both with dark, lustrous eyes that were saved from being doe-like by strong, dark brows.

The stranger gaped. At one level, Carlos supposed it was most droll, this meeting between two men so alike as to seem twins, no doubt with identical expressions of disbelief painted on their faces. At another level, it was so disquieting it made Carlos' good leg dip somewhat, causing him to have to hop for a couple of steps to regain his balance. The stranger inhaled, barked a laugh, and to Carlos' bemusement, pinched himself – multiple times.

"Where am I?" the stranger finally said.

Carlos studied this double of his in silence while smoothing down his cassock. Might the man be an English spy? But no, if anything the stranger seemed utterly confused.

"*En Sevilla*," Carlos said.

The stranger groaned, tore at his hair and groaned some more. "Bloody, bloody, bloody hell! This can't be happening. I'm just drunk – really drunk – and soon…oh God!" The man swayed, steadied himself against the nearby wall, thereby coming to stand in a patch of moonlight.

Carlos had never seen a man dressed like this before. With interest, he took in the long wet breeches, the odd footwear in some kind of fabric, and the rather more normal shirt, even if it was very narrow in fit and had small buttons along the front rather than laces. One of the sleeves was burnt, the skin below looking very red and irritated. A leather belt but no knife, no sword – not even a pouch; no cloak, no hat, and hands as narrow and long as his own but with the fingers liberally smudged with ink and paint.

The stranger folded his hands together under Carlos' open inspection. "I can't get it off," he muttered.

"Are you a painter?"

The man nodded and looked about the courtyard. "I got it just right," he muttered, and a shiver ran through him. "The arches, the fountain – shit, even the crumbling plaster is just as I painted it."

Painted it? Carlos followed the man's gaze round the small courtyard, smiling as he always did as he took in this his favourite place: the arches in soft sandstone, worn to smoothness through very many years, the whitewash of the walls, the irregular stones of the walkways – all of it spoke of permanence. A huge stand of ivy clambered its way up to the latticed first floor shutters, in a circle surrounding the fountain grew straggling roses and high tufts of lavender, and set into a niche in the wall stood the abbot's pride and joy: an ancient statue of the Virgin.

"What is this place?" the man asked.

"A Dominican monastery," Carlos said "San Pablo el Real." He shifted into English, and the stranger's eyes grew round with astonishment. "My home for the past two years, a resting place for a battered soul." He nodded at the man. "It would seem you are in need of some rest as well."

"Rest? No way! I have to find a way back home." The stranger scowled at the surrounding walls and went over to stare intently into the waters of the fountain, as if he were looking for something in the shallow basin.

"Hmm," Carlos said, and then recalled his original question at finding the man. "How did you get here?"

The man shrugged. "I have no idea, I just—" He broke off. "I just fell."

"Fell?" Carlos looked at the sky. There was nothing to fall from.

"I know," the stranger said, his eyes full of anguish. He shook himself like a wet dog, and extended his hand. "I'm Isaac, Isaac Lind."

"Carlos Muñoz," Carlos replied, and grasped the hand. Isaac Lind? He recognised the name. He tried to place it but came up with a blank.

"Muñoz, you say?" Isaac said, and it seemed to Carlos the name had some relevance for him. Ah well, in truth, not an uncommon name.

"Yes, Carlos Benito Muñoz." Not Muñoz de Hojeda,

like his uncle and his cousins, not for a bastard this illustri-
ous name.

"Pleased to meet you," Isaac said.

"Likewise," Carlos replied.

Isaac shoved his hands into his pockets and turned his
back on Carlos, the slow, casual pivoting of a man taking in
new surroundings.

"This may seem a strange question," he said, "but what
year is it?"

Carlos gave the slender back a surprised look, and all
along his arms his hair rose to bristle in fear. What was this
man, dropping out of nowhere in strange vestments to land
in their courtyard? He crossed himself.

"1688," he answered as calmly as he could.

Isaac closed his eyes. A strangled sound escaped him, and
his frame bowed. Carlos was well familiar with dejection,
and saw it now in every line of the man before him. His
heart filled with compassion, and he decided that for now
the important thing was to get this unexpected visitor dry
and out of the beady eyesight of the abbot, who no doubt
would shortly be about.

For a Historical Note and more information about
Matthew and Alex, please visit Anna Belfrage's
website at www.annabelfrage.com

9 781781 322413

The ACE Advantage